T0197037

Printed in the United States
by Baker & Taylor Publisher Services

SLAVE

SLAVE
30 STINGING TALES
FROM THE BOTTOM

edited by N. T. Morley

HEAT
NEW YORK, NY

THE BERKLEY PUBLISHING GROUP
Published by the Penguin Group
Penguin Group (USA) Inc.
375 Hudson Street, New York, New York 10014, USA
Penguin Group (Canada), 90 Eglinton Avenue East, Suite 700, Toronto, Ontario M4P 2Y3, Canada
(a division of Pearson Penguin Canada Inc.)
Penguin Books Ltd., 80 Strand, London WC2R 0RL, England
Penguin Group Ireland, 25 St. Stephen's Green, Dublin 2, Ireland (a division of Penguin Books Ltd.)
Penguin Group (Australia), 250 Camberwell Road, Camberwell, Victoria 3124, Australia
(a division of Pearson Australia Group Pty. Ltd.)
Penguin Books India Pvt. Ltd., 11 Community Centre, Panchsheel Park, New Delhi—110 017, India
Penguin Group (NZ), 67 Apollo Drive, Rosedale, North Shore 0632, New Zealand
(a division of Pearson New Zealand Ltd.)
Penguin Books (South Africa) (Pty.) Ltd., 24 Sturdee Avenue, Rosebank, Johannesburg 2196,
South Africa

Penguin Books Ltd., Registered Offices: 80 Strand, London WC2R 0RL, England

Published by arrangement with Bookspan.
Slave copyright © 2004 by N. T. Morley.
Master/Slave copyright © 2004 by N. T. Morley.
Interior text design by Stacy Irwin.

"Zombie Love" first appeared on goodvibes.com. It is copyright © 2002 by Elizabeth Colvin and is reprinted by permission from the author.
"Lucky" first appeared in *Sweet Life 2: More Erotic Fantasies for Couples*, edited by Violet Blue, published by Cleis Press. It is copyright © 2003 by Elle McCaul and is reprinted by permission of the author.
"Blind" first appeared in *Torn Shapes of Desire*, published by Intangible Assets Manufacturing. It is copyright © 1997 by Mary Anne Mohanraj and is reprinted by permission of the author.
"Day 1,617: The Inevitability of Isabel" first appeared on alt.sex.bondage.com. It is copyright © 1994 by Adrian Hunter and is reprinted by permission of the author.
The remaining stories in this collection are copyright © 2004 by their respective authors. They are used by permission.

PRINTING HISTORY
Venus Book Club hardcover edition / 2004
Heat trade paperback edition / July 2005

Library of Congress Cataloging-in-Publication Data

Master/slave / edited by N. T. Morley.
    p. cm.
    Originally published by Venus Book Club (Garden City, N.Y.) as two separate works:
Master (2004) and Slave (2004), but here combined into one.
    ISBN 0-425-20269-0
    1. Sadomasochism—Fiction. 2. Erotic stories, American. I. Morley, N. T. II. Master III. Slave.
PS648.S24M37 2005
813'01083538'090511—dc22

                                    2005040425

CONTENTS

Introduction
by N. T. Morley

What is it about a submissive woman that makes her experience so compelling? So much erotica, regardless of style or orientation, is about the descent into submission as a woman surrenders to her most secret desires. My own writing focuses almost exclusively on the naive virgin character getting her comeuppance—both because and in spite of her own clever machinations as she simultaneously seeks and shies away from the submission she so desperately craves.

In *slave*, I have collected thirty stories where a woman enjoys and even celebrates her submission—but there is often, in these sizzling stories, the hint of reluctance. For me that only makes the heat rise, as I suspect it will for many of the readers, both male and female. Whether you're identifying with the woman's surrender or placing yourself in the shoes of her forceful seducer, I'm sure you'll agree with me that the women in these stories are so tempting, so alluring, so exciting precisely because they are being pushed to their limits—and beyond. While I have stayed away from openly nonconsensual stories, all the stories in this book play with the resistance of the submissive—after all, what fun is being overwhelmed if you can't fight back?

But these are more than simple sweets intended to satisfy for a moment. They leave a lasting impression, because if one theme runs through these stories, it's that submission is a profound act of love. Whether that love is self-directed (the woman getting exactly what she wants, as most of these women do) or other-directed (the poor girl submitting willingly only to please her lover) makes little difference, since the beauty of much BDSM play is that both partners get what they want precisely because their (presumed) negotiation has freed them from the sticky necessities of lovers being equal in bed. Here, women are controlled, captured, bound, punished, humiliated, degraded, treated as property. And they love it. Willingness to surrender to, or even beg for, such treatment *is* a magnificent kind of love, and it implies a trust of one's lover greater than that shown anywhere outside the bedroom.

In no uncertain terms, however, let me remind you that I refer to the bedroom in figurative terms only. The women in *slave* are far too hungry, horny, and willing to let their lusts be confined to the boudoir. Rather, the femmes herein turn entire apartment buildings into palaces for their pleasure; they kneel and beg and strip and surrender everywhere they can; they put their asses in the air in restaurants, libraries, and nightclubs, in speeding automobiles and '50s-style diners, on their best friends' beds while partygoers mingle outside, in warehouses filled with strange men who use them in every way possible, to everyone's dark delight. And, it almost goes without saying, they submit to their well-deserved and much-longed-for punishments in dungeons, those modern palaces we've built in basements, garages, and back rooms; these women experience their ecstasy bound to crosses and hanging from rafters and bent deliciously over strange men's knees. But there are bedrooms here, too—women who succumb to their desperate ecstasy with their arms and legs tied to four-poster beds, behinds raised high to receive their lovers' forceful attentions, whether from hand or paddle or flogger or cock. There are even, believe it or not, girls who do it missionary style, but that makes them no less kinky—if there's a hint of vanilla in here, I'll drown myself in chocolate sauce.

I've brought these stories together with a sense of great love, profound affection, and deep respect for the naughty girls who kneel, bow down, and bend over for what they want, what they need, and—perhaps more importantly—what they deserve. They deserve pleasure, as much as they can stand and more, and freedom, no matter what the cost—because pleasure often hurts, and freedom, even more often, comes in its most profound form with leather cuffs around your wrists and ankles, a collar around your throat, and a rubber ball gag filling your mouth.

And these ladies, bless them, like it like that.

In fact, they wouldn't have it any other way.

—N. T. Morley
San Francisco, Summer 2003

The Super
by Alison Tyler

Alison Tyler is undeniably a naughty girl. With best friend Dante Davidson, she is the coeditor of the best-selling collection of short stories *Bondage on a Budget*. Her short stories have appeared in anthologies including *Erotic Travel Tales 1* and *2, Sweet Life 1* and *2, Wicked Words 4, 5, 6,* and *8, Best Women's Erotica 2002* and *2003, Guilty Pleasures,* and *Sex Toy Tales*. With Thomas S. Roche she is the coauthor of *His* and *Hers*, both from Pretty Things Press.

In our first story, "The Super," Tyler delves into the kind of taboo sexual roles and spanking-good fun that make so many of her stories sizzle. Of this story, Tyler writes: "I've always been into role-playing with my beaus. Undergoing a transforming can make a sexual encounter vibrate with intensity. But it doesn't matter what costume I slide into—naughty school girl, tarty nurse, slovenly secretary—my stories generally have the same moral: bad girls get spanked." "The Super" reaches the inevitable ending with a bit of humor and plenty of powerful paddling.

His wife-beater T-shirt caught my eye first. The tight-ribbed cotton showed off his muscular arms and broad chest. I turned slightly to look at him, my hand on the small copper mailbox key, my whole body still, like a deer, appraising the chances of crossing the street safely. If he noticed me, would that be a good thing or a bad thing? The connection happened suddenly. His eyes made forceful contact with my legs, and I felt each moment as he took his time appraising my outfit: slim short skirt in classic Burberry "Nova" plaid, opaque black stockings, shiny patent-leather penny loafers, and lace shirt with a Johnny collar that was probably a bit too sheer for work, but I paired it with a skimpy peach-colored camisole and nobody said anything. Maybe somebody should have.

He did.

"Wore that to work today, did you?"

I blushed, instantly, automatically, and pretended there was dire importance in the action of checking my mail. My fingers felt slippery on the multitude of magazines and catalogs stuffed inside the tiny box, and I hoped I wouldn't drop the whole handful of mail. I could feel him moving closer, and now I could smell him, as well. Some masculine scent, mentholated shaving cream, or aftershave. Not cologne. Wouldn't be his style.

His hands were on me now, thick fingers smoothing the collar of the shirt, then caressing the nape of my neck, his thumb running up and down until I leaned my head back against his large hand. Crazy, right? In the lobby of the apartment building, letting this man touch me. But I couldn't help myself.

"A little slutty," he said, "don't you think?"

My mind reeled at the insult. Slutty? The entire outfit cost more than a thousand dollars. The skirt alone was worth nearly half of that. Now, his hand became a fist around my hair, gathering my black-cherry curls into a makeshift ponytail and holding me tight.

"Don't you think?" he repeated, his voice tighter, as tight as his fist around my long hair. With his free hand, he pushed my mail back into the box and flipped shut the door. I dropped my hands to my sides, not needing to pretend to busy myself any longer.

"Yes," I murmured, agreeing suddenly. It *was* slutty, the skirt far too short for a professional woman, the shirt sheer enough to be lingerie. The whole outfit was much more appropriate for bedroom games than office politics. What had I been thinking when I got dressed that morning?

"Yes—" he repeated, his voice tighter still.

"Yes, Sir," came just as automatically as my agreement, as automatically as my feet began to move as he pushed me forward to the apartment at the end of the long, narrow hallway. I stumbled once on the blue and maroon Oriental runner, but he caught me, his other hand high up on my arm, so firmly gripping me that I could feel the indents of his fingers digging into my skin. I'd have marks, I knew it, dark purple bruises showing each place his fingers made contact, but I said nothing.

He hurried me through the door to the living room, then kicked the door closed and hauled me quickly to the sofa. I saw everything swirling around me. The chocolate leather of the sofa, the bare shiny wood of the floor. He sat down and looked at me, and I shifted uncomfortably before him. I knew better than to sit, knew better than to do anything but wait. Yet waiting was the worst. Waiting and wondering. And hoping.

Of course, hoping—

"Dressed like a naughty little schoolgirl," he hissed through his teeth. "Dressed in public like that," he continued, shaking his head now, as if he couldn't fucking believe it.

I looked down at my feet, head bowed, curls falling free now around my face, and all I could see were my polished loafers and his scuffed work boots, the dark denim blue of his Levi's, the wood floor . . .

"Do you have anything to say for yourself?" he asked. "Anything to say in your defense?" I shook my head no. Immediately, he was standing, his hand around my hair again, my face pulled fiercely back so that I was looking up into his gaze. The way he held my hair hurt now, and I clearly understood the message he was sending me.

"No, Sir—" I said, quickly, but not quickly enough. He had me bent over the side of the sofa in an instant, my skirt roughly pulled up to reveal the lilac rosettes adorning the tops of my garters, then yanked even higher to show my black satin panties. I heard the whisper-hiss of his belt as he pulled it free from the loops of his jeans, and then I felt the air—that crackle-shiver of moving air—before the leather connected with my upturned ass.

Fire. That was the instant vision alive in my brain. Fire. Pain like fire, so hot and hard that I gasped for air. The pain seemed to grow, spreading through me, flowing over me. He struck me six times with the belt over my panties before sliding his meaty fingers under the waistband and pulling them down. I closed my eyes now, knowing the pain would intensify without that filmy shield, and trying to prepare myself for this—even though I knew that was impossible.

"Say, 'Thank you, Sir,' after every blow," he commanded.

"Thank you—" I started, but he hadn't struck me yet.

His lips were against my ear as he hissed, "Are you messing with me, girl?"

"No, Sir!" Louder than I'd thought. Louder than I'd heard the words in my head. I sounded like a soldier. No, Sir! Punctuated fiercely with my inherent willingness to obey.

"Don't mess with me, young lady," he said. "Don't test me." He then kissed me, high up on my cheek, and I trembled even more. The feeling of his gentle lips pressed to me, combined with the knowledge that he was about to grant me a serious hiding, left me twisted and shuddering inside.

The thrashing continued, now with the belt meeting my bare ass, and I did my best to choke out, "Thank you, Sir," after each blow. Didn't do quite well enough, though, because he had to continually up the intensity of the blows to keep me in line. Until finally, he moved forward, grabbing my arms and using the belt now to bind my wrists behind my back. Against the couch, I balanced, body arched, waiting, waiting for what came next.

I'd thought about this moment all day, and it had been difficult for me to get any work done. Every time I tried to concentrate, I envisioned myself with my knickers at my ankles, ass in the air, submitting to the punishment I so desperately craved. Needed. Yearned for. Deserved. Every time I opened a new file, or clicked my mouse on a spreadsheet, I lost myself in forbidden daydreams. Now, those daydreams were coming true.

I sighed, inwardly delighted, when he tested between my legs for the wetness. I felt as if only one stroke of his calloused thumb against my clit would get me off. But he didn't touch me the way I needed, changing my sighs to desperate mews.

"Not done, yet," he hissed at me. "Not quite done, yet—"

Before I fully understood what he was doing, he had me over his lap, my wrists still captured, head turned on a sofa cushion, my body in perfect position for a bare-hand spanking on my naked behind. I was already smarting, so hot from the belt, but that didn't stop him from delivering another series of stinging blows on my throbbing ass.

I squirmed my hips against his knees to gain the contact I craved, and this time, he didn't admonish me. He let me leave a wet spot on his jeans before undoing the buckle of his belt, freeing my wrists, and repositioning me over the edge of the sofa. This is the way he was going to fuck me, with my ass so hot and red from the belt and his hand, with my pussy swimming in sex juices.

He slid in and I gripped him immediately, and then he placed one hand in between the sofa and my body and began to stroke and tickle my clit as he fucked me. The sensations were almost too powerful to handle. I closed my eyes and thought about how I'd spent my day. From the second I woke up, still in bed when I planned my outfit, I'd thought of this moment. At work, when he'd called to check and see if I had been a good girl or a bad girl, I'd nearly lost it—hurrying to the bathroom to rub and rub at my clit, but unable to make myself come without the pain that he so generously dispenses.

The pain and the pleasure.

Now, as I came, I thought about our arrangement. Whenever I wear my schoolgirl skirt out of the house, I know I'm going to get a spanking, know that I'm going to have to be taught a lesson when I get home. That my man will have left his expensive suit in the closet and changed into the working-class superintendent of our building, ready to dole out punishment to any needy young lady. Truth is, I can hardly get through a week without wearing something that will catch his eye and make him shake his head.

"I love it when you wear that skirt, baby—" Mark said.

I smiled as I looked down at the rumpled Burberry plaid, then imagined what I might sneak out of the house in tomorrow . . .

Blind
by Mary Anne Mohanraj

One of erotica's brightest lights, **Mary Anne Mohanraj** is known as the author of *Torn Shapes of Desire*, *Kathryn in the City*, and *The Classics Professor*. She also edited the very popular erotica collections *Aqua Erotica* and *Wet*. Her writing has appeared in a wide variety of anthologies and magazines, including *Herotica 6*, *Best American Erotica 1999*, and *Best Women's Erotica 2000* and *2001*.

Mohanraj also founded the erotic webzine *Clean Sheets* (www.cleansheets.com) and serves as editor-in-chief for the Hugo-nominated speculative fiction webzine *Strange Horizons* (www.strangehorizons.com). She is currently a doctoral student in fiction and literature at the University of Utah. She has received the Scowcroft Prize for Fiction, a Neff fellowship in English, and currently holds a Steffenson-Canon fellowship in the Humanities.

Mohanraj tells us that "Blind" is "pure fantasy, through and through. If only we all had partners willing and able to fulfill our fantasies so thoroughly!"

I wake to darkness.

The champagne lingers in my body, and I do not know how long I have been asleep. Perhaps I dozed off briefly during the birthday celebration—I am not used to so much champagne. Maybe I have been asleep for hours, and Joshua has ushered out the guests and turned out the lights.

There is a heaviness across my eyes, something pressing against the skin. I try to bring my hand to my face, to test what feels like silk, or chiffon . . . and discover my hands are bound behind me. Gently, comfortably, but without any extra give at all. I am curled on my side, my arms behind me, my legs tucked under, blind.

This is probably one of his little games, but I hear no voices, feel no touch of callused hand or stubbled chin. I breathe deeply and open my mouth to scream for him . . . and a finger lands softly on it, as a feather might, and a stranger's voice whispers, "Hush."

I do not know who is here. I do not know who is here with me, in my blue-painted room, in my flannel-sheeted bed. I do not know whether to scream or smile or wait. Maybe I am dreaming.

A hand slips between my legs, parting them gently. This hand is soft, testing, and I am dry as desert, and I do not know if that is what the stranger wants. Apparently not, for he/she parts my legs even more, and a wet mouth is suddenly moving on me. The mouth plays me like an old friend, tracing a delicate path from inner thigh to hipbone to circle around my clit and back again. This is not Joshua's touch. This is not a rapist's touch.

I try to remember the tongues of all my lovers. All of them, every one, did this at one time or another. It's hard to distinguish once you're past your fourth or fifth, and the growing fire between my damp thighs is making it hard to think. I am trembling now, as soft hair brushes my hip and a warm tongue thrusts in and out, followed swiftly by one, two, three fingers. And then I am arching, moaning, begging this stranger, and a tongue is tasting my neck and this, this is Joshua, biting softly and the world is starting to dissolve around me . . . they stop.

Cold hands grasp my breasts and squeeze, hard, forcing a gasp. They twist my nipples cruelly, and I am helpless against this. Tighter and tighter, and then the fingers are replaced by two mouths, biting softer, then harder, until I am pleading, no, don't, nooo . . .

I do not say stop. One continues and the other slides behind me, and I cannot tell who it is. Male, though, his hairless chest pressed hard against my thin shirt, his erection hard against me. My skirt must be pushed out of the way; I can feel the texture of his warm skin against my own shivering.

Fingers gently probe my asshole, and I contract, tense. The mouth on my breast stops its assault suddenly, and it is kissing me, a stranger's kiss on my lips and so it is Joshua behind me, unless there are more than two here. Fingers return to squeezing nipples, and gentle lips drop butterfly kisses against my mouth, my cheeks, my chin. Joshua's fingers, I hope, are cold and wet between my cheeks, sliding in and out and around, going deeper and deeper each moment.

A cock slides between my thighs, rubbing gently against my clit as his hips move forward to meet mine. The man in front of me, a man I do not know, continues to kiss me as his cock strokes me, his mouth gently promising, not asking.

I do not remember when I first started telling Joshua my fantasies. The one about sex with a stranger. The one about two people at once. The one about two men at once, two cocks inside me. The one about pain. The one about being blind.

A cock presses against my asshole, insistent, demanding. It pushes forward, and I cannot tell how long an eternity it takes to make its way inside. The stranger alternates breast and breast and mouth and neck, at one moment his teeth and Joshua's on opposite sides of my neck, at another so close they might be kissing. Fingers tease my nipples, my clit, rake fiercely along my back and sides and always the cock in my ass is sliding further and further, until it is lodged inside me and I am almost weeping.

Then the stranger slams into me, his cock in my cunt, his smooth chest crushing my breasts and I am crushed between them, and they are kissing me everywhere. The cocks slide in and out, slowly at first, alternating then synchronous and back again. And the stranger is gripping my head between his hands, his thumbs pressed firmly through the cloth against my shut eyes, and Joshua's leg wraps around us both as he thrusts harder and harder; as my moans get louder and louder and he is whispering words of love and the stranger is silent, his chest against my breasts, rubbing and rubbing. And the world once again begins to dissolve, to slow, to freeze with that particular peculiar stillness, as they slam my body between them, and the two cocks erupt, one after another and I cannot tell which is first and the stranger suddenly tears the blindfold from my eyes.

And I come screaming into the light.

In the Stacks
by Kristina Wright

Kristina Wright is a full-time writer and a part-time assistant librarian. Her erotica has appeared in the anthologies *Best Women's Erotica 2000; Sweet Life: Erotic Fantasies for Couples; Best Lesbian Erotica 2002; Ripe Fruit: Well-Seasoned Erotica; Bedroom Eyes: Stories of Lesbians in the Boudoir*; and the forthcoming *Sex Toy Tales 2*. Her stories have appeared on the websites *Scarlet Letters* (www.scarletletters.com), *Good Vibes Magazine* (www.goodvibes.com), *Clean Sheets* (www.cleansheets.com), *Libida* (www.Libida.com), and Blowfish e-mail newsletter (www.Blowfish.com). Her work has also appeared in novel length from Silhouette Books.

About "In the Stacks," Wright says: "As an independent, self-assured, sexually confident woman, I've always been intrigued (and, early on, a little frightened) by the side of me that longs to be dominated. It is neither politically correct nor socially acceptable, but it is powerful and very, very arousing. Mixing my own submissive desires with the reality of my job in a library, I wrote 'In the Stacks' in a heated rush and with a smirk on my face. I wanted to capture the revelation of submission in the so-called 'mild-mannered librarian' who is forced to face her true nature, much as I've come to terms with mine. What makes this story especially hot, in my opinion, is the context of the relationship. A stranger walks into her life and captures her imagination, awakening the sleeping dragon of her submission and enslaving her for as long as he holds the key to her desire. It's the perfect storybook tale, complete with a dominant hero and a kinky twist. What better bedtime story than that?"

He came in one evening shortly before the library closed, looking for information on nautical knots. I pushed my glasses up on my nose and searched the database. Four titles, all about knots. He smiled, this quirky little smile that hinted at some secret I couldn't begin to fathom, thanked me, and left with three of the books. The fourth didn't have enough pictures, he said. He liked pictures.

I forgot about him. You tend to forget the ones that only come in occasionally, who ask one question and never come back. But he came back. I don't remember how long it was. A month, maybe two? But he came back and something about that little smile reminded me of the knots.

He wasn't handsome in the classical sense. He was average look-ing, average height. The kind of guy who could be really cute if you liked him or nondescript if you'd only met him once or twice. But the smile—that made him stand out. It would be a while before I'd notice that his eyes held the same secretive amusement as his smile.

The next time he came to the reference desk he asked about the Marquis de Sade. Not his fiction, a biography. Not a usual request for a small-town library in the heart of Virginia. I checked the database. Just two biographies on the Marquis. He took them both. I felt a little strange leading him back toward the biography section, deep in the shadows of the nonfiction stacks. Maybe it was the smile.

I pulled the books and handed them to him.

"Ever read him?" he asked, tapping the cover of the top book.

I could feel myself blush as I shook my head. "Uh, no."

That smile again. Amused, knowing. "But you know who he is."

Not a question, but I nodded. Then I hurried out of the stacks and back to the refuge of my desk with a muttered, "I have patrons waiting." I didn't, and he knew it. I think I heard him laugh.

After he left, I looked him up. It's against the rules, but I needed to know. His name was Justin Brant and he was forty-one years old. I knew the neighborhood he lived in; it wasn't far from my own town-house. I also knew the types of books he liked—historical biogra-phies of questionable characters and action-adventure. Harmless enough. Yet something about him stayed with me long after he left.

I'm embarrassed to say I checked the status on the Sade biographies for the next couple of weeks. He renewed them both once. I found that interesting. Either he didn't have time to read them or he was being very thorough in his research.

He came in one night just before closing. I didn't see him at first; I was reading over some paperwork when I felt his gaze like a weight on my shoulders. I glanced up to see him staring intently at me.

"May I help you?" I asked, sounding colder than I felt. My palms were already beginning to sweat and he hadn't yet said anything to me.

He smirked. "No, I found what I was looking for this time." He gestured at the stack of books in his hand. The title of the one on top mentioned nude photography.

"Oh."

The smirk deepened. "I was wondering if you'd like to have coffee sometime, maybe one night after work?"

"I don't think so," I said quickly, glancing around to see if anyone had heard him. "I mean—thank you, but I don't think we really have much in common."

The smirk never faltered. "No? What a pity. I thought I turned you on."

He was gone before I could pick my jaw off the floor.

I was curious, I admit it. So when I pulled out of the parking lot half an hour later, I turned left instead of right. I drove the five miles to the street where he lived. I turned onto the street in a very nice subdivision and drove along the main road that circled the hundred or so houses. I found his house, tucked in a cul-de-sac. I was so intent on making sure I had the right house number, I didn't realize someone was getting out of the Mercedes in the driveway. It was him!

I sped away, heart hammering in my chest. He couldn't have seen me, as he wasn't looking in my direction. Still, I could feel my cheeks flush hotly as I drove the few miles to my house. Whatever his charm, I wouldn't do that again.

I almost dreaded seeing him at the library again. Almost. Here I was, thirty-seven and hopelessly single, mooning over some pervert who used the library as his dirty bookstore.

Still, there was something about him that suggested he'd be able to tell me all the secrets I'd been wanting to know. Questions I wasn't even sure how to ask. Maybe he was a pervert, but if he was, so was I. Because he had my mind going down a road it had never been, and my willing cunt followed.

By the time I saw him again, I was debating the idea of calling him. It would have been highly inappropriate and I could have lost my job for it, but desperate times call for desperate measures, to my way of thinking. Who am I kidding? I wasn't thinking, I was only feeling. And it felt good.

Strangely enough, it wasn't the library where I saw him next, but the grocery store. I was standing at the bakery counter, choosing a loaf of bread, when I heard a familiar laugh. I jerked my head around just in time to catch his smile as he turned and walked away. My cheeks flushed hotly, but instead of ignoring him, I followed him, bread forgotten.

"Wait. Hey! Mr. Brant, Justin—wait."

He turned and looked at me. We were standing alone in the wine aisle. It was after ten o'clock and there were few people in the store.

"Yes?"

I stopped in front of him, suddenly speechless. "I was just—I mean—"

He arched an eyebrow. "How did you know my name?"

My face felt like it was on fire. I couldn't think of a good lie quick enough. "I looked you up," I blurted.

"I like that."

That made me feel warm for an entirely different reason. "Can we go someplace?" I asked, emboldened. "To talk?"

"Talk?"

I felt like he was teasing me. "Yes, talk," I said, suddenly angry. Not at him, at myself for being so foolish. "Never mind, forget I asked."

He grabbed my wrist with a gentle but insistent pressure that was impossible to ignore. "I don't forget anything," he said. "Ask me again."

Part of me screamed to get out of there and away from him. Part of me never wanted him to let go of my wrist. "Would you like to go somewhere and talk?" My voice was soft, I could barely hear myself, but he didn't seem to have a problem.

"Good. You're learning."

There was a condescension in his voice I wouldn't have tolerated from anyone else. So why was I taking it from him? Something about his confidence, maybe. Or maybe I was just ready for someone like him. In any case, his approval sent a little thrill through me that I hadn't experienced in a long, long time.

We each paid for our groceries, waiting in line silently. Then he told me to follow him. I liked that better than going with him. I was curious, but I wasn't stupid.

He drove to a coffee shop about a mile from the library. I'd passed the place a thousand times, but I'd never been there. I parked next to him and followed him inside.

The waitress nodded to him as if he was a regular. We sat in a booth near the back, the only other patron an elderly man sitting at the counter. Justin sat across from me, studying me with dark, unblinking eyes.

"What?" I said, fidgeting nervously.

"Sit still."

Like an obedient dog, I immediately quieted. Then I frowned.

"What's the matter?" he asked.

I shook my head. "I don't know."

"Yes, you do. Tell me."

I started to say I really didn't know, but I could feel my frown deepening. "I don't like you."

He chuckled and it was a soft, seductive sound that washed over my skin like a touch. "No. What you don't like is how you respond to me."

I opened my mouth to deny it and he held up his hand.

"Don't. Don't lie to me and don't lie to yourself. You respond to me and it confuses you."

I thought about that for a moment. "Yes," I said, though it hadn't been a question.

The waitress came over and took our order—a black coffee for him and a hot chocolate for me. When she was gone, he stared at me once more.

"Why do you think that is?" he asked.

I'd lost track of our conversation for a moment, so caught up in his steady gaze. "What?"

His lips thinned to a straight line. "Pay attention. Why do you think it bothers you to respond to me?"

I didn't like the conversation, but I knew if I continued to argue with him, he would leave. I wasn't sure how I knew it, but I did. I thought hard for a moment, trying to put my feelings into words. "Because I'm used to being in control."

"And I make you feel out of control?"

I played with the salt and pepper shakers. "You make me question myself."

"Interesting."

I felt like a science project. I also felt a need to clarify myself. "It's mostly curiosity," I said, sounding defensive even to my own ears. "It's not like this is going anywhere."

Again, that soft, sexy laugh. "Oh, really? Is that what you think?"

I didn't get a chance to respond because the waitress brought our drinks. I waited until she'd gone off behind the counter once more before saying anything.

"I think I'm going to be very careful around you."

He nodded. "Smart girl."

We talked then, about inconsequential things. My job as a librarian, his as a college professor. I wasn't surprised he taught college. He had the air of a man comfortable in academia, in instruction. I wondered, almost jealously, if any of his female students had experienced his disciplining side. Somehow, I didn't doubt it.

An hour slipped by and my cocoa grew cold. He pulled a few bills from his wallet and tossed them on the table. I felt an irrational disappointment to know our time together was over.

"Don't frown," he said.

"I didn't know I was."

He reached across the scarred table and circled my wrist with his fingers. I could feel my pulse jump and I knew he could, too. "You're upset it's time to go."

I swallowed hard, but I nodded.

"So, don't leave me just yet. Come to my house."

I gently tugged my wrist free of his grasp. "I can't go with you. I don't even know you."

He studied me carefully, as if memorizing me. "You know me. And you're afraid of what I know about you."

Almost against my will, I asked, "What do you know about me?"

His fingers took my wrist once more. "I know you're nervous, a little afraid." His grip tightened. "I also know if I asked you to go to the restroom and remove your panties, they would be soaking wet."

I gasped, but I didn't attempt to pull away. Nor did I deny his statement. How could I? I'd been wet since I'd spotted him in the grocery store.

He smiled. "Good. I didn't want another argument." He rubbed his thumb over the pulse in my wrist. "Now, do you want to come with me?"

I didn't miss the double entendre. "I don't know."

"Honest enough. Would it make you feel more comfortable to go to your place?"

I thought for a moment before I shook my head. "I don't think so."

A frown line creased his brow. The pressure on my wrist grew tighter. "Then what?" Then, a smile. "Oh, I think I know."

Again, my pulse began to race. "What?"

"Do you have a key to the library?"

"Oh, God."

More pressure. "Answer me, please."

I nodded.

"And there's a security system, I'm sure. You know the code?"

"Yes," I whispered hoarsely.

My mind was racing as quickly as my pulse. Could I get away with it? Yes, probably. The library was tucked away off the main street through town; no one would be likely to notice if we slipped in through the back door and didn't turn on the lights. But just because I could get away with it didn't make it a good idea.

"Don't think about it. Just feel. React. Respond. The only consequences are the ones you make for yourself."

I didn't believe him for a minute, but I knew I was in too deep to say no. Even the threat of losing my job wasn't enough to keep me from sliding out of the booth and walking toward the door. I was going to do it. Not because he told me to, but because I wanted it.

The library was dark and silent, the parking lot empty, just as I knew it would be. He'd followed in his car and parked beside me in the employee parking area. I led the way to the employee entrance, keys jingling in my trembling fingers. At the door, he put his hand over mine as I went to insert the key in the lock.

"This is it. If you don't want to do this, say so now and it's over." He caressed my hand with the most delicate of touches. "But if we go inside, be prepared to give up your control."

I'd already worked it out in my mind, but when he put it that way, I hesitated.

He smiled, and it was a wicked smile. "But if we do go inside, I promise you won't regret it."

I turned the key and entered the security code. My hands were hardly trembling by the time I led him into my office behind the circulation desk. Now that I'd committed to this, I was feeling calmer.

He sat in the comfy chair in the corner, leaving me standing in the middle of the room between my desk and the door. He looked around, studying the pictures of Paris and Milan hanging over my desk. My office window looked out onto a pretty garden area with reading benches. At this hour, all I could see were the lights from the parking lot.

"Close the blinds," he said.

I didn't argue or question. The last thing I needed was a nosy teenager, or worse, a cop, driving by and peeking in the window. While I wasn't quite sure what was going to happen, I was pretty sure I didn't want anyone watching.

When the blinds were closed, he nodded. "Good. Now turn on the desk lamp."

The lamp he was referring to was more decorative than functional. I quickly obeyed and the parchment lampshade cast an intimate golden glow across my office.

"Now, strip."

Whatever I'd expected, it hadn't been that.

I fumbled with the buttons on my blouse. There was still some rational part of my brain that couldn't believe I was undressing in front of a stranger. In my office, no less.

The blouse fell away, leaving me in my bra and conservative skirt. I paused, waiting for him to say more, but he didn't. He only stared.

I reached behind me and unzipped my skirt. The motion forced my breasts up and out, and I watched his eyes drift to my chest. My nipples responded to his gaze as if he touched me. I felt them tighten, pushing out the material of my bra.

The skirt pooled at my feet. I reached for the clasp of my bra, afraid that if I hesitated, I wouldn't be able to do it.

Justin watched as I removed the bra. He watched as I slipped out of my shoes. My legs were bare, the summer weather and a good tan making stockings unnecessary. My panties glided down my thighs and then I stood before him naked.

"Very nice," he said. His voice was cool and distant, as if he was admiring a piece of artwork. "How do you feel?"

"Vulnerable," I whispered.

"And?"

"Excited." The confession came at a price. I could feel myself blushing and knew he could see it on my neck and breasts.

"Good. That's how you should feel."

A long moment went by as he stared at me and I resisted the urge to fidget. Finally, when I couldn't take his silence any longer, I said, "Now what?"

"Impatient?"

I nodded, though I wasn't sure what he was asking for.

"Do you like pain?"

The question took me by surprise and I blurted, "No!"

He tsked. "Get dressed."

"What? Why? What did I do?"

Justin stood quickly and I took a step back. "You misled me. I thought you shared my interests."

"I don't know—"

He closed the distance between us in two long strides. My back was up against the wall, the soft brush of his shirt against my bare breasts. My breathing was ragged and harsh. I realized I sounded like a woman in arousal, not someone who was afraid.

"You know exactly what I'm talking about. I'm interested in exploring pain. Namely, yours." He took my nipples between his fingers. "If you want me to stop, simply pull away."

I couldn't have moved if the security alarm had gone off.

"If you want me to continue, ask me to hurt you."

His words were soft and surprisingly arousing. I lowered my head, ashamed and embarrassed by my feelings, my gaze falling to my nipples imprisoned in his fingers. The sight of my pink nipples against his tanned fingers brought a soft moan to my lips.

"Well?"

"Please."

"Please what?" His fingers just barely held my nipples. "Don't play games with me, little one. You won't win."

I raised my head until I met his gaze. "Please hurt me, Justin."

Almost immediately, he began to twist my nipples. If I had thought about it, I might have said the pain began even before I asked for it, as if he knew I would ask. The pain intensified, a warmth flowing from the tips of my breasts across my chest, radiating a steady, constant pressure that became more and more intense.

I wanted to squirm, to cry out, but something in his expression made me stay still and quiet, my back pressed to the hard wall while he tortured my tender breasts. He gave my nipples a particularly vicious twist and I bit my lip until I tasted blood. It hurt, no doubt about it, but there was also a heaviness in my cunt, a corresponding tingle in my clit with every painful twist of my nipples.

"You please me," he whispered. He leaned close and gave me a chaste kiss on the lips that seemed incongruous with the rest of the situation. "Your threshold for pain is going to be a delightful challenge."

I wasn't sure I liked the sound of that, yet I felt myself smiling in spite of the pain. "Thank you."

He tugged my nipples out from my breasts, stretching the already pained skin, then released them. The ache began as the blood flowed back into them and I moaned softly.

"Nice."

Before I could respond, his hand was between my thighs, squeezing my cunt. The sensation was pleasurable at first and I pressed against his palm. Then he exerted the same pressure on my pussy that he had on my nipples and I gasped.

"Pain with pleasure," he murmured. "There's nothing like it."

I wanted to ask him how he knew, if he'd ever felt pain during sexual arousal or if he only liked to inflict it. The words died in my throat as his fingers found my clit. With a quick, steady motion he kneaded my swollen flesh roughly. So rough, in fact, my body couldn't decide whether it felt good or hurt. My hips moved of their own accord, alternately thrusting against his wrist and pulling back as far as the wall would allow.

"Don't think about it," he said. "Let your body decide what it likes."

I closed my eyes and rested my head against the wall. My body was aching for release; that much I knew. Justin seemed to realize that, because each time my body would tense for orgasm, he would pinch my clit that much harder.

"Please," I begged, though I could barely speak loud enough to hear myself. "I can't take any more."

He chuckled softly and rolled my swollen clit. "You'll be surprised how much you can take."

I shook my head, denying him—or denying myself? I couldn't be sure.

"You're going to come on my hand," he said, matter-of-factly. "You're going to come and it's going to be stronger and harder than anything you've ever experienced."

I kept shaking my head.

"Yes, you are. And it's going to hurt, which is going to confuse you more." He pushed a finger in my drenched cunt, then slid another one in for good measure. "But you're going to love it and you won't want it to stop."

He was finger-fucking me now, hard. Hard enough to lift me up on my toes with each thrust of his hand. I whimpered and moaned, clutching at his shoulders with my hands, but not pushing him away.

"That's it," he coaxed. "Feel it, feel everything. Come on my hand. Let your body have what it needs."

I was moaning now, almost screaming with the intensity of the sensations he was causing. I could feel his cock, hard and insistent, pressing against my hip bone as he angled his fingers higher into my cunt. He wanted me. He was giving me pleasure and hurting me at the same time and he wanted to fuck me. The fact that he wasn't as distant as he sounded made me relax.

"Come," he said. And though his voice was as harsh and cold as his fingers in my cunt, I knew he was enjoying me.

With his fingers driving into my cunt and my clit rubbing against his wrist, I came. I clung to him, whimpering and sobbing as I rode a powerful orgasm, his demanding cock bruising my hip, wanting me.

"Yes," he hissed, close to my ear. "It's what you need. Show me what you need."

I sagged against him, no longer caring I was naked and vulnerable in my own office. All that mattered was the orgasm, the release. What he had given me, what he had taken from me. They were one and the same. I came and whimpered and said his name like a prayer.

He lowered me to my knees, his hand cradling my head against his erection. The fabric of his pants was soft against my cheek and I nuzzled him, weak and satisfied and still craving more.

He pressed my head against his cock, hard, then harder still, until I thought he might leave a mark on my skin from the zipper. I let him rub his crotch against my face, wanting only to please him.

He gave my hair a tug, forcing me to look up at him. "What do you say?"

My brain felt fuzzy, my speech slow and thick when it finally came. But I knew what he wanted. I knew it instinctively. "Thank you."

"Your pain arouses me," he said, holding me against his cock as proof. "That's the first lesson."

"Will there be more lessons?" I dared to ask, looking up at him. My heart was throbbing in my chest, afraid he was going to leave me now that he'd proven he could have me.

He smiled. It wasn't a pleasant smile. "We've only just begun."

Zombie Love
by Elizabeth Colvin

Elizabeth Colvin is a journalist and sex educator who has written fiction and nonfiction for Good Vibes Magazine (www.goodvibes.com) and fiction for the anthologies *Sweet Life 2: More Erotic Fantasies for Couples* and the forthcoming *Naughty Stories 3*. She says: "I have always loved horror movies, because there's something incredibly hot about monsters. They're sexy, gross, and threatening, but the best horror movies are about how that monster reveals his (or her!) humanity. 'Zombie Love' is about that sense of the grotesque. I guess that's a pretentious way of talking about a monster-fucking story!"

Jake was dressed up like a zombie: that's how it started.

I mean, not that I've got a thing for monsters or anything, but you remember *Young Frankenstein*? "A creature like that would have a very large *schwanzstucker.*" Know what a *schwanzstucker* is? I didn't either. But you get the idea. Jake had one, all right, but I already knew that.

It wouldn't have tempted me so much if I wasn't dressed up like a damsel in distress. White fluffy dress, cut very close and showing a lot of cleavage, drawing stares from everyone at the party, women and men alike. Not to mention the dual slits up my legs, so high that they almost reached my hips. My blonde hair was in pigtails, my eyes painted so they looked even bigger than they are—big and bright and utterly without guile. Very sexy, but virginal.

I mean, the whole innocence gone wrong thing really appealed to me, and it was kind of turning me on knowing I looked sexy enough to draw stares from everyone. Usually Halloween is when people break out their sexy personas, the schoolgirls and sluts and cheerleaders and vamps and French maids they always wish they could be. Not this crowd.

There weren't even that many costumes—maybe half of the guests were dressed up, and those who did had gone for . . . you know, the usual lame costumes selected by people without much creative time. Lawyer types dressed as James Bond. Computer-geek army men. One woman dressed like a judge, waxing philosophic on the importance of having women on the Supreme Court.

It's not like we planned it that way, but when a party gets boring enough, you need something to keep you occupied. And Jake's always good at keeping me occupied.

Jake? He's into costumes. He found me the dress, even bought it for me. So maybe it was his idea to begin with. His costume was better than mine. He'd gone for the face paint and even a bit of a rubber prosthesis—a big gash in his head, running from his pallid chin to his pallid forehead, oozing what looked like blood. Really, really gross. It *was* Halloween, after all.

Jake's a big guy, 6'6", more than a foot taller than me with broad shoulders and muscles. He doesn't even work out and stays in perfect shape, his chest developed and his belly and legs slim and sinewy. I hate him for that. But then again, I love him for that.

"Ugh," Jake grunted at me, leaning over and nuzzling my ear as we sat on the couch listening to some loser spin another tale of dot-com riches gone poof.

I swatted his arm. "Don't get friendly," I whispered. "If you think I'm going to make it with a zombie, you're dead wrong, mister."

"Dead," he grunted into my ear. Then, quieter, "Zombies have supernatural strength," he said. "You'd be helpless to resist."

I elbowed his hard-muscled six-pack abs and put my lips to his ear. I whispered: "Just try it, Maggot Man. We'll see who's helpless to resist."

"Zombies need love, too," he whispered.

"Some zombies need a spanking."

"That, too," I heard him say.

"What are you two whispering about?" sighed Annette, one of the hosts, as she breezed by the sofa picking up discarded plastic cups. She was dressed as a fairy princess, her high-peaked cap smacking the chandelier and falling off every time she passed under it. "Care to share it with the rest of the class?"

"We were just discussing zombie love," said Jake.

"I hear it's quite compelling," winked Annette, and flitted away.

"What's with her?" I wondered in a whisper.

"She said we could use their bedroom," Jake said softly.

"For what?"

"I told her you had a headache," he whispered. "I said you might want to lie down."

"I don't have a headache," I hissed.

"I'll give you one," Jake said.

"You are already."

"Good," he said, and got up from the couch. Grasping my hand, he all but dragged me with him.

"Excuse me," he said to the other guests clustered around the couch. "I've got to go fix my makeup."

"Jake," I protested, as he dragged me along the hallway. "This is rude."

"It's a scientific fact that zombies have no social skills," he said, pushing me toward the staircase. "But they have enormous sex drives."

I felt a quiver go through me as he said that; was he really being that blatant? He was telling me that he was going to take me upstairs and fuck me in his zombie costume?

I looked at him, admiring the weirdness he'd poured into his costume: the caked blood on the tattered suit coat, the big gash in his head. But more than that, I admired the way the black, threadbare suit matched the contours of his body.

I turned and hurried up the stairs.

I had never been in Annette and Mike's bedroom; they were friends of Jake's, not mine. It smelled unfamiliar, a mix of potpourri and incense with the hint of strange bodies underneath—unique, the way every lover's bedroom smells different the first time you walk into it. They had framed prints of Klimt on the walls and a smattering of candles around the bed. The candles had been lit. More importantly, they had a big king-sized bed with an enormous, heavy wooden frame. At the head of the frame, they'd Velcro'ed three different kinds of lube in big pump bottles.

And right there in each corner, metal restraints were bolted directly to the frame.

Jake closed the door and locked it.

I turned, my eyes wide. "Wait a minute," I said. "I didn't know Annette and Mike were kinky!"

"Very much so," he said. "Even kinkier than us."

"You're not thinking . . ."

"Zombies have inordinate strength," he said, and grabbed me.

I felt like I should argue with him, but instead I sort of melted into him. When Jake and I make love, I adore the feeling of his huge bulk on top of me, his strong arms crushing me to him. I love the feeling of losing myself in his hugeness. The only problem is that he really does have an enormous *schwanzstucker*. And as for me, I'm not exactly built like the Bride of Frankenstein, know what I mean? Jake's the most patient, understanding, gentle lover I've ever had, though, so it's all good.

But this was a zombie, right? A monster. He's supposed to have an enormous one, in any event.

More importantly, there was something hot about Jake's costume. Dangerous. Scary. Don't they say fear is an aphrodisiac?

"What if Mike and Annette walk in?" I asked as Jake began to untie the back of my innocent-virgin dress.

"They won't," Jake said. "I told them I was bringing you up here to fuck you."

"Um, excuse me? Come again?"

"They're cool," he said, as he pulled the last fastener and my dress slipped off my shoulders, pooling around my feet. I stood there in a white thong and no bra, white four-inch heels on my feet lifting my head to only a foot lower than Jake's.

I could feel my nipples hardening against the wool of his thrift-store suit.

"On the bed, prisoner of love," he told me.

"Or what?"

Jake and I like to play games a little, and that was all the opening he needed. He seized me, his hands firmly gripping my shoulders, and pushed me back onto the bed. I gasped as I went bouncing onto it.

Under Jake's bulk, I was helpless as he fitted my wrists into the cool metal restraints and clicked them closed.

"I hope you have the key," I whispered.

"Nope," the zombie said cheerfully. "Annette has it."

"What?" I hissed, pulling against the restraints—but by that time, Jake was down at my legs, forcing my ankles into the manacles.

He had to stretch my legs wide, very wide, to get them to fit.

"I think the bed's too big," I squeaked. "Can you loosen them at all?

"Annette's taller than you," said Zombie Jake. "That's as loose as they get."

I lay there, utterly immobilized, stretched out on a stranger's bed, manacled. I was stretched so tight I couldn't move even a little bit. I was spread wide, my pussy exposed except for the thin slip of fabric that made up my thong.

Jake stood next to the bed and surveyed his conquest: me, spread-eagled in an X of surrender, slim breasts peaked with hard nipples as it sank in that my boyfriend was going to fuck me like this. I was about to be taken.

I was still in the innocent-virgin mode, and discovering it was a huge turn-on for me.

"Please," I whispered breathlessly. "Be gentle."

"Zombies never gentle," he grunted. "Zombie love is hard love. Zombies eat human flesh." He made a dramatic face, which got me giggling a little.

Jake shrugged off his blood-spattered suit coat and pulled his T-shirt over his head, careful not to disrupt his head wound. He quickly undid his pants and let them fall, then stripped off his boxers and kicked off his shoes.

Standing there nude except for face paint, a prosthetic head wound, zombie face makeup with whiteface, and trickles of blood running out of his mouth—I have to admit it, but Jake looked strangely compelling.

More compelling, though, was his hard cock, standing full and hard and huge, with its gentle curve beckoning to me.

Whenever I see it hard, I have to admit my mouth just starts watering. I squirmed against the steel manacles, feeling helpless, wholly owned. I could feel my pussy getting wet as my eyes ran up and down Jake's hard cock. I could feel my throat aching for it, could feel a thin dribble of saliva forming at the edge of my mouth. I slurped, perhaps a little louder than I needed to, and licked my lips.

Jake could see me looking at it. He knew what I wanted.

"Zombie need virgin," he grunted. "Evil jungle zombie god need virgin sacrifice."

"Cut the zombie crap," I breathed, "and come over here and put that thing in my mouth."

Zombie Jake crawled onto the bed, holding me down with his bulk as he squeezed his knees and his folded legs awkwardly into the space between the top of my head and the headboard. I opened wide and he guided his cock to my mouth, sliding it in until the head reached the back of my throat.

It tasted divine. I wanted to moan, but my mouth was so full. I ran my tongue along the underside and swirled it over the head, tasting his pre-come. I felt my pussy throbbing, hot and dripping, as I pressed my face up against him, coaxing him to press deeper into me.

It was a good position for doing it. Deep throating, I mean. Some girls aren't into that, I know. But nothing turns me on more. I've been working on it ever since I started going out with Jake. All I have to do is take a deep breath, hold my neck straight and swallow.

And I swallowed Jake smoothly, filling my throat as he slid into me.

I was so lost in the taste of Jake's cock and the feel of it sliding down my throat that, even though I heard him grunt "Zombie must eat human flesh," it didn't register until I felt him pulling my thong aside.

By then, his tongue was so close to my pussy that there wasn't even any time to anticipate it. It slid hard against my flesh, and he knew then—if he'd had any doubt—just how wet I was.

I laid back, neck straight, and felt Jake slowly grinding on top of me as he slid his cock down my throat. It's a more complicated sort of motion than one might think, but my favorite zombie has gotten very coordinated. So much so that he was able to fuck me slowly, smoothly, sensuously while his tongue found my clit.

If I hadn't been so full, I would have gasped; I would have moaned. As it was, I couldn't make a sound, not even low in my throat, as I felt the tip of his tongue starting to work my throbbing, swollen clitoris. I felt my body straining instinctively, trying to arch my back, lift my ass off the bed, press my pussy more firmly into his face. But I couldn't; locked in Annette's restraints, I was stretched to the limit. All I could do was lay there and let Jake use my mouth as he licked me, mercilessly, knowing exactly the touch that would make me explode into the stratosphere.

I wanted to say it. I wanted to moan it. I wanted to tell him, "Jake, baby, I'm going to come," but I couldn't. All I could do was lay there, dissolve into the sensation of his tongue on my clit and let him slide down my throat, pulling back every few seconds to let me breathe before sliding in again.

But he knew it was approaching. He could read my body, could tell from the way I tensed and struggled against the bonds that I was getting very, very close.

Which is good, because he slid his cock out of my mouth, leaving me panting and drooling, spittle covering my face and running down my chin, my mouth wide open as I finally let the wrenching moans explode from my mouth, let him know that I was only seconds away.

When I came, I tried to buck, tried to fuck my pussy against his face. It was my body, moving, like a zombie's, no brain to tell it to stop.

But it didn't matter. It was hopeless, because I was stretched so tight I couldn't move. All I could do was pull on the chains, moaning and whimpering and coming as Jake's tongue drove my clit over the edge.

When my moans quieted, I gave Jake's cock one last, savory lick, running my lips up and down its enormous length. Then he pulled away and crawled on top of me.

Between my legs.

I knew what was coming, and I felt that momentary pang of vague fear and intense, overwhelming arousal that comes from knowing that Jake is going to enter me. I didn't even realize it until I felt him guiding his thick cockhead to my pussy, though. Didn't realize that he'd reached up to the headboard and squeezed a thick glob of lube into his hand, smeared it over his cockhead, slicked more of it around the entrance to my pussy.

Usually we use lube when he fucks me—lots of it—but I guess it still caught me off guard. I was still wrapped in the costume of an innocent virgin, naive, about to be taken by a huge, scary monster—even though the costume itself, all but the thong, lay in a limpid pool at the foot of the bed.

"Zombie god demand virgin sacrifice," growled Jake, and entered me in one smooth, hard, well-lubricated thrust.

I was so wet, so turned-on, so opened, that it went into me easily; his cock took me in a single rapturous push, possessing every inch of my cunt as his big zombie body settled on top of me. I always get a little tighter right after I come, but everything feels so much better—so even the taut embrace of my pussy around Jake's huge cock made me moan with delight. I would have pushed up against him, would have lifted my ass to meet his thrust—but I couldn't move. I was his prisoner.

Jake began fucking me as I looked up into his zombie eyes. The prosthetic head wound was beginning to melt, and his face glistened with sweat, making the makeup run. Coagulated stage blood went liquid again and dripped down onto my face. The gash was disintegrating, pulling free from his flesh and turning into a mass of goo as he fucked me harder.

He looked ridiculous. I didn't laugh, though, because all I could say was, "Fuck me, zombie master. Make me your zombie princess."

Jake ground his hips slowly, leaning heavily so that his pubic bone pressed against my clit. I gasped as he did that—he knows it's the perfect way to make me come.

"Fuck," I moaned. "Fuck, yes . . ."

I was going to do it again, maybe before he did. I wished I could grind against him, wish I could push up and help him take me, help him fuck me, help him make me come. But I was immobile, and as I dissolved into the sensation of being fucked helpless, I felt my orgasm building, utterly out of my control—and then I came, stretching my limbs against the manacles, my breath choking in my throat as I closed my eyes as tight as I could. My climax exploded through me.

An instant later, my zombie lover grunted, this time not a stage grunt but a real one, an uncontrolled rumble of pleasure followed by a monster howl as he came inside me. The sensations of my pussy contracting around his thickness mingled with the feeling of slickness as he filled me with his come.

Still moaning, bathed in afterglow, I opened my eyes.

Jake's head wound finally dislodged from his head and went glop on the pillow next to me in a wet, red mass.

"Oh, fuck," he sighed.

"See?" I giggled. "It's true what they say. Love heals all wounds."

"I don't think Annette and Mike are going to see it that way," he said, eyeing the stage-bloodstain he'd made on their pillow.

"Tell you what," I whispered. "I'll convince them."

Time for a Spanking
by Sara DeMuci

In "Time for a Spanking," new writer **Sara DeMuci** places herself in the first-person narrative role, describing what she says is a semi-true relationship where she is expected to submit to punishment whenever her Master deems it necessary or—more commonly—enjoyable. What I love about this story is the palpable sense of both dread and erotic excitement, and the loving way in which Sara describes her punishment. Obviously she's learned her lessons well.

"Bend over, Sara," you tell me, and a shiver goes through me as you say my name. "It's time for a spanking."

I know what it means; I know how you want me. Naked, and bent over the bench. Way over, my arms grasping the eyebolts on the far side. My legs spread wide. My pussy exposed.

I walk meekly over to the bench and take off my clothes. First the blouse, then the skirt. I stand there in my bra and panties feeling your hungry gaze all over me. You've already selected the implement of my punishment: A long, thick paddle I've felt many times before. I unhitch the front clasp of my bra and take it off. Then I pull my panties down to my ankles and step out of them. I kick off my shoes and now I'm the way you want me: Naked.

I bend over the spanking bench, which has been built specially for me. It's exactly the right height to support my belly as I lean over, far over—so far my heels leave the ground and I stand on my tiptoes as I grasp the tie-downs. My long hair hangs down over my face. You come around the side and wrap leather restraints around my wrists, then padlock me to the eyebolts.

Then you pull up my hair and rubber-band it behind my head so you can see my face. I redden. There's no hiding from your devouring stare.

"Open your mouth," you say.

I obey, and you pop a gag into my mouth, buckling it at the back of my head. I run my tongue over it; I know the contour well. It's shaped like a cock. Even when you're punishing me you want a cock in my mouth.

And it's a very big cock. It forces my mouth wide open; I can't even beg for mercy. The gag presses deep into my mouth, almost reaching my throat. It stifles my breath and I have to take great, slow breaths through my nose.

Your fingers caress my face, reminding me that I belong to you. Your hand grasps the bun you've formed of my hair. Then, without warning, your other hand slaps me, across the face, hard. Tears form in my eyes. You slap me again, and twice more until you feel the tears drizzle out of my eyes and onto your hand. You touch them and put your fingertips in your mouth. Tasting my tears.

You hold my head firmly, and slap me three more times. A sob bursts through me, muffled by the thick gag. Five more, six, seven, eight, ten, twelve, and I'm sobbing uncontrollably behind the gag. Just the way you want me.

When you've reduced me to nothing, you're ready to continue.

You get behind me and my ankles get the same treatment as my wrists. I'm suspended, now, hanging over the spanking bench, defenseless and sobbing. Before you've even started. Before you've even spanked me once.

Your hand slides up my inner thigh until it touches my shaved pussy. I'm dripping. Gushing. You dip your fingers in my juice and smear it over my thighs. I feel its coolness as it dries, growing tacky. Reminding me that I want this, no matter how much I sob.

Tears leak out of my eyes and form a pool underneath me. You tease my clit and I try to squirm out of the restraints.

It's hopeless. I'm bound fast.

You run the edge of the paddle over my cunt. You gently stroke my sweet spot with the flat of it. I moan. I sob. You strike me.

Hard. No warm-up. No warm-up at all.

There's a brief flash of nothingness, and then the pain thunders through me. My whole naked body shudders. Another sob comes. You strike me again, harder. I throw back my head and wail. I make only a distant groan through the cock-shaped gag. You push up close to me, leaning on the bench so hard it creaks. You raise the paddle and bring it down on my ass. Now you're warming me up. Slow, at first, building until I'm thrashing and pulling against my bonds. Harder, now, making me scream behind the gag. My tongue feels the pressure of the swollen cockhead in my mouth, pushing toward the back. You paddle me harder. Harder. Faster. I scream.

I hear the paddle drop between my feet and your fingers rove over my cunt. I'm so wet that droplets of it ooze out onto your fingers. You draw back your hand and spank my cunt.

My naked body spasms, and I try to pull free of the restraints. You spank my cunt again. And again. Your middle finger strikes my clit, right at the bony ridge at the underside of your knuckle. I scream. I try to get free. You spank my cunt. Harder.

I come.

It's so overwhelming it feels like the room is spinning around me. Pleasure rips through my body and I pull at the restraints, sobbing with release. You start to rub my clit, which only makes my orgasm mount higher. I hang over the bench, my naked body slack. You spank my cunt again, and right after an orgasm it's always so sensitive that you know exactly what you're doing to me. You're hurting me. Hurting me terribly.

You spank my cunt again.

Then I feel your hand caressing my reddened cheeks, stroking their curves, petting my sweet spot. You draw back your hand and spank me. My ass, this time. Right on my sweet spot. Right where the vibrations go rumbling directly into my too-sensitive clit. Right where it feels like you're fucking me.

You spank me again, and again, each blow rising in intensity as my cheeks get hot. Tears run out of my eyes and over my forehead, onto the floor. My ass pumps back and forth as you spank me.

Now you ball up your hand into a fist, and hit my ass, lightly at first. The punch sends waves of sensation into my cunt. I push my ass up to meet your next blow. Harder. You punch me. Again. Your hand opens wide and you start spanking me again. My ass is now raised as

high as I can make it, and I'm standing on tiptoes, straining the manacles. You alternate hard spanks and light punches, slow caresses of
my pussy as it gets wetter and wetter. Touches to my clit, testing the
way I twitch and moan behind the gag. Testing how close I am to
coming again.

I'm very, very close.

You open your pants and press up behind me. You enter me so
fiercely, savagely, that I don't expect it. I also don't expect the powerful response that pulses through my naked, bound body. I don't expect the orgasm that explodes through me as you start to fuck me.
You pound me without care for my pleasure, using my cunt, using
me. I'm just a hole to you. Just a thing you use to get yourself off. That
makes me come harder, harder, my orgasm swirling all around me as
I come and come and come and come and come. When you moan
with your own release, I feel my pussy flooding with you and I'm not
sure when or if my own second orgasm has ended. All I know is that
my entire naked body is humming with pleasure.

You unlock my wrists and ankles, unbuckle the gag. You lift me
off the bench and carry me to bed. You take off your clothes and wrap
yourself around me. I lay there, spent, useless. But you've another use
for me. You touch me all over, your hands tracing a path from my
breasts to my belly to my cunt. You're hard again. You enter me slowly
this time, and fuck me in great long strokes deep into my body. When
I arch my back and come again, you let yourself go inside me for the
second time. You lay on top of me and breathe hard.

My arms lay limp at my sides. My legs are wrapped around your
body, the stretch of their muscles making my well-spanked ass feel
warm and sore. My mouth hangs open, and as tears run down my
face I taste them: salty and sweet. I whisper that I love you, Master,
but you've already fallen asleep.

Just My Type
by Emilie Paris

Emilie Paris is a writer and editor. Her first novel, *Valentine,* published by Blue Moon, is available on audiotape by Passion Press. She abridged the seventeenth-century novel *The Carnal Prayer Mat* for Passion Press. The audiotape won a *Publishers Weekly* best audio award in the "Sexcapades" category. Her short stories have also appeared in *Naughty Stories from A to Z, Volume I* (Pretty Things Press) and *Sweet Life I & II* (Cleis), and on the website www.goodvibes.com.

Of this story, Paris says: "When I went off to college, I became instructed in far more interesting subjects than chemistry or calculus. I learned the world of slave and Master from one of the scene's best teachers. While my fellow dorm mates made plans to attend ice-cream socials at sorority row, I made plans to obey my dorm-floor Master, to do everything and anything he could possibly wish. Getting into the spirit of dorm living has never been quite so decadent or debauched before."

John was my friend. From day one in the dorms, he was my friend. I don't know what made him choose me. Maybe he sensed that I was scrambling for balance. Maybe he had a yearning to do a good deed for the day, helping out the most obviously less fortunate, at least socially speaking. Or maybe he knew when he saw me that we'd be good together.

I was too confused to know much of anything.

As soon as I entered the dormitory building and found myself on my own—*really* on my own—I learned that I was clueless. Yes, I'd been craving this moment for years, my first time of total freedom from parental control ever, but that didn't make the situation any less disconcerting. Looking around my dorm room, I realized that I had no idea what I was doing, which way was up, who to talk to, how to act. I was a little girl lost, standing in the center of the long, narrow room, gazing at the one poster I'd put up on the wall, wishing that I could climb into the safety of the black-and-white picture, no matter how X-rated, and disappear. Somehow, John discovered me at the exact moment, poking his head through my open door and saying, "Hey, I'm your neighbor. I live right there—" a nod across the hall. "Wanna get a bite?"

"A bite?" I asked, staring away from the bulletin board to look at the tall, lean, handsome man in the dark blue T-shirt who was talking to me. First person to talk to me since I'd arrived on campus.

"Cafeteria's open. First come, first able to choose a meal that doesn't completely suck."

I looked dizzily around at the multitude of overflowing boxes scattered on the floor—*Where was I going to put all of that shit? What the fuck had I been thinking when I packed it all?*—looked down at my unmade and unattractive twin bed, at the angry emptiness of my side of the dorm room in general. The place needed a serious transformation. In truth, it needed a miracle, and I had no mental energy to attack the project. The only thing on my wall so far was a Mapplethorpe print that I'd had in my closet for years. One my mother had forbidden me to put up until I had a place of my own.

"Come on," he said, glancing at the vibrantly colorful nameplate on the door that the R.A. had kindly posted—I either had to be Mirabella or J. C. He took a wild shot and said, "Come on, Mira," naming me correctly. "I'll help you unpack later. Promise." I hadn't gotten a look yet at my roommate, but from the way she'd decorated her side of the room, all olive green camouflage and military-esque posters, I wasn't sure how well we were going to get along. Still, I had high hopes. High hopes for new friends, for eye-opening college experiences, for taking risks. Risks like nodding to John and following obediently after him down the hallway.

John was a junior, and he knew everyone, nodding hellos to the staff, waving at other students he recognized from the previous year. He understood the system, and he helped me choose the best the cafeteria had to offer before telling me how the year would play out.

"People opt to live on coed floors because they either like to party, or they're terrified of being deemed gay." He took a sip of soda before continuing in a lower voice: "*Or* they appreciate the pleasures of the opposite sex."

I glanced up at him from my pasta primavera, waiting to see which type he thought *I* was.

"You don't seem uptight," he said, "and I saw the Mapplethorpe picture on your bulletin board, so you're no homophobe." He tilted his head, continuing his assessment, while I took him in. He had straight blonde hair, that white-blonde color that goes perfectly with clear blue eyes. He was dressed casually, but not surfer-casual, and he looked smart. That was the one word that fit him immediately in my mind from the very beginning: smart.

"You don't have the appearance of a major partier," John continued, "I can usually tell. So . . ."

Now, I smirked. For the first time since arriving at the university, I felt myself starting to relax. Did I like the pleasures of the opposite sex? Based on the sizzling European tryst I'd had the summer after graduating high school, a month-long fling with the dark-eyed waiter in the cafe at the École Français, the answer was most definitely yes. John grinned back at me, and I felt his leg brush mine under the table, felt his heavy engineer boot press firmly against my jeans, making serious contact.

We joked while we ate, sharing favorite TV shows and worst dates ever, and I left my unpacking for the next day when John invited me to watch a movie in his room. He was all set up, had the high-tech DVD entertainment center, the twin beds already stacked bunk-bed style to make more room in the small environment. His own roommate wasn't in town yet, wouldn't arrive until the next day, so we had time. Plenty of time. Time for John to show me more of the high-tech systems he had already incorporated into his decor: the heavy leather thongs on his bed frame and the carefully placed metal hook to place handcuffed limbs. The assortments of sex toys, vibrators, dildos, blindfolds, feathers, and candles kept neatly stored in an opaque Rubbermaid container. I couldn't believe it. Someone who looked so upstanding, who was actually a *third*, as in Jonathan Francis Walker III, had such a deviant streak. Even more impressive was that he'd recognized a similar streak in me.

I spent high school in hell, understanding my cravings but not able to locate a match. High-school boys have no imagination. They only want a hole. Nobody I met came remotely close to understanding what I wanted. I'd thought, hoped, and yearned that at some point I'd discover someone who would answer the fantasies in my head. Someone who was just my type.

That someone was John.

I was his from that first day. Simple as that. I was *his*. To use, to adorn, to abuse, to create—all as he saw fit. When his roommate was away studying in the engineering library—which was often—I would be tied down to his bed, awaiting the pleasures and pains he had in store. On campus, I wore the delicate silver nipple clamps he bought me, under my rah-rah!-style maroon-colored university T-shirt. In class, I shifted in my seat to find the right position for taking notes while wearing a butt plug. Late in the evening, I found myself bound to his bed frame, mouth open, ready to suck his towering cock as he straddled me high up on my chest, ready to bathe his balls between my sweetly parted lips, to bounce them gently on my tongue.

And the best part?

Nobody knew. Not my militant-fanatic lesbian roommate. Not John's overachieving roomie from abroad. Not any of the motley assortment of winners and losers on the dormitory floor. Just us. We reveled in our slyly seductive secret life. While others partied in the hallways on the weekends, getting wild in coed showers and drinking cheap beer in the lobby between the two wings on the floor, we double-locked the door and lost ourselves in the fantasy world of S and M and B and D. While everyone around us acted the way college kids are "supposed to," we created a complicated lifestyle based on rules—*his* rules—and obedience—*my* obedience. I obeyed him, from that very first moment when I followed after him down the hall, I obeyed. He liked the way I looked at him, up from under my fringe of dark bangs. He liked how shy I'd get when he'd tell me how he was going to use a tool on me, and then wait until I'd quiver, begging him to start no matter how frightened I might be.

John had no boundaries as to how he would use me. If he wanted anal sex, he'd flip me over on the bed, generously lube up my asshole, and plunge in. If he wanted to punish me, and his roommate was around, he'd find some deserted corner of the building or outdoors in the parking garage and take care of his needs swiftly and efficiently, dealing immediately with me whenever I failed him. And punishing me sometimes for not giving him a good reason to whip me. He was a marvel with the belt, a pro with his hand. He knew all about my personal barriers, and vowed to topple every one.

We fit each other perfectly, craved each other. Swallowed everything that the other had to offer.

But finally, near the end of the year, I needed to know how he'd recognized me. How he'd pegged me so quickly as a like-minded soul.

"I saw you come in that morning, Mira," he said, stroking my glossy black hair out of my eyes because I couldn't do it for myself. Not with my hands bound so firmly over my head. I was accustomed to this position now. It was as comfortable for me as any other. "Your indigo-dyed jeans, artsy look. Soulful eyes. Long dark hair. No California beach bunny. That was for sure."

"But you could have a bunny if you wanted one." I thought about all the sorority girls on the floor, the ones with their ice-cream socials, gooey flavored lip glosses, and pastel eye shadows. The ones who didn't understand why I wouldn't rush their houses, why I didn't want to date a football player.

He shook his head. "They're interesting for half an hour. And then you realize that their minds are as sheer as the little sundresses they like to wear. But not you—"

I still didn't understand. "But why?" I asked again, tied so firmly to his bed, waiting to see whether he'd use his crop or his belt or the deceptively innocent-looking wooden paddle that stung so fiercely and left marks afterward for hours, sometimes days. Marks that I'd have to be careful not to reveal when taking a shower or dressing. Marks that I adored staring at in the mirror, that I felt as if I earned. "Come on, John. Tell me why."

Pressing him could be dangerous. I knew that from experience. I might be opening myself up for more than I was prepared to accept, but I couldn't stop the questions. I had to hear his reasons.

John got a faraway look in his blue eyes, as if he were seeing something I couldn't. Then he started to explain. "I saw you circling in your room, trying to make it work. You looked like a caged animal. I stood out in the hall, in the corner, so you wouldn't notice me. And I saw how you riffled through your bags and boxes until you found that poster, and how relaxed you seemed once you had your art on the wall. Unsure of your place, yeah, maybe. But at ease with yourself. I knew you were different. That leather wristband, those pouty lips."

He paused and kissed me before reaching for his pair of jeans tossed over the edge of his bed. I gazed at him longingly, lovingly, as I watched him extract the leather belt from the loops.

"I don't know how, exactly," he said, shrugging in a charming way as he easily positioned me exactly how he wanted me, dead in the center of the mattress. Then he said the words that had echoed my own assessment of him: "But I knew you were just my type."

Liar
by Julia Moore

Julia Moore is the coauthor of the best-selling book *The Other Rules: Never Wear Panties on a First Date and Other Tips* (Masquerade), a spoof of the tragic dating guide *The Rules*. Her short stories have appeared in *Sweet Life I & II, Naughty Stories from A to Z, Batteries Not Included,* and on the website www.goodvibes.com.

She writes about "Liar": "My taste for bad boys began with my very first relationship, way the hell back when I was still in high school. I've always had a yearning for rebels, and my beau back then fit the description exactly. He was everything I needed, everything I was looking for, right down to the tattoos and motorcycle jacket. And even today, so many years later, I find that I can get wet simply from hearing the rev of a Harley engine."

I had sex for the first time when I was in college. I'm lying. I had sex for the first time when I was eighteen, a senior at Fairfax High School, with my very first real boyfriend.

I'm lying.

He wasn't a boy; he was a man. He was twenty-seven and he let me touch his cock and stroke it and look at it and put it in my mouth. We did everything *but*, until our last date at his apartment, on the bed with white cotton sheets, when he pinned my wrists above my head, spread my legs apart, and took me.

I'm lying.

I did love him, though. I did. I loved the way he looked at me. That rebel glance. I loved the leather jacket he wore and the smell of beer and cigarettes that warmed my mouth when he kissed me. The shadow of his beard scraped my face, and the pain awoke something within me.

We met at Kanter's diner. He ignored me for an hour before coming over to ask for my number. I debated about telling him that I was still in school, and opted out. Instead, I told him I worked as a secretary at a bank on Wilshire. He said he was in importing and exporting. I pictured handwoven baskets and throw rugs from faraway places. What did I know?

Jason took me for rides on the back of his Harley. Or someone's Harley. Never the same Harley. He never had keys for the motorcycles he drove. He always rubbed two wires together to get the bikes started. His explanations strayed toward the unbelievable, but it didn't bother me. We were both okay with the situation, and if I didn't come clean with him, it didn't really matter. He never came clean with me, either.

Liars bond. They stick together.

After school, then work, I took the bus to his tiny apartment on Sunset, painting my face on the way. I became an expert at applying lipstick in a moving vehicle, cherry-red glosses, dark eyeliner. Other passengers watched in awe as I made the transformation from student to harlot.

Jason saw me as no one had before, as no one has since. "You're bad," he would tell me, greeting me at the door in faded black jeans and a shirt. "You're a bad girl." Just what I wanted to hear.

Attached to his mattress, on each of the four corners, were silk ties to capture trembling limbs. Hidden behind a small photograph above the bed was a hook, for hanging handcuffed wrists.

"Tell me your fantasy," he'd whisper, his voice husky and smoke-filled. "You can tell me, baby. You can tell me anything."

Now you see me, now you don't.

On his well-worn couch, one denim-clad leg scissored over both of my bare thighs, he'd say, "You're such a naughty girl," continuing the trip with his probing fingers, continuing to speak in a soft croon. "You're my bad girl, aren't'cha?"

My panties wet, I'd lean back on the couch as his relentless fingers found the source of my pleasure. Staring into his eyes, I saw myself looking back.

"I'm gonna tie you down," he'd tell me, playing, capturing both of my wrists in one of his large hands. "I'm gonna show you the type of girl you really are. You're going to be loud for me. You're going to scream."

I'd shake my head, even at the same time as my hips arched upward, uncontrollably. I knew the screamers in my high school. I wasn't one of them.

"You're going to come undone," Jason would tell me. "You can't even imagine."

I was addicted. I went to his house every night. My parents thought I was at the library, studying. They were so trusting. But when you're eighteen and a senior, the world is large, and high school is small.

I would cut class and follow him, trying to figure out what he did during the day. Importing. Exporting. What did that mean? I'd take my older brother's car and weave after Jason through the traffic, watch him enter the Oasis Burger Joint. Sit outside, in the car, and stare at him through the tinted windows.

I saw the girls that liked him. The waitresses, batting their mascara-drenched lashes. I'd get out of the car and come into the restaurant, sitting at a booth behind him, but close enough to hear them bantering with him. They stretched out his name, "Jason," smiling as they said it. You could imagine them in his bed, saying it. You could picture them on the back of his bike, sighing it.

But I rode on the back of Jason's bike. I smiled as I said his name. I stroked that glossy dark hair away from chocolate brown eyes. I was the girl tied to the bed.

Jason told me he only had to work part-time, that his business was so successful it didn't require his full attention. He gave me a list of names and numbers where I could reach him if I ever needed to find him off hours.

And then he disappeared.

"Liar," my best friend said when I told her what happened, when I tearfully confessed the whole deal. "He was a liar. He used you."

I dialed the first number. The person refused to admit knowing Jason. I called the second. The man said he would contact the police if I bothered him again. I tried Jason's house over and over. Finally, a stranger answered the phone. The man told me never to call Jason again.

"Never?" I couldn't hear what he was saying.

"He's bad news," the man said. "He's in over his head. There are people who want to kill him. I'm doing you a favor."

I didn't believe him. I drove to the Oasis, to the Beverly Hills 24-hour diner, to Rae's, to all the hangouts I had followed him to in the past. I promised myself that if I found him, I would tell him what he wanted to hear. Would tell him what I had to say.

But he was nowhere.

Every day, I read the paper from cover to cover, searching for news of a drug deal gone bad. I called the hospitals. I called the mortuaries.

And then, outside of my high school, on a brand new Harley, I saw him. His face was cut. One eye was purple-toned, puffy. His knuckles were scraped and I caught his grimace when he sat up straight on his bike. I walked to his side.

"Bad girl," he said, a smile lost somewhere in his voice. "You lied."

I climbed onto the back of his bike, put my arms around his flat waist, laid my face against the smooth warm leather of his jacket. "You, too," I whispered as he gunned the engine and took off.

At his apartment, a different apartment, with different furnishings but the same ties on the bed, he bound me down, cut my clothes away from my body. He said, "You deserve this," taunting me, his damaged face still unbelievably handsome. The scars enhancing his rebel looks. "You're just like me," a hiss, a whisper. "You're just like me. Pretending to be good. Wearing your little twinset, your charm bracelet. Pretending to be on the other side of the line. When really, you're just . . . like . . . me . . ."

His words made me wet, and when he opened his jeans and positioned himself above me, I took him in, grabbing him, squeezing him.

"Now, say it . . ."

He pushed up on his arms above me, filling me with steady strokes, then moving his hips in small circles that sent me reeling with pleasure.

"Tell me," he said, "tell me what you've never said out loud."

I opened my mouth, but made no sound. I tried, he could see it in my eyes. He had to have been able to see it. But I couldn't say anything. He kissed me fiercely. He kissed my mouth and met my tongue with his. Then he parted his lips, his mouth just a sliver from mine, and whispered, "Tell me."

I wished my hands were loose so I could stroke his face. I wished I were bruised so I could feel what he felt. Did that make me dirty? Did that make me bad? I wanted to know his pain, it was why I liked him from the start. Damaged, on edge, so different from the people in my perfect world.

"Please," I said, swallowing hard, closing my eyes and waiting. But nothing. "Please," I said again, "Jason, please. Make me feel it like you feel it."

"How?" he asked, stroking the underside of my chin with his fingers, the way you'd pet a cat. "How, Jodie?"

I closed my eyes, whispered the words, "Hurt me," and he brought his hand back and slapped me, hard, so that I knew. Like he said I would. And he dug into me, his sex hard and powerful, cutting me.

He brought his lips to my ear and said softly, "Scream for me. I'm gonna come and I want to hear you scream as I come."

His cock moved in and out of me piston-fast, thrusting inside me, filling me up. His hands turned my head so that I could see our reflections in the mirror on the closet door. My cheeks were flushed, and while I watched, he slapped me again, openhanded. And then again, with the back of his hand, hard enough to make me cry out.

I was dizzy from it, the vision melding with the action, my mouth opening, watching as the scream poured from my lips. It sounded decadent, rich, and I kept on screaming, until I wasn't thinking anymore. Until I couldn't think anymore. I moaned and sobbed as those vibrations washed over me, as he pulled out, as he stood on the bed and looked down at me.

His eyes were dark brown, but they glowed. His teeth bit into his bottom lip. His head went back and his hair fell away from his face. I watched as the world slowed on its axis. I watched as his come rained down on me. It was hot and sticky, but it cooled me just the same. He bent and traced his fingers through it, drawing figure eights, curving designs with the tips of his fingers.

He lay at my side, put his arms around me, and we slept, joined, my wrists still captured above my head. My ankles still bound to the posters of the bed.

In the morning, I was alone. My shredded clothes were folded as well as they could be and stacked at my side. My wrists and ankles were cut loose. It was as if he'd never come back. Or as if he'd always been gone.

There was a small piece about him in the paper the next day. There was a write-up on the back page and as my father read the newspaper, he muttered to himself about what can you expect when these druggies want to kill each other. When that is what they want.

That's not what he wanted. It's just what he was. Too much, and not enough. I loved him. I did. With everything I was and everything I am. And they say all you need is love.

But they're lying.

Halloween
by Cecilia Tan

Boston-based **Cecilia Tan** is a well-known name in erotic fiction, having attracted attention from science fiction fans, erotica readers, and literati alike for her anthologies of erotic science fiction and fantasy published by her company, Circlet Press. Her own erotic short stories have been collected in her book *Black Feathers.* Cecilia is also an accomplished organizer and speaker in the leather community, having been active for years with New England's National Leather Association.

About "Halloween," Cecilia says: "I suppose this is my version of the 'mysterious stranger' fantasy. Every woman has one, right? This is also another one of those stories I write from time to time about two people who are not really connecting in a traditional way. That is, it isn't love at first sight, and they aren't 'perfect for each other,' not in the romantic sense. It's more like when you take two characters, two personalities, and rub them together like sticks and see if sparks fly off. You get more sparks when the personalities are a little weird, when the people have hang-ups and attitudes and gaps in their manners. That's what makes it interesting and fulfilling for me. They end up connecting, but it is more about their tangents as individuals than about a twosome.

"I have no idea now where the idea for this story came from. I sat down at the computer one morning and I must have been hanging onto some scrap of a dream . . . I wrote the first few paragraphs and then left it alone for a few days. When I went back to it I couldn't be sure I had intended to write an erotic story, but I guess I was horny or something, because that is what came out."

You wouldn't believe the stuff they do around here in the name of Halloween. Actually, it isn't even Halloween. It's any time. You walk into The Strand for their supposed Goth night any Wednesday and you'll find stupid shit like fake cobwebs hanging above the bar and a lame little fog machine trying to make it "spooky." Spooky is a good name for a dog, not the atmosphere for Goths. Or maybe it's just me. Twenty-one years old and jaded as fuck. Maybe I'm like those super-pious Christians, for whom Christmas is ruined by over-commercialism and hokey dumb crap for kids. Same thing, right? Halloween should be the Goth Christmas, except who cares anyway?

So it was that on Halloween night I was at The Strand, sneering at a bunch of the newcomers who were slumming with the Halloween theme. Let's go hang out with the spooky vampire chicks. Fuck off. Go play pool or watch a ballgame or something. I was all in white to confuse the fuck out of them—the dress looked like a little girl's first communion dress, not like a wedding gown. Simpler, smaller. I wore a white wig. Some tourist asked me what I was supposed to be and I was going to tell him "a Goth, fuckface" but for some reason I decided to take the high road, and told him I was Cathy from *Wuthering Heights*. He replied he'd never seen that show and I wanted to beat him over the head with a book. Any book would do, but how about a nice fat one, like a leather-bound edition of *Moby Dick*? Yeah, so I have weird fantasies, get used to it.

Micah was there that night, and Jeana, and Ash. All people I was desperately tired of. I resolved to spend most of the night on the dance floor where idiots wouldn't talk to me and I wouldn't have to listen to Ash mooning over some girl he'd never touch. But I ended up at the bar on the far side of the floor instead, nursing a Grand Marnier and pushing some stupid plastic spiders around on the bar top.

The guy next to me was perhaps the only interesting thing about the night, and that was only because I couldn't read him. People wear all sorts of stuff to Goth clubs. We have the punks in chains, high Goths in velvet, fetish crowd in latex and leather, and then on Halloween you can mix in a lot of other randoms in black. This one was in leather, but he wasn't done up like the fetishwear people usually are. It's hard to explain. He wasn't projecting an image with what he wore, unlike everybody else in the place. He was in black leather pants, a black silk shirt, a leather vest, a leather jacket. He projected an air of ease, like this was what he wore every day. He was drinking water, leaning against the bar next to me, looking utterly relaxed and calm in the hubbub of the club. Relaxed, yes. Like he belonged there?

No.

I guess you could say I got a bug up my ass about him. I set about tormenting him. It was pretty crowded; even where we were on the far side of the bar close to the wall people were jostling past us, taking the long way around to the dance floor. I grabbed some kid I barely knew, Gary or Gerry or something, on the shoulder as he went by, just so I could bump into Mister Leather, step on his soft riding boots with my hard combat boots. "Sorry," I said in his general direction as I got back in place at the bar. I did a bunch of shit like that. I guess he'd decided he had had enough when I ordered water myself. I was perched on my knees on a barstool then, and reached way over him to grab it from Dessa when she poured it.

My plan was to dump it down his back and play drunk, all oopsy, but as I pulled my hand back toward me, suddenly his hand was on my wrist, his other hand on the cup, pulling me forward off my tipsy stool. I didn't see where the water went but I ended up stretched out across his chest. One of his arms was under me, and he hitched us both onto my bar stool, me flat across his knees. One elbow pressed between my shoulder blades. The other arm swept my little dress up onto my back and then the flat, hard side of his hand came down on my ass.

I was so shocked that for a second I couldn't think of what to do. Kick my feet and squeal like a little brat? Curse him out? He had hit me four or five more times while I lay there, limp, before I decided to slip out of his grip and just get out of there.

Decided. But he had that elbow pinning me and one fist wrapped tight in the excess of my dress. Four, five more smacks. Just enough to make it really hurt. Then he let me go and I tumbled into the legs of the people making their way past. Jaded fucks, no one even gave me a second glance. I climbed up his leg, ready to give him a piece of my mind, but as I tried to get my feet under me, my fingers grabbing at his thigh, his hand was on mine. He slid it onto his fly, his eyes burning down at mine. I had the "W" of "What the fuck is wrong with you" already bowing my lip, but instead I just stared. He moved my hand forward and back on the hard spine of his dick inside his leather pants, never taking his eyes off mine.

And where were my fucking friends to see this gorgeous fucking spectacle? Nowhere. No one was even looking. No one had even noticed. I narrowed my eyes and made my hand into a claw, squeezing him through the pants. His fingers went all the way around my wrist. Fucking hell. I should be kicking him in the shins right now, is what I was thinking, but it's not every day you meet somebody like that. I mean somebody who is just so outside the normal, so whacked out, different . . . I could feel his dick throb under my hand and his eyes flared a little when it did. You don't say no to a gift like that, to the challenge of which of us was crazier or more out there. My other hand came up and started tugging at his belt.

He leaned forward on the stool. His jacket swung open and he let my other hand go. As I got his belt unbuckled, his pants unbuttoned, I could feel the bones of his hips. Under that jacket I hadn't expected to find him so underfed.

His dick wasn't so skinny, though. I fit my lips over the head and smeared my pearlescent lipstick up and down the shaft. Delish. I was down there in the dark, the smell of leather, the taste of it on the veal-soft layer of his skin, salty and sweet at the same time. I held his erection in my hands and swirled the wetness of my mouth all around the crown. The shaft was so fat I couldn't get any more of him into my mouth.

Was I loving every second of it? Yes. Was I even then thinking of how to get the motherfucker good? Yes. And I knew how. I knew if I could make him come it would undo him. My feet were tangled with his somewhere under us, my knees had come to rest against the legs of the stool, and my head was completely hidden from the pandemonium of lights and music and fake fog and jostling that was The Strand. Just my mouth and his cock, my tongue working and my hands pumping at the same time since no way was that horse cock going any deeper. Wet. Hot. No air in there, really, nowhere in that damned building but especially not down there, not while I was working. It felt like a bone in my mouth, like something supple wrapped around something else.

He was like a marble statue. He didn't move. Maybe he couldn't, jammed onto the stool in the crowd. If he was breathing heavy, I couldn't hear it. I couldn't hear anything, duh. I couldn't tell how close he was, and for a while it didn't matter. For a while it was like I wasn't even there, my whole body broken apart into sound and darkness and motion, like dancing, like those moments on the dance floor when the music eats you.

But I couldn't forget myself completely, now could I? After a while, I wondered how much time had passed with his cock in my mouth. Fatigue burned my jaw, and I realized I had no way of telling how much longer it might go on. What was it I had thought when I had first seen him? That he was hard to read?

So, could I stop? Would my pride let me? No fucking way. I kept sucking him, licking him, pumping him, the thump of an industrial beat through the floor keeping me going. Come on, motherfucker, give it to me.

His hand in my hair, jerking me back, my eyes aperturing open to see his again, his face close to mine, waiting for a kiss, bastard. He leaned in close, his mouth opening for a small breath, but never quite touched me. His other hand was getting his fly together again, dammit. And then he was pushing me into the crowd, his hand on the back of my neck. Where are we going, fucker? What's your plan?

The men's room. I should have known. You think it's the first time I ever sucked somebody off in the men's room of The Strand?

The truth?

Of course it was the first time I'd sucked a man's dick in The Strand. That's what I'm trying to tell you. This kind of crazy, fucked-up shit doesn't happen every day. If only. I was sick to death of the mundane crap that lurked just under the fishnets, the velvet, the tattoos. I wanted a bite of something weird and wonderful in life, I'd been looking for it for a couple of years—god, had I found it? It was my first year of drinking legally, but not my first year of being a freak. My heart thumped as loud as the bass as he pushed me through the black doorway, to the back, to the last stall and its door scarred with reverse graffiti, scratched out of the black paint with car keys and wristband spikes. He shut the door, and I was amazed the latch worked.

The sound in here was muffled, the light dim but steady, but my nerves made it seem as loud and confusing as it had been out there. He knocked the lid down, and sat on it, his cock standing up again. He dug in his jacket pocket a second while I wondered whether I was going to get down on my knees on the damp floor or what. But no. He pulled something shiny and square out of his pocket. Gimme that.

I ripped open the foil packet of the condom and held it up in front of me, pinching the tip between my finger and thumb. I kept looking in his eyes and I can't really tell you what he was saying through them. Do it. Go on. You know you want to. It sounds stupid when I try to translate it. I rolled it onto that stallion dick, planted my feet on either side of his, my hands around his neck, and tried to lower myself down. Yes, I was dripping, honey heavy, and I got one hand down there and moved the rubberized tip of him back and forth along my wet slit. Okay motherfucker, here it comes.

I settled the head between my lips and sank down an inch and had to stop. God, so big. I backed off and slid down again. Just the tip fucking me felt nice, but two inches only does so much, for me, for him. I wasn't trying to be a tease. Suddenly I didn't want him thinking that was my game. "Okay, okay," I said to myself, to his ear, trying to get it deeper in. Oh god, this is just not going to work. Not like this, not this position. I tried to jam myself down, just get it in there and everything will be fine, right? Or would it? I felt like something literally might have ripped. I was frightened to look, but at the same time I thought, fuck, nothing bad is going to happen. That just wouldn't happen. It just wouldn't.

I kept thinking that. But I couldn't get him in. It hurt too much. And the friction right around the opening to my vagina seemed to be making me all the more aroused, and all the tighter. I gasped every time I had to pull off of him, until the gasps were sobs, and the sobs were me crying into his overlong hair, draped over his ears, my legs shaking because I could hardly hold myself up anymore, and I wanted to fuck him so bad, I wanted to lose myself on that prong the way I had when I was sucking him, but this time I couldn't use my hands to cover all but the last few inches of him, this time I couldn't be satisfied with that. "I'm sorry," I was saying into his ear, "I'm sorry, I can't, I can't, I'm sorry," unable to say more than two words at a time between sobs.

His hand on my back, bracing me, holding me, HUGGING me. The other hand moving his cock out of the way. He turned me on his lap then, my feet scrambling to catch up with the rotation of my upper body, until I was sitting on his lap facing the other way, his chest to my back, his cock sticking up between my legs.

His hand turning my head back so our tongues could meet, so hungry, so much wanting him. His other hand sliding in the wetness between my legs, his fingers sliding into me then, deep into me, long slender fingers so kind, seeking their way in, two of them it felt like, two merciful fingers, reaching into me, while his thumb or the palm of his hand or something ground my wet clit.

Oh my god, he was making me come. This is wrong, I thought, this isn't how it's supposed to be. How did I know how it was supposed to be? What were the rules? I had no idea, I just knew it was wrong. "No, no," I said, even as my body was beginning to shudder. "This isn't how it's supposed to go . . ." I was supposed to make him come, make him lose it, out there by the bar. "Not supposed to . . ." Barely being able to speak because of my lips still touching his, my neck still craned back, my chest still heaving with sobs. Off the map. Crazy. I cried from guilt, from failure, from how I couldn't stand the kindness of his touch after all that. But here it was coming, like a tidal wave, nowhere to run. He let my head go and I began to buck on his lap, his mouth at my ear, and I heard his voice for the first time. I couldn't hear what he said, but a shock went through me, almost like the shock of recognition. I think he was telling me to come, ordering me, even while his hands gave me no choice.

The come hit me hard, climbing up the front of my body, shaking me on his lap, bent back by his hand now on my throat, holding me to him. Wanting to kick my feet and squeal like a little girl. Or curse. Instead, I just wailed.

When it subsided, he held me to him until my muscles started working again. He tore off some toilet paper and handed it to me and I wiped up the puddle that was mostly on him. I wanted to go home and cry myself to sleep and I didn't even know why. The pit of my stomach felt empty and I was dizzy.

I thought, fuck, I ought to dash out of here right now. That's what I would have thought I was going to do anyway. But I wanted to hear his voice again. I wanted something more. So I stayed. So I stayed, and waited to see what would happen next.

He zipped himself up, looking at me the whole time. I had to look away, that staring, who'll blink first game . . . I felt like he could look through my skin, like his fingers had been so deep inside me he must have known what was in every nook and cranny. He reached for me then, his arms enfolding me, until my face was against his breastbone and his mouth was making soft sounds in my ear.

And again, his voice, his arms wrapped tight around my back, he said just one word, "Come," and my body writhed in his embrace, rubbing against the long spike of his body, my scream muffled by his chest, his jacket, as I convulsed against him. The sensation was like pain, opening and blossoming in my stomach, but not a full orgasm—a quickening, a spasm, that left me still hungry. I ground myself against him, my whole body buzzing and shaking with the crescendo of coming, or almost coming, whatever it was. I slid my own hands along my thighs, and found my clit too slippery to handle, so hard and swollen I didn't know how to make myself come with it like that. I wanted his hand, his rough fingers, rubbing it raw. And I wanted to take that horse cock inside me. I wanted it and yet I couldn't bring myself to do it.

He loosened his hold and held me at arm's length. I was afraid he was going to say it again, order me to come, and this time watch me twitch helplessly without even his leg to rub against. Like I was under some kind of a spell. All he had to do was say it. I reached for his fly of my own accord this time, pressing my palm into the protrusion. I felt like I should be begging for it just then, but I didn't know how, didn't know the words, didn't know how this ritual worked. So I just rubbed him until he took a deep breath, and then carried me out.

He carried me right out of the club, and I smiled when I caught a glimpse of Ash jabbing Micah in the shoulder, pointing for him to look! He carried me to a small black car that beeped as we approached. He settled me into one snug-fitting seat, then came around the other side and got into the driver's seat.

I don't even remember the drive. Maybe five minutes later he

pulled into a driveway and then led me by the hand from the car to a
doorway in the back of a house. In the outdoor October air I could
smell The Strand on us, the cigarette smoke and fake fog and sweaty
sex smell, and then I was following him into the back stairwell of an
old house, the smell of old wood and lead paint and the stairs creaking as we went up.

Inside his bedroom he lit a candle and turned on a small bedside
light. I could make out shelves of books, small heaps of laundry on
the carpet, but not much else. The window was dark and the bed itself
was a mattress and box spring set directly onto the rug, no frame. I
could almost feel a wisecrack about that bubbling up in my throat.
But I kept it there. He had not said a word and I was not going to
speak first.

He sat down on the edge of the mattress. And yes, he spoke first.
"I want you to take off your boots," he said. I bent over and the wig,
which had stayed with me thus far, finally slipped completely off my
head, revealing my dark bob underneath. It took what seemed like
too long to undo the knots in my laces, and then another forever to
loosen the laces enough to step out of them. Now I was barefoot in
that little girl dress. He stood up and let his jacket slip to the floor. I
stared as he unbuttoned the silk shirt, undid his cuff buttons, and let
it fall also. I knelt down to get a hold of his boot to let him step out of
it. I don't know why I did. It just seemed right. Then the other one.
And then I was helping him out of his pants.

Standing naked in front of me, he seemed no more vulnerable
than he had when clothed. His cock seemed even wider because of
the narrowness of his hips. From where I was on the floor it seemed
very large and very close and I reached up to kiss it. Yes, I want it, I
was trying to tell him with the kisses, the hungry nibbles.

He understood. He took my hand and we turned in place like a
pair of ballroom dancers, and then he backed me to the bed. I sat
down, which put my mouth near him again and reached out with my
tongue to suck him. There was the residual sweetness of the old condom, and the musk of him, making me tremble all over again. He was
already steely hard but I sought to delay him another minute.

A minute, but a minute only. Then he pushed me back onto the
bed, and wrapped my wrists in straps of soft leather. His voice was

only a whisper as his body covered mine and it seemed to me like the words came out of the darkness I was floating in: "If you need to get out, say 'I'm not worthy' and I'll release you. Otherwise, I'll release you when I come."

And what came out of my mouth was "Oh, yes please," which really made no sense. But it did: emotional sense. I quivered under him and he lingered there a while, kissing my neck, running his hands under the dress that I was still wearing for no reason other than neither of us had taken it off. Then he slid down to secure my ankles, my legs spread wide. My heart hammered in my chest and I examined the emotions flying around in the dark. Fear. I gasped, and fear felt like an old friend. Little girl on Halloween night waiting for the ghouls to come eat her soul. His tongue found my clit and lapped at it like a cat, rough and methodical. His fingers searched inside me again and I found I could grind my hips despite the bonds.

And then he was leaning his bony hip against my thigh, one of his hands moving that tree trunk of a rubber-covered cock up and down against me, against my wet spot, and I froze. His hands coaxed me to relax, kneading my ribs through the virgin cotton of the dress, his lips on my neck again, the tip of him slipping in and all of me seizing it. My shoulders strained as my arms tried to hold onto him, but they were held fast against the bed. His face was above mine now, his eyes looking down into mine as he held himself up on his arms. His hips moved in a circle and I moaned, but he came in no deeper. I rocked my pelvis upward, and he slid an inch, like a seismic shift, two huge pieces of the earth being pried apart. My breathing grew rapid as I anticipated the pain, and I gritted my teeth and squeezed my eyes closed against it. But he held still. His lips brushed mine and I heard my breathing begin to squeak in and out of my throat. Terrified. Like that moment when you are hiding behind the closet door, and any moment the monster is going to rip it open.

He paused, one arm holding him up still as the other reached down between us. Those fingers, pinching my swollen clit. My eyes flew open at the surprising sensation, like pain but not a pain I expected, a shock. When I was a little girl I used to put clothespins on my clit and try to masturbate, and I could always make myself come. And then I knew what he was going to do.

"Come," he said, and my body began to writhe, trying to leap up off the bed, against gravity, against the bonds, trying to press myself against him. My eyes rolled up into my head and my sense of what was up and what was down faded.

"Come," he said, as ripples and waves of shock and heat and other things ran up and down my skin and through my belly.

"Come," he said, as our breastbones came together like they were magnetized, as his lips followed and I lost myself in the smothering sensation of his mouth on mine.

And of course, in all this, he had plunged himself deep and was somehow keeping himself to long slow strokes, despite my frenzy. When my spasms subsided and I could open my eyes and take deep breaths again, he was pulling himself within an inch of out and then rocking forward, up my body, running the whole length of him into me until he was buried, and then starting again. We were both breathing deep and I felt like my insides were moving aside for him to let him go deeper.

"Fu-u-u-u-u-ck," I said then, without thinking, and he began to laugh. That made me laugh, like two actors on a stage who had just made a blooper—the masks fell right off, and all we could do was laugh.

"That's exactly what I'm doing," he said, when he could. "You crazy little brat."

That made me absolutely squeal with laughter. I would have kicked my feet except they were tied down. And damn if his blood didn't quicken when everything tightened up on me like that. The next thing I knew he was tickling me, I was squirming as much as I could, laughing myself hoarse, half-orgasms flitting across me here and there, and then he wasn't laughing, he was bellowing, gripping me by the shoulders as he jammed himself into me, one, two, three, four, five . . . and then he slumped. I think we both saw stars. And then it was over.

"Jesus fucking Christ on a pogo stick," I said, as he untied me. "Where the fuck did you come from?"

His chuckle was soft. "I could ask you the same thing."

"No, no, no, Mister I-have-leather-straps-attached-to-my-bed . . ."

"Was that your first time?"

"My first time, what, getting banged with a telephone pole? I guess you could say so." His dick looked big even shriveled inside the condom, which he wrapped in a tissue and tossed out of my sight.

"First time being tied up?" His voice went quiet and he sat on the edge of the bed, one finger trailing my arm.

I'm telling you, it was like a spell he could cast. A spooky Halloween bewitchment. It made my voice quiet, too. And truthful. "Yes."

"Did you like it?" he said, even lower, even quieter, like music descending.

"Yes." I was trying to get my baby bitch face back on, but it wasn't coming.

"Do you want to do it again sometime?" The quietest of all. I could only nod. He nodded back and lay down next to me. I rolled over and he wrapped around me spoonwise, pulling a blanket up from the floor with his long arm.

I could see then how it was going to go. He was going to ask me if I wanted to spend the night, and I was going to chicken out and say what he wanted me to say, "I'm not worthy," and then leave. Except he didn't ask. And I didn't chicken out. And we exchanged names in the morning.

Not Until Dawn
by Marie Sudac

Marie Sudac is one of my favorite new erotic writers, having contributed delightfully naughty fiction to *Best Bisexual Women's Erotica* and the *Sweet Life* series. She's never afraid to push the boundaries of "acceptable" fantasies, and here she writes of a surreptitious all-night date where a submissive is tormented with desire until she's ready to explode, and made to wait until she can't stand it anymore before she is granted sexual release. Luckily for the narrator, dawn is never too far away.

Tonight is the night you're going to make me wait all night. All night for your cock. All night for my come. All night for what I need, most of all, you inside me.

You take me out to a late movie, a foreign film everyone's been raving about. It's filled with sex, the steamy tale of multiple seductions. I don't see much of the movie, though, just the beautiful press of flesh as the European actors writhe together in bed. We sit in the back row of the near-empty theater and make out, my hand resting casually in your lap, stroking your hard cock through your pants. Your tongue explores my mouth, your teeth nipping at my lips. You slip your hand under my dress and fingerfuck me, first one finger, then two. But you don't let me come, even though I'm very close. You can tell when I'm close, and you make me wait, letting me cool down before you start to finger me again. I beg you to let me come, but you won't. "You're going to wait," you tell me. "You're going to wait all night."

"Please," I whimper, and you slip your hand out from under my dress and bring it to my lips, making me lick it clean. The taste is sharp, tangy, delicious; it sends a warm surge through me. I never would have tasted pussy before the night you made me yours. Never, ever. I'd never even dreamed about it. Now, when you put your fingers in my mouth I suck on them hungrily. My cunt is yours, and so it tastes beautiful to me.

You kiss me again, deeply, and my hand gently rubs your cock as your mouth takes me more aggressively this time. You finger me again, and I'm dying from need. I start to unfasten your belt and un-zip your pants. I lower my face into your lap—I've got to have you. I've got to have your cock.

You grasp my hair and pull me back up, pressing me into the creaking theater seat. Your mouth is on mine again, forcing my lips wide open, taking my tongue and possessing it.

"All night," you tell me. "You're going to wait all night."

"Please," I beg you, but you shake your head.

"Zip it up," you say, and I draw your zipper back up, awkwardly buckle your belt.

I look into your eyes and you kiss me again, your hand sliding once more up my dress and fingering me as I beg you to stop. "I can't take it any more," I breathe, but you know that I can. And even if I couldn't, you wouldn't care. You finger me until I'm right on the edge, until just the slightest touch of my thighs together would make me come harder than I've ever come before.

"All night," you tell me as your hand eases up my shirt and begins to play with my nipples. "You're going to wait all night."

We leave the theater after the movie and drive to a nice restaurant you've selected—one that's open late. As we eat, your foot stretches out and rests casually between mine, checking the distance between them—making sure I'm keeping my legs spread. Not too far—not far enough to draw attention. Just far enough to let me know that my pussy is exposed, that you can see it if you look under the table. You drop your fork several times, I notice. Each time I feel the heat of your gaze on me, shooting right up my dress. It makes me want you, right here. And the feel of your foot against mine, ensuring that I don't close my legs, drives me crazy. You're just letting me know that you own me. Letting me know that my legs are yours, to spread as you see fit.

You take me for a long drive through the beautiful hills above town, the city lights spread out below us, glimmering like diamonds.

You reach over and slide your hand up my dress, casually, never tak-ing your eyes off the road. Your middle finger penetrates me, careless, almost disinterested. I moan. "Moan as loud as you want," you tell me. "You're going to wait all night." You finger me until you hear my moans change, feel my hips bucking against you, and then you pull away and casually change gears, downshifting into second. We've reached the summit.

Before you let me out of the car you make me lick you clean, slip-ping your middle finger into my mouth. I suck on it, the taste pulsing through me and making my tortured clit hurt bad. "Please," I beg.

"Please what?"

"Please," I beg you. "I need to come."

"Not until dawn," you say.

I slide up against you, my hand on your belt buckle.

"Please," I whisper. "Please let me suck it."

You shake your head. "Not until dawn," you tell me.

We get out of the car. You drape your jacket over my shoulders and lead me over to the railing that overlooks the city, the lights so brilliant they blind me. You push me hard against the railing, and I feel like I'm hanging over the city. Your arms go around me and you cradle me tight, crushing me against you. Your cock rubs through my dress, against my ass. I want it so badly I moan. I whimper. I grind my ass against yours. You kiss the back of my neck and make me shiver. You slip your hand up my dress and start to rub my clit. You put your middle finger into me and start to fingerfuck me again. I shudder and whimper, begging. No. Please. Please stop. No. I can't stand it. My nipples are hard against your jacket. You tease those, too, your hand up my shirt and moving from one nipple to the other to ensure they both stay hard. Your feet are planted firmly between mine, making sure I keep my legs spread. Your cock remains motionless as you let me grind my ass against it. The city lights swim in front of me. My breath comes in great gasping sobs.

"It would be so easy," I moan. "Just pull my dress up and . . ."

"Not until dawn," you tell me, and start to fingerfuck me harder, making me lean against the railing and moan at the top of my lungs.

You drive me to a bar for a nightcap. It's close to last call, and we find a booth near the back where almost no one can see us. You lean against me and slide your hand up my dress again, but this time you don't touch me. I relax into the soft cushions of the booth, my legs spread, and beg you. "Please. Please. Please." But you won't touch me. You just let your fingers hover there, inches from my pussy, and it's worse torture than I've ever felt. Within moments I'm on the edge of orgasm again, and you've never even touched me. The pink champagne tastes sickly sweet and it makes my stomach tingle. The smoke of the bar swirls around me and I lose all sense of direction. Am I awake or asleep?

You kiss me, and I know I'm asleep: and dreaming. A nightmare. A nightmare of want, of need, of desire. You slip your hands into my mouth and I would swear I can taste my cunt. I lick you eagerly. I beg you for more. I run my hand up the swell of your cock and whimper for what I need.

"Please," I whisper. "Let me suck your cock. Right here. Let me suck it right here in the bar."

You shake your head and kiss me. "Not until dawn."

You drive me back to our apartment and lead me up the stairs. You grab me and push me hard against the wall right by the door, before you've even closed it. I moan as I melt into your grasp. You grind your cock against my front and I reach down to cup it. I try to slide my hand down your pants as you kiss me. You seize my wrist and pull it away.

Leaning firmly against me, you undress me right there. You slip my dress over my shoulder and let it shimmy down my body, revealing me. I'm not wearing panties or a bra. My small breasts feel so tender against the rough wool of your jacket. My nipples ache like they're going to explode. You take me over there, pressed against your body, wriggling up and down as you savage my mouth with yours. "Please," I beg you. "Please let me suck it?"

You pull me off the wall and guide me toward the bedroom, one hand on my shoulder and the other on my hip. I can hardly walk, I'm so turned on. I can barely stand, my cunt hurts so much. I stumble into the bedroom and you push me across the bed, forcing my legs open wide, this time with your hands. I see what you're doing and the terror grips me. No. No, you can't. You can't do this to me. It's too much. I can't stand it. No, please.

But what I say is simply: "Please."

Your mouth descends between my legs.

From the first touch of your hot tongue on my aching clit, I know I'm going to come. You know it, too, and it's only that first touch you let me have. Your breath tickles me, sizzling my flesh. Your tongue undulates an inch from my clit. I beg you, tears streaming down my face. I need it. I have to have it. But you make me lay there, spread wide, until you know my orgasm has subsided. Then, cruelly, you begin to eat my pussy.

I sprawl across the bed, clawing the sheets viciously. Moaning "No, no, no, no, no," unable to stand it. About to die. About to disintegrate. About to explode.

Your tongue swirls around my clit in exactly the way that makes me come—then stops. You tease my pussy lips. You lick down to my entrance, slipping the tip of your tongue in. You lick around my clit, blow on it, tease it with your breath. You do everything but make me come.

"Please," I beg you.

I feel your fingers inside me again, and my moan comes louder than ever. My back arches. I push my cunt down onto you, taking as many of your fingers as you'll give me. You finger me until I'm on the edge again. I've lost all perspective. I've lost all sense of time. I know I'm going to die if I don't come. I know you're going to kill me by torturing me like this.

"Please," I beg. "I can't take it. Oh God, I can't take it . . ."

And then my wide-open, glossy eyes see it: the first hint of light through the window. I want to tell you it's dawn. I want to ask you to fuck me. I want to beg you to make me come. But I can't. I can't say anything but "Please, please . . . no, no, no, no, no." I'm so far beyond speech I can barely even manage that. My body writhes under you as you start to eat my pussy again.

And I'm on the edge again. You stop.

But this time you stand up, towering over me at the foot of the bed. I watch you, eyes wide, as you take off your clothes. All of them. Your cock stands out, straight and hard. I would give anything to touch it. Anything at all to taste it. Everything I have to feel it inside me, thrusting. Fucking me. Taking me. Making me come.

You slide on top of me, naked. My body presses up against yours, seeking. My legs spread still wider. My ass lifts off the bed.

"Please," I say as the streams of light tear through the blinds and savage me.

I come the second I feel your cockhead penetrate me. I come a second time as I feel your shaft sliding into me. I come a third time as you grind your hips hard against me, forcing your cock in and out against my desperate flesh. I come a fourth time as I thrust my body up against yours, wailing, sobbing, taking each hard thrust you give me and begging for more. My arms and legs are slack; only my hips and my cunt exist. And my mouth, wailing in hunger. More, more, more, more, more.

The fifth and final time I come is when I realize you're about to come, too. Hours of pent-up need. Your cock filled with semen, about to flood my pussy. That drives me over the edge one final time, and as the sunlight bathes us I rise onto you, lifting you wholly off the bed until nothing is touching but your knees. Then your body tightens, and you come—deep, deep inside me, deeper than you've ever been before.

"Not until dawn," you promised, and you made me wait. "Not until dawn," you told me, and you gave it to me. I came hard at dawn, harder than I've ever come before. More times than I've ever come. My arms come into being again and I wrap them around you—my legs, too. I clutch you close as you heave a great sigh of exhaustion.

"Thank you," I whisper, but you're already fading. The sun feels cool on my flesh, and your breath on my face feels warm. I close my eyes and vanish into your heat.

Confessions
by Sally McGowan

Sally McGowan's writing has appeared in anthologies, including *Come Quickly for Girls on the Go* (Masquerade) and *Down & Dirty* (Pretty Things Press). She is a part-time gymnastics teacher and a full-time slave.

"Now!" Mick demands, irritated by how long it takes me. He wants me to confess. He *likes* it when I confess. But I never fail to irk him when I take so long to get my nerve up.

"I'm a masochist," I finally squeak out.

"That's right," he says, nodding, his close-cropped hair slicked back to his head so that the smooth, lovely lines of his skull are visible. He's dressed in a black turtleneck, tight against his spare form, and black leather pants that were made to suit a sadist. "Now, say it again," he says, this time punctuating his words with a slap of a paddle against the palm of his hand.

I flinch at the sound, which makes him laugh. He steps forward, then uses the paddle to lift my chin upward. "Say it again," Mick says, his voice gone in that low, hoarse tone that lets me know he's turned on. "Say it . . . louder!"

I'm scarlet, I know it. My cheeks are flaming pink, my eyes are watering with effort. I barely speak above a whisper in our "normal" life. During sex-play scenes I lose my voice almost entirely. "I'm a . . ." I hesitate again. Bad move. Or good move, for a cunning masochist such as myself. He has me standing in an instant. It's easy to stand quickly when someone is yanking on your collar.

"Are you being difficult on purpose?" he asks, all the while turning me, so that I am bent over his knee, lifting my stupid frilly white dress, dragging the ruffled baby-doll panties down my trembling thighs. "Are you trying to get a reaction from me?"

No answer is needed. I've succeeded. The paddle whisks through the air to land with a crack of pain against my left buttock. He paddles my right without asking his question again. And then follows the two bursts of punishment with a series of powerful blows that leave me hanging onto him for support. I am breathless, but not crying, when he shoves me back onto the floor.

"Fix your dress," Mick hisses, and I yank up my panties and arrange my dress, as before, so that it falls neatly around my body. "Does your bottom hurt?" he asks next. I nod, knowing this is not what he wants, and then, open my mouth to respond. As I part my lips, he parts his slacks, immediately sliding his cock into my mouth. This is not what I expected, and my eyes bulge wide as I try to accommodate his sudden, harsh thrusts. When he pulls away from me and tucks himself back into his slacks, I am still wide-eyed, disheveled.

"Answer quicker when you are spoken to," he advises and then, because he is getting worked up and wants to play hard, he motions to one of his friends from the group gathered quietly around the room to come and fasten me to the leather horse.

"You will receive ten lashes," my Master says. "Ten from me, that is. Then the others will have a turn with you." I want desperately to get away, to beg forgiveness. I want more desperately to climb over the horse and be whipped until I cry. I want most of all to thank my Master, my most cruel and understanding Master, my savior who knows me better than I know myself.

But thanking him comes after.

His assistant binds me to the horse and then cuts away my dress and panties. The others gather closer together to watch. I feel the heat of their bodies around me. I love that they are watching me. I am more than a masochist. I am an exhibitionist.

My Master doubles his belt and gives me ten, blindingly painful strokes against my naked ass and thighs. I moan for him, but do not cry. I have a pain tolerance that makes him extremely proud. Another takes his place, this time wielding a crop. This hurts more. This leaves marks. This makes me dig in my breath after each blow, but still, no tears mark my face.

"Who's next?" my Master asks, his voice taunting. "Who can make my little bitch shed real tears? That's what she needs, you know. Real, honest to goodness tears of pain."

There's silence in the room. Then a voice I know and fear, the voice of the man who was my Master's own trainer, responds in the affirmative. Master Victor uses a cane, and I know before even receiving the first blow, that he will be the one to bring me to my pinnacle. He will make me cry and he will make me come.

The first stroke doesn't even register as pain until he hits me a second time. The first blow sounds throughout the room and I am aware of it, but the pain doesn't come, doesn't fill my body with a ringing, vibrating howl until he has lined up a second stroke below it. Now, my ass is on fire. I bite my bottom lip, but cannot stifle the low groan that escapes. The third stroke makes me bite my lip harder. The fourth brings tears.

That doesn't stop him, of course. He doesn't stop until I am sobbing, as I should be, and coming, as I don't deserve to be but am grateful for.

And, as I come, as my hips pound against the leather, I whisper the words to my Master. I whisper, "Thank you," and then close my eyes, the tears dripping slowly down my face and dropping to the wooden floor below.

All Tied Down
by Ayre Riley

Several stories by **Ayre Riley** appear in the new collection *Down & Dirty* (Pretty Things Press). She lives in San Antonio, Texas, with her husband, Jason. He's truly tickled by his wife's dirty mind.

Of this story, the author says: "I've always believed that people who write in their journals do so only with the hope that someone else will someday read the words. In 'All Tied Down,' a girl gets precisely what she wants, after her boyfriend devours every sexy description she's ever had the nerve to pen."

It started simple enough. Gabriel said he wanted to tie me down. Just tie me down and fuck me. No chains. No whips. Nothing scary.

"Let's try it, Gracie," he whispered to me, his face pressed against my long auburn hair, his strong arms holding me tight. "We can stop any time you want. We won't have to do anything more than that—" His voice was both patient and hesitant, as if he were scared that I might not agree, but he needn't have worried. I've always been into playing with new ideas. I had no problem with doing it outdoors, fucking in the back of his shiny black pickup truck after a rock concert at The Greek Amphitheater, making love on the aerial ride at the amusement park at the beach, the little blue metal car swinging and swaying with our raucous movements. And even though I'd never told him about my fantasies—well, deep down, I'd always wanted to play a little more kinky. Or a *lot* more kinky. Even if I never told *any-one*, I'd always had these urges that went unfulfilled by all of my past good-guy boyfriends.

"Are you game, Gracie?" Gabriel asked me, his arms around my slim waist, pulling me even closer to his muscular body in a spoon embrace. "Are you, baby?"

I rolled out of his grip to look over at him, and I realized as I stared at his gentle, yearning expression that I've always been with the good guys. You know how some girls always go for the bad boys? The ones who treat them cruelly, who don't call when they say they will, don't act like a gentleman in any manner of speaking. I've never fallen for that type. The Mickey Rourke type. The Colin Farrell type. Unlike many of my friends, I never saw the appeal in dating a guy who could only think about racing motorcycles and wearing well-worn leather. I never yearned for rough whiskers and whiskey breath. But in the back of my head, I always wondered, *Does it take a bad boy to give me what I crave?* Would it take going in for that sort of sickly twisted relationship in order to get what I needed? I hoped not. That's all I could do—just hope.

I never mentioned my sexual daydreams to Gabriel. I liked him too much, and I was scared I'd frighten him off if he ever saw the real me. But now, *he* was the one bringing up the idea. He was the one saying that he wanted to tie me down. Just tie me down and fuck me. Nothing scary. So why not? Why would I say no to something that he promised would bring me great pleasure?

And he was right—it did.

Being tied to the mattress was divine. I lay in the center of the bed, my wrists over my head, my ankles spread wide apart. Gabriel used his own work ties to fasten my trembling limbs, and when I turned my head I saw that he'd chosen a tie I'd given him for Valentine's Day on my wrists. A navy blue one decorated with miniature crimson hearts. That made me smile and relax. Yes, we were dabbling in bondage, but this was my sweetheart, my one and only. Even when tying me down, he played nice.

He took a moment to look at me, and I could tell that he was admiring my naked form bound for his own personal pleasure. When he was ready, he climbed onto the bed and made me come with his mouth on the very center of my body. Made me come like I never have before. He used his tongue to trace pictures up and over my clit. He took his time, moving away from me when I was desperate for him to let me climax. Only giving in when he was good and ready.

But he didn't want to stop there.

"You liked that, right?" he asked, his sex-glazed mouth so close to my ear that his breath warmed my skin. "Didn't you, Gracie?"

I nodded, my whole body still alive and tingling with pleasure. "Yeah, I did." Being bound was even better than I'd pictured, better than I'd fantasized about alone, my fingers moving quickly and making their magic circles up and over my clit, up and over, until it happened. In my head, I hadn't understood the power of being powerless. Now, I was starting to figure everything out.

"So let's take things up a notch."

"Meaning?"

"You tell me, Gracie. What would that mean to you? What visions does that idea conjure up for you?"

I closed my eyes, trying to guess what he expected me to say, trying to read his fantasies solely from the way he was asking the question. What would a good boy like Gabriel fantasize about? What would an all-American guy like my sandy-haired boyfriend think was pushing the edge? Gabriel's a devoted son with an upstanding job. He's a man who's never once forgotten my birthday, or our anniversary, or any special occasion at all. What would *he* think was kinky? I was already tied down—and he had ravaged me without me being able to do anything about it. Not that I'd wanted to do anything about it. He'd started by kissing my lips, letting me return his passion beat for beat, and then he'd moved slowly down, working his way along my entire body until he had reached that place between my legs, the place so desperate to feel the wetness of his kisses, and—well, what could be better than that?

"Blindfold," he suggested, breaking into my thoughts. "A blindfold, Gracie?"

So, yeah, as soon as he said the word, I thought that I should have known to say it myself. I've spent many pleasurable hours imagining the appeal in the abandonment of a sense, picturing how it would feel not to know where he was going to go next, what he was going to do, when he was going to fuck me.

"Sure," I said, trying not to sound as excited as I really was. I didn't want to spoil the effort he'd put into creating this exotic encounter. Would he possibly think less of me if he knew that sometimes, just sometimes, I take one of my extremely expensive silk scarves, the ones I wear when I go to conventions, and blindfold myself before allowing myself to come? I close my eyes tightly under the fabric and pretend that Gabriel is the one placing the blindfold over my eyes, that he is the one plunging my world into darkness.

"Really?" Gabriel asked.

"Yeah," I said slowly, "that would be okay."

I was still agreeing when he brought the purple velvet blindfold out of the dresser drawer and held it up for me to see before positioning it over my eyes and fastening the back beneath my heavy hair. I had only long enough to realize that he'd gone out and purchased this particular toy for our use, that he'd planned this event for me, that it wasn't in the least bit spontaneous—and then we started again, with Gabriel kissing me all over, alternating the places he paid attention to and the pressure of his kisses, so I had no concept of what to expect. His mouth was wet and open, and I shivered at every connection of that wet heat with my naked skin.

Then, suddenly, he moved over my body, reaching in the drawer again. After a moment, I felt something different, something that I recognized instantly as a feather, caressing and playfully tickling the bottoms of my feet, my inner thighs, working right up over my clit, which still hummed from my first orgasm of the night.

"You trust me, right?" he murmured. "Right, Gracie?"

Deep breath. Did I trust him? Yeah. Of course, I did. I nodded.

"Say it."

"I trust you, Gabriel."

"Mean it."

"I do," I said quickly. "I do trust you. Of course, I do."

"Then confess to me—"

"What—" I stuttered. "What do you mean?" All at once, the fact that I couldn't see him made me feel off balance. This idea of being captured, a concept I'd had explored in my head for years, took on a deeper meaning. I couldn't see him with the blindfold in place. I couldn't get free without his assistance. What expression was on his face? Precisely how intently was he staring at me?

"Now, tell me the secrets you've been keeping."

My breath came faster now. I tested the binds with my wrists and my ankles, for some reason feeling intensely confined when before I'd only felt erotically captured. As I squirmed, he brought that feather back into play, so that I was wildly squirming and laughing even as my mind scrambled desperately to figure out what he wanted me to say.

"I read your journal, Gracie," he said—the one to actually confess. "So I know. I know all about it, baby. So now you tell me . . ."

Oh, Christ. Oh, Jesus. Oh, fuck.

"I know what you think about when you take that naughty little hand of yours and bring it between your legs late at night. I know you wait for me to fall asleep, listen for my breathing to go soft and heavy, and then the sticky sap starts to flow down your thighs as you crest the waves of those silent orgasms. I know everything. But I need you to tell me. I need to hear you say it."

So he *did* know. He knew. Knew more than I was willing to tell even myself. That what I wanted was this. But more than this. Far beyond this. What I wanted was for him to take control. Total control. Not to ask me anymore if this was okay, or if that was okay, but to just do it. To do everything. To do whatever he wanted with me. Using me. Taking me. Forcing me. No more nice and sweet and gentle lovemaking for his pretty girlfriend. But real and hard and fast and raw. And I understood even more than that, before he started, I had to say it all out loud. Creating truth from fantasy. Making it all real.

"Say it," he insisted.

"I want—" but the words died right there.

"Say it, Gracie."

"I want to be yours."

"You are mine."

"More than that."

"Say it."

"I want you to do things to me."

He sighed. "Oh, yes, baby, I know." My request unleashed a torrent from him. As if he'd been waiting forever for me to say the words that would set his own fantasies free. "You want me to fuck you hard. Isn't that right? Harder than I do now. Harder than I've dared. You want me to take you doggy-style, my hand in your hair, holding you steady for my pace. You want me to slam you up against the wall and just fuck you, holding your wrists over your head, keeping you right where I want you. You want me to make you masturbate when we're caught in traffic, right there in the car, where everyone can see you, if they'd only look. You want to have to do what I tell you. Is that right? You want me to make you do things."

I nodded.

"Is that right?" he said again, his voice more softly menacing than I'd ever heard before.

"Yes, Sir," I managed to respond. "Yes, yes, yes."

"But what if you fail me?"

And now we were at the fantasies that I'd written so quickly in my journal but refused to reread. The parts that gave me the most pleasure, as well as the most shame.

"Then—" I started.

"Yes, Gracie? What, then?" His whisper was almost menacing. A hiss. A demand for more information.

"Then I want you to punish me."

"Punish you how?"

I couldn't turn back now. I had it within my grasp to get everything I'd ever wanted. I had to come clean. I had to do exactly what Gabriel insisted. I had to confess. "I want you to spank me with your hand and your belt. With a Ping-Pong paddle. With whatever you need to use. A wooden spoon. A ruler. A hard-backed hairbrush. I want you to make my ass smart so seriously from the blows, and then I want you to stand me in the corner with my panties dangling around my ankles so I can think about how I might better please you in the future."

"What else?" Gabriel asked me. "What else should I do to you if you disobey me?"

I took a deep breath. "I want you to call me names, to slap my face, to use clothespins on me."

"Clothespins?"

"You know, on my nipples, and my pussy lips, and my clit—" Now, I was grateful for the blindfold, so I wouldn't have to see the look on his face. Would he leave? Was he disgusted with me? "I want you to make me beg and—"

"And—"

"I want you to make me cry—"

"Oh, Gracie. Who would have thought? Who would have thought that my good girl could be such a bad girl at heart?"

I didn't have an answer for that. I didn't have an answer for anything. I was waiting, my breath held, to see what he'd say next. To see how he'd deal with all I'd just confessed to. He'd read my fantasies, but could he handle them now that I'd said everything out loud? Now that I'd really come clean, just as he'd asked me to? Now that I'd confessed?

"Of course, I will," my good-guy boyfriend said. "Anything you need, baby," my all-American man promised me. And I suddenly realized that maybe you don't need to date a rough-and-tumble guy in order to find a master. You only need a kindred spirit. And that maybe Gabriel was looking the whole time for someone like me, a good-sort-of-girl, fine and upstanding, sweet and even-tempered, who wanted only to serve and obey and be disciplined for failing her master.

And so here I am, exactly where I always wanted to be, all tied down and nowhere to go . . .

I Will Not Fail
by Lizbeth Dusseau

Fans of BDSM erotica will recognize the name **Lizbeth Dusseau** — and if they don't, they should. She published her first erotic novel, *Alexandra's Awakening,* in 1990; it was followed by seven Masquerade Books titles in the next several years. Though she's a wonderfully skilled and passionate writer of erotica in her own right, she wasn't satisfied there. Since 1994, she has not only published her work through Pink Flamingo Publications (www.pinkflamingo.com), the company she founded with her husband, Ken, but has also served as the principal editor and web designer for that imprint, which has published the work of more than fifty erotica authors. Dusseau has authored more than one hundred erotic novels and short story collections. She and Ken live in rural Michigan.

I was quite pleased to net a story by Dusseau for both this collection and its companion, *MASTER,* and this tale lives up to Dusseau's reputation for excellence. Of it, she says: "In my writing, I most enjoy delving into the heart and mind of the submissive woman . . . I suppose that is only natural since I consider myself a natural-born submissive. Submission for me is not a static characteristic, but one that changes, evolves, and grows just as the individual grows. It can be a position of great strength but it can also be a challenge to understand and accept, as it is for Sandra in this story."

I feel him near. It's now the quiet hours of the morning before dawn. The world around me is silent, shaded by the remains of night and a day beginning to crawl toward its birth. I can see this new dawn about to break as the horizon begins to pale in anticipation.

"There's unfinished business," he says.

I've been sitting at my dressing table, watching the sky's changing palette, and now turn at the sound of his voice—mellifluous, but jarring in its rising vibration.

"Reg . . ." I speak his name, but then let it fall away. The house has been so voiceless since he left. There's been no mirth in my heart. "How do I pay for my negligence?" I finally have the courage to ask, but I still can't face him. Chilling shivers run along my back in sensuous waves. With a whiff of his cologne, another one darts up my spine. I finally turn in my seat.

He stands like a pillar of granite, bathed by the expanding morning. Disheveled blonde hair, suit jacket thrown over his shoulder. I wonder where he's been.

"Get out of my house," he says, coldly.

I shrink back with alarm.

His eyebrows rise mockingly. "You look surprised. You think I'd let you stay after what you've done?"

There was a time when I would have sunk to my knees at his feet, kissed his shoes as a lowly penitent and begged his forgiveness. But we seem so many miles, so many years beyond that now.

"I thought we might . . ." I start and stop. I can't even finish the thought.

"You thought wrong. I've been away. I needed time to collect my thoughts."

Of course. Time to brood as he does so well, to put on the cloak of despondency he wears with ease. There was a time when I could pull him from that gloom of character by my submissive presence. But so many years have come and gone.

"But what do I do, Reg? Where do I go?"

"I don't really care. Go back to your lover, walk the streets, sell your body for cash, whatever a slut like you does." His face entertains a twisted smirk. "Or maybe I should just let you stay here since you've ruined this house, this bedroom, this bed."

I feel my stomach clench as a remorseful pang of guilt stabs my gut.

He scowls derisively as he scans the rumpled sheets and tossed pillows where he found me with my ass bouncing on the breeze, as

I wet-hot fucked the man beneath me. The screaming, grunting, groaning fiasco was not half as pleasurable as it must have looked to him.

"Is there no way we can mend this?"

"And what do you propose? I see no way that works for me. You're an easy woman. I'm sure you could find lots of methods for your redemption. But I'm not interested in redeeming you."

I'm losing him fast—the man, the lover, the master I have adored—and I feel my emotions start to spark with fear.

"No, Reg! Your heart can't be this cold."

He walks by me to the closet where he hangs his coat, and begins, hanger by hanger, ejecting my clothes, tossing them in a pile on the floor.

"I'll have a taxi pick you up in two hours." He consults his watch to see that it's nearly six A.M. "It'll take you where you want to go, on my dime. After that, it's up to you."

What if I were to fall at his feet again? What if I were to beg? My mind thinks so fast that my head hurts. Desire, need, remembrance flood my body, urging me forward like a prodding friend. "Do it, Sandra!" I hear that anxious friend scream. She is as desperate as I am now. But I still can't move. It is no use; he is immovable.

Hours later. I've checked into a cheap hotel; I've walked the streets; I've combed my thoughts, my life, my past, and what looks to be a bleak, unpromising future. The day lingers in this mood of weariness. How did I come to this sad end? What happened to take away the light, the mirth, the joy in my heart? When did my master lose his allure? When did I forget myself and the substance of who I am?

When walking fails to lift my spirits, I hail a taxi and direct it to the brick house near the water. Bright lights gleam from inside. Is this a sign? The mood of welcome I'm looking for? I know what this step means, this return, what Roger will demand—if he'll take me. The desire to surrender sweeps me again like it did in the bedroom with Reg, but this time, I won't let the cobwebs of doubt keep me from acting on impulse.

My former master, the man who trained me in the art of submis-

sion, who nurtured it in its infancy, is the only one who will understand me now and know what to do. When he answers the door, his
enormous aura sweeps over me and I drop to my knees, sobbing. All
the tears that wouldn't surface with Reg are streaming from my eyes.

"What the hell, Sandra? Not now. Get off your knees." He impatiently draws me to my feet and pushes me toward his study, away
from the drawing room and the sounds of laughter and music.

Before I have a chance to explain, he lets me know that he's already heard the news.

"You really blew it this time," he says, with an edge of judgment in
his voice as crisp and incisive as Reggie's cool rebuke.

"I know," I agree, my tone heaped with suffering.

He paces before me, shaking his head despairingly. "You know
this is a terrible time. I have fifty guests in the next room, and I'm
here with you."

"I'm sorry, I'll go. I only hoped—"

"No," he cuts me off, "there's no hope for you, Sandra."

I slink into a chair, despondent, then gaze up submissively, praying for compassion I do not deserve. He eyes me with a curious com-
bination of interest and contempt and I fear the worst as he sums up
his present dilemma: "So, what do I do with you? Deal with your deception or throw you in the street?"

"Oh, please, Roger! Give me the hell he won't. It will satisfy us
both."

His eyes narrow. "Are you sure you know what you're asking?"

"Yes, I'm very sure," I say with unwavering control, even as every
nerve in me trembles with fright.

"And you mean what you say?"

"I do, with my whole heart," I answer, as I lurch forward with the
hope in my heart preceding me.

He wears a look of consternation as if in thoughtful contempla-
tion and finally states: "The shame is, you really are a submissive
woman."

"Oh, I am. I just got off track and I'm desperate now." I hadn't
planned to say any of these things. In fact, I hadn't even envisioned
the outcome I wanted before I knocked on Roger's door. But now I'm
traveling headlong down familiar paths of sub-speak, forced there by

regret and need—deep need—that for reasons I can't even recall now, I put aside like a pair of worn shoes.

"Exactly how desperate are you?" he asks.

"Roger, please. Don't deny me." I'm ready to humbly sink to my knees, but that would be too contrived for this practical man.

"Deny you, hmm . . ." He smiles darkly, as the devious passageways in his brain light with inspiration. I know it's been a long time since he had a woman like me. Is he as needy for this as I am?

"You need to be punished thoroughly before I consider anything further," he warns.

My body reacts in raw, tumultuous fashion, craving the retribution, my only salvation from my savage guilt. "I know that," I concede, "and I'll submit as you require."

His face lightens as he sighs. "But, my dear, there's a party going on outside these doors and you've interrupted me." He then stops. Zeros in on my humbled gaze. I can feel the tug of war inside him. And then, he suggests exactly what I fear the most. "How about you take your punishment in front of my guests?"

"Oh, dear!" I gasp. Yes. I should have expected as much. How inspired! How humiliating! How cruel a test! My mind races and my stomach sours as it tumbles nervously. My palms begin to sweat. I can feel my body heat soaring from the thought of a humbling exhibition.

Roger feels my hesitation. "I thought you were serious," he says, to fill the silence.

"I am serious. And yes, I will do anything to reclaim even a small place in your life."

He laughs. "Don't get melodramatic, Sandra."

"But I will take my punishment before your friends, if that's what you desire. I have to." I can feel the demeaning scene drawing me to it with the force of an ocean tide submerging me in its dangerous waters. I spiral downward at a dizzying speed.

"But it won't be over in one night," he adds. "You'll serve me here, collared and naked. You'll accompany me decked out like the slave you are. You'll become the woman you try to hide from the world. You want the retribution you've earned, you'll show your truth like a badge of honor. It's about time, isn't it?" He pauses as I soak up his words. "But, you make your choice now; there will be no retreating."

He stares me down with a cruelty I've not seen from him before. Does he hate me, or is this just his version of master? And what has this hard approach done for me but turn my insides into jelly, reaffirmed the fact of who I am, and made my randy crotch stir in anticipation?

"What will it be, Sandra? I don't have time to waste while you haggle with yourself. You either know, or you don't know, no in-between."

I don't have time to consider carefully what I agree to. "I have to, Roger, I must." I say what he needs to hear, committing myself with words that are easily spoken.

He laughs like Satan's evil twin. "Ah! What else would I expect you to say? You always had the words down pat, the attitude, the persuasive line. You fooled a lot of people—Reggie, for one. But me, you don't fool me. You're going to have to prove yourself with your body, in acts that speak loudly, that declare, announce, broadcast who you are with no reluctance, no dithering about, as you did with Reg."

"I promise. I won't fail you."

His eyebrows rise, as if he knows something I do not. "Well, then, let's get started," he states coolly. "My guests are waiting for my return."

Roger did not lie. His massive living room vibrates with the sound of fifty opulently dressed guests mingling, chatting, sipping wine, reeking of elegant perfumes and expensive liquor. As Roger leads me, collared, leashed, and naked into their company, their eyes turn to me in wonder. Expressions of shock and curiosity break out across the room. Breathy gasps sweep all conversation aside.

My legs tremble, weakened by embarrassment, and yet I can smell the redolent aroma of my sexual pheromones as my body heats with lewd excitement.

I could be one of them—the makeup-laden, silk-dressed snobbish nouveau riche, who delight in the unusual, the eccentric, the bizarre. Truth is, I have been one of them in my other life—the life I wrecked.

"If you'll indulge me, my dear friends," Roger begins. "I have a necessary task that must be attended to. This woman has committed a grievous act against the man she loved. She is an adulteress, a headstrong, incorrigible harlot in need of castigation." He pauses, to allow the stunning announcement to sink in. "But she begs absolution, and so I've agreed to begin that task tonight, here, in your company.

"For those of you offended by corporal punishment, I urge you to move into the dining room now for coffee and dessert. But the rest of you, even if you're just curious, I welcome you to witness the act. This woman will be hurt. She may scream and she may well beg me to stop. But, she has also put herself in my hands with the understanding that I may attend to her disgraceful behavior as I see fit. This is her choice. She came to me." He turns my way. "Isn't that so, Sandra? Tell them."

"Yes, he is correct," I answer softly. My body quakes as I speak; I lust for the humiliation I've earned.

I note that not a single soul is headed for the door.

As Roger pushes on my shoulder, I drop to my knees and crawl at his command, until I'm poised before a leather footstool placed in front of the fireplace. The fire roars, heating the room, heating my skin, making perspiration collect beneath my breasts and between my thighs. He taps me with the toe of his Italian loafer and I move forward, draping my torso on top of the stool. My arms and breasts dangle on one side, while at the other end, my bare, exposed posterior waits for the cruelty to begin. Clenching in fear, I hang on to the footstool's stubby legs and try to breathe calmly.

But there is no calm for a woman on the verge of punishment, on the verge of awesome pain, on the verge of a new beginning. I hear the familiar rustling sounds that precede a punishment, but I close my eyes so I see nothing of his preparations. Does he remove his coat and roll up his sleeves? Does he address the crowd with his eyes or remain focused solely on me? And what weapon does he choose? I imagine the smell of leather—perhaps a whip, a flogger, a tawse. Or perhaps I'm wrong, and he has chosen a wooden paddle.

I feel him near as he readies himself, and then my master of the hour rains blows in perfect cadence against the flesh of my ass. He's chosen a leather tawse; its biting intensity is unmistakable. What is instantly warmed turns hot, starts to sting, then begins to burn within seconds. I squirm, bite my tongue, and prevail as the good submissive. He punishes not just my flesh, but a soul long in need of such chastisement.

Even as practiced as I am in the art of silence in the midst of pain, I can't contain the cry that lurches from my mouth in a garbled sob. My entire body heaves with anguish. I'm barely hanging on as his scourge scorches my skin.

And then he pauses.

I think the worst is over as Roger puts his tawse aside. But how naive I am to think I'd get off so easily!

Forced by curiosity to peek, I spy his cane from the corner of my eye. The thin rattan cuts air, cuts skin, cuts through to the core of a rebuked submissive like nothing else can. I close my eyes again, hold on to the legs of the stool tighter still, then send my mind away, while praying that I'll contain myself like the good submissive I once believed I was.

Despite what follows, I manage to keep my wits about me. There will be no all-out mutiny, no rebellion of any kind, no screaming for an end. That would defeat my aim here. I may whimper with each cut that sears my ass and wish myself elsewhere, but once the third cut slices my skin, as if in the twinkling of an eye, that cut transforms me, his cane transforms me. The succeeding strikes become my friend; they give me hope. I can feel them work out the anguish, the guilt, the self-torment, and touch what really matters in my life. At least for this one hour, the remorse that makes my heart ache will be satisfied.

Roger finishes his work, leaving me poised over the footstool to contemplate my punishment.

"What will happen to her now?" someone asks.

"Ultimately, that is up to her," he replies. "But if she places herself in my care, as she's sworn to do, she will become my slave. She'll start over where she began with me some time ago, and relearn the rudiments of submission. She'll be chattel and nothing more to me for months before I offer her even the slightest kindness or simple reward."

"And she wants that?" another someone asks.

"She needs that," he returns. "She'll face tomorrow differently than she did today, seeing through the eyes of her surrendered self. The power of her submission is what she lost and what she must reclaim. Without it, she'll continue to hurt herself and those she loves. I consider her wise to have realized the truth. And it is my job as her master to keep her closely contained so that she can be the woman she was meant to be."

His words caress me as surely as the touch of his hand soothes me. I am, again, where I belong and I will not fail this time.

Diary of a Masochist
by Fiona Hall

Fiona Hall is the pseudonym of a well-known writer. She assures us that every word in "Diary of a Masochist" is absolutely true. She writes: "It's the shy ones like me who have everybody fooled. The stern-looking researchers. The mild-mannered librarian types. But don't kid yourself into thinking we have fantasies as staid as our outfits . . . because beneath the surface, in our hidden worlds, you have no idea what we're thinking." "Diary of a Masochist" gives a tiny view into the world of a closet pain-craver.

When I first learned how to use a dictionary, I'd take one to my desk at school and look up the words that thrilled me the most, finding the definitions that were suitable to my "needs." The ones that resonated in my head even after I put the book away.

Discipline: punishment designed to control an offender and to eliminate or reform unacceptable conduct.

Punish: subjecting someone to loss of freedom or money or to *physical pain* for wrongdoing.

Chastise: refers to corporal punishment as a means of improving behavior.

Spank: to slap on the buttocks with a flat object or with the open hand in punishment.

At nineteen, when I was with my second lover, he asked me, "What's your fantasy? You can tell me, darling. You can tell me anything . . ."

Blindly, frightened, I shook my head.

"Name one. Just one."

"I can't."

"Sometime I'll have to tie you up and beat you. You know? Would you like that? Would you like me to give you a spanking?"

I blushed, so innocent, so scared, and I looked at him with hopeful eyes, but I couldn't get any words out. He seemed to understand. He stroked my hair and kissed my lips, and he said, "Maybe tomorrow. Maybe you'll find your voice tomorrow night."

After he left, I poured out everything into my diary. In smeared purple ink, the words screamed the answer to his question: *YES! Okay? That's what I want. I don't know why. God knows why I need to be punished. But that's what I want. Okay? Tie me up. Spank me. Hard. Then fuck me. Just fuck me. Okay? Please . . . I need the heat. I need the electricity/excitement/danger. Maybe it'll straighten me out.*

And then in smaller letters, these questions: *Why do I look so vulnerable, innocent? Am I really?*

The next night, he asked the same questions again. In that same, sultry voice, same soothing tone. I took a deep breath. I tried to respond. He said, "Let me make it easier on you. Let me do all the work."

I shrugged. I trembled.

"All I need from you is the answer to my question. Do you want it?"

I couldn't speak. Didn't dare speak. So instead, he came over to my side in his living room. Turned off the light. Pulled down my top and suckled my breasts. Suckled until I arched and moaned, feeling wetness spread between my legs. After kissing me and licking me and getting me ready, he fucked me with my legs wrapped around his waist, his hands cradling my ass. I could imagine just what it would be like to have those big hands spanking me, but I couldn't say the words.

Afterward, walking me to my car, he asked again, "Have you been naughty, baby? Should I give you a spanking? You've been a naughty girl, haven't you?"

Yes. Yes. Yes. Okay? Goddamn it!

That's what my diary says.

Yes. Just do it. Don't make me say it!

But I had more problems than simply speaking my fantasies out loud. There were two men in my life. The one who might make my

X-rated dreams come true, and the other who was exactly the type of man I'd been groomed to marry. My ingrained good-girl attitude made my life hell. I couldn't decide between the nice boy who worked at my office—the one who took me out to dinner and plays and introduced me to culture—and the one who worked night shift at the grocery store, the one who wanted to whip me, beat me, hurt me.

So I saw them both. There are lines in this diary that read like this: *I'm meeting J's mom and stepdad at dinner (eek) tonight. What will I wear? Kelly wants to lick me all over. He wants to spank me. He says I deserve it.*

That has always been my word: deserve. And I have always wanted to do this: to TAKE it. To bear the overwhelming force of another's power. To lie still, or be tied still, and to take it.

But I couldn't speak. Couldn't say no to J, when I realized things were wrong. Couldn't say yes to Kelly when I wanted him to strip me and fuck me, to tie me down, to spank me until I cried.

It took Kelly finding my diary before I came to terms with my true life. It took him devouring every word, then tying me down to his bed as he read those words to me. "Back and forth," he sneered. "Between him and me, when you know the life you were destined to lead. Don't you, bad girl?"

I nodded.

"Then say it."

With my eyes focused on him, I finally found the power in truth. And I knew that I wouldn't see J again, no matter how nice he was, and I knew that I would stay with Kelly, because he'd give me everything I ever wanted. So I took a breath, my eyes on his, the power flickering between us, and I said, "I'm yours. Do with me what you will. Spank me. Fuck me. Use me. No code words needed, no safe words used, no stopping until it's over."

There aren't any entries in my diary after that. I didn't have anything left that I needed to say.

Day 1,617:
The Inevitability of Isabel
by Adrian Hunter

Adrian Hunter began posting his fiction on the Internet in 1993. Four years later, he published his stories on a website, www.adrianhunter.com, which has attracted more than one million visitors. In 2000, he was the recipient of the "Best Bondage Writer" SIGNY award. His short stories, novellas, and poetry have been compiled in four volumes: *Chain Reaction, Come True, Crash Your Party Dress,* and *Something Just Clicked.* He has also coauthored two novels with Chelsea Shepard, *Association* and *Once Bitten.* Hunter's books can be purchased at major booksellers, as well as through the author's website.

What this editor loves about "The Inevitability of Isabel" is the idea of death and rebirth—here, a life of full-time submission is a fresh start, and absolute and overwhelming bondage is its midwife. Of this story, Hunter writes: "The saga of 'Isabel' began in late 1994, when I posted the first chapters on Usenet's alt.sex.bondage. Ostensibly chronicling the week-long adventures of a couple who meet on the Internet, the novella was really a long personal ad from me; as with the Rolling Stones' similarly themed 'Satisfaction,' it is my best-known and most popular story.

"More than a series of sizzling bondage scenes, 'Isabel' is a reflection of the desperate yearning known so well to those whose DNA compels them to explore erotic power exchange. It also serves as a map of the dangerous rapids to be navigated by couples of all flavors before reaching the safe harbor of togetherness. Over the years, I've resisted the urge to rewrite 'Isabel,' but the time has come to properly finish it. This coda finds our heroine and her hero still together four years later, taking the logical (to me, anyway) final step in a BDSM relationship where all wishes come (in every sense of the word) true."

What a bitch. Oh well, Caroline had no one to blame but herself. She had her chance. And it wasn't Isabel's fault the stupid cunt wouldn't let Ron do his worse.

Much, much worse.

Just listen to her prattle and pander, Isabel thought to herself. Boo hoo, it's so bloody sad, poor girl, you must be brokenhearted, may she rest in peace . . .

Fat fucking chance of that, Isabel duly noted, as Ron pressed the button on the remote-control key fob hidden in the jacket pocket of his Sunday suit, complementing the compliment via infrared ("just like your Palm") to the tiny vibrator nestled against her clitoris. The device sported four buttons to control speed: fast, faster, fastest, blur . . .

Whoo hoo, let's hear it for "Song 2." Isabel tried to scream, but nothing but prayers was getting past the overinflated bladder in her mouth tonight.

Then again, begging the forgiveness of gods was always appropriate behavior at a wake.

At least it's not velvet, she had consoled herself when Ron opened the lid of the long trunk that would serve as their new coffee table. Its interior was padded with the kind of foam that molded itself to her contours like the lining of a ski boot; the perfect shape required multiple fitting sessions, first measured in hours, soon extended into days.

Not that she had anything better to do. Not anymore.

Four years of living with Ron had taught Isabel many things. How to touch her elbows behind her back. How to walk in ballet heels. How to pee around a chastity belt. How to come at the sound of his voice.

But one accomplishment eluded her best intentions: how to 24/7. For real.

Slavery was not supposed to be optional, even for those who chose it willfully. But reality had a boring habit of safewording her efforts to craft a full-blown submissive lifestyle. Deadlines at the office, family obligations, phone calls from fast-fading friends . . . social relevance was disappearing in direct proportion to her zeal to kneel. And the object of Isabel's devotion was only too happy to justify her piety in ways that often made her reach out to steady herself against the nearest wall.

She had long since come to grips with the symptoms of fatal affection, as well as the psychological imperatives of her genetics that compelled her to be owned and operated. Isabel knew exactly what she wanted—leather cuffs, as supple as an old hippie's Levi's—and she kept them, as well as her pockmarked gag, in the garage next to the clothes she was forbidden to wear in the house.

No, Isabel's only problem was her passive past making the present tense at the expense of the future perfect. So why not give yesterday a proper burial, like the grief counselors always suggested?

Isabel clenched her toes in glee, partially to celebrate the success of their Tom Sawyer scheme, and partially because they were the only parts of her body she could move right now.

When it came to reincarnation, she decided the Egyptians definitely had the right idea about how to begin the journey. Over the years, Ron had experimented with everything from Clysar industrial shrinkfilm ("suitable for all grades of meat") to Petflex elasticized fetlock wraps, but nothing put the "mmmmph!" in mummy quite like Ace bandages followed by a layer of duct tape.

Or two. Silver first, then black. Like the Raiders said, "Commitment to excellence." No missed spots. Each limb encased separately. Before it was fused to its neighbor. Including her fingers. But not, as noted, her toes.

"A tragedy. She was a beautiful girl, always smiling and . . ."

Despite the quality of the microphones under the table connected to her hearing aids, Isabel missed the rest of Fred's spontaneous eulogy as the vibrator droned back to life.

Faint dribbles began to coalesce in her bladder, but practice had trained her to push away such thoughts with the same firm insistence as the tapered silicon probe distending the entrance to her rectum. In these circumstances, she knew there were greater pleasures than water for which to thirst. Starting with a proper orgasm. Maybe tomorrow. Maybe next month. Not for her to decide.

When the intermittent attacks on her sex finally ceased, Isabel gasped through the plastic pipes extending down from her nostrils to her exposed nipples, which were stretched almost an inch high by cages of slender brass posts supporting crossbeams that passed through her piercing holes. Every expelled breath channeled past her pinkish-brown flesh—splitting the difference between tissue and membrane—threatened to trigger a distant contraction; another reminder that Ron was not one to overlook the smallest facet in his favorite diamond.

This was one of several thousand stellar qualities that had spurred Isabel's decision to entrust Ron with her very life by ending it (although they couldn't decide if it was murder or suicide). Her soul had been permanently branded (the other parts would come later) by his confession that he would never find another partner so willing to be his canvas, whether stretched between the edges of a frame or belted like a straightjacket. Everything else was logistics.

It was no secret that she was a nervous driver, especially when road conditions were even slightly icy. The authorities warned Ron it was unlikely they'd recover anything from the ravine after the spring thaw. Best not to be too hopeful. Animals got awfully hungry this time of year.

"So you really think you can run your business from there?" someone asked Ron. "I didn't think wetbacks had real phones, much less T1 lines."

Actually, Cabo San Lucas was extremely civilized by Mexican standards, thanks to the luxury villas that dotted the surrounding hills overlooking the Gulf of California, the Sea of Cortez, and the Pacific Ocean. Fishing, diving, blue agave tequila, the weather report permanently stuck on fair and warmer . . . when it came to splendid isolation, the southernmost tip of the Baja peninsula was pretty much paradise.

Current conditions excepted, Isabel tried to grin to herself as her extended ears hoped for more homilies from the assembled friends and relations.

She'd visited their new casa—well, technically, it was hers, since it was her life insurance that would pay off the mortgage early—only once, which suited her fine. Ron was much more qualified to boss around surly subcontractors, especially ones who only spoke Spanish.

And it wasn't like she had any say in the design or the decor. Gas or electric on the range, the tile pattern in the Jacuzzi, the curve of the cage hanging from the ceiling . . . totally his call. Like everything else in her life from now on.

Despite the pump gag, Isabel smiled as she realized she was destined to become the first person in the history of the Western Hemisphere to be smuggled *into* Mexico in the trunk of a car.

Apparently, the infrared worked both ways; Ron started to unroll the blueprints on top of her well-sanded sarcophagus, showing his friends the layout of his new "bachelor pad" being built into the side of a mountain he now owned from base to summit. He was awfully convincing as he rapturously described the views of the water to the east, south, and west from the great room that housed the living, dining, and kitchen areas, as well as the rooftop terrace, complete with swimming pool, and the three-car garage where he could stash his off-road toys, like a vintage Husqvarna 450 Desertmaster (ahem) dirt bike.

What he didn't mention was the mirrored glass in the picture windows, the privacy hedge surrounding the deck, and the gigantic basement, lackadaisically identified on the architect's plans as "storage." While he trusted the local crews to put the finishing touches on the rest of the villa, Ron had already relocated his sawhorses, lathes, and drills onsite to personally craft the interior of the dungeon; the walls, floor, and ceiling were to be covered in thick slabs of polished lumber so hooks, pulleys, and suspension bars could be secured wherever he pleased. As for furniture, what they didn't already own in the way of spanking benches (five), stockades (four), St. Andrew's crosses (three, including one with a center beam to better support her back, torso, neck, and head), discipline thrones (two), and her favorite new coffin would wait until Ron finished the fence surrounding the perimeter of the property.

It isn't easy twisting razor wire by hand, but you know how it goes with him and details, Isabel thought to herself as a guest said something about how happy Ron always seemed around her, which led to another round of launch-the-missiles with the pocket rocket.

Besides, Isabel wasn't altogether certain Ron's intention was to keep people out of their compound, or keep her in. Not that she would get very far in the one piece of clothing she would be allowed to wear in public, a string bikini consisting of three latex straps no more than an inch wide, barely sufficient to cover her nipples, much less the space between her legs, which was due for another bout of electrolysis before they left.

People won't even notice, Ron had assured her. The village was infamous for its flocks of crazy rock-star wannabes and their groupies pounding top-shelf margaritas at the Cabo Wabo cantina. You'll just be another *muchacha loca* in high heels who wants to fuck Sammy Hagar.

Accent on "high." Just like the vibrator. Again.

Not that she was anticipating a lot of local interaction. Besides annual visits to the doctor and dentist, "out on the town" was pretty much out of the question for a person without a passport, or, presumably, a pulse.

"What's in the table, Ron?" Isabel heard Caroline titter, her voice dangerously close to the hidden mikes. "Is this where you hide your secrets?"

"Just my porn," Ron replied, much too casually for Isabel's tastes, although it was hard for her to concentrate on their conversation due to Ron's elephantine touch on button 4.

"Oooh, I'll bet it's the nasty kind," Caroline purred, presumably for Ron's benefit alone. "But why just look when you can touch?"

Despite the adhesive patches under layers of elastic wrap and reinforced tape, the blackness in front of Isabel's eyes burst into a rainbow of angry reds and greens. What kind of monster hits on a man in the process of burying his girlfriend?

"Actually, it's the BDSM kind," Ron said, his voice practically jaunty. "Wanna see?"

"Oh, you don't have to tie me up to do whatever you want to me," Isabel heard Caroline say in a low whisper.

"Oh, I think I do," Ron whispered back as his fingers began jabbing buttons on the vibrator's remote at random. "Because after I strap your arms and legs to the sides of this box, I'm going to slice off your clothes with a razor, then stuff your underwear in your mouth and seal it shut with what's left of your pantyhose, because I wouldn't want to be distracted while we're finding out how many clothespins I can fit on your nipples and your pretty little pussy. Tell you what: when we get to fifty, I promise I'll whip them all off with a riding crop before I flip you over and fuck you in the ass, nice and slow and deep, and after I'm done, I'll keep on fucking you back there with a fag dildo . . . you know, the really fat ones they use when their assholes get too stretched out . . ."

Isabel's brain exploded in a thousand white stars from the spine-wrenching detonation of the first in what promised to be a D-Day parade of clitoral orgasms, the super-sized kind that often made her pass out from . . .

"Isabel? Honey, wake up."

Eyelids, engage. Pupils, dilate. Vision, focus. A familiar wooden tray. Scrambled eggs, thick bacon, hot tomatoes . . . are we in London? No, too sunny outside.

"Were you having that dream about the funeral again?"

Coffee, juice . . . funny, there's no silverware.

"Here, let me help you up."

No hands, either. A jingle behind her back. Another good sign.

"Comfy?"

She nodded, her scanner grids shifting to Ron sitting on the edge of the bed. Alone. Naked.

And very tan.

"Close your eyes."

Sí, señor, Isabel happily complied. There's no place like casa.

"Open your mouth."

Refried beans for breakfast had never tasted so sweet.

Inexorable
by Carol Queen

Carol Queen got a doctorate in sexology so she could impart more realistic detail to her smut. She is an award-winning erotic author and also writes personal essays about sexual diversity. For a complete listing of her work, see www.carolqueen.com. Her classic erotic novel *The Leather Daddy and the Femme* was reissued in 2003 by Down There Press. She works at San Francisco's Good Vibrations (www.goodvibes.com).

About her story in *slave*, Queen writes: "'Inexorable' explores something I've always been fascinated by: the phenomenon of women who fall for prisoners. I have all kinds of 'How could she?' judgments about it—but at the same time I see that kind of relationship as needing an erotic logic all its own, and that interests me. I also had fun depicting a D/s relationship that doesn't exist in real time, but escalates through letters. I once got a steamy letter from a prisoner—I didn't write back, but what erotic focus it must take to try to seduce a stranger when you're locked up!"

Unsolicited letters arrive in Angie's mailbox all the time. She's a minor talk radio personality in a major market, plus she writes a column once a month for a mid-circulation magazine. A postage-stamp-sized color picture tops the column, her a few years ago, with fewer pounds and hair a little less gray. The women she knows in local TV have to sweat at the gym every day, color and tuck and lipo, or else they'll lose their jobs. Radio is a little more forgiving, and no one really knows how out of date that magazine photo really is.

Angie gets mail from her listeners, though they mostly call when she's on the air. Her readers write to her, though. Reading and writing—well, of course they go together, like listening and talking. Angie likes getting mail. Likes knowing she's making an impression. Why else have a job where she connects with the public? It's not like the fame, if that's what it is, is matched by the money.

Angie opens her mail today and notices one return address—strange, like most of them are—that has numbers following the name. A man's name, out of state. Angie has a ritual with her mail—she slits each envelope in turn, then reads the letters while sipping the glass of wine she has every night before dinner.

Dear Angie, this one begins. *I hope it's not a problem that I address you so informally. I have been reading your column for several months now and have decided it's time to get in touch to tell you how much I like the way you think about modern life. I have unfortunately not been able to participate fully in this life for several years now, but I try to stay as current as I can thru reading and television. I have been incarcerated for over seven years, so you see your insight is very important to me—it helps me remain out in the free world, you might say, vicariously. Also, I like the picture of you that runs with your work. It gives me the impression that you are both thoughtful and at the same time fully engaged with life.*

Seven years, Angie thinks without meaning to. Isn't that when that photo was taken?

Angie, I am on death row, but it is a mistake—a severe one, to be sure, but I feel hopeful it will be rectified one day. In the meantime, I read and try to correspond with interesting people on the outside. I need to keep my mind sharp, and don't have people from my former life who have stayed in touch. I value the new friends I've made through letters and hope you, too, will be one of them. I find myself talking to you in my head after I read one of your interesting columns. It would mean a lot to me to make that conversation a little more real. Seeing your little tiny picture there helps me keep you in my mind's eye, and I can imagine talking to you as we walked along or shared a glass of wine.

Angie takes a bigger than usual sip.

I know you must be busy, but I think I could make you a good friend, and I hope you'll write me a note in reply. I'll await the day I hear from you.

Your admirer, Steve

Angie doesn't have any admirers at the moment. Most men assume she's spoken for. She can't bring herself to approach them, and so it's been months, or more than months, since the last time she had more than a business meeting with a male editor or station manager. Angie tries to answer all her letters, anyhow, even if only a brief note thanking her correspondent for their thoughts. So after dinner, when she pulls out stationery to reply to today's mail, she doesn't think twice about addressing one envelope to Steve Green in Joliet, Illinois. The next morning the letter vanishes into the corner mailbox.

Dear Angie, the next letter, postmarked less than a week after the first one, begins. *What a pleasure to get your letter. It is always a roll of the dice writing to a public figure such as yourself. I never know if I'll get a reply. But I had a feeling you would respond—it is something about the look in your eyes in this picture. I save your columns, you know, so I can always look at that picture, and small as it is, I feel that it tells me a lot about you. Being in here has definitely been a lesson in understanding character—it is not the lesson I would have chosen, but we have to make the best of everything. And there was a new ray of sun in my gray world today when I got your letter.*

Angie, I would love to have a larger picture of you to keep me company here. I don't know if you send photos to fans. But would you send one to me? Signed?

Yours, Steve

Angie has some PR photos in a drawer somewhere. They are almost as old as the picture from her column. The radio station had them printed up when her show switched to prime time. No one really asks for them.

She gets out a manila envelope and addresses it to Joliet.

She finds a Sharpie and writes her name on the photo, not quite obscuring her décolletage. Another quick note thanking Steve for his interest.

Angie, this picture is beautiful! Steve writes. *You don't know how much it means for an intelligent woman like yourself to correspond with me—it's not like I get to interact with women in here! It helps life feel more normal. And of course every contact from outside feels great. Incarceration is a little easier to take when I feel that I am remembered. I have your photo hung up over my desk. It brightens my day!*

Your devoted Steve

Angie doesn't really plan to do it, but at the drugstore she sees a rack of cards with beautiful little colored pictures, photos almost as small as the one on her column. She picks out a card with vivid flowers, a whole garden in miniature. She writes some kind of vague "Hang in there" message and the next day, it's in the mail to Joliet.

Oh, dearest Angie, You are my angel! What a beautiful bunch of flowers. I have them taped over my desk. (I moved your picture closer to my bed. I like to look into your beautiful eyes at the end of the day.)

Knowing that you are in the world makes this waiting game so much easier to bear.

Love, Steve

Angie writes a little more each time. I've got a pen pal, she thinks—she had a couple of pen pals when she was a kid, too. It's better to get letters with familiar handwriting.

Angie, you are making me such a happy man. Now I want to ask you for something really special. I want something personal from you. Do you have a Polaroid or a digital camera? I want a photo you take just for me. Do you understand?

This will mean so much to me.

Love always, Steve

Angie is pretty sure she knows what Steve means. She gets her old Polaroid out and figures out a way to get a picture out of it with half her face and all her cleavage, wearing her best bra. It comes out a little fuzzy, but she figures that's good.

Angie! Baby! He is writing her at least two letters a week.

What magnificent tits you have, excuse my French. Oh, you know exactly how to please me! A lot of the guys here want porn, but I'm not interested in that. I see no point in looking at pictures of someone I don't know and don't care about. Only a woman who wants to give herself to me can really get my attention—and you do want that, don't you? I could tell when I first wrote to you what a special woman you are.

Always, Steve

Angie isn't sure if Steve expects an answer to that question. She carefully writes a reply that says he is special to her, and that it is precious to have a friend, no matter where you found them. When she goes out to get stamps the postmistress gives her the ones with "love" on them, without being asked. Angie buys them.

Angie, baby—

You can be real with me. Remember, I'm in here where I have to keep it real day in and day out. I guess that makes me a little different from the men you meet outside. You know you are the most precious thing to me, ever. I look at your picture at night and my cock fills with longing for you. I dream of getting a picture of you in the pose I like the best—bent over, showing me your ass. Looking over your shoulder at me so I can see what's in your eyes. Send me a picture of you like that, Angie. God, my cock is so hard as I write this, I'm afraid to touch it.

Make me happy, Angie.

All my love, Steve

I don't know, Angie thinks as she lays out all her lingerie on the bed, why life goes off in these funny directions. None of the real men in my life were ever this passionate. That's all a woman really wants, after all—a passionate love.

Angie puts on a black garter belt, sets the timer on the camera, and bends over. The lights are a little dim, but when the flash goes off, she makes sure her eyes are open.

Angie, you good girl! I love this photo. But I have to tell you, my beautiful baby, I don't dream about you in black. Oh, you look hot in this picture, but I know underneath the sophisticated front you always put on for your public, there's a little girl who needs a strong man. There's a woman wearing white. I don't care what else you've done in your life, Angie, with me it's all new. I'm going to be the first real man you ever had. I want you to send me that picture again—in white.

Angie does not ask herself why she complies with the erotic instructions of a death row prisoner. This behavior only works if she doesn't examine it too closely—that's what she'd say if you tapped her on the shoulder as she enters the Victoria's Secret shop at the mall, or if she were a guest commentator on someone else's radio show. Fantasies are evanescent and you can't scrutinize them too hard. They melt away like fog. Angie has been feeling meltingly womanly lately, and she isn't willing to give this feeling up. She has taken to getting dressed each morning pretending that Steve is sitting across the room, watching her choose her lingerie, watching her put it on.

And now she needs more white.

Angie, darling girl, what a gift this most recent picture is. I can't keep my hands off my cock now. It's not just your lovely ass framed for me, or the look in your eyes. It's that you complied. I told you to do something for me, Angie, and you did it. Such a good girl! But I don't want this to be all about me. I can't be there with you right now, but if you'll do as I tell you, I can pleasure you all the way from here.

Write back to me and tell me, "Yes, Daddy, I will do what you say."
I know what you need. Be a good girl, Angie.

Angie whispers the words out loud as she writes them. "Yes, Daddy . . ."

She encloses the rest of the "love" stamps in the letter.

Angie, be a good girl and do exactly as I say. Go pour yourself a glass of wine and get on the bed. Wear what you want, but nothing over your pussy. Now this part is very important: Keep the blinds open. I want your legs spread and your pussy visible from the window. I want you to stroke your clit for me, honey, stroke it until you come. It doesn't matter if anyone looks in and sees you. You are showing off for me, and that's all you are to think about. You want to be beautiful and sexy for me, don't you? Come on, show it to your daddy.

Then write back and tell me about it.

Love and kisses for my good little girl.

Steve

Angie wonders if, and how, Steve knows her bedroom has a big window. She wonders who can see into it; while she is in her bedroom, unless she's cleaning it, the drapes are always fully closed. Angie doesn't mind the public attention she gets—she likes it, in fact. But she doesn't like getting attention out in the world when people don't know who she is and don't care. She doesn't really like being just any other woman on the street—or visible, and masturbating, on a bed.

Anyway, Angie doesn't masturbate very much, under normal conditions. A thought slips through her mind like a small slick fish in the shallows: These are not normal conditions at all.

She could just write back and tell him she did it. She could write back and tell him she can't. She could even just stop writing back at all.

Instead, Angie—a little defiantly—puts on the black lingerie. She pours the wine. She plumps the pillows up so they're soft, so she can lean back on them. She opens the blinds wide. She lies on the bed, spreads her legs.

She strokes.

Angie's pussy is almost not part of her body on most days. Tonight it is the center of everything: hot, drippingly wet, so responsive to her first tentative clitoral stroke that her brain practically shuts down—that part of her brain, that is, that usually obscures the part that ascends now, and feels, and wants nothing but more feeling.

She dips her fingers into her cunt to wet them. She would ordinarily be amazed that she is so wet, so fast—Angie normally takes quite a while to respond to the hopefully patient ministrations of the men she dates, or rather, has dated in the past. The slick fish swims by again, all but too fast to notice: *not normal.* Anyway, she is past feeling amazement about anything except sensation, past processing anything but pleasure.

"Time stands still," she'll think later, "it's such a cliché, and yet it really feels that way when it's happening." Time stands still for Angie, the quick little movements of the second hand replaced by an internal clock whose movements are also circular, but whose center is her clit, whose chimes at the hour are big climaxes that make her fold in half, roll on her side, whimper or catch herself yelling out loud—but not stop. After the third one, or is it the fifth, still tumbled on her side with her ass stuck out as if she's waiting for Steve to slip into bed behind her, thrust his hungry cock into the dripping place that waits for him to take her, her free hand, which has been clutching at her tits, snakes back behind her and she burrows a finger into her own asshole.

Angie has never, ever done this before, but it causes the fourth, or maybe it's the sixth, orgasm to hit her like a train. In its wake she whimpers again, but words: "Look, Steve—watch me. Look at me, Daddy."

. . .

Her hands still tremble and her legs still feel wobbly and worked-out when she gets up and goes to her writing desk. There she keeps a stash of envelopes already addressed to Steve. She has just had more orgasms in a row than she's had in the past year, maybe more, and she makes sure to touch the paper all over with her hands, still pussy-damp, before she begins to write.

*Angie, Daddy's angel, you little whore, I knew you would come that hard. I know exactly what you need, baby. If I were with you I would have turned you on your face and held you down with my weight so you couldn't move at all. I would have shoved my big cock into you so hard you'd scream with need. Someone like you needs to get fucked every single day, Angie. Did I ever tell you how big my cock is? Some women can't even take it, but **you** could. You'd have to, because I wouldn't let you up until I was finished with you, and Angie, you know how long it's been since I fucked anyone, don't you? Seven years, one month, and six days, Angie. And a few hours. And when I get out of this hellhole to come fuck you, I am not going to stop thrusting and biting the back of your neck until I'm good and done. I told you I would be the first real man you ever had, Angie. I mean every word. I'll roll you over and look into your eyes while I hold you down, and you won't be able to look away. I want you to see what's in my eyes, and in my soul, girl. I'm going to put your legs over my shoulders and hold your hands over your head and get my cock up into you so deep I'll be able to feel your heart beat. When I'm good and wet with your cunt juice I'll slide slowly into your ass, Angie, which I know is as tight as any ass on earth, open you wider than you thought you could stretch, I'll go slow but never, ever stop shoving my big meat into your tight hole. I want to make you cry and scream, Angie. I want you to **know** I'm inside you. I never want to let you up.*

All my love, Steve

Shaken, Angie reads the letter over and over. Then she searches her apartment for something, anything, to fuck herself with. Why doesn't she have a dildo? What can she use to force into herself the way Steve promises to do?

She rejects a bottle and a round deodorant stick before remembering the vegetable bin, and soon is on her bed using both hands to get the cucumber deep and deeper. She doesn't even need him to tell her to open the blinds.

In fact, as days pass, Angie keeps them open to the world.

*All right, Angie, this is a very important letter. I don't know how soon I will be with you in the flesh. Only a miracle will get me by your side soon, but miracles do happen. You are with me every night when the lights go out and I take my cock in my hand. I lie on top of you and fuck your cunt, your ass, your mouth. I make you mine every night, and every night in your own bed I want you to **be** mine, do you understand? **Every single night.** I want to know that all those miles away you are writhing with need. I want to know that only I can give it to you as hard and as thick and as fast and as unending as I will when I am with you, but until I am, there is something else I want you to do. Now that you know how much you need to get fucked, I know you'll be able to do this, and just remember, you are doing it for me. For **me**, Angie, not even for yourself. Tonight, dress as provocatively as you can. Go out to a bar. Not a classy bar, a bar with real men. Pick out a man and walk up to him. Tell him you need to get fucked to within an inch of sanity. Tell him your cunt is empty and needs to be filled. Pick the guy you want, and go tell him. Pick the one who looks the most like me. As soon as you put this letter down, go get dressed and go do it. I don't care if you bring him home to our bed or fuck him in the alley. I don't care if he brings all his biker friends and they do you one at a time or take you one down your throat and one in your ass. Just remember whatever happens, it's **my** cock you're feeling splitting you open. **I** am holding you down. Come on, Angie. Be Daddy's little fuck kitten. Remember, you are with me, no matter who is fucking you.*

Just in case, Angie puts a bottle of wine next to the bed. Maybe some other woman would not feel herself tonight in the throes of romance, but so what? She belongs to someone. Inexorably, she thinks, it's the word she always wants Steve to use in his letters, because it means inevitably, unavoidably, inescapably. Inescapably—like she would ever want to get away from these feelings. She puts on the white lingerie and pulls a short black dress over her head. What jewelry to wear? What looks slutty? Angie has never, ever tried to look slutty before.

Extra liner around her eyes. In the brightly lit bathroom mirror she sees a look on her face she has never seen. This is inexorable, she says to herself, inexorable. Inevitable. Unavoidable. Inescapable.

Tonight the only escape she wants is Steve's.

Ecstasy
by Nancy Kilpatrick

Award-winning author **Nancy Kilpatrick** has just published her fourteenth novel, *Eternal City* (5 Star Books). Her nonfiction book *The Goth Bible* is coming out from St. Martin's Press in 2004. She is coediting with Nancy Holder a new anthology for Roc/NAL called *Goth Gurrls and Boiz* (is there a theme here?). In addition, her popular vampire series *Power of the Blood* is about to be reprinted by Mosaic Press, and one of the books, *Near Death*, has been optioned for film. Nancy writes mainly horror, dark fantasy, mysteries, and erotica under the name Amarantha Knight. She is responsible for the hot tongue-in-cheek S and M classics in *The Darker Passions* series, originally published in the 1990s by Masquerade Books, all seven of which are being reprinted by Circlet Press. *Dracula* and *Frankenstein* are out now, and *Dr. Jekyll and Mr. Hyde* is coming later in 2004.

She says of this story: "The charge for me with 'Ecstasy' is trying to convey the excitement and outsider-looking-in feeling I had the first time I ventured into an S and M club, lo those many years ago. There is a club in Montreal where I live with the physical layout of 'Ecstasy.' And there used to be a club here with a similar sense of strangeness and an otherworldly quality to the clientele but it is, alas, no more—everything becomes mundane in the end, it seems, and what was avant-garde yesterday is passé today. I have seen people like the characters in 'Ecstasy,' and even befriended a few who have touched this realm, and I know the effect they have had on me, and on others. I don't think everyone can or should live on the edge of time and space. But anyone who comes face to face with those who do is going to be altered in some manner because they are brushing against potency and intoxication in the largest meaning of those words.

Extremes force us to cope with paradox. Not an easy task, but nobody said life is easy, and if they do, don't trust them; they're lying!"

The world, it seems, is bound for hell. You grip the handbasket tighter, holding onto your life.

This is the first time you have come for him, and that unnerves you. With luck you will find him. With more luck, you won't. Either way, intuition implies you are not in a good position, despite what you now believe.

Everywhere you turn, white light assaults your eyes as if it were the white light tunnel of death instead of moonlight glinting knife-blade sharp off snow. Harsh air forces you to pull inward, shrinking back to yourself, shriveling, becoming smaller to hide from the cold. Nowhere you have been was the environment this inhospitable to human survival, although you realize other places on the planet are worse. Still, you haven't been there, and in the midst of this trauma where your cells suffer from the possibility of freezing to death, speculation seems pointless.

You have searched for hours with this lanky, sexy prostitute by your side. Together, you visited places where Kevin has been seen. Inquiries here, there, his identity verified by photo, all paints a fresh trail, or so your companion assures you. "Listen, Fran," Didi said at the last transvestite bookstore, your name on his crimson lips sounding far too intimate, "we'll find him. There are only so many places a broken boy can hide." That was many hours ago. Between then and now, dozens of taxi rides taken, club entrance fees paid, drinks bought in bars, seedy hotel clerks questioned, meals eaten and coffees drunk in restaurants and diners frequented by "she-males" as Kevin likes to identify himself. You are not naive; this world is not the one you glide through ordinarily, yet it is not entirely alien. So many personas, each in its own way demanding love and acceptance. How you envy their seduction techniques; how they terrify you.

The last club was in the middle of nowhere, and as you left it, once again, you congratulated yourself that you only paid this pretty hustler a fraction of the promised money—he will make efforts to keep you unharmed to get the rest. "Listen, sweetie, taxis won't answer calls to this neighborhood," Didi assured you. "We'll hike it. Just you and me romping through the snow!" She said this with a Madonna-like toss of the head and a devilish sparkle to almond eyes. That he plays with you, laughs at your expense, does not bother you. Since long before Kevin's treatments began, before his breasts swelled and his voice rose an octave and his body hair thinned, all of it leading to "the change," as he calls it, you have been to hell and back many times. Nothing bothers you anymore. Except for one thing. The nightmare.

This northern city's mean winter streets leave you hopeless. Life does not exist here in the dead of a cold night. No one sane walks around at 3:00 A.M. The last vehicle to pass inspired a fantasy of jumping in front of the bumper and pleading with the driver, "Take me home! I just want to go home!" But there is no home, not anymore. Mother is gone. Father was too often there. Kevin is all you have. You do not even care that your baby brother is becoming your baby sister. You just want to find him before—as the nightmare leaves you feeling—it is too late.

Hands and feet half frozen, you finally reach a wide street, but you are so far from downtown that it is deserted of people, vehicles, shops. Life has ended, or so it seems. What must it be like in daylight? You shudder to think about the corruption that will be exposed when the ice melts. Now, a ridge of danger lingers, danger and desolation, two emotions that when combined, combust and leave a raw scar from a wound that runs deep to the marrow. A wound you have suffered. A scar you still possess. You know it is the same with Kevin.

Your companion points ahead gleefully. "See! I told you!" he cries, as if you did not believe he would find this place, and in truth, you had doubts.

The building resembles a burnt-out factory. The windows not boarded up are blacked out, the bricks smoked and much of the char and aluminum siding covered by graffiti in various languages. It amuses you to think that tagging might bridge linguistic solitudes.

There appears to be no door, no sign. "It's here somewhere," Didi insists, voice reeking with false confidence that relaxes into real confidence the moment a cab pulls up and two persons of indistinguishable gender emerge. They know right where the door is, a crack in the aluminum wall, a spike for a handle. "This is the place, Fran," Didi says, as if you are dim, unable to see the world for what it is.

This door would go unconsidered if you hadn't seen for yourself that it could be opened. Apparently, no secret code is needed to enter. You open it now. Heat rushes out at you, and sound, loud, a cacophony of panting and beating heart and angry, fist-pounding flesh. Once you step inside, the sound swallows you.

You fight hard to hold onto yourself, caught in an auditory intensity that forces you beyond your normal rhythm and into a power-drill mode of being. Remember why you're here, you remind yourself. Kevin is more lost than you are. He needs you more than ever. The bad dream told you this, and more.

A man, or a large woman skimpily dressed, glares at you as if you are an insect to be crushed, definitely not worthy of admittance. You know the look is real, but the true function is other. The function involves money. Didi whispers "Fifty. Each," in your ear. Reluctantly, you pull large bills from your nearly depleted wallet and slap them onto the hot hand this monolith shoves inches from your chest. A smile erupts on the heavily made-up face, one more sinister than sweet. The cash is theatrically slipped down between the breasts encased in black latex, down further past the exposed stomach, down into the leather pants, up under the crotch. All the while dark eyes mock you, patiently awaiting a reaction, but you show none. Life holds few surprises. A flicker of disappointment accompanies the thumb pointing behind.

Didi removes his fur, and his dress, leaving his body clad only in a white-lace bra, G-string panties, and garter belt of the same fabric, the last holding up white hose. He hands everything else over the counter with a "No Drugs!" sign attached to the wall that almost brings a cynical smile to your lips. A muscular tattooed arm reaches out of the darkness toward you, waiting. Didi turns. You shake your head. You have no intention of leaving your coat, let alone undressing. Fabric is the only protection you might have here, and fifty dollars should pay for your eccentricity. "Whatever," Didi says, obviously disappointed by not seeing you near naked. "Still got a tip, sweetie?" he smiles, and you hand over five dollars and do not receive change.

A dark plastic barrier is held open, like a vulva, or the entrance to a womb. You follow Didi in, the Amazon making sure you brush against him or her, but your coat protects you from contact.

Sound slams into you, louder, raping your body through every orifice, beating your pulse into submission, racing toward the target, your heart. You gulp in oxygen to ensure you are still alive. The air is clotted with smoke that chokes you, and you cough uncontrollably. Your eyes tear, then blur, and you realize you cannot distinguish anything here, objects or people; and although the room is lit with red and blue lights, the colors do not make things discernible.

You have come this far, and you know Didi has no more ideas. To retreat is unthinkable. You must find Kevin. For once in your life, you need to act on his behalf, and on your own.

You step further into the room. Suddenly the floor shifts down a level, half as deep as a step, and you fall forward. Your knee buckles and you struggle for balance. You have always been sharp on your feet, thank god, and right yourself, feeling not so much foolish as vulnerable—what you cannot see *can* hurt you, mother! But she never would hear you, or Kevin, and now cannot.

The throbbing techno drives you to the edge of insanity. It makes you angry. At life, for inflicting all this craziness from birth onward. At your parents, for solidifying the madness. At Kevin, for being weak, for leaving you to struggle alone. You are furious at yourself and your misguided hands-off philosophy that gave your brother carte blanche, immersing him in unconditional love, extending extreme unction for his soul to pass into other worlds. You destroyed the power of conditions that lead to self-responsibility. The degree to which you reign yourself in is the same extreme of permission he enjoys.

Your senses cringe in terror. You argue with your optic nerve, willing it to clear your vision. When it does, shapes become apparent. Bodies dot the walls like giant cockroaches. One nearby drags on a cigarette, the yellow glow of fire casting a hellish illumination onto harshly angled features. Not a friendly face, but the eyes look too distant for this to be an enemy.

You inch forward, now feeling with your feet for dips in the floor that seem to be everywhere. The mallet sound changes, like a hammer passed from one hand to the other of an ambidextrous person. The beat is the same. It punches through your nervous system, producing more fury that you battle, and a throbbing at your genitals. Most of these patrons must be high on ecstasy. This music would stimulate them in a different way, or so you've read about . . .

Finally, you stumble upon the bar, close by the dance floor. A girl—or a good imitation—leans over, her Nazi cap low over kohl-lined eyes, minimal breasts bare, tiny nipples erect and staring at you. She does not ask you what you want. You have an impression of deep disinterest. Didi shouts his order and gestures for you to do the same. You lean in and her face shows distaste as she eyes the coat you clutch to your body, her look implying you are not brave enough to be here. Above the pounding, you scream "Jack, straight up!" Without a nod, she turns her back on you, and fades into the darkness. You glance to the right to watch the dozen or so dancers.

Young. Slim. Naked. Sweat dripping down sinewy bodies that have never known fat. These danse macabre figures writhe and jump to the beating noise, eyes rolled up so whites glow in flashing black light strobe, tongues lolling, corpses like puppets yanked on strings. One penis, erect, suddenly shoots into the air like a fountain. Two dancers fall to their knees to lap up the cum.

The light allows you to see patrons next to you at the bar, others across the dance floor, stripped of clothing, waiting, watching, fondling themselves and one another. All are skeletal, ribs jutting, hip bones prominent, many bald, skulls so large compared to the child-like bodies, like fetuses. They resemble drawings of aliens, photos you've seen of victims in Nazi concentration camps. Watching them makes you hot, and you feel like a pedophile. Or a necrophile. You wonder when it became sexy to look as if you're starving to death.

The harsh tapping on your shoulder goes almost unfelt—the rhythm is the same as the music, the same as the fingers around you groping, the same as your heartbeat forced to synchronize to all of this. But you do notice, eventually, and turn to find your drink. Behind it, one hand still on the glass, the other fondling a ringed nipple, the capped bartender releases your shot to hold out an open palm in much the same way as the door person, the coat check. You have the impression of beggars, starving, willing to take anything from any-one, but of course they will not take less than they demand. The image is titillating in its obscenity. You offer bills that are snatched away even before reaching the palm.

You want to ask Didi questions, about this place, about the preponderance of the thin, the beautiful, who may live fast and die young for all you know, but the music prohibits verbalization. You only know this place is called Ecstasy, a 24/7 club that is more than a club, it is a "lifestyle," Didi assured you, frequented by transvestites, transsexuals, gay men, lesbians, bisexuals, straight couples and singles, fetishists, hardcore S and M players, everyone with the "need to be ecstatic," in Didi's words.

Kevin, you know, loved to get high. Most of his life he gravitated toward anything that would obliterate his pain. You watched your brother transit sexual preferences, chemical intoxicants, liquid libations, extreme physical ritualistic practices, various cults, endless trendy diets to reduce the bulk he is prone to, all designed to take him out of the mud of this physical realm he loathes and lift him to spirit. You stood by helplessly for the thirty years you have known Kevin, unable to even aid yourself, let alone him. Each of his ventures was "the answer," the salve to soothe the wound of living in a terribly imperfect world. Each would bring him the love and acceptance he longs for. Each was abandoned, or incorporated into Kevin's perpetual morphing. You understand him only too well. He acts out the inner turmoil you silently endure daily, that has driven you to three quiet suicide attempts, that causes you to sleep more hours each day than you are awake, that leaves you alienated and too depressed to make contact, or even to exhibit symptoms of your despair. Only the anorexia you battle in secret is evidence of your pain, and that goes unnoticed in a twisted world that values minimalism in everything to the point of praising your rejection of nourishment.

Kevin has tried it all, and you have watched like a voyeur, living vicariously through his efforts. Someone getting the thrills without the risks. You encouraged him, perhaps to placate the demon within you that demands extremes. When Kevin told you about his plans for the operation, and how if he were female instead of male, if he had been you instead of himself, life would be different, fulfilling, accepting. That night, you had the first of what would become a recurring nightmare.

Stuck at the bottom of a dark empty well, you look through a soulless mirror that liquefies. This noir river begins to flow into you, your nose, mouth, ears, anus, vagina, even your pores. Little animals with barbed bodies scratch this tender penetrated flesh, stimulating you almost beyond endurance. You are poised in midair, air black as night, body throbbing with desires that will not allow release. And only when the black fire of passion forces a scream of exquisite agony from your lips do you wake in your lonely bed, covered with sweat and tears, thighs slick with juices. And no amount of stimulation releases your volatile frustration.

Eventually, when you had dreamed this enough, and cried miserable tears until your ducts emptied, it dawned on you what had been happening all along. And now, like the religion you both turned away from when it failed you, you have come with no answers to save Kevin from himself. But in the process of trying, perhaps you will be rescued as well.

Didi nudges you and you follow, away from the safety of the bar, around the outer corners of the room. You pass between people, and hands reach out to touch you, finding fabric instead of flesh. You smile, happy to have thwarted their expectations. But then one hand discovers your secret and worms beneath the fabric, inside your blouse, down under your bra, the body pressed hard against your own, following, in step, bony fingers tweaking your nipple in time to the pounding beat, forcing your head back, your mouth open, the black river flowing once again . . .

"This is it, what we came for," Didi says. The hand is gone, leaving your nipple burning, your body freezing. Didi opens a door and enters. You step into a cathedral of ice, with lighted grottos on each side of you. As you walk down the aisle, you pass these "rooms." On the left a man is suspended by his wrists and ankles. Four naked attendants shave his head, strip the hairs from his torso with wax, pluck out his eyebrows, and the hairs around his anus . . . To the right, a bald woman's bare body is cut with a scalpel, little cuts, deep enough to bleed, not enough for permanent injury, her flesh a canvas of tiny crosses, out of her mouth deep erotic pleas for forgiveness . . . A genderless being is having finger and toenails clipped very very short, eyelashes singed, dead skin cut from the feet . . . You bend to peer inside a small door to find three pale and slender bodies prone on blonde wood shelves, sweat pouring off them as an attendant splashes water onto steaming rocks . . . Another grotto, a woman with her finger down her throat, vomiting, peeing, shitting, bleeding from her vagina, all at the same time . . .

You have seen each of these worlds in one way or another, and they do not shock you. All your life, you have known that to rid the body of everything leads to purification, to spirit. Every major religion reinforces this value. The culture in which you reside prays for the destruction of the flesh.

At the end of this corridor of pain and humiliation is a white door with a white Gothic arch above folding inward. Didi opens the door, and you realize that somewhere along the way she has discarded the rest of her clothes. You move up the three steps to this altar of rejuvenation.

The inner sanctum glows with twinkling lights, bright as stars. All here is colorless, odorless, pure and uncorrupted: walls, floor, hospital gurney, sheets atop it. The frail woman lies as still as death, attended by skinny hairless beings dressed only in white latex gloves and shoes.

Didi puts a finger to lips, and you stare into her liquid eyes, realizing that they remind you of the black liquid fire. Her body is lean, angular, the dead refusing to die. Your vagina spasms.

This sideshow is interesting, but you remind yourself of the purpose of this quest. The pounding techno is a fraction dimmer here, enough to allow thought. Kevin is not here. You turn to leave.

"Fran?"

The voice catches you in a net of fragility. You glance back at the gurney, and the languid corpselike form lifts its skull. Unnaturally bright eyes—familiar—peer into yours from deep in their sockets, as if beckoning. "Kevin?"

"I'm Fran now," he tells you, and your body jolts with this confirmation.

"I need you for the reinventing."

It is Kevin, or what is left of him. Instantly, you move beside the gurney as if it is a coffin. He has no hair, no eyebrows, lashes, no fingernails or toenails. His body is covered with pale stitches, like a rag doll repaired too many times.

"What's . . . happening to you?" you ask.

"Ecstasy," he says, his voice more feminine than masculine, the tone otherworldly.

"Drugs—"

"No. True ecstasy."

You stare along his body, breasts plumped like white plums. His penis gone, replaced by . . . by . . . nothing! This is disturbing, but what leaves you unable to speak is his once thick-fleshed frame, now lighter than air, an exoskeleton.

"I'm thinner than you are," he whispers, with a smile so grotesque you shudder.

You can only shake your head, confused, horrified, resigned in your failure.

Suddenly, as if they are meant to distract, you notice the apparatus—white and clear tubes removing blood, suctioning fat from the body, washing out the intestine's contents. You watch as one of the attendants pulls skin together over Kevin's stomach where fat cells have been taken, cuts the flab, stretches the skin taut, sutures . . .

"My stomach is stapled now, so I don't need to eat," Kevin whispers, eyes gleaming.

"What? . . . why? . . ." But you can no longer form sentences.

"To be you," he says, the words so simple. The message clear as crystal. This is your nightmare, your legacy. What you have created in your own distorted image. What you cannot show the world but what Kevin displays on your behalf. You gave him permission to reflect your darkness. Now that you see yourself with clarity, you cannot bear the sight.

He stares at the ceiling as if seeing God, as if he is ascending, and your eyes fill with tears. Didi gently pulls the coat from your ravaged body, your clothes, and fingers find you through all your barren openings.

At long last, the basket slips from your grip. Finally, you descend.

Pins and Needles
by Rachel Kramer Bussel

Rachel Kramer Bussel is a freelance writer focusing on sexuality and pop culture. She is the reviser of *The Lesbian Sex Book*, coauthor of *The Erotic Writer's Market Guide*, and coeditor of the forthcoming lesbian erotica anthology *Up All Night*. Her writing has been published in *AVN, AVN Online, Bust, Curve, Diva, Girlfriends, Playgirl, On Our Backs, The San Francisco Chronicle, Best Lesbian Erotica 2001, Best Women's Erotica 2003, Tough Girls, Faster Pussycats,* and *Juicy Erotica,* among others, and she has appeared on the TV shows *In The Life* and *Naked New York.* Find out more at www.rachelkramerbussel.com

Of her story in *slave,* Rachel Kramer Bussel writes: " 'Pins and Needles' was inspired first and foremost by my messy room, which on a daily basis looks like a tornado has hit it. I often wonder whether I need a Top who will force me to clean my room (or just a personal organizer). I try to imagine what a stranger would think about my room and I just wanted to have some fun with that; I'm not one of those people who have all their toys categorized and sorted and stored all neatly. I'm as likely to find a paddle or riding crop lying on the floor as hanging on the wall or tucked away in a drawer. I'd say I've been interested in BDSM for about five years, and love exploring and learning about new things, even if I might not actually want to try them.

I have to be out of my apartment in three days, and I need help. Severe help. At this point, my room looks like a tornado has hit it. Which is not unusual in my case, but not a good sign considering that

I have to be one hundred percent gone, as in no trace of my having lived here, in a mere seventy-two hours. My friend Kyle is here helping me sort through my many belongings, though I'm not sure he was the best choice to assist me, given his own none-too-neat living space. However, he was my only option after all my other friends bailed on me. I'm not sure if it's because it's the week before Christmas (I'm also not sure why I need to be out before the end of the month, but when your landlord is as stern and intimidating as mine, you don't argue), or if my friends know just how daunting a task this will be and don't want to get involved, but they all came up with various semi-legitimate excuses not to help.

So I'm sitting on my bed sorting the piles of papers, books, and magazines on my bedside table while Kyle rummages through whatever area of the room he fancies at any particular moment; there's so much stuff in here, he can take his pick as long as he sticks around until the end. He's quite strict with me, not letting me get away with packing things that will most likely be discarded as soon as the box is opened. But I'm also a very stubborn pack rat, and have found myself physically wrestling him for items he wants to put in the trash pile, like my favorite beat-up sweater that is so raggedy I don't even wear it out of the house anymore. But he doesn't understand the sweater's *history*, its place in my life. I've worn that sweater through some of the best, and worst, times of my life, like my first date with Brad, the trip to Vermont in the dead of winter where I found myself wishing I had my ugly heavy wool sweater rather than this light but gorgeous one. I was wearing it the day I got fired (it's one of those casual but serious sweaters that can do double duty for work or play), and I'd gotten into lots of trouble at various clubs while wearing it. We've had a few differences of opinion, but things are proceeding fairly well. I'm trying to stick to the task at hand, rather than look around in despair, worrying that the deadline will arrive and my room will still look like a teenage boy's beloved getaway. I'm deep into a pile of papers, sorting them into categories such as bills, personal, contracts, etc., when Kyle interrupts me. "What's this?" From the edge in his voice, I know it's something unusual, though I can't imagine what it could be. We've been friends for over five years and don't keep too many secrets from each other. But when I look up, I blush fiercely.

"Oh, just, you know . . ." I let my voice trail away. He's obviously not really asking me what the offending items are, but what they're *for*. Anybody can recognize a clothespin, but living in a twenty-story apartment in New York with a laundry room (which I rarely use because I send most of my laundry out, to be washed, folded, and then picked up in a neat and tidy bundle, in the utmost of urban extravagance), I don't need them for laundry.

"No, actually, I don't." He pauses and stops working, so I can't just ignore him and continue with my papers.

"Well, you know, okay, you don't know, but anyway, sometimes, well, sometimes I've used them during sex."

Even from halfway across the room, I can see Kyle's eyes light up. "For sex? How?"

"Never mind, it's not important, can we please just get on with this? I now have only sixty-eight hours to get everything in this entire apartment packed, plus whatever cleaning needs to be done." I try to stress the urgent nature of what we're doing, but Kyle has already heard my panicked tone plenty of times over the last two weeks to know how serious I am about this.

"We'll get it done, have no fear. You think it's a lot because you live here and this is your stuff, but from an outsider's point of view, it's a piece of cake. So don't give me that. I want to know what you do with these." He swings them in the air, taunting me with the dozen or so black plastic clips encased in a plastic bag.

I roll my eyes and try to move us along as quickly as possible. "Well, you know that I'm kind of into some kinky things, and sometimes Derek and I used to use them. He'd tie me up once in a while and then put them on me." I try to make "on me" as loaded as possible, so we can end the discussion and not have to get into exactly where "on me" means, but Kyle is adamant, insisting on a more detailed explanation. "On, like, my nipples, or sometimes on my clit, or my thighs. They can go anywhere really, and it's very intense, while they're on and then again when you take them off." Despite my resolve to stay in the here and now and focus, I can't help closing my eyes for a moment. A shiver runs through my body as I recall the last time I'd played with them. Derek had had to gag me, the only time we'd ever done that, because I'd been screaming so loud, and I'd come so hard we were both stunned and a little scared. Afterward, we'd held each other and stared into each other's eyes, not needing to say a word to know we were both awed by what had just happened. Despite myself, my nipples harden at the memory.

I open my eyes to find that Kyle has walked across the room. He sits down on the bed, the package resting lightly in his hand. I swallow heavily, suddenly feeling the need to open the window and get some fresh air. He keeps his eyes on mine while he opens the plastic bag and removes one of the pins. Though I generally consider myself a starving artist, I'd bought special plastic clothespins to avoid splinters or any other mishaps. He opens the pin a few times, testing it out. Without speaking, he moves in closer to me and kisses my neck before moving downward. He licks and kisses his way across my chest before suckling my nipples, one at a time. His tongue flicks back and forth, fast as a snake, darting and teasing. Then he clamps down with his lips, pressing firmly. I can't help but arch back, urging my nipple further. His knee makes its way between my legs, pressing against the dampness of my jeans. He moves back and forth, from one nipple to the next, moving from tongue to teeth as my nipples adjust to the delicious pain. Then, right when I'm almost ready to scream, he stops. He takes the lone clothespin and holds it in front of my lips, and before I can even think about it, I open my mouth. He slides it in, pressing it along my tongue like a kinky doctor. In and out goes the pin before he replaces it with his tongue. He rams it into my mouth, sensuality forgotten as he grabs the back of my head and fucks my mouth with his tongue, swirling and thrusting, laying claim to my body while I feel myself start to go weak with shock and arousal. When he's done, he lets go, and I have to struggle to stay balanced.

"Wow," is all I can manage to say. I've never thought of Kyle in a sexual way, he's just always been around, kind of like a big brother, always willing to help me out and listen to my stories. He's cute enough, but not the kind of guy I'd consider going out with. But now he's someone different, not the easygoing, protective, all-around nice guy, but a guy with a bit of an edge, a boldness that's making me wet. He's doing things to me with the clips that had never even been hinted at all those times with Derek, and seems totally at ease taking control of our imminent fuck. Maybe he knew what the pins were for all along, or maybe he's just been overtaken by an unexpected bout of lust. I don't really care which is the case; I'm ready to surrender to him. I stare at him in wonder for a moment, then slide out of my clothes and clear the papers off the bed. I crawl over to him, staring up at him as I slither against him. I bring his hand with the clothespin up to my breast, rubbing my nipple against the plastic. He stares at me for a few moments, silently, looking like he's trying to decide what to do next. I nod at him, then lean my head back and let out a sigh. My clit tingling with anticipation, I look at him, then can't help but moan and writhe as he teases me by lightly tracing the plastic over my nipple. My face, twisted in aroused frustration, begs him to do much more to my sensitive, hardened buds.

"Okay, I'll give you what you want," he finally says, opening the pin and clasping it around my firm, protruding nipple. He places another on my other nipple and stares as they stay right where he's clipped them. I start breathing faster, almost panting, and even though I'm trying to stay as still as I can, my arousal is clear, from my trembling breathing to the wetness glistening from my pussy. My nipples are still and silent, the pain settling in slowly, as if in layers. His fingers slide down past my stomach, teasing me as they dance around my thighs, avoiding the place I most want them to be. "Don't worry, Jo, I can see how wet you are. I'll fuck you in a little while. Right now I just want to make sure you're ready for me. Turn over."

His words have made me even wetter, and I automatically turn over, willing to do anything to get him to touch me. I roll over, and immediately feel the already painful clamps pressing into my skin. My nipples burn with the pain—a deep, intense, relentless pulsing. "You look so beautiful like that, with your ass in the air, knowing those clothespins are doing their job. You like that, don't you, Joanna? You like the pain and it's making you so wet you're starting to drip onto the bed, aren't you? You want me to fuck you really hard right now, to slam your body back and forth and rock the bed and make those pins pull your nipples back and forth, right? Is that what you want?" He slides two fingers inside me and I gasp, biting the pillow in order not to scream. I squeeze his fingers tightly with my pussy, not wanting to let go, yet wanting more fingers filling and stretching me. "That's good, now keep doing that, keep squeezing me. You're so wet

I'm sliding right in, which is good because I want you to be nice and ready for my cock. Have you ever thought about my cock before? 'Cause I've thought about fucking you, Joanna. I wasn't going to tell you that because I thought you weren't interested, but I had a feeling you were a naughty girl. A very naughty one." He slides a third finger into me as he says this, but by now I'm desperately craving his cock. "I pictured you tied up while Derek did all sorts of dirty things to you, and you liked all of it. And I guess I was right, huh, Jo? Are you ready? Really? I don't really know if you are. You're very wet and you're pushing back against me like you want to be fucked, but I'm just not sure yet. Turn over again for me." I make a whine of protest, but do it anyway. He stands up and strips down out of his jeans, no underwear, his cock hard and proud in front of him.

"Do you want me to fuck you now, Jo? Yes? Are you ready?" I spread my legs as wide as I can, trying to beckon him to me. "I felt how wet you are, baby, but I don't know if you're really ready. Why don't we check?" He takes another pin out and pinches some of my stomach's skin. I gasp as he places the pin around my flesh. It hurts, in a different way than my nipples do, but it also sends sparks straight to my cunt, making me even slicker. "Is that better, does that get you even more excited? I thought it might." He takes another pin and traces it along my arms, then down the middle of my body, between my breasts, down over my stomach, through my pubic hair. He runs it over my clit, and my head sinks back against the pillow. He slides it over my wet pussy lips, teasing me by pushing it in slightly, then removing it. By this time, I'm pushing my hips up, so eager for his cock inside me I feel like I'll combust without it. "Soon, soon, Joanna." He takes the clip, now wet with my juices, and sucks on it, noisily smacking his lips, then lifting one of my breasts and placing it on the tender outside of my breast. At this point I don't care what he does with the pins as long as he fucks me soon. "I think you're ready now, my dear." He's talking to me so gently and calmly, but my body is anything but gentle and calm.

He gets onto the bed and kneels before my spread legs, putting on a condom and rubbing his cock against my wet slit, teasing me for just a few more moments before sliding, slowly, all the way in. I clench my eyes shut, feeling his cock find its way into the deepest reaches of my body. I slide my legs upward so they're balanced on his shoulders, and as he pushes down against me, I feel all the clothespins pressing into my skin while he slides back and forth. I've been primed so well that in only a few thrusts I'm gone, screaming as I feel my body erupt, my stomach knotting and my cunt spasming fiercely as I come, his cock still hard inside me. He's stopped his dirty talk, which apparently wasn't just for my benefit, and is thrusting quickly in and out of me. I toy with one of the pins, making sure he's watching as I close and open it around my now nicely mashed nipple. With his eyes on me, I lean forward and push my nipple toward my mouth with the end of the pin, licking it and sending tingles throughout my body. The sight of my pink tongue and nipple converging is too much for him, and he pushes into me one last time, letting out a yell as his cock shoots its hot liquid. He collapses onto me, his head resting on my breast, breathing raggedly. I stroke his hair and close my eyes, not wanting to look at the state of my room. He quietly removes the clothespins, and I'm so worn out I barely move, just relax into the painful warmth of the blood rushing back to my skin. After a few minutes, he slowly sits up, dresses, and claps his hands in a brisk, serious, let's-get-back-to-work signal.

"Well, I think we'll be keeping these. Now, what's next?" He's back to business. I nod, my body still trembling, and we continue packing. When he gets to the package of hypodermic needles, he doesn't say a word. With a small smile, he packs them neatly into a box, careful to make sure they're protected. We both know there'll be plenty of time to unpack when I get to my new place.

Late Lunch
by N. T. Morley

My own contribution to this collection is something I've always wanted to write in short form: an abduction scenario where a submissive woman submits, at her Master's behest, to her own secret desire to be taken and used by a large group of men. While the story itself isn't based in reality, I must say that I had a particular person in mind when I invented the main character—and that she showed me, in no uncertain terms, just how much she appreciated my letting her live out her fantasy on the written page.

When the third man enters her—that's when she comes. Comes hard. Uncontrollably. Moaning and shuddering, thrusting her body back onto his cock.

Or, rather, that's when she finally gives it up. That's when she lets them know that she's come. She tries not to, fighting off her pleasure, struggling against it as if it were the force holding her down, pushing her ass into the air, pushing her tits against the metal freezer, spreading her legs wide and making her take it. She struggles against her oncoming orgasm until it overwhelms her, until she throws back her head and howls in sobbing release.

And that's what makes the men laugh. The three who've had her, and the three more waiting. They start to laugh, and talk about how bad she wants it, how she's begging for three more guys to take her. They start to comment on how she's bucking against them, forcing herself onto their cocks, moaning in pleasure even through her sobs of humiliation.

And they're right: She is. Her body, uncontrolled, is striving to force her against them harder, to push her onto their cocks even as they hold her down, her blouse ripped wide-open, her bra yanked up, her skirt bunched around her waist and her panties around one ankle. It's pumping, her ass writhing, her cuffed wrists pulling against the restraints in the small of her back, her thighs spreading wider and her thigh muscles tensing as she humps back onto the man who's violating her.

But that's not what humiliates her. It's not the sound of their laughter, or the comments they make about the juice of her pussy running down her inner thighs. It's not their remarks about how they should take her ass next, since she's probably going to like that twice as much. It's not even the fact that they're right—about her wanting it, about her coming, about her wanting them to take her ass as well, use every hole she has, violate every part of her defenseless body.

No, that's not what humiliates her.

What humiliates her is that she's normally so good at hiding it. She's normally so good at coming without making a sound. She's masturbated on airplanes, silently pressing her thighs together until she climaxed several times in a row, never letting the person in the seat next to her know about it. She's masturbated at work, sneaking a quick rub under her desk—in a cubicle, mind you, not a private office—after a surreptitious glance at porn sites between sales calls. She's climaxed many, many times in a room with a roommate—practically every night in the dorms in college, many times when visiting her sister, even a few times with her husband when he was watching TV. She's normally excellent at coming—coming hard—without letting anyone know.

And she was doing so well. When the first man had taken her, and the second—even the second, who reached underneath and rubbed her clit while he fucked her, like he knew it intimately, like he'd touched that particular clit for years—she was doing so, so well.

She'd hidden it twice. Two intense, fiery orgasms exploding into her body while the men watched, waiting their turn to use her.

And nobody had known. Nobody had known that being used, taken, violated like this made her come. Nobody had known how hard she'd had to fight to keep from coming even faster than she had. Nobody had known how good it felt to feel them holding her down, to feel them all taking her, wanting her, waiting their turn to invade her body.

Now, they know. They all know. Everybody knows that she loves it, she wants it—she's begging for more.

It had happened so fast, like it does in the movies. She'd been walking to her car. She'd been distracted, thinking of something else, feeling sorry for herself about how heavy the bag of groceries was. She was dressed for the office, perhaps a little sexier than usual, because she'd had a round of sales calls to make in the afternoon, and a woman selling perfume wholesale really has to look sexy, doesn't she? The black wool skirt a little tighter around the hips and thighs than she would have worn on a day in the office; it was also a little shorter, short enough that you could see the lace tops of her stockings where they clasped to her garters. The blouse, too, was a little low-cut, showing a hint of her cleavage and the string of pearls she liked to wear to remember her last, and very happy, wedding anniversary in Fiji.

But today she'd gone a little further than usual. She and her husband had planned a quick lunch meeting at a favorite restaurant very close to her work, as they did every few weeks. On those days, she often played a naughty little trick in the hopes that he might be able to sneak an extra half hour away from work and slip into the executive washroom at her office—she knew the back entrance.

But her husband had had to cancel, and so she hadn't gotten to use her clever trick, which she'd read about in this year's "Slut" issue of *Bonne Femme* magazine.

So even at 9:00 at night, when the van had pulled up alongside her, she still had her thong panties worn on the outside of her garters—facilitating quick removal.

The van had pulled up alongside her without her notice. Her first hint that something was wrong—very wrong—came about one second before the hood went over her head, before she felt the strong hands grasping her wrists, forcing them behind her back. Before the muscled bodies pressed her into the stink and darkness of the van, the door slamming behind her and the wheels squealing as the van took off.

She'd heard their voices in the van, drifting to her over the loud industrial music they played to cover her screams. She heard them talking loudly about what a prize she was, how sexy she was dressed, how they'd been watching her for weeks. She heard them talking about what they were going to do her. She heard her own heart pounding in her ears as she felt their hands roving all over her, groping her, invading her. She heard her own sobbing as hands found their way under her short skirt, down her thong panties.

They found them wet, perhaps from the slow post-sales-call afternoon in the office, stealing glances at porn sites. Or perhaps still moist from her morning anticipation of a quick visit by her husband.

Or perhaps, just perhaps, wet in that fraction of an instant when she realized that she was about to be violently, hatefully taken, and that nothing she was capable of doing could save her.

After her climax—her third climax, but the first one they all know about—they treat her different. They know she'll cooperate. They know she won't resist. She tries to, but she can't. She tries to struggle when they strip off the tattered remains of her clothing, rendering her naked and helpless. She won't look them in the eye, even when they push her to her knees in front of a straight-backed chair and one of them sits there, plants her face in his lap, supporting her shoulders with his thighs, his cock hard and ready, still smelling of her pussy. When he puts his hand under her chin and tips her head back, forcing her to look into his face as he says "Suck my dick."

She lowers her eyes, looking instead at his cock—huge, hard, imposing.

When she doesn't comply immediately, he puts his thumb into her mouth and forces it open. Then he guides his cock into her mouth and presses it all the way back—entering her throat even as she gags.

As he does that, another man mounts her from behind. She feels his cock going into her pussy as her throat fills with another, and she comes. She wasn't expecting this one, and she doesn't even try to hide it. But if she were to try, she would be unsuccessful. Her hips are pumping back, forcing her onto his cock before he has completed even the first thrust. And despite the fact that her moans are muffled by the thick cock filling her throat, it's quite clear to the men what's happened.

She tries to resist for a second, two seconds, as she feels the cock filling her from both ends. She tries not to do it, but she can't stop herself. She tries to remain passive, to perhaps let them use her but not encourage them, to allow them to take their pleasure with her body but not to possess her mind. She tries to stop herself from servicing them, but she knows that it is hopeless. She gives in to her hunger and starts sucking cock. Her tongue presses against the underside and she desperately takes it down her throat, now wide open from being forced. She closes her eyes and tells herself over and over again what's happening. *I'm being taken*, she thinks. *I'm being raped, ravished, possessed by strangers. By a gang of them. And I'm not just being used—I'm letting them use me. I'm begging them to use me by the way I fuck my body back against them. I'm sucking their cocks. I'm servicing them. There are so many of them, so many cocks violating me, and waiting in line to violate me. How many are there? A dozen? Two dozen? I've lost count. I've lost count of how many men have used me.*

Were her mind clear, perhaps she would remember that it's six—only six. But her mind is not clear, and in any event the six men could have summoned more. There could be a line of men out the door, waiting to make use of her defenseless body.

Lost in her reverie, she's shocked when she feels the man in her mouth pulsing, when she feels the first hot stream of come hit her tongue. She does not have time to pull away—and she couldn't if she did, because the man she's sucking has his hands tangled in her hair, forcing her head into position on his cock. She cannot stop him from coming in her mouth—she cannot stop him from doing anything. So she gulps his semen down her throat. A little still drizzles out and runs down her chin. She licks at it hungrily when he pulls out of her. But there's another man waiting, his cock hard in his hand. This one doesn't have to force her mouth open. She lets him shove his cock into her mouth, taking her—but then, before she knows what's happening, she's sucking it. She's sucking his cock.

The man inside her pussy comes, moaning, holding stock still and letting her pump herself onto his cock as she milks his come. She can't believe she's doing it. She's fucking herself onto his cock while he stands there. She can feel his cock pulsing inside her, feel her pussy growing even slicker with his come. She can feel him pulling out and another man taking his place, entering her quickly, finding her open and receptive.

She returns her attention to the cock she's sucking, lavishing sensation on it, but that doesn't last long. After only a few thrusts, she feels the man behind her pulling out of her pussy.

He's going to enter her ass.

She wants to protest, wants to beg him not to take her that way. She does it so rarely, only when her husband asks for it or she's feeling particularly naughty. She realizes with a rush of shame that she wants it, now, she wants to be taken in every hole. She wants him to fuck her ass, but she still wishes she could beg him to stop.

But the man in her mouth won't let her up. He's holding her head, forcing her quiet, her compliance, as she feels her anus heartlessly violated.

Her whole body, naked now, shudders as she feels her asshole taken. She's now been despoiled in every way, and she feels the tension fill her body as she struggles to let her asshole accept the invading cock. Then he's pumping, and she loses herself in sucking cock as her body relaxes into the sensations.

The man inside her grips her hair and comes, filling her mouth. This time she does not spill a drop, but swallows it all. Moments later, the man in her ass releases himself inside her, and she feels her back door, slick with his come, dripping semen as he pulls his cock out of her.

It seems to her as if she's become a rag doll, a thing for them to manipulate. So when she feels the cock slip out of her ass and is pushed forward, frog-walked onto another man now laying on the ground, she knows what is to come and she doesn't have the strength, will, or desire to resist.

Instead, she lets the men position her, thighs spread wide over the man on the floor, her pussy hovering over his cock.

And, rather than make them force her, she lowers herself onto him.

She wants to moan when she feels him enter her, but the spell has been broken and she manages to resist her need. But that changes quickly when she feels a second man take his position behind her.

They're going to enter her both places at once.

Her moan is deafening, rising almost into a scream as she feels the thick head of his cock against her asshole. This man is larger than the last, and it's hard for her to accept him, especially with her pussy stretched to capacity like that. But as she feels his lubricated cock entering deep into her asshole, she surrenders—or, rather, is forced to surrender, by her body, which wants it more than her mind ever could.

She comes.

She's still moaning with her climax, her mouth wide open, as a third man enters her—this time, her mouth. Pressed between three bodies, she closes her eyes and gives herself over, completely, to the men using her. She cannot push herself back onto them, now, only because her position is too awkward and to fuck herself onto the cock in her ass would be to sacrifice the rapid thrusts of the man underneath her. So she concentrates on sucking cock, and finds herself taking it deep into her throat, anticipating a mouth full of come with an excitement she has rarely felt in her life.

But she doesn't get it. The men fucking her want something else.

She can hear them talking, planning something. Her fear has dissolved into the knowledge that she is a thing, that she is but a body for them to invade and violate. She wants whatever they're planning. She wants them to do it to her—whatever it is, whatever it means.

She feels all cocks leave her at once. She slumps forward onto the concrete floor, her wrists still cuffed behind her. They turn her over, face up, her legs tucked awkwardly under her ass as she tries to curl into a ball. The three who were just fucking her crowd over her upper body, while two more grab her legs and one holds down her shoulders.

Their hands are on their cocks, all hard and glistening from her body.

She feels the first stream hit her face and breasts, and a rush goes through her as it dawns on her just what they're doing. Stream after stream pour out of the hard cocks above her, covering her with their come. She's horrified at first, in a split second, and then a shiver over-takes her body as she surrenders to it.

She doesn't even realize she's doing it.

She opens her mouth wide.

A thick stream hits her outstretched tongue. Another. And an-other. More come. There must be more than just the three. Were the other men masturbating, waiting to use her? Her eyes are closed, and she accepts each load of come onto her tongue and face, into her mouth, onto her breasts. She moans softly as she is covered in it.

Sprawled on the ground as their hands leave her, she feels sud-denly alone. No longer held down, she could curl into a ball if she wanted to—but she doesn't. She stays, face up, her cuffed arms tucked awkwardly into the small of her back, her legs spread wide as if inviting the next man to take her.

But he is not there; there is no man to use her that way now. In-stead, she is pulled to her hands and knees, her head swimming as they guide her to a chair where a new man is sitting.

She looks up at him, taking in his face, perhaps, to her eyes, the most beautiful face in the world. He smiles softly at her.

She does not smile back.

He has to push her head down onto his cock, but only because she does not want to take her eyes off that gorgeous face. The mo-ment she feels his cock in her mouth, she starts sucking eagerly, want-ing it—wanting his come. Wanting it to wash away the taste of all the others—wash it away, and compliment it.

His hands rest gently on her head, in contrast to the other men, who pulled her hair. She's now on her knees, her ass in the air, her legs spread wide, both her pussy and her ass available for use. But no man comes forward to use her.

Instead, they let the man in the chair enjoy her full prowess. She takes his cock down her throat, works her tongue all over it, brings her eyes up to meet his and uses them to beg him for his orgasm.

The man comes in her mouth, his fingers running through her hair. This time she is even more greedy, swallowing it all and sucking him hungrily, as if asking for more. He pushes her gently off his cock, and she remains there, hovering over it, her lips and tongue still working, her breath coming hard and heavy. She looks up at him, desperately, wanting more.

She hears the footsteps behind her, feels the hand grabbing her hair, the hood going back over her head. They lift her naked body in their arms and carry her away. She feels the rough carpet of the van floor against her body, hears the engine starting. Exhausted, she falls asleep before the van starts moving.

She has no memory of how she is bathed, toweled dry, placed in her own bed with clean sheets. She luxuriates in the feeling of clean, cold muslin, its surface smooth against her nipples. She opens her eyes.

He is there, above her, stroking her hair.

"Did you enjoy your late lunch?"

"I thought it would never happen."

"Would I let you down?"

"I was suspicious when you didn't show for lunch—you never cancel on me."

"And I didn't. I just had to eat later."

"How long did it take you to plan?"

"That's a trade secret," he says. "I hope that wasn't a good dress."

"You know it was," she says.

He smiles.

"You've got lots of nice dresses," he says.

She shivers under the covers, curls up her body clutching his thighs, and moans softly.

"Yes," she says. "I do. Lots of good dresses. Lots and lots and lots of them . . . and lots of lunch dates to wear them to, yes?"

"Yes," he says. "But none of them are in your appointment book."

She feels a quiver go through her naked body.

Flannel Nightgowns and White Cotton Panties
by Patrick Califia

For anyone who writes on the cutting edge of BDSM fiction, **Patrick Califia** is an inspiration, the boundary-pushing writer who, in some ways, started it all. My personal admiration for Patrick started when I read his early book of short stories, *Macho Sluts,* one of the best collections of hot, smart, and smutty fiction ever published and a big influence on my own work. (A dubious honor, I know—Patrick, I apologize!)

Califia's two subsequent collections of erotic BDSM fiction, *Melting Point* and *No Mercy,* are every bit as hot as that influential first volume. Califia also authored *Sensuous Magic,* which I consider to be the world's most accessible and best-written guide to BDSM for beginners. Other books of Patrick's include a book of gay male leather fiction, *Hard Men,* forthcoming from Alyson Publications, and *Speaking Sex to Power,* Califia's second superlative collection of essays (the first was *Public Sex*). Both are published by Cleis Press. He is working on a vampire novel, *Mortal Companion,* for Suspect Thoughts. Patrick lives in San Francisco with Hecate, his tortoiseshell cat, and a large collection of whips and unfinished quilts.

This story is based on one of Patrick's favorite sexual fantasies, and he says he is happy to hold spontaneous auditions for aspiring Daddy's Little Girls of all genders. The editor will be happy to forward any requests.

This story is for Tim Woodward

My master has told me that we must start all over, from the very beginning. I will be spending my vacation at his house, taking nothing of my own with me but the clothes on my back. We will be together for every hour of every day. I will eat what he gives me, wear what he has for me, sleep when he allows it. If there is a deity that looks after slave girls, I pray to that deity for grace. Let me fit myself to him as easily as water curves around a stone in its path. Perhaps even more than grace, I need courage. Since I received his written orders, the time when I am to present myself and the place, fear has opened a vast cold cavern in the center of my being. Even when I am holding perfectly still, I am vibrating to the secret rhythm of this terror.

Perhaps he would be infuriated to hear me call him my master, even though I have taken that liberty with his face and form only in the silence of my own heart. It is easy to displease the powerful. He is so far above me that he has probably lost all sense of how much power he has. Some gesture or word that means no more to him than clearing his throat could crush all my hopes and dreams, drain my life of meaning. I lived in a state of frustration before, gnawed at by a conviction that I was not like other women, afraid to look too hard at that difference, lest it prove to be tainted with madness. It is bad enough to live in the blinders of ignorance, but if those blinders have been removed, how could you go on if you knew no rider would ever appear to take your reins and spur you toward his stable?

This time that we will spend together is a test. It will determine whether he will accept me as his own, and train me to become the living image of that ownership.

I met this man through the good graces of my sister-slave, the friend who gently helped me to untangle the snarl of doubt and prudishness that choked my sexuality. She already had a master of her own, and out of love for her, he showed me enough to be taken out with the two of them, in the realm where it was safe for her to openly wear the tokens of her slavery. I know when and how to kneel, a few appropriate positions in which to display myself, the respectful forms of speech, the rudiments of service in the drawing room and bedside. But she is the slave of his heart. I would not want to be his second girl, even if that position had been offered to me.

Once I knew enough not to embarrass them in public, my friend and her master took me to a party. I was distracted by equal parts of arousal and intimidation. So the fantasies that I had really could become a reality—for women as beautiful as these! He encountered a colleague who expressed an interest in me. I went through my paces with a pounding heart and a dry mouth, painfully aroused by the screams of girls in duress and far happier than I. How does one contrive to be artless when so much is at stake? This new man was less than ten years older than myself, soft-spoken but authoritative, with what seemed to be a well-built body. He was wearing leather pants, a turtleneck shirt, and a professorial jacket. His graying hair was close-cropped, and there were laugh lines around his blue eyes. His two front teeth were slightly crooked. Not that I had more than a split second to assess him out of the corner of my eye.

My sister-slave's owner had taught me a simple routine. As my body bent and twisted, extended and retreated in submissive choreography, I felt a surprising amount of gratitude toward him, this master who would not collar me. He had created an opportunity for me to be examined. And he displayed me well, using hand signals rather than verbal commands. After my dance, I was sent away with my friend to do some little task for him, and when we came back, the stranger was gone.

Now it was dark, and I was outside his house, ringing the bell. He came to the door and brought me inside, taking one of my hands between his own. "You're here," was all he said, but his voice was a deep, subtle instrument that conveyed welcome and perhaps a little relief. The possibility that he had feared I would not obey his summons—that he actually needed me to be here—settled my stomach and stiffened my resolve. This was a master of good repute and great experience, a man who had been recommended to me by people I trusted, and I thought every molecule of him was handsome. *Please*, some part of me was crying, hammering at the clear but immovable walls that held my slave-self back, *please rescue me, set me free.*

I realized that he had placed something in my hands. "Put this on," he said, showing me down the hall and into a bedroom. "Then come back into the living room. Whenever you feel ready."

He closed the door, leaving me in a room that was a little girl's fairy princess dream. The bed was sized for two adult bodies, but it had frothy, girlish white lace curtains and linens to match. The flocked, white velvet wallpaper was flecked with rhinestones, and the moldings were painted birthday-cake-frosting pink. There was a shelf full of character dolls, expensive collectors' items, and some first editions of two fiction series for young adults. One featured a girl detective; the other, a nurse. I sternly suppressed the impulse to go to these books, pick them up, look at the illustrations, lose myself in them. The double doors of the closet were sliding mirrors. Avoiding their judgment, I turned my back and stripped off and folded everything I wore, then stashed the small stack (shoes on the bottom) in the last drawer of a dresser decorated with stenciled golden crowns. Curiosity led me to open a door, and it led to a bathroom with art deco fixtures of nude women posing in sprays of flowers and black-and-white tile. Since he had not told me to get my ass into the living room as quickly as possible, I took the liberty of a quick shower.

Walking back into the bedroom, which I assumed was to be mine, I thought again about his statement: *We must go back to the beginning.* My hands shook a little as I approached the bundle of fabric that he had given me. It had not had the sleazy feel of nylon stockings, a spandex dress, or silk lingerie. Nevertheless, the garment that shook out from the folds could not have surprised me more. It was a simple flannel nightgown, red hearts on a white background. I pulled it over my head, and as it fell around my shoulders, I felt something land against my right foot. A pair of white cotton panties had been folded up with the nightgown. I slid them up over my legs and hips, a little embarrassed by their snug fit and full, 1950s cut. I was completely covered in the most modest outfit possible. The contrast between it and the desire that simmered in my belly was indecent. There was a pair of fuzzy slippers by the bedroom door, and since my feet were cold, I put them on. No one had handed me a script, but I was in costume, and I knew where the stage was. So I went toward the living room, frosty stage fright nipping at my heels, herding me forward.

My master was sitting on a large, comfortable leather sofa, wearing red silk pajamas and a heavy paisley brocade dressing gown. A cigarette smoldered in an ashtray on the end table, a bit of bad-boy insolence in politically correct northern California. There was also a glass full of red wine. The lights in the room had been lowered, and the dimness leached some of the tension out of my shoulders. He did not turn to acknowledge me. It was as if he didn't realize I was there. The wide sofa faced a large screen television, and as I watched him, hungry for more knowledge of him, he lifted his right hand and pressed a button on the remote control.

The screen was suddenly occupied with the life-sized bodies of beautiful young men and women copulating in front of us with what looked like genuine enthusiasm. From time to time one of them would turn to stare at us, as if they knew we were there, privy to their revels. I was shocked, first by the pornography, and then by the fact that it had shocked me. I was rooted to the spot, short-circuited.

"What are you doing up so late at night?" he asked with patient tenderness.

It was enough of a hint for me to guess what was required of me, and I fell naturally into the role that was consistent with the flannel nightgown and the glamorous, if juvenile, bedroom. "I couldn't sleep, Daddy," I whispered.

One corner of his mouth quirked up. He was pleased with me, then. But this amusement at my quick wit was not part of the fantasy, and he quickly assumed a more neutral expression. He patted the sofa. "Do you want to sit down?" he asked.

When you are a slave, there is no "want" about it. You must go where the hand of your owner beckons. And so I went, albeit awkwardly. The ultrasoft flannel caressed my naked breasts. I parked my hopefully cute little butt in the middle of the end cushion. He turned to regard me thoughtfully, taking a drag on his cigarette, a sip of wine. "I don't know if you should see this," he said, and lifted the controls.

"Why not, Daddy?" I asked, staring at the screen with my mouth slightly open. I had come into the room in a state of arousal, and all of this sex, even though it was relentlessly equal and cheerful, made me uncomfortably aware of my panties and what was inside of them.

"I guess you're old enough to be able to watch an X-rated movie," he said, carefully flattering my imaginary adolescence. "If there's anything going on up there that you haven't seen already."

If I left that coarse comment alone, the evening would take a different turn, I sensed. But I did not feel like a promiscuous teenage wildcat in the presence of this strong and quiet man. I was a novice, and a beginner, just as he had dictated. "I never saw anything like this before, Daddy," I said breathlessly.

I could not take my eyes off the screen. A man was undressing a woman, running his hands across her breasts, his fingers dragging at her nipples. Then things got more interesting, less bubblegum-happy. He turned her so that her back was to the camera as he tore her dress down the back, exposing the curves of her ass. Then she was facing the camera again, hands behind her back (held there by him?). Only one of his hands was visible, and it roamed across her breasts, pawing at them, squeezing crudely, leaving red marks behind. The woman twisted in his grasp and moaned, her legs separating as if against her will.

My imagination was not powerful enough to reproduce the feeling of those hands upon my own skin, but I was leaning forward, trying to find that touch. The rising emotions in my body were entrancing, but there was another reason to keep my eyes forward. My skin on the right side of my body tingled, sensing his approaching warmth. He was coming toward me, settling his greater weight on the cushion next to mine.

"Never?" he asked, and I had trouble remembering our earlier exchange.

"No, never," I exhaled.

Was he touching me? I thought that he was, but what control he must have, to put hands on me so lightly that I could wonder if contact had been made. I looked down and saw that he was simply holding his hands near my shoulders and my arms. What I felt was the energy between us. I was being stroked by the mere probability of his skin meeting mine.

The couple on the screen were kissing, deeply, ferociously, her head twisted back to meet his mouth. Strands of her long black hair flew through the air, partially hiding the things his fingers were doing to her nipples. I was breathing more quickly, panting, and when the tips of my master's fingers touched my lips, I gasped, frightened by the sudden incandescence. The porn actress slid down her man's body, pivoted, and seemed to put her head into his hand. His fingers twisted in her hair, and the camera focused on the hard cock that he bounced in his other hand. He slowly brought it forward while she halfheartedly struggled, not seeming to realize that when she opened her mouth to protest, it only made her more available for the lesson he was determined to teach.

As his cock head slid between those beautiful, swollen lips, my own parted. My master was looking at me with pure hunger in his eyes, and he had slipped his thumb into my mouth. My groan was silent, blocked. A callus rubbed the roof of my mouth. He didn't move his thumb much, just barely rocked it to and fro, but I had let him into my mouth, and I sucked on what he gave me. Suckled, rather, and titillated with supple strokes of my tongue. Kissing and sucking upon the dream of someday being fed his cock. Intoxicated by the presage of that initiation.

I dared swivel my eyes to look at him. My knowing mate grinned back at me from his cruel, appraising blue eyes. What a relief it was to see no sympathy there, no hesitation, no possibility of reprieve or mercy. *He's real,* I thought, and my heart sped up, throwing itself against the cage of my ribs. *This is really going to happen. He will make it happen. He will use me for his pleasure, and at last I will know what it is like to have real pleasure of my own.*

He took his thumb out of my mouth, settled deeper into the sofa, and took a gulp of wine. It must have been the reflected shadow of the thick red liquid that made his face seem flushed. I kept my eyes front and center, trying to look nonchalant, but I knew my body was flinching slightly every time a woman on the screen was caressed, bitten, or penetrated. When his hands settled on my shoulders, I willed myself to ignore him. "Your shoulders are so tight," he murmured, and his fingers dug into my muscles, massaging me. "Let me see if I can loosen you up. Then maybe you can go back to bed and sleep." I adjusted my body slightly to give him access as his hands wandered further down my back, fingers grazing the top of my buttocks. Then he was focusing on my upper arms, and as I continued to watch the orgy on screen, a light tickling pressure melted across my breasts. He was sneaking up on my nipples, touching the flannel that lay upon my skin rather than the skin itself. But I still felt him, and his intentions, and my breasts seemed to swell to an uncomfortable size. I could feel my nipples crinkling painfully, and between my legs a sharp sensation made me want to excuse myself and run back to the bathroom.

Since I permitted this much, he grew bolder, until there was no denying that he was fondling my breasts. I could not help it, my legs parted slightly. The tight crotch of the white panties was digging into me. "You're getting to be such a big girl now," he crooned. "Do you like it when I massage you?" As he spoke, he was unbuttoning the yoke of the flannel nightgown and sticking his hand inside it, rubbing my collarbones.

"Oh, yes, Daddy," I whispered, as a nameless blonde was made to suck one man's cock while another man entered her from behind. The man who was fucking her struck her on the ass. Lucky bitch.

"Massage is really good for you. It helps your body to develop properly. And you know I want you to grow up to be a beautiful young lady. Would you like a breast massage?"

Before I could reply, he skillfully peeled the front of my unbuttoned nightie over my arms, effectively pinning them at my sides. My breasts were exposed. He put one hand around my throat while the other explored me freely. My body surprised even me with its hunger.

"What beautiful big titties you have," he said, escalating. "I'd love to kiss them." It wasn't a request for permission, just a warning. When his mouth closed over my nipple, I thought at first I could not stand the intensity of the sensation. Then it took me over, and I yielded to his mouth, even when he sucked roughly at the hard nubs and bit them. He came up for air and smiled at me. "Daddy sometimes gets a little rough, doesn't he?" he said. "But you don't mind, do you?"

"No, Daddy, I don't," I stuttered.

"Of course not," he sneered. "I think it would be a good idea for me to see how the rest of your development is coming along, don't you?"

I thought a shadow of resistance might prevent my surrender from becoming tedious. "What do you mean, Daddy?"

He kissed me then, still squeezing and twisting my breasts, then took his mouth away and said in my ear, "Spread your legs, you little bitch."

I tried to comply, but in my haste, forgot how long the nightgown was. So my knees were stuck only a foot and a half apart. He wound his fingers in my hair, grown long in lonely hope that it might someday be used in just this fashion, and he pulled just enough to create a delicious pressure on my scalp. "Pull your nightie up for Daddy," he suggested, licking my ear and my neck like a big lascivious dog. With numb fingers, I complied, inching it up a little at a time. As soon as it cleared my knees, he gently edged his hand along the inside of my nearest thigh, as if he was warming it.

"Do you ever massage yourself?" he asked, sharply tweaking my left nipple.

"I don't know what you mean, Daddy," I gasped, struggling to stay put despite the pain.

"Really. Well, then you should spread your legs a little further, baby, because Daddy is going to masturbate you."

I acted as if I had never heard the word. "*What* are you going to do, Daddy?"

"This," he said, coming close to kiss me again. Then his finger went under the edge of my panties, between my inner lips, scooped up a little of the moisture that was running freely there, and took it up to my clit, where he gently rubbed it into the top and sides of the hood. I could hardly kiss him back, I was moaning so much. How could a man know this much about a woman's body? Within minutes he had taken me to the very edge of an orgasm, and he kept me there for an insufferably long time. "What's going to happen if I keep on doing this?" he asked, taunting me.

"I—I don't know—I don't know—" I lied, so deep in character that I almost believed it.

"Do you want to find out?" The finger was tracing figure eights within my labia, outlining clitoris and opening, over and over again. He sucked on my nipples, hard, then told me, "Say it. Ask me."

My tongue was twice the size of my mouth. So he slapped me on the inside of one thigh, then the other. I could not catch my breath. The reality of the pain was not anything like what I had imagined, but I was prepared to adapt to what my body told me, and fall in love with it. He kept slapping me until he was tired of it, then he gently stroked the burning skin, giving me a chance to find my voice.

"Please—Daddy—please masturbate me," I whimpered.

It took only a slight increase in pressure and speed for his fingers to reduce me to a babbling orgasmic mess. "Sweet baby," he groaned, taking me in his arms. He lifted his fingers to my mouth, made me suck them again, then put his hand between my legs and forced them back into an open position.

"Do you see what's happening to that lady in the movie?" he asked me. We were currently being shown a close-up of a huge torpedo of a cock, housed inside a shaved pussy, pummeling it. How the actor came all the way out and then accurately found her hole again without the guidance of his hands was a marvel to me.

"Ye—es," I replied, reaching for him. He pinned my hand down.

"Would you like to know how that feels?" he asked, and went into me without waiting for me to reply. I didn't know how many fingers he had put into me, but it was as if no one had ever finger-fucked me before. I suddenly had feeling where there had been little or no sensation before. And I understood, in my flesh, why the woman on the screen might not be feigning her insatiability.

"Oh!" was the only response I could make. One word that could not begin to contain all that I was discovering at his behest.

"Say it again," he told me, tongue once more against my ear, a sultry insult. "Say the words. The words that Daddy taught you."

I repeated the phrases he had used already, and he introduced more of them, key groups of dirty words that we both found enormously exciting. I was such a spoiled girl, receiving all of this physical attention. None of the men who had wanted to fuck me had touched me this much before getting down to what they saw as the main event. With his thumb on my clit and the rest of his fingers engaged within me, he showed me again and again that I was the very opposite of what I had often been called—cold, frigid, withholding. Through much of this, we were eye-to-eye, and I could feel him learning me, appreciating my responsiveness, but seeing much more of me than my shudders and gasps. Sometimes my reactions were so pronounced that I was afraid he would think I was overacting, but his expression told me that he knew I was truthful, and he was excited by my openness.

"You like looking at the men's things, don't you?" he asked, pulling his hand away, leaving me shockingly empty. This time he would not proceed until I agreed. "Don't you want to know what a real one looks like?" he asked me, taking one of my hands in his own.

I nodded, and he guided me to the lap of his silky dressing gown. There beneath the heavy fabric lurked an equally heavy shaft. But before I could touch it directly or heft his ball sack, he made me circle it with my hand on top of the brocade, and slowly jack him off while he made me repeat all the names he could think of for his parts. Baby talk, adult slang, and medical terms were all deliciously sacrilegious as they went back and forth between us in stage whispers. Any guilt I might have felt about enacting a fantasy like this one, which would have been so offensive if it were real, was absolved during this exchange. We were so clearly playacting, two adults turning each other on in what might have seemed a farce if we were not so engrossed in it. We even giggled together, a time or two, but I think he sensed that if he allowed too much levity, I might become hysterical.

When he finally showed his swollen penis to me, I bent toward him of my own accord, and he allowed my approach. I stared at the stalk and crown of his sex, wondering if I had ever really looked at a cock before. How many billions of heterosexual women are there on this battered planet of ours? And how few of them have ever really studied a rigid prick—or one in repose, for that matter? Much as I desired him, I realized I was afraid of his erection. Some of this was the shame that had been drummed into me from childhood, but some of it was based on a long experience of disappointment, and perhaps I had also picked up on my lovers' ambivalence about their own genitals. But this man had his cock screwed on nice and tight; he knew exactly what it could do, and he preened beneath my gaze.

"I'm going to teach you some important things about growing up," my master told me, taking his tool in hand and pointing it toward my lips. "This is what you're here for, to worship my cock. To worship the thing that gives you pleasure and rules your heart. Do you love me, baby? You love me, don't you, my favorite little girl? So kiss it, just do that for me, kiss it. Kiss it the way that I kiss you."

It was a salty kiss, because the head of his cock was drooling precome, and he deliberately smeared the stuff across my mouth, then told me to lick my lips and swallow it with a smile, and come back for more. The kiss led of course to other things, and soon he was riding back and forth within my throat, coaxing me to do what the women in the movie were doing. "They like it," he said. "You've seen how much they like it. And once you get good at doing it, you'll like it too. But even if you didn't like it, you would still have to do it, and do you know why? Because I am your daddy, that's why, and little girls always do what their daddies tell them to do. I made you, so I own you."

Soon my eyes were running with tears and the back of my throat was sore. The thick, sour taste of his secretions lined my mouth. "I know what you're thinking about," he said, rocking his hips. "You're thinking about what it feels like to have this inside of you someplace else. Are you making Daddy's cock get hard so he can . . . fuck you with it?"

I took the risk of letting his cock slide out of my mouth so that I could stare at him wide-eyed. "What does 'fuck' mean?" I asked. I was no virgin, true, but it was also true that I had no idea what it would mean to be fucked by this man. His power over me was so complete and welcome, I didn't think there could be such a thing as vanilla sex with him.

He chuckled and rubbed his gray crew cut. "It's better if I show you rather than tell you," he decided. "Slide off the couch and kneel by the foot of the coffee table. Take off your nightgown. Bend forward. That's right. Now, I want to make sure that we're not interrupted. This is a very important lesson. So I want to make sure you can hold still."

"I'll hold still for you, Daddy," I vowed, my breasts pressed uncomfortably flat by the cold slick wood of the coffee table's surface. Black leather bumpers ran around all of its edges, padding my hips. He ignored me, walked to the head of the table, and buckled straps around my wrists, chained them to the legs of the table. I pulled once (of course), but I was well-tied. The cuffs were snug and the chains sunk deep into the wood. I could not free myself. He was behind me, taking off his dressing gown, and peeling my panties down. Cold air humiliated me with pimples of goose bumps all over my bum. The tight panties were made out of fabric that was thick enough to keep my legs together. But I felt as if my pussy peeked out anyway, she was so swollen, the sweet slick mouth of a siren.

When he rubbed the head of his cock against my tender slit, I began to cry. Sob, actually. I struggled with my bonds. I really did try to escape. He had been wise to tie me. But even as I thrashed around, I knew it would have upset me to break free. The frenzied motions I made were somehow a part of giving way to him. I could not go to him quietly, I suppose, as if it were no little matter. Perhaps it was *my* way of testing *him*, to see if he really was the lighthouse and harbor that I needed.

"Shush," he soothed me, stroking my flanks. "Daddy's here. I'll take care of you. Don't cry. Are you afraid it's going to hurt? Don't worry. If it hurts I'll stop. But you've been wet for so long, and you know what it means when you get wet. It means you're ready to be fucked. It means you need it. And I want you to have everything you need, honey. That's what daddies are for."

There was an introductory thrust, a shallow one, and then a slow, steady push that seemed to fill me to my heart. I cried out, and the sound of it was so poignant that it made me cry afresh. Yes, I cried out with no small amount of grief for the freedom I was about to lose, my autonomy, the illusion that I did not need anybody else in order to be happy. But I also mourned for the years that I had lived without this glory, the weight of his body upon me, his steady and sinister intentions, the goodness of his erotic selfishness.

"Does it hurt?" he asked, moving a little.

"Oh, yes," I said, quick to take up my cue. "It hurts, Daddy. Oh, please stop! Please stop, Daddy. You said you would if it hurt." He really did feel bigger than any other man who had taken me, perhaps because he was plowing me from behind, perhaps because of the way my legs had been pinioned.

"Shush," he exhaled. "Shush, now, my little slut. Daddy's little sex slave. Daddy knows what's best for you. You're just a little hole for me to use. My tight little whore in training. And it doesn't hurt that much. You need to be stretched wide. It's about to feel better—much, much better. Oh, yes. It is. Better and better."

Well, I could tell that it felt better for him. And I almost lost myself in the old habit of withdrawing from my body, watching the man who was fucking me, allowing him to get off without participating. There was something oddly maternal about loaning a man my body that way, and some enjoyment or warmth resulted from knowing I had pleased him. But my master was not going to be taken in that way, or should I say, patronized? He put one hand under me and reminded me that he knew how the little button down there worked. Before long it was pretty clear that I would come before he did, and he rode me skillfully all the way through that climax, down into the valley, and up the hill into another. It wasn't until I had collapsed on the table, resting all of my weight limply upon it, that he put both hands on the cheeks of my ass, spread them so that he could watch what he was doing to me, and gave it to me at a tempo and depth calculated to please no one but himself. Still, at the end, when he told me to beg for his come, I meant every word.

He left me restrained while he cleaned himself and tied his robe. Then he unbuckled the straps, lifted me onto my feet, and took me into the bedroom. There, he peeled back the covers and put me on the clean lace-edged sheet. But I was to get more than a kiss goodnight. He said, "From now on, you can't come unless you have something inside of you. Do you understand? It isn't good for little girls to do without that. You need to be opened up, and you need to be kept filled up. That way you'll always be aware of your sex, and always ready to be used by your master. And I don't want you touching yourself, either. When you need to come you have to ask me. And I'll decide if I want you to get off or not."

So he tied my hands above my head, to the rails of the canopied bed, and spread my ankles and tied those apart as well. Before he covered me up, he said, "I have a surprise for you," and showed me a small dildo. "Tonight I used your mouth and your cunt," he said. "But you have to learn how to make all of your holes available to me." I gasped as a doubled length of rope was cinched tight around my waist. He greased up the imitation cock and pushed it carefully up my unhappy ass, where startled muscles did all they could to push it out. Then the rope came between my legs, holding the plug in place. The harness was finished with a large, intricate knot that rested on my clit. He slapped lightly at my pussy to show me how accurately it was placed.

He leaned forward to give me a good-night kiss on the cheek (oh! his star-blue eyes), and left my side without covering me up. He paused by the door, but he did not turn off the light. "I'm turning on the security camera now," he said. "I'll review the tape in the morning, so I'll know if you made yourself come or not. Sweet dreams, little slave. You played your part to perfection. It takes an intelligent girl to assume a persona of such simplicity. Tomorrow, you will have your reward: a sound spanking, before breakfast. Then you will get to meet some of Daddy's friends."

I wanted him to spank me. But I didn't think I could say thank you, any more than I had been able to just spread my legs for him and placidly accept that first firestorm of a fuck. "Sleep well, master," I said, trying not to make it sound like a curse as I writhed, unable to silence the prong within my bowels.

Despite the bright light and the insistent pressure within me, I fell asleep at once, as soon as his eyes no longer provoked me. Without thinking about it or being told, I had learned one of the slave's most valuable skills: to rest whenever an opportunity to do so is given. I would need every hour of slumber I could scavenge from his schedule, for the next day was to be a demanding one. He had already hung another outfit on the back of the bathroom door: a hooker's leather micro-miniskirt and a fishnet halter top. I was so tired, I didn't even twist my head up to see if I could catch a glimpse of my shoes.

I Should Not Want This
by Midori

Author of the book *The Seductive Art of Japanese Bondage*, **Midori** is an educator and writer on S and M, fetish, and human sexuality, and she travels the world presenting to university students, S and M clubs, and the general public. Raised in a feminist intellectual Tokyo household, Midori holds a degree in psychology from the University of California at Berkeley. Her work has appeared on HBO and the BBC, and in *Mademoiselle*, *Playboy*, *Der Spiegel*, *Wired*, *British Esquire*, *Vogue*, *Surface*, and many other publications. She is currently working on three new books, including a collection of her essays, a volume of erotic science-fiction stories, and another how-to kink book.

I should not want this.

This is wrong.

I am an independent, self-made woman. I did not get to this place in the firm by bowing down to anyone, especially a man.

All through the jury selection all I could think of was being on my knees. In the judge's chamber, my face steeled to the world, no one knew my secret. No one knew that under the charcoal gray Donna Karan suit, my cunt soaked the white lace thong panties. I faced off bitterly with the burly police detective, even as part of me remained bound in tight, cruel ropes. The attorney for the defense—could he smell my sex as we barked our cases at one another?

The court day crawled excruciatingly slowly to its end, finally bringing to me the much-anticipated weekend. I dreaded its arrival as much as I craved it. He would make me wallow in the filth of my darkest mind. He would strip me of my dignity until I was completely naked, to the core of my soul. I could not bear the thought. But I could not bear the thought of going without it, either. For two long months I buried myself in unending work, ignoring my gnawing hunger. He's now returned to claim his throne and to claim me.

He was already in town. The FedEx package arrived in the morning with its usual contents: a hotel key, a slip of paper with the room number scrawled on it, and the collar. I pulled the package out of the desk drawer where it lay hidden. He no longer sent instructions with the packages. It wasn't necessary. He had trained me thoroughly.

I had long since learned to surrender any attachment to material things. I had also learned to leave anything that I gave a damn about at the office: the ring my grandmother gave me, case and client documents, identification, my cell phone, and most of all, my pride. In his domain, my needs were irrelevant. That, after all, was precisely my need. I hated him for knowing me that well.

I tucked the leather collar into the pocket of my Burberry mac.

The rain streaked down the dirty taxi window, blurring the city lights, melting away the forms like waves on a sandcastle. Sharp edges began to melt away inside me as well. In a haze I paid the cabbie and walked through the tasteful lobby. I placed the key card into the elevator control panel, lighting up the top-floor button. The elevator climbed to the penthouse suite with what seemed like unbearable slowness, mocking and teasing me. Did his domain and control extend to the machinery around him?

I stood before his door and stared at it until my dry eyes began to water from the strain. Gingerly, I knocked twice. I waited five counts before sliding the plastic key card into the slot. The red security light turned green. A heavy sigh escaped my mouth as my knees weakened. Before I could fall to the ground I found the strength to turn the handle and push the door open. An elegant suite opened before me. Beyond that, the vast window showed the city twinkling and glowing in the soft blackness of the rainy night. The warmth of the room caressed me. The lights were low, and a gas fire roared in the fireplace on the other end of the room. The dining table was scattered with the remains of dinner for two. I resisted the urge to check the wineglass for lipstick stains. That would be unbecoming of an independent woman of my power, and unbecoming of a slave. An enormous vase sat on the coffee table, overflowing with dozens of long-stemmed red roses. The *Herald Tribune* and *Economist* were scattered on the floor by the overstuffed leather armchair next to the fire. I caressed the arm of the chair, remembering the musculature of his strong arms and the maleness of his scent. Then I saw the leather-wrapped cane leaning against the arm of the chair, its silver-capped handle gleaming in the firelight. I pulled my hand away, as if reprimanded by his invisible gaze. Startled out of my revelry, I remembered my duties.

I put the wet mac into the cloak closet, doing my best to ignore the master bedroom. How appropriate its name was. I found the glass of red wine on a tray on the floor next to the fireplace, opposite to the armchair. That was my place to begin tonight: to begin my surrender.

I sipped the wine slowly, letting the day slip further away. As I drank the crimson fluid, it was as if I was drinking his will and desire, taking it into me slowly. I let him saturate my flesh. He was going to anyway.

I put the emptied glass away, and replaced its space with my body. I laid the thick black-leather collar carefully on the tray before me. The heavy steel O-ring clinked once against the metal of the tray. Still fully clothed in my suit, I kneeled, facing the door. I kneeled as comfortably as possible, taking into consideration the stiffness of the Blahnik pumps and the possibility of a long stay in this position. One night he left me kneeling for four agonizing hours. One learned to endure gracefully . . . eventually. I focused on the pain in my legs. I focused on the misery of the loneliness of being without him. I focused on the aching pain of my desire for what was about to come. I focused on all this, so I'd have something to hold onto when he pushed me to that breaking point. I'd need to remember the true pain of loneliness so that I could savor the pain of his love.

Deliberate shifts of my weight from left to right became a slow, rhythmic dance. I lost track of time. The clothes felt alien and uncomfortable to me, an armor now ill-fitting on this flesh that needed to become naked and defenseless.

How long had he been watching me? I didn't hear him come in. Somewhere, lost in the pain of my flesh and agony of my longing, I became deaf. I sat mute, mid-gasp, with my eyes startled wide. How handsome he was, leaning against the entryway column. His powerful frame was hidden under the smooth black Italian silk cashmere suit, his dark eyes gazed down at me with intense focus. Soft black hair, styled in perfect nonchalance, framed his chiseled dark olive face. Supple lips parted in a predatory grin, showing gleaming white teeth. He seemed more panther than human. Had he always been so breathtakingly handsome?

I felt more prey than human.

When our gazes locked, my cunt throbbed. Then, suddenly remembering my training, I looked down, ashamed for behaving in such an untrained way. I knew better. But it was too late. Before I could regain composure, he stood before me, my face grasped in his powerful hand.

"Look at my face, my pet. Go ahead, look at it." He spat out the words. "Take a good long look, because that mistake's going to cost you dearly."

I tried to turn my face away, but his hand would not let me. Fear shuddered my flesh. What am I doing screwing up so badly, so early? I feared the loss of his cruelty. Silently, wordlessly, I begged, "Don't banish me." Would he hear my voiceless plea?

He shoved my face away like some discarded object, turned on his heel and sat down into the armchair. A long silence passed. My eyes gazed down to a spot on the carpet. I did not breathe hard, in fear that my body may move. Finally he spoke, much to my relief, in soft words.

"Gift yourself to me."

I leaned forward and took the collar between my teeth, careful not to mark it with my crimson-painted lips. Keeping my head bowed, I crawled across the space between us. A space so vast that I thought I'd never reach him. I just wanted to leap onto my feet and run toward him, wrap my arms around him, and smother him in kisses. But I could not. I crawled. I crawled as slowly and gracefully as possible, letting my hips sway slowly under the fine wool skirt. The carpet burned my knees, even beneath the stockings. With each sway of my hip, I hoped to please him a bit more. His cordovan wingtips in my field of vision, I finally reached him. Keeping my gaze and head

down, I rose from all fours onto my knees and clasped my hands behind my back. His hands opened, just below my mouth. I parted my
teeth, dropped the collar into his waiting hands, and bowed forward
from the waist. He placed the collar around my neck, buckled it, and
I heard the loud click of a padlock. My soul flooded with relief and
dread. It was the sound of heaven's gate opening before me and hell's
gate shutting behind me. I was now free in my captivity. The muscles
of my shoulders relaxed while my heart beat uncontrollably.

I should not want this.

Then the cutting began. From the recesses of the finest Italian suit
danced into his hand the crude implement of terror, a common
street-thug's switchblade. It flashed cold and menacing into my face.
The flat of the blade pressed into my jugular, just above the collar. I
breathed slowly to still my quaking body. With expert handling he caressed my face with the sharp blade.

I was his. Not moving, I simply let him.

A part of me wondered, "How could I allow this?"

Another part of me answered, "Because this is my Truth."

He straightened my posture for better access. The blade traveled
down my throat, past my clavicle and to my cleavage. He slid it between the lapel of my single-breasted suit and cut off the silver buttons with ease. They rolled onto the floor. His free hand slid the jacket
off and tossed it on the floor behind me. That hand cupped my ample
breast and fondled it gently through the cream silk blouse. Then,
pulling a handful of silk into his hands and pulling it away from my
body, he stabbed at the blouse with the tip of the switchblade, crudely
cutting the cloth away from my breast. Then he slashed the white lace
bra cup away, exposing my right breast. My nipples stood hard,
aching without the protective cover. He repeated the slashing on the
left side, cutting away the silk and lace. The blade now traveled down
my torso and found the place where my sex lay hidden. With a swift
kick from his fine shoes, he forced my knees as far apart as the narrow
skirt would allow. Stabbing the cloth at my crotch, he ripped the knife
down the front of my skirt, making a most indecent slit. With the tip
of the blade he scratched at the white lace of the panties and nicked

my skin just a bit, then sliced a gash-like opening on the panties. My shaved cunt lips blossomed obscenely from the torn white petals of my underwear. My breasts jutted out and sex exposed in the lawyer's suit now made into rags, I was a mockery of my professional decorum. As I said, I'd long since learned to surrender any attachment to material things.

A moment of silence followed. He was studying my form. Did I please him?

The answer to my thoughts came suddenly, as he grasped a handful of my thick black hair and shoved my face into the carpet and rubbed to remove the lipstick. Then my face was forced into his highly polished wingtips. Relieved at his attention upon me, I breathed in deeply the warm scent of his leather shoes. I pressed my face hard into his shoe and nudged him.

"Go ahead," his husky voice murmured. I parted my lips and kissed the leather, open mouthed, then I licked and tasted his shoes with the full length of my tongue. Pressing into him with each lick so that he could feel my gratitude. Then I felt the pressure of the other foot on my back, pressing me into his shoe, pressing me into the floor, and pressing me into oblivion.

I could stay here forever.

Suddenly, without notice, he simply kicked me away. Despondent, I tried to crawl back to him. Silently, he kicked me away again, standing to step over me. I was in agony again. I heard him in the master bedroom, after which he returned quickly. With one foot he kicked me over, then grasped the ring on the collar, yanking me up onto my feet, almost choking me. Keeping one hand on my collar, he picked up the cane with the other. Knowing what was to come, I gulped tightly against the collar. Barely able to keep up on my high-heeled feet, he dragged me into his bedroom by the collar. He spun me around to face the bed, then shoved me unceremoniously onto it. "Click," snapped the switchblade, and then he tore away at the skirt, cutting off all that covered my ass. My garter belt framed my dripping cunt, exposing my true nature like a common bitch in heat. I heard the swoosh of the air, but before I could prepare, the burning cane stroke seared my ass cheeks. *Oh god, this hurts.* Before the pain subsided he brought down another full blow. I began to hyperventilate. He didn't stop for me to catch my breath. It's his prerogative. I forced myself to remember the true pain of loneliness. I forced my ears to love the swooshing sound. My breathing slowed to a labored pace. He struck my ass and thighs over and over. My whole body ached and my cunt was throbbing. Each stroke now vibrated through my pussy, G-spot, and uterus, starting the first shudder of that familiar earthquake that would invade my mind and body.

As my head turned to the left, I realized that I was watching myself in a wall of mirrors. His profile was just barely in my field of vision. He was shirtless now, and his sculpted back gleamed and rippled under a light coat of sweat. Cruelty and lust darkened his face. My flesh melted under his cane strokes. I began to drift in a high induced by rhythmic, deep, throbbing pain.

I realized that he was no longer holding the cane, but was holding handfuls of the roses. Like an opium eater, I became lost in the grandeur, the vision, color, and form, until suddenly, the world exploded in rose petals, and I felt the thorns digging into and tearing at my tenderized ass cheeks. I cried out in pain, only to be met with his laughter.

Then came the sound of his zipper.

Yes, oh, yes, take my aching cunt! Let me cum. I raised my ass to receive his pumping cock to my pussy. He simply pushed me back down onto the bed. To my horror I felt his cock, lubed and pressing into my ass.

"NO!" I shouted, before I could hold my tongue. *I will not take this.* I struggled to get up.

His cock pulled away and I felt a strong, talon grip on my shoulder turning me over onto my back. Eyes full of lust and fury, he spat into my face. He raised his hand, and I reverberated from the hot, fierce slap across my face.

The storm in me was suddenly calmed. The fight in me, my resistance, drained away with that single slap. I sank into the mattress, like meat. I was meat. This was his flesh. The self slipped away and this meat was the extension of his desire. I was calmed, peaceful, and contented in my fate.

He rolled me back onto my belly, and took his place at my ass. I breathed slowly, to open to his enormity. A sweet little pain vibrated through me. I began to sob. He pressed his cock slowly into me, deeper into me. Then he began to pump my ass. I sobbed loudly and freely as he fucked my ass and claimed his meat—his property. The shudder within me built bigger and bigger as he fucked me deeper and deeper.

"Take your flesh," I cried.

"You're my meat," he growled. "My slave . . ." he moaned.

The earthquake built closer to the surface. I wallowed in this annihilation of pleasure. I bucked my ass against his invasion. His hand pressed my head hard into the bed, and he buried his cock deep in my ass and I bucked, came, and shuddered, speared on his dick. He growled like a panther tearing into flesh and thrust into me, as if to split me in two. My flesh seared as he collapsed on top of me.

Before my mind faded to the blackness of sweet oblivion and exhaustion, I felt his powerful arms wrap around me and his lips press on the back of my neck.

How could I have not wanted this?

Live Transmission
by Alex S. Johnson

Alex S. Johnson is a thirtysomething music journalist and grad student who lives in Torrance, California. He is the former editor of *Juggernaut: The Magazine of Extreme Music,* and is currently a staff writer for *Brave Words & Bloody Knuckles,* in addition to contributing to half a dozen other periodicals, including *MK Ultra.* He spends his rare free hours watching Italian Giallo films, listening to lots of Cradle of Filth and Darkthrone, and occasionally writing short fiction, some of which has been published in places like *Bloodsongs* and the *Noirotica 3* anthology.

About "Live Transmission," Johnson says, "I've recently concluded that my life would have made more sense if I'd been allowed to live it as a character Jennifer Jason Leigh might play. Whether it's *Georgia* or *Skipped Parts* or *Flesh and Blood*, Leigh has this wonderful fucked-up endurance and a dark, fatalistic quality I've always found very sexy. But since I can't be a character played by Ms. Leigh, at least not on a twenty-four-hour basis, I'm resigned to being an overeducated white guy who finds the notion of forced submission, especially as imagined from a female perspective, incredibly erotic.

"I always enjoyed stories by the late, great horror writer Karl Edward Wagner for this specific reason—I think he nailed latent male masochism on the head; the movie *Sick,* about Bob Flanagan, and a short film by R. Kern also contribute to the hothouse mental climate in which I dwell more than I care to admit, and produce fantasies very much like the ones described in this story. There's also a not-so-subtle tribute to a legendary proto-deathrock band (which has nothing to do with the above)."

For GRS

Iona Cortese buffed her nails till she could see herself in them, practically. It was a Saturday morning, and by 5:30 she had awakened to a loud splash in the pool that occupied the center of her apartment complex in Westbrook. She hoped it was some built guy, but not some built guy wearing nuthuggers, more like a boxer style. Even if the dude had enough to justify wrapping his thing like a Christmas sausage, that whole look still turned her off. Iona parted the curtains with one freshly buffed hand and stole a peek.

He was doing laps, sluicing through the water like a shark. She could see the muscles pop from his neck when he turned his head for a quick breath. The guy was smoothly bronzed, tall, broad shoulders, short blonde hair—not a faggy butch, just neat and practical, the way she liked 'em. A perfect swimmer's body. He had to be on some team. When he finally pulled himself out of the pool and slipped into flip-flops and a T-shirt, she let the curtain go, but not before sneaking one last peek at the way his swim trunks clung to a hard, shapely butt.

She sat back at the kitchen table and decided her nails would stand up to inspection. It was hard to believe that her broadcast debut was just two days away. Even though it was only cable, community access stuff, everybody would be watching—her professors, friends, and maybe, who knew, somebody from a local station. Iona wanted to start her video portfolio early and seriously.

At nineteen, a sophomore at California U, she already knew what she wanted to be, and had it planned with a fair amount of detail. Broadcast journalism was practically in her blood—Daddy's uncle been a correspondent in Korea, and she could remember sitting in his study, decorated with black-and-white photos of artillery and men in uniform, watching a video compilation of combat footage over and over. She could see herself hunkered down in the sand, snapping exclusive photos of some Mideast war and zapping them over to UPI with a cellular modem. It was kind of a romantic fantasy, and she knew it, but Daddy had always been big on her living her dreams—finding out which parts were real and how she could become whatever she wanted to be.

Back in Boston, where Daddy had worked hard as a plumber and Mom played the good wife role as best she could, there'd been plenty of encouragement. They were proud she was going to college, the first in her family, proud of the scholarship. What they didn't know would never have to hurt them—the kinky thoughts she'd have, coming in a rush until she had to find some way to release the pressure. Goody Two-Shoes, they'd called her in high school, and she'd always been secretly proud of the tag. If only they knew.

Iona tested the shower water before slipping off her terrycloth bathrobe and hanging it neatly. She let the water just flow over her body before doing anything else, before reaching for the little shampoo bottle, before the coconut-smelling moisturizing soap, before allowing herself to rub, then tweak her nipples—one, then the other—with her right hand, while her left found its way down to her clit.

Between the studly swimmer and her mental excursions into Saudi Arabia, Iona had started to get wet. This was the way it always happened—two ideas jammed up against each other and made her hot in some unexpected way. She'd been working as an undercover photojournalist—with Mom's black Irish blood and Dad's Sicilian, Iona had passed herself off as a Saudi woman, learning Arabic, rising at dawn for prayers and prostration to Mecca, while infiltrating an international terrorist organization. Only she'd slipped; one of the women caught her at her laptop and turned her in.

Naturally, they would be unmerciful to her—an American, an infidel, a spy. Pushed down, blindfolded and gagged, for an endless bumpy ride in a jeep, her head buried in a blanket that smelled like camel piss and gasoline; pulled to her feet, led into a tent, passed from hand to hand until somebody removed the blindfold. Sitting behind a low, long table in semidarkness she saw a man, his face mostly hidden by a white robe, cleaning a powerful semiautomatic—a Glock, maybe.

He wheeled around, stood up and pulled back the robe. The dude from the pool, Mr. All-American! What was he doing in this captured-by-Saudi-slave-traders fantasy, a personal favorite? But then more hands had pushed her roughly to her knees, and a voice whispered in broken English, "Not to look at the face." Pool guy sat on the edge of the table and opened his robe, revealing about ten inches of thick pink cock. She felt cold metal meet her right temple; the man behind her pulled loose the gag and pressed her mouth against the pool guy's swollen cockhead.

They'd probably torture her and kill her anyway, or so went the standard scenario. She tried to balance herself on her knees and launch her head forward as far as it would go without her tipping over, but it was tough to keep a center of gravity with her hands firmly tied behind her back. He was already oozing pre-come as she wrapped her lips around his cock and began a steady rhythm, trying to lap as much of the shaft as she could with her tongue. Again, the hands pushed her mouth down on cock, and she had to suppress the sudden gag reflex. If she showed disrespect, they might just kill her. Iona squeezed her eyes shut, filled her lungs with air and took as much cock as she could down her throat. Pool guy's breath had become more ragged as she steadily took his inches; he had his own hands clamped around the nape of her neck and she felt them dig in harder as he pulled her roughly down, so she almost couldn't breathe.

She sucked his slick shaft up and down, faster and faster, until at last he erupted, his hot come dashing the back of her throat. But there was more—the hands behind her twisted into her long, dark hair and pulled—and pool guy's cock popped out of her mouth like a cork, jetting hot come over her upturned face. Flecks of it got in her hair, her eyebrows, trickled down the side of her mouth, and she knew without being told that she would have to eat as much come as she could reach. When she'd finished licking him like a cat, cleaning the come off his shaft and balls, the hands from behind shoved the gag in her mouth again and she was lifted to her feet.

With her left hand working her clit, she'd gotten herself so hot she was able to move three, four fingers in her pussy and wriggle them; Iona then came so hard she immediately felt faint, and had to gingerly ease herself down into the tub. The shower shot a steady stream of warm water across her chest as she slowly lathered herself, barely able to touch her engorged nipples, moving in semicircles down her stomach and down to her pussy.

Iona's head felt like a freshly popped balloon, and as she stared at the water trickling down her ankles, she suddenly remembered that she'd signed up for a slot at the editing bay in the communications department, and needed to haul ass to campus. There was no point in shampooing now—she felt too drained to do it properly, anyway. She steadied herself against the shower rail and pulled herself regretfully out of the tub, toweled off, and slipped into denim cutoffs.

Normally, Iona wouldn't dream of showing up at school without the usual beautification process. But this was a weekend, she had commitments to meet, and she probably wouldn't run into too many people in the basement of Olsen Hall, where they kept the editing equipment. As she glided through Westbrook Village on her twelve-speed, she thought about her fantasy with the mystery guy from the pool.

Ever since she hit puberty, she'd had these imaginary encounters, and they'd gotten more detailed and complicated; more twisted. Like nothing she'd ever done in real life. With a heavy Catholic upbringing, Iona had been raised to be careful around boys. In fact, she was still only a few steps away from virginity, and those encounters had been frantic, slipshod scramblings with her senior year boyfriend in the back of his battered Ford pickup.

Kent was a quarterback, popular, and made good grades in school. She admired him because she knew that he had a job at a machine shop to help out his sick Mom, and sometimes came to classes so tired he would fall asleep in the back of the class. She'd found out about his extracurricular labor one lazy summer afternoon at the Dairy Queen, when he came in wearing grease-stained overalls and had his hair done up in a red bandanna.

He looked embarrassed, although she didn't know why. Maybe because she was in all the AP classes, wore glasses, and had a reputation as a brainiac, he thought she was stuck-up. Actually, Iona went out of her way to efface her working-class roots, hoping people would mistake her for one of the prepsters. The socialites, of course, knew she came from the wrong neighborhood and shunned her; the other smart kids were mostly misfits and tormented geeks, and the jocks weren't aware she existed. It had always been important to her to be thought of first for her mind, even as her body filled out into an object of pure lust. She knew she was way beyond cute, and the stupid girls in gym made a point of snubbing her. So when she saw Kent that day, she expected him to treat her the way everyone else did.

When he actually talked to her, and they had downed a few sodas together, Iona felt something give way in her carefully prepared world. But after they'd dated for a few months and things got hot and heavier, she discovered that a chasm had formed between the things she fantasized of doing and what her body was capable of doing.

At eighteen, she wanted to give it up to him, and did, but she'd also wanted to open up to him completely, and couldn't. It was the ultimate irony—she liked him so much, thought he was fine, and the perfect gentleman to boot. And that was the problem. As much as she thought she wanted a guy who'd treat her with respect, she only came when she imagined some stranger yanking up her skirt and forcing her arms behind her back with one meaty paw, slapping her over the hood of a muscle car and fucking her senseless.

Kent never understood why she had to drop him. She tried to explain that it was not him or anything he was doing. "Girls always say that," he said, uncharacteristically forlorn. She held his hands tightly in her own and said some bullshit about a life lesson, how she was changing and confused and had to spend some energy on herself for a change.

She knew as the words sped from her mouth that it was all lies, and hated herself for doing this to a guy she really cared about. She also knew that, just as the cliché said, it was for his own good. He didn't need to learn what she really wanted, what she simultaneously feared and desired. It would blow his sweet mind.

Iona locked her bike and walked down to the basement of Olsen, skipping the elevator. Opening the door of the editing bay, she was surprised to find somebody else was already there, hunkered down in front of a computer and pushing a stream of images back and forth with his mouse. Even more surprising, she recognized the guy—but from where? He could be any clean-cut blonde jock, except—and her breathing got shallow suddenly—that he was a specific blonde jock, the one from the morning, the one who'd set things in motion like a binary chemical bomb and made her explode in the shower without having laid eyes on her.

"Hey," she said.

He turned half his face to her, eyes still following the movement on his screen. "Hey." Up close, he reminded her of that actor who'd been in *American Pie* and *Rollerball*, the same hunky slice of Americana, with an ever-so-slight sneer in his smile that said he knew it. Iona sat at a computer on the opposite side of his, about three rows down.

She needed to concentrate on the task at hand. Fishing for a CDR from her tote bag, she fed it into the machine and clicked on the clapper icon. A toolbox came up and she began to run footage back and forth, some things she and Sandy had filmed at her Brentwood apartment just to get some raw material she could play around with.

Sandy had a handheld digital camcorder, the same thing they'd shot most of *The Blair Witch Project* with. There was some major dopey stuff on the disc, real amateur-hour shots of neighborhood kids running back and forth chasing a dog, somebody throwing a Frisbee, a BBQ, and then some tricky dolly shots down the hallway. Sandy was going through a whole Brian De Palma period, and Iona didn't care as long as they could capture some images and mess with them. In two days, Sandy was going to be her techie, producer, and camera gal, and the real test of their collaborative talents would commence. Iona couldn't wait.

The task before her now was essentially an equipment check. Sandy had discovered this warehouse in Lincoln Heights where they could rent the entire top floor for practically nothing. Of course, it was a crime-ridden neighborhood—so bad that nobody dared whitewash the graffiti splashed over every free inch of the building. That was a good way to get yourself shot.

The warehouse would be their studio for the community access cable program they were going to launch. Over the past few weeks, they'd hauled over monitors and DAT machines, cameras, a digital mixing board, and boom mikes, with Sandy's friend from the drama department fabricating a set out of corkboard. They'd lugged up a sofa from a yard sale in Pasadena, perfectly serviceable except for some minor scratches in the vinyl, laid down some throw rugs, and before long had crafted something that would fool the cameras. On the show, Iona would profile local artists and politicos and introduce segments she and Sandy had shot.

Iona clicked on some footage they'd compiled while fitting out the warehouse. One shot showed them pushing the sofa up a 45-degree ramp to the freight elevator. It had been an exceptionally hot day and they were both wearing shorts and tank tops. Sandy was a fire engine redhead with a hot little body and dragon tattoos crawling over her shoulders, a truly fearless individual with a dark sense of humor. She was also the only one who knew about Iona's secret fantasies.

Sandy had started the vodka and orange juice breaks as a way for them to relax from the stress of the broadcast project, but they had become something else, too. They were Truth or Dare sessions. Iona had never had a friend like Sandy Gold, a true free spirit, and since they'd met at freshman orientation and discovered they shared majors, they did most things together—homework, hunting boys, and partying. Iona knew she needed someone like Sandy to shake things up for her, because left to her own devices she usually found herself staring back at the long rut she'd made in the earth.

On the third week's vodka break, they were lounging around Sandy's apartment, fresh from a dip in the pool, when Sandy started talking about doing things with girls. At first, Iona thought she was joking—Sandy mixed so much kidding with the serious stuff sometimes it was hard to tell which was which. But when she saw Sandy's wicked grin and the faraway look in her dark jade eyes, Iona knew this was one of those for real moments.

Which was why she needed to focus on broadcast journalism, making her debut clean and professional. Iona spliced together a rough cut from shots of the set, the hallway dolly footage and a scene from Sandy's kitchen. The digital editing came so effortlessly, not like the laborious strips of film and microscopic splicing tape she'd started with long ago. It was easy to see tangible results with a few strokes of the keyboard, a swipe of the mouse, easy to undo mistakes and try new things without worrying about wasting valuable resources.

Feeling sufficiently prepared, Iona sat up and recovered the CDR, then walked toward the door. She snuck a glance at Blondie, who seemed to have finished whatever he was doing and had also gotten up to go.

Their eyes met for a second that seemed to last forever. "Hey, aren't you—" they both started, and Iona flashed him one of her patented quick grins that showed all her sparkling whites. "We both live at Elmwood, don't we," he said. "Hi, I'm Brent." He stuck out his hand.

"Iona," she said, trying to ignore flashbacks from the morning's shower scene. "I guess we're both in communications. I just moved out of the dorms, 'cause they had some reconstruction going on." As usual, she was explaining too much to a cute guy. What the hell—he wasn't telepathic. "A couple of us got vouchers to move into off-campus housing. I'm actually glad—it beats all hell out of the dorms."

"Yeah," Brent said with a broad smile. "Bet you don't miss the food."

She nodded, trying not to giggle.

"So I heard that you and Sandy were doing a show."

"You know Sandy? She's never mentioned you before."

"We met a couple of weeks ago. I'm actually new to the program—transferred from up north. Needed the change of scenery, you know?"

"Change is always good," said Iona, thinking that she sounded incredibly dorky. "So—did Sandy tell you we're looking for a crew guy?"

"Yeah?"

"Yeah," she said, feeling bolder and more flirtatious by the second. "Know anybody, maybe, I don't know, 6'3", strong, good with his hands?"

"I've hustled some equipment in my time," Brent said. "When do you need an extra set of hands?"

"Monday. Sandy can give you the directions. That would be nice—I mean, I'd, we'd both really appreciate the help." She was getting tongue-tied, thinking about him in that bizarre scene. "Well, I hope to see you then!"

"Sounds good—catch you Monday!"

He walked out the door. Iona took a few seconds to breathe and get herself together before she slung her tote bag over her shoulder and left, walking in the opposite direction as Brent.

Monday afternoon Iona nearly missed the off-ramp as she approached Lincoln Heights and broadcasting history. Ever since Saturday her brain had been trying to replay the scene with Sandy in the kitchen, and she had managed to keep it semi-subconscious. But as she tooled down the road in her black Mazda Miata, keeping time on the steering wheel with an industrial dance mix Sandy had burned for her—KMFDM, Nine Inch Nails and White Zombie—she couldn't tell one from the other. It was as if something was adjusting the signal in her head, sending sharp squawks of feedback the further away her mind tried to stray. Finally she had to give in, because the thoughts weren't going away. Thoughts about Sandy, about her questions, and Iona's revelations; about the way Sandy suddenly wriggled out of her yellow bikini bottoms and pushed her red bush in Iona's face. Hands on hips, she'd suddenly assumed a commanding tone. "Eat me," she said.

Had she, though? Had that happened? Whenever Iona drank, which had been practically never before college, things went on she later had to disentangle—reality from fantasy, truth from lies. What was really going on in front of her and what she wanted. The lines blurred at those moments; it was as if she could see the veil drop and the inner workings of a situation revealed. She would remember a drunken wisdom—that most interactions she had with people were just thin masks. If you dropped one step below the surface, you could see the masks for what they were, and what lay beneath them, the same needs everywhere, the same longings.

She didn't need to tell Sandy she wanted to eat her pussy like a little bitch, could smell the sharp tang of it mixed together with her own hunger. And Sandy, bless her heart, knew when to stop too before things got out of hand. "That's a dare you can give me a rain check on, if you like," she had said, hoisting up her briefs and changing the subject to sports or something equally neutral.

A rain check. Funny, because the radio had said something that morning about drizzle, and the skies had been clouding up. As she pulled into the parking lot beside the dumpster, Iona scanned to see if Sandy had arrived yet. Sandy's Lexus was not in sight, instead there was just some white panel truck with tinted windows. That was odd, but not scary odd; maybe it was the building manager or a maintenance person. As she stepped out of the car, Iona put out a hand and was only half-surprised to see a fat raindrop splash in the center of her palm.

Then she remembered her conversation with Brent. Maybe that was his vehicle, even though it looked more like something Ted Bundy would drive, not the wheels of a babe athlete. Anyway, she was a little early, as usual. Glad she'd remembered to bring an umbrella, she opened it and punched the security code on the panel next to the stairway door. She fished in her purse for the keys and found the right one, a slightly bent silver key. When it twisted all the way around, she tried the door and found it was already unlocked.

Slightly annoyed, she folded the umbrella and walked to the stairs. Whoever had come in wasn't big on safety precautions; nor, apparently, did they need much light. She pulled out her pen flashlight and trained a thin sliver of illumination along the right-hand wall until she found the light switch. Then she heard something heavy drop in the darkness next to her, and things began to happen very quickly.

The attack was efficient and well-coordinated. Iona's arms were roughly yanked behind her; at the same instant, somebody else stifled her scream with duct tape. She tried to put up a struggle, but couldn't tell which direction her abductors were coming from, and after her hands and feet had been cinched tight, she couldn't even move an elbow.

"Live one," said a familiar female voice. As somebody hoisted her over their shoulder like a sack of laundry, Iona scanned the dark, but only saw strobe-like fragments. There were at least three of them, all wearing white utility jumpsuits and shiny reflective masks. The one who had just spoken leaned in close and she could see herself as in a distorted mirror, big eyes and a ragged gray rectangle over her mouth. "It's your big moment, Iona—are you excited?"

Iona didn't know if she was excited or scared, ready to shit herself or come her brains out. Even though she could start to see the scenario, the plan Sandy and Brent had built out of scraps of drunken confessionals and their own perversity, she'd never in a million years imagined that they would act on it. The freight elevator arrived and suddenly they were going up. She figured Brent was carrying her, and, of course, Sandy owned the voice. But who was the other person? Nobody said a word as they ascended; the doors opened and they carried her out.

Several million watts glowed over the set, which shone like a large jewel in the vast darkness of the room. Soon more lights flickered on, and she could see the banks of monitors, all showing the same scene from slightly different angles. Five cameras took a live feed. The floor was swathed in gaffer's tape, holding down dozens of cables—some going into the DAT machine, others hooked to the video mixing board, others of unknown purpose.

They plonked her down on the sofa, on her back. The stranger undid the rope around her ankles, and as she flexed her feet, Sandy tilted the mask up and let down her hair down—it looked for a second like flowing fire. "Surprise!" she said, ripping the tape from Iona's mouth. It stung for a second. Her tongue felt like a wad of cotton.

"Okay, funny funny," Iona said. "Damn." She let out a long breath. "You took me completely by surprise. So are we going to joke around or do we have a show to do?"

Brent now took off his mask. "We definitely have a show to do."

"So untie my hands," said Iona. "I can't be a proper hostess and a kidnap victim all at the same time." This was all fun and games, but people would be watching who weren't in on the joke. Her dad had rigged up some kind of satellite deal so he and Mom could watch their daughter do her first live broadcast. Not only that, but a grade, and more importantly, her career, were all riding on this moment. "I really do have a sense of humor, guys," she said, looking around. "It's just that you know how much I need to do this right. *We* need to do this right."

Sandy was still smiling, that slightly cruel, definitely wicked, smile she'd had after giving Iona that pussy snapshot. "You're absolutely right. But you can't be a proper hostess if you're wound up like a spring, either. Let me help you relax."

She came in closer, and Iona could smell her perfume, like night-blooming jasmine. She'd unzipped the jumper down to her navel and was totally nude underneath, her big, firm tits inches from Iona's face. "Let me help you relaaax," she said, purring, taking Iona's left earlobe in her mouth. She felt a sudden blush of pleasure cascade down her body and realized she was starting to breathe harder.

Sandy's soothing tone continued as she worked her way down Iona's neck, softly suckling and blowing on her skin. Iona let out a low moan. She felt as if she were underwater, like none of this was happening, but she still couldn't move her hands, and her best friend was kissing her full on the lips now. She caught the sudden phosphorescent flash of a white lozenge on Sandy's tongue, and before she realized what had happened, swallowed the tab of X. "Good girl," said Sandy.

Iona had never taken a drug harder than aspirin in her life. She'd researched the rave scene for an article in the school newspaper, but what she'd found out scared her away. Would she get brain damage now? Would her neurons implode? Would she wind up some slaphappy party girl, a zombie blowup doll? And God, her parents, the show—she looked up at the monitors and saw that the cameras had been recording the entire scene. Was this going out live?

"It *is* a live broadcast," Sandy said, answering her unspoken question. "And I'm sure it will be, um, educational for all concerned." Brent chuckled at that one, as did her other abductor, who still hadn't spoken a word. "How do you feel now, girlie?"

Iona was feeling streams of sensation glide across every nerve ending. Her brain was prattling nonsense like a silly mushroom. The lights were suddenly more sharply in focus and cooler on her eyes, and the colors—so intense. She nodded rather than speaking. "I'm kind of funny."

"We're all very amused," said Sandy. "Although—" and here she placed an index finger to her chin à la Marilyn Monroe—"your parents may not see things in quite the same light."

"You're not seriously, I mean, we're not on the air, right?"

"Are we on the air?"

Brent nodded.

Iona's next protest came out like "Glorf" as the unknown guy— she guessed it was a guy—strapped a ball gag into her mouth. Sandy opened her blouse. "My my, what fancy underwear," she said. And traveling down, lower, "Are those French-cut lace panties?" She tugged Iona out of her panties as two pairs of hands pinioned open her legs. Sandy slid a long wet tongue into her pussy. "Shaved, yet," she said, coming up for air. "You will never cease to surprise me." She began to lick around Iona's clit while her hands gingerly explored her pussy. "So wet, yet so young!" she said. "Gllmph" came Iona's indignant reply. "Exactly," nodded Sandy, as if this was the sagest wisdom she'd heard in years.

Iona could only stare dumbly as Sandy found the zipper in back of her skirt and slid it down past the flesh-colored stockings.

Not being able to resist, move, or speak, Iona didn't know what to do. It wasn't her fault, not at all, when she'd shared those intimate fantasies with Sandy. It had just been girl talk. This was kidnapping, abduction, illegal confinement, and God—what Sandy could do with her tongue. She wanted to clamp her legs around Sandy's head and drive her pussy into her mouth, make her suckle it, kiss it, annihilate her. Iona was dizzy and silly and angry and crazy with pleasure all at the same time.

Then Sandy stood up, a glistening thread of spit hanging in the air between them as she did. The guy who'd been holding her left leg let go for a second and Sandy's hands clamped down to replace his while he walked around to the front of the sofa.

"Iona, we'd like you to meet a new friend of ours. His name's Rudolfo. We met him today, selling, what was it, oranges?"

Rudolfo was a big-shouldered Mexican guy with a network of tattoos embroidering his entire upper chest and flowing down to his rock-hard stomach. He was nude now, except for a crucifix on a silver chain. "Si, naranjas," he answered, flashing a gold-plated grin. He held his huge cock toward Iona as the other two suspended her from her ankles. Sandy reached over and undid the ball gag. "Now be a good girl and eat everything that's served."

Iona could only move her head back and from side to side, but she still had control over her mouth. They could treat her like a whore, but she wasn't going to suck off some fucking Mexican. She clamped her jaw tight.

"A little cooperation here would be nice," said Rudolfo.

She shook her head.

"Oh I get it—just 'cause I'm Mexican, I'm not good enough for you. You're not going to let the brown bomber past your *gringa* lips, right? Have to drink a gallon of disinfectant just to get that taste out." He patted his stomach. "See that, that's from the Army. I served my country in Desert Storm while dumb bitches like you were showing your little ass off to Daddy's friends just to give them a thrill." Rudolfo laid a quick, flat slap on Iona's cheek. "I'm not going to wait all day for you, *ruca*."

Just below his ribcage, Rudolfo had a Sacred Heart, tangled in barbed wire that wrapped around the legend "Born to Raise Hell" in fiery letters. "I see you're admiring the artwork. Come in for a closer look, bitch." He pinched her nostrils and wrapped a hand around her throat. Eventually she had to breathe.

Rudolfo guided his cock into her mouth. Slowly they slid her down from the sofa until she was lying on the floor; they retied the rope around her ankles and attached it to her wrists. That gave her just enough room to perch herself on her elbows.

"Just up and down," said Rudolfo, and Iona obliged. She didn't have a ghost of a choice. As she sucked, her bonds were again removed and she felt something big and hard press against her ass. Deft fingers slicked her asshole with lube, and as she struggled to gain her balance yet again, holding Rudolfo's cock for support, she felt Brent slide up her ass.

It hurt a lot at first. Iona thought she was going to be torn to shreds, her bowels ripped open. She forced herself not to think, just follow instructions. Rudolfo's cock swelled as she steadily ate; there was so much she had to manage the rest by locking her elbows as close as they would go and stroking the base with both hands.

As she did, she felt her asshole begin to tingle and warm like it was thawing out, and then she wanted it so bad she could scream. She pushed her haunches back against Brent as he gripped her ass cheeks and sank his cock to the hilt. It felt so good, her pussy began to throb.

Oh God, please fuck my ass, she thought. Brent was grinding against her tailbone, slamming her, and every movement he made in her opened a new need, a new pain. She was going to come and there was nothing she could do about it; pussy juices were already oozing down her leg.

"You like it, princess?" asked Rudolfo. "You want some genuine south of the border flavor?" He pulled his cock out of her mouth and began to jack himself off—the length of his shaft was already slick with pre-come. He squeezed his eyes shut and the first load shot directly into her surprised, open mouth. "Bull's-eye!" he said, laughing. Come was dribbling off her chin, and she felt Brent driving it faster and harder until he exploded, filling her asshole with hot jizz. Rudolfo kept spurting, hitting her in the cheek, in the eyebrows, in her carefully teased and treated hair. "Just think of it as conditioner."

She looked up for a second and saw Sandy scoping the scene with her handheld. What she saw, the monitors caught, and what was going out to the world was not Iona Cortese, pro newscaster and girl next door, but a drugged-out slut, mouth and ass full of cock, who looked like she was loving every minute of it.

With Open Arms
by Chelsea Shepard

Chelsea Shepard has coauthored two novels with Adrian Hunter: *Association* and *Once Bitten*. About "With Open Arms," Shepard writes: "Submission is in the mind. The smell of leather, the tightness of rubber, the cold touch of metal links may bring out interesting reactions, but only if your brain will allow them. Floggers and clothespins will turn into pleasurable toys, but only if your mind is set upon that goal. Physical restraints are nothing compared to our mental barriers. In fact, cuffs and chains often liberate us from ourselves and allow us to submit, feel, enjoy. Without them, the journey into submission may be surprisingly harder, although more rewarding. 'With Open Arms' tells about such a journey."

A bird trapped in a sea of black oil, pointlessly flapping its wings and getting more exhausted by the minute. Frustrated and pathetic, that's me. But more than that, I'm confused. Why, of all body parts, did he leave my arms free?

The scene started in a typical way. Very promising, too. It was a rainy Sunday—our favorite kind—and Malcolm summoned me straight after breakfast. I had been waiting for this moment all week, and my excitement grew exponentially with each step down to the basement.

When I entered the quiet room bathed in dark orangey light, my lover was already at work transforming our multipurpose wooden cross into a single, sturdy beam. The top portion was firmly bolted to the wall, and he was screwing the opposite end to a bracket mounted on the floor, leaving the beam at an exact angle of 45 degrees.

We had done this before.

He liked to tie me to the beam from head to toe, then tease and torture me for hours, safe in the knowledge that the bondage was comfortable, yet totally inescapable. I always loved every second of it.

When I realized it was time for an encore, I smiled. No suspension, no hogtie, no bending over . . . this was going to be easy.

And fun.

Impulsively, I looked around to see if he had already retrieved any floggers, crops, or whips from one of the closets, but I caught his eye instead. He was grinning in that mischievous way of his, when he's up to something so evil, even my wild imagination cannot envision it.

My smile disappeared under his lips as he kissed me hard.

"Are you ready?" he whispered.

As I nodded, he motioned me to the beam. I lay against it, naked, still and silent, as per my permanent instructions when I was in this room.

Malcolm is a practical and efficient dom. With the help of the series of heavy leather straps fixed to the back of the beam, he secured my legs, hips, and torso in a matter of minutes.

After that, he did something peculiar; he locked leather cuffs around my wrists, then chained them to the ceiling, leaving my arms perpendicular to my body. This was weird. Sensing a challenge, I tried to guess his nefarious plan.

When he began uniting my body with the beam in Saran Wrap, I figured I'd sussed his strategy. He was going to mummify me—another big hit in our Top 40—and was saving my arms for the end, where he would wrap them over my chest on top of the first layer of cellophane. I silently approved. This was a neat idea, and I am certainly one for redundant bondage. As I always say, the more, the merrier.

At peace with the procedure, I relaxed and watched him do the heavy work. My heartbeat accelerated for a few minutes while he swathed my head, but we were nothing if not prudent; once I knew I could breathe normally, I reveled in the warm comfort of the soft helmet he had created for me.

After the first layer was finished, Malcolm added a second one, this time with black electrical tape applied even more methodically, careful not to miss a single spot. The confinement was as tight as I could hope for. No slack at all, except around my neck where I felt a layer of air between my skin and the thick coating formed by the cellophane and the tape. But my head was enveloped as meticulously as my toes; only my eyes, nostrils, and mouth were exposed.

At that moment, I realized he hadn't plugged me, nor had he left any open spaces that provided easy access to my sex, or even my breasts. I felt a sharp pinch of disappointment. I was not in the mood for complete isolation. I wanted to feel something. Pain or pleasure, just something.

I debated telling Malcolm about my feelings, but this was against the rules. I was allowed to speak if I was in trouble—he usually left me ungagged during a heavy bondage process until he felt certain I could stay in that position for hours without an errant strap numbing my limbs—but not if I disagreed with his decision. Such a breach was likely to get me in more trouble. If he had chosen to leave me isolated for two hours, a single complaint might encourage him to double that time.

So I stayed silent and resolved to make the most out of an unwanted situation. After all, I was comfortable, and I could always rest, if not fall asleep. There were worse fates in my complicated lifestyle.

When Malcolm finished with the tape, my body looked like a glittering black missile. Ready for launch, sir.

Well, not quite ready, apparently. To my surprise, he added another layer of tape. Now, that was completely redundant. I was already so tightly wrapped, a third coat didn't make any difference. Such a waste of time, I reflected. So unlike him, too. And when was he going to do something about my still-naked arms anyway?

He stopped packaging my immobile body after he had exhausted the fifth roll of tape. He let me sip a bit of water, and then decided to shut me down. The big trainer gag was purchased specifically for use with the cross, as he was able to buckle the mouth strap behind the beam, pinning my head tight against the polished wood. Again, he had done this before. But he was full of surprises today.

First, he hadn't blindfolded me. Not too unusual, but a must for an isolation scene. However, this oversight wasn't nearly as confusing as the sound of hammering behind my head. He was nailing the mouth strap to the beam! Okay, I knew I was constantly asking for stricter bondage, but wasn't this a wee bit out of line?

Slightly agitated, I pulled at my arms and the rattling of the chains caught his attention. At last.

Malcolm unlocked the chains, as well as the cuffs, and then . . . left.

"Have fun," he snorted, before he closed the door.

Stupor doesn't begin to describe my feeling as he deserted me in one of the best bondages ever . . . with my arms free! He hadn't even bothered to confine them in mittens. My fingers, "my dancing digits," as he would affectionately call them, were free to pry as they pleased.

Had I missed something here? We sometimes played "damsel in distress" scenes, where he tied me up, only to give me a chance to escape. And he always timed my efforts. If I didn't break free, I was in trouble. If I did, I was in trouble, too. I could never lose.

However, we always discussed that option beforehand. I knew I was allowed to escape. Heck, that was the whole point of the scene. But he hadn't mentioned the possibility at all. I tried to remember our chat during breakfast, even the hints sprinkled in our conversations the day before, but nothing, absolutely nothing, had intimated DID.

Besides, leaving my arms free made no sense, even in the framework of such a scene. No villain or kidnapper would leave his captive's hands free. If anything, hands were the only part he would tie up.

Malcolm couldn't have forgotten, could he? No, that was by far the most unlikely explanation.

Eventually, I decided this was a test. To see if I would stay still when temptation was so strong. That was evil enough for him. He had outsmarted me yet again.

Well, I was going to show him. Yes, I was able to control myself, and yes, I would turn the awkward situation to my advantage since, with my arms free, I could scratch the itch when it popped up. Literally. It's something few bondage stories mention, but an unscratchable itch may become the worst aspect of a scene. Especially when you have long hair like I do, and a stray strand escapes. How wonderful to be able to flip it off my nose at will.

After what felt like half an hour, my good mood deteriorated, and my rebellious side took over. I could no longer resist the urge, nor the challenge. If I showed him I could stay still without ropes, why would he bother to tie me up properly in the future? I was going to show him what a bad girl I was.

I started to work on the tape near my hips, tearing, digging, squeezing. I tried other places, like the junctions at my neck and armpits where I figured the tape wouldn't be so tight. But the layers were too thick to break through, and all the end pieces were plastered against my back and thus impossible to reach.

Revising my tactics, I tried to remove the gag. Ha. Now I knew why he had nailed the strap. My fingers would bleed before I could pull those nails back an inch.

Giving up on the trainer, I tried the tape again and again, getting more frustrated by the minute. Angrier, too. What was the point here?

I was sweating and breathing much too hard. My arms were tired, my fingers sore. I broke two nails. The ones on my fingers, of course.

I got desperate. I wanted to stop and ask him what he expected from me.

I looked at the tiny camera that hung from the opposite corner of the room. I had hated that digital spy since the day Malcolm installed it. It was an intrusion on my solitude, and I resented it. I didn't understand the point of watching me when I was tied up so severely, I could barely move my eyelids. Even when I was lost in a frenzy of orgasms caused by an unstoppable vibrator, my body was trapped in bonds that prevented any visible movement. So could I have at least a bit of privacy? Even blindfolded, I was aware of its presence. It seemed to spoil all the fun.

After a few weeks, however, I stopped caring. If he enjoyed watching me lie still or squirm an inch or two, who was I to argue when all my needs were so wonderfully taken care of?

Eventually, I got so used to the tiny eye in the corner, it became my best friend and the only ally I had when things went too far. I knew Malcolm had learned to interpret my slightest moves, and he always returned to the room promptly whenever he felt I was too sore or too bored.

Now I was staring at the lens, pleading with my eyes. What do you want me to do? Why won't you come back and tie up my arms? Or at least play with me?

My silent pleas were useless. The basement door remained inexorably shut on my growing misery.

Tears welled up, as they always did when I couldn't deal with a situation any longer. This was silly, too. Crying because my arms were untied and I didn't know why? We were, after all, professionals. But it must have been hours by then, and anyone who's been left in isolation will tell you that a moment eventually comes when the restlessness and frustration grow so strong, you simply lose it and become wretched, eager for a human touch, a word, eye contact. This is the normal cue for the sadistic top to return and exploit that vulnerability by turning it into sheer erotic power. A simple caress of the calf could send pre-orgasmic shivers up to your womb.

Yet there was no such excitement for me to enjoy. After another hour, I was still on my own, all cried out and, finally, resigned. Whatever he wanted, I would accept it. I had reached deepest subspace, a mindset that took some effort, or, as in this case, utter desolation to reach.

When Malcolm opened the door, one look in each other's eyes confirmed what we both knew. I was his, to do as he pleased.

My arms lay still down my sides, as if bound by the most restrictive straps.

First, he cautiously cut two large strips of tape to expose my breasts and sex. I sighed deeply, already grateful.

The first whiplash on the side of my breast was so severe, I gasped, but took it bravely, undoubtedly helped by my near-hypnotic state. He repeated the assault on my other breast. Then he moved to my sex, and struck it with equal ferocity.

The pain was intense, but not entirely unwelcome. I was craving for relief, and it didn't take long for the first orgasm to strike in perfect synch with the whip. Untied, I would have arched and bent like a rubber band, unable to stop those natural contractions all over my body. But here, the only signs revealing my inner turmoil were the mad movements of my eyes, muffled moans, and the faint creaks in the beam. The rest of me was motionless.

Even my arms.

When the realization hit, I opened my eyes wide and stared at my executioner. He was already smiling, knowing before I did the amazing accomplishment we had reached today.

Although I know that pain is an expressway to extreme pleasure, it's hard for me to acknowledge it and not resist. If it wasn't for the bondage, I would run away, or at least cover myself to escape it. I know there's a prize waiting for me beyond the well-known threshold. Only I need ropes and straps to help me get there.

Not today. While I couldn't escape the beam, I could have used my arms to protect myself, and I didn't. I accepted the pain and took the journey boldly, certain of reaching my goal, no longer afraid or ashamed of my own special needs.

I returned Malcolm's smile as best as I could behind the gag, and he rightly took it as a request for more.

Before returning to my chaotic bliss, I made a mental note to ask him next time to leave my legs free. And wait eight hours instead of four.

Erin's Rules
by Erin Sanders

The author of "Erin's Rules" wrote this story under a pseudonym, she says, because "While my biggest fantasy is to be in a 24/7 relationship like the one I describe, I'd rather everyone not know that."

Like many successful professional women, she enjoys the dream of relinquishing control full-time. "Erin's Rules" describes one submissive's ideal.

RULE 1: When I am in the house, I am naked. I must remove all my clothing when I come home. The only time I'm allowed to put it back on while I'm home is if someone comes to the door who wouldn't understand or doesn't need to understand my status— a delivery person, neighbor, or friend who doesn't know that I am a slave. Then, if it is warm outside, I put on a very tight pair of shorts and a crop-top, without bra, panties, or shoes. If it is cold outside, I put on a very tight pair of white sweatpants, a tight white thermal undershirt, and a pair of fur-lined slippers, with no bra or panties. The shirt must be light enough to reveal my nipples and areolae underneath.

RULE 2: I shave my pussy each week. Immediately after shaving, I masturbate to orgasm, to remind me that what pleases Master pleases me.

RULE 3: I wear only skirts and shorts. I am not allowed to wear slacks or jeans.

RULE 4: I do not wear underwear. As my breasts are small, I also do not wear a bra. If my nipples become visible while I am in public, I may not cross my arms to hide them.

RULE 5: I will be wet at all times, so that Master may fuck me whenever he wants. If I am not sexually aroused, I will make sure that my pussy stays wet with lubricant.

RULE 6: I am not allowed to sit on the furniture at home. I may kneel or sit cross-legged on the floor. If I lay on the floor, I may only lay face down and must keep my legs spread.

RULE 7: When I am at home, there will be pornography playing on the television unless guests are over. Master has selected an assortment of discs that are acceptable for me to watch. I may not watch anything else without his permission.

RULE 8: When Master returns home after being away, I will greet him at the door on my knees and offer him oral gratification. If he chooses, he may use me right there in the hallway, with the door still open if he so wishes.

RULE 9: When we are together for the evening or on the weekend, I will ask Master each hour if he would like oral sex. If he says yes, I will give it without hesitation.

RULE 10: Before I make Master come with my mouth, I will ask him if he wishes to come in me or on me. If he wishes to come in my mouth, I will swallow. If he wishes to come on my face, I will not wipe it off until he instructs me to.

RULE 11: Before bed each night, I must ask Master's permission to occupy his bed. If he withholds it, I will sleep on the floor next to his bed.

RULE 12: When Master has a male houseguest who understands and accepts my status, I must offer him the same obedience that I give Master. Upon entering the house, he will be greeted by me on my knees and offered oral sex. For each hour that he is in the house, he will be offered oral sex, and if he accepts, I will provide it without hesitation, up to and including his ejaculation. I will then swallow his come and thank him for it.

RULE 13: Master may allow any man or woman he wishes to use me in whatever way he deems appropriate.

RULE 14: Master may take whatever photographs or videotapes of me he wishes, and may share them in person or electronically with anyone he wants. Master may also instruct me to write erotic letters or e-mails to anyone he wishes to whatever specifications or scenarios he assigns, and I will do my best to make them erotic, exciting, and interesting. I will sign my name.

RULE 15: When Master is traveling, I will call him at least once per day and offer him phone sex. If he accepts, I will do my best to invent a scenario that excites him.

RULE 16: When I am traveling, I will call Master at least three times per day from a private location and ask him if he wishes me to masturbate. If he says yes, I will do so while he listens, and will tell him exactly what I am fantasizing about, in detail. If Master wishes me to engage in sexual activity while I am traveling, I will without question find a partner and do whatever Master has ordered me to do with him (or her), calling Master immediately afterward to describe what a slut I have made of myself.

RULE 17: Master may pierce or tattoo any part of my body he wishes, in any manner he chooses. I will not express reluctance for any modification Master imposes upon me.

RULE 18: Master may instruct me to write down the rules for my behavior and publish them under my real name or a pseudonym, as he sees fit.

RULE 19: I will always love Master no matter what he does.

RULE 20: Master may love me as he sees fit.

Rituals
by Kate Dominic

Kate Dominic has written erotic stories for a large number of publications under many different pen names. In her strikingly original first solo collection, *Any 2 People, Kissing,* released in 2003 by Down There Press, she explores many different sexual orientations and proclivities in both male and female voices.

Of "Rituals," Kate Dominic writes: "Introducing BDSM into a many-years vanilla marriage takes a lot of soul-searching and sometimes difficult (but ultimately rewarding) communication. This story is fiction, written at a time when I was searching for ways to understand the emotions of submission. The writing helped me realize just how not submissive I am—and how that makes a 'switch' relationship a continuing adventure."

Every Friday evening, Don wheels his chair into our bathroom and parks quietly by the door. The movement triggers a quick flash of memory. I see him standing there instead, in the tight black jeans and leather vest and sexy white shirt he was wearing the night we met. His arms were folded on his chest, his cool gray eyes watching me with what I hoped was approval. He'd paid handsomely for me at the slave auction at our local club. I'd knelt naked at his feet, hoping he wouldn't notice my entirely too proud expression at having commanded the highest price of the evening. Just looking at him made my pussy wet. His thick dark curls were shot through with a hint of silver that reminded me of black leather and handcuffs and the severe bondage for which he was famous. He was sadistic and tender and his eyes glinted with arousal when he comforted the crying women he tormented. I'd blushed just thinking about what my body would love to endure to please him. Back then, belonging to him was barely a dream.

The memory fades with the whir of his chair. My master still wears black pants and a white shirt and the same sexy leather vest. His dark hair has much more silver now. He is seated, in his omnipresent chair, his arms lying on the armrests, near his control panels. His face is the same, though. A few more lines, perhaps, but his eyes still glitter with the command that makes my pussy hum when he calls me to his side. It is for his voyeuristic pleasure, as well as my own need for submission, that we make my weekly enema sessions into a ritual of obedience.

Last night, as always, I walked naked to him and knelt beside his chair. I kissed his motionless feet and his now-wasted legs, and the soft, heavy cock resting against his scrotum. I brushed my lips up to where his muscles grew taut and firm over his chest. Then I lifted my head and waited for him to bless me with the warm, controlled strength of his kiss.

"You know what to do, wench," he growled, his breath hot and spicy from his mouthwash.

Even as I whispered, "Yes, sir," I blushed. Don laughed and kissed me on the tip of my nose. I knew better than to stall. I rose and put on a glove. I took a glycerin suppository from the same jar I take into our bedroom each evening for his bedtime ritual. Turning so he could see me, I bent over the counter, swiping lube over my anus and wiggling when I slid my finger in and out. Then I pressed the waxy spike deep into my rectum and stripped off the glove.

"My anus tingles, sir," I flushed, wiggling my hips again. I had standing orders to describe the step-by-step details he couldn't feel anymore. "I'm really going to have to go in a little bit." I batted my eyelashes, giving him my most innocent smile, pretending I thought he might go easy on me, even after all this time together. "How long should I hold it, sir?"

"Two minutes longer than when you really have to go," he said, smiling softly. I stuck out my tongue at him and giggled at his low chuckle. We both knew how short-lived my nervous brattiness is on Friday evenings.

I'd been Don's sub since the night of the auction, long before I'd been his wife. The car accident two years after our wedding had turned our lives doubly upside down. He was paralyzed from his waist down, and even the intense rehab program had been unable to restore full function to his lacerated hands. While his shoulders and upper arms were unbelievably strong, he had almost no fine muscle control below the top of his wrists.

It had taken a lot of negotiation and counseling with a rather unique therapist for us to reach a balance that kept our kinky psyches healthy and happy. I'd learned not to allow my submission and masochism to drain me to the point where I had nothing left to give to the husband and dominant I loved with all my heart. We had a housekeeper, and I worked nine-to-five at a paralegal job I truly enjoyed. Don had a personal attendant twelve hours a day and a college intern who worked half-time as his hands for the architectural designs he still drew for the city.

Our sex life was as kinky as ever. Friday nights were just for us. The suppository was making me fidgety, but I didn't really have to go yet. At Don's direction, I took out the two-quart enema bag. I filled it with water that was almost hot, so it would still be warm by the time I was ready for it. Having my hands in the water made me have to go even more. I told Don, and he laughed. By the time I was ready to screw on the top of the bag, I was clenching my bottom.

"Shall I close the bag, sir?" I held the cap in my hand, hoping the answer was yes. The gleam in his eye told me otherwise even before he shook his head.

"Two teaspoons of soap, pretty one," he said firmly. As I pursed my lips, he added, "Make sure they're full ones, or you'll be punished in a way you don't like, rather than in one you do."

He knew me so well, and he was smiling fiendishly. I muttered "Yes, sir" and took the bottle of enema soap from the cupboard. I turned so he could see me dutifully measuring two full doses into the bag. Then, I attached the cap and tipped the bag over, running the cloudy water through the line. As I closed the clamp, my belly tensed hard and I gasped.

"The sensation is getting intense, sir!"

"Come here," he said quietly. When I stood beside him, he said only, "Straddle me." I took a deep breath, bracing my arms on his shoulders and stepping over his legs. At his command, I lowered myself, until my legs and bottom were spread wide over him and my breasts were even with his mouth. He licked my nipple and I groaned. My breasts were still incredibly tender from his attentions the night before. The need to go was getting so much stronger. In this position, I had to really clench my bottom.

"Tell me how it feels," he ordered. Then he sucked my nipple into his mouth. I gasped, my eyes tearing at the intense stimulation.

"The sensation is m-much stronger now, sir." I squeezed my butt cheeks together hard. "Each time you suck, I feel it all the way down to my cunt. It makes my whole belly contract. Oh, sir!" I stiffened and leaned into his shoulders. "I'm cramping!" I moaned as a wave of peristaltic action flowed over me and I struggled to control my bowels. "I have to go, sir." I clenched my muscles as hard as I could. "I really do!"

"Then you only have two more minutes to wait," he said firmly. I groaned and looked at the bathroom clock, willing the second hand to move faster. It didn't. If anything, each time he sucked, time seemed to stand still.

"I'm so afraid I'm going to have an accident," I gasped. "I'm trying so hard to hold it, but the suppository is working so well. Each time you suck it makes the cramps so intense. Oh!" I rose up slightly, tipping forward yet dutifully keeping my nipple on his merciless tongue. Tears streamed down my face as Don moved his head from one side to the other, sucking my nipples until I was beside myself.

Just as I wailed that I was going to lose control, he bit me and said, "Time's up, wench. Go!"

I scrambled over him and around the divider to the toilet. As I sat there, I sobbed out, "Thank you, sir. Oh, thank you!" I smiled through my tears as his softly chuckled, "You're welcome."

As always, the suppository did exactly what it was supposed to do. When I was finally done and had cleaned up, I picked up the enema bag and carried it over to him. I lowered my eyes, my face blushing hot.

"Straddle me," he said again. I did, resting the bag between us, so we were sharing the warmth.

"Tonight, you will take your enema in the shower, love. You will hang the bag so it is barely a foot above your bottom." He licked my well-sucked nipple. I squirmed at the pain. "You will lube yourself and the nozzle, which you will then insert well into your eager little rectum. At my command, you will open the clamp. The enema will flow into you very slowly. You will tell me exactly how it feels."

As he sucked my nipple, I tightened my grip on his shoulders. "Even though you're well cleaned out, pretty one, the warm soapy water will make you have to go very badly." His lips moved to my other nipple. I was so sore tears stung my eyes. "While you cry out your pain and humiliation to me, you will also enjoy the wicked feeling of water flowing into your ass. Your vulva will become engorged from the pressure. It will stimulate your pussy." He suckled both breasts again, so hard the tears rolled down my face. "You will tell me every sensation, in explicit shameful detail, so I may torment you as befits one so lovely as you." As I trembled against him, he smiled and put a chaste kiss on each tender nipple.

"Take your enema bag to the shower, love. It's time to put this warm soapy water up your bottom."

I moved off of him, my legs trembling and my belly suddenly cold. Our shower had no door and was wide enough for Don's chair, so I had plenty of room. I hung the bag and turned to see his eyes glinting at me like sparks on steel. God, I have loved that look for so long. My heart overflowed with longing for him as I ran the cooled water through the line. When the stream was running warm and viciously cloudy, I closed the clamp.

"I'm ready, sir."

He nodded. "Speak while you lube your anus."

I have standing orders to use petroleum jelly. Don wants my anus well-protected from irritation. I scooped a glob onto my fingers.

"I have two fingers greased. I'm sliding them through my sphincter." I paused, breathing deeply as I worked my fingers in. "I'm playing with my anus a little bit, sir. My fingers feel very good, sliding in and out." I felt my face heat and looked at him from under my eyelashes. "I feel very embarrassed saying that, sir."

Don's eyes were burning into me. I raised my head to look him fully in the face, giving him the honesty that has always been the cornerstone of our relationship. "When I put three fingers in, it reminds me of how your fingers used to feel, sir, when you were teasing my ass open, making it feel so good so you could use me so roughly later. Your touch made me want to come." I put every bit of my love for him into my look as I quietly said. "Now, I feel my own fingers in my ass, but I still want to come. I know you're letting me feel this good so you can torment me later for your pleasure."

God, oh god, I love that man. He looked at me for a long time, his eyes glittering, giving me the look that had always been just for me alone. When he finally spoke, his voice was thick and husky.

"Lube the nozzle and slide it in, beautiful girl. As soon as it's in, look into my eyes and release the clamp. Count slowly to ten, out loud, taking the enema into you, no matter what. At ten, close the clamp. Make no other sound until I command you."

I obeyed instantly. I looked into the steel gray of his eyes and released the clamp. Warm water surged up into me. I felt the soap immediately.

"One," I gasped. My anus trembled and my rectum contracted, but I kept the clamp open, slowly saying "two," then "three." By ten, I was breathing hard. I stared into Don's eyes, drawing strength from his intensity, from the inherent power in his gaze as I closed the valve. My hand started toward my belly, to soothe the waves of tension rolling over me. I caught myself in time and lowered my arm, panting hard as I concentrated on watching his eyes, only his eyes.

"Do you want to rub your belly?" he asked quietly.

"Yes, sir," I gasped, squeezing my cheeks around the nozzle as another wave rolled over me.

"Tell me why as you rub."

"Thank you, sir," I sighed in relief, even though I knew it would be short-lived. "My rectum feels very full. The water has moved well up into my colon. I-I'm . . ." I gasped and straightened, tightening my cheeks desperately. "I want to expel the water, sir. The cramps are intense."

"But not unbearable," he said softly. Tears filled my eyes and I shook my head.

"They're just very . . . intense, sir." I panted, as another wave passed quietly over me.

"If the pain becomes unbearable, you will release immediately. Do you understand?"

"Yes, sir," I said, still rubbing, though the cramps had mostly passed now. Don settled back in his chair and nodded.

"You will take the rest of the bag at your leisure. You may stop five times." His eyes narrowed. "But only five. And you must stimulate your nipples whenever you are resting." As I stared at him, open-mouthed, he continued. "If you need to close your eyes, you may. You may knead your belly as you please. You may cry as you wish. But when your eyes are open . . ." His look was so hot, it made my mouth dry. "When your eyes are open, you must look into mine. You must tell me everything you are feeling, every dirty, shameful detail. And when you have taken the whole bag, you may not release until you climax." He quirked his eyebrow, his eyes radiating pure, delicious cruelty.

"One more thing, my love," he said quietly. "Turn the shower on, slow and warm, and stand in it while you take your enema. Let the water run over your belly and your breasts, so they are stimulated even more by the heat flowing over them. I will take great pleasure in watching your responses."

I whispered, "Yes, sir," so turned-on I had to force myself not to rub my cunt. With one hand holding the nozzle firmly in my bottom, I turned on the shower. When the water ran warm, I stepped into the spray, wincing as it streamed down over my nipples and onto my belly.

"My nipples are very tender, sir. Even the shower hurts. The sensation echoes all the way into my pussy." I looked at him and took a deep breath. "I'm opening the clamp now." I gasped as the water once more flowed into me. It was warm and filling and I tried to pretend it wasn't going to do what I knew it was going to.

"I have to go already, sir, but I'm not closing the nozzle." I moaned, letting him see my discomfort as I kept the water flowing into me and waited for the feeling to pass. "The water's moving up into my colon now, sir. The pressure is less. Oh!" I closed my eyes, arching forward. "I can really feel the soap, sir. My colon is contracting. It wants to flush the soap out, but I'm keeping the valve open." I panted heavily. "It's very unpleasant, sir. The warm water flowing over my belly is making me have to go even more."

A cramp passed over me so hard I had to close the clamp. I glanced at the bag, relieved to see almost a third was gone. I wanted to save my stops for later, when the urge would be worse. But I needed a rest now. With one hand holding the nozzle firmly in my anus, I dutifully put my other hand to my breast and lifted my head to the water, letting it flow down over me as I tugged on the nipple. I cried out loudly, first at the pain from my fingers, then at the cramp that had me almost doubling over.

The feelings were so intense I couldn't speak. I moaned loudly, letting him hear my torment as my belly clenched. I turned so the water was falling full on my nipples, keeping the torturous stimulation my master demanded as I panted through the seemingly endless spasm. As it passed, I released the clamp, cupping my swelling belly in my palm, kneading and rubbing, trying to ease the flow of water further up to relieve the pressure on my lower colon.

"You are so beautiful in your pain," Don said quietly. "Turn so that the water falls even more on your abdomen. Then massage deep into your belly, so the warmth relaxes your muscles. It will open your colon so you can take more of your enema for me."

I did as he ordered, tears streaming down my face as I kneaded. When I finally stopped again, I kept my face in the water, crying into the shower as I waited for the cramp to pass, knowing the stimulation on my nipples was just bringing on another painful spasm. They were sore beyond speaking. When I could breathe again without panting, I reached back and opened the clamp, mercifully moving so my nipples were out of the shower flow, but letting my master hear my voice break as I described the feel of the water again surging forward to meet the warmth flowing over my skin and the pressure of my hand urging the enema deeper into me. I took it as long as I could, then I once more stopped the clamp, moaning as I lifted my hand to my other breast.

"My nipples hurt so much when the water hits them, sir. It makes my pussy leak. I have to go so badly!" I panted and tugged my nipple, opening the valve again. "The cramp is passing, sir. I'm opening the nozzle right away, because I want to be done with my enema quicker." I moaned as the water again flowed in and I was able to turn my nipple from the spray. I lifted my face into the shower, crying and rubbing as the warm water flowed in and over me again. I couldn't take it long. I stopped once more, quivering as I turned to tug on my nipples.

"Please, sir!" I panted. I wasn't sure what I was asking for anymore. I wanted my torment to stop, yet my pussy was so engorged I was desperate to climax.

"Look at me, love," Master's voice flowed over my ears. I opened my eyes to him, tears streaming down my face as I pulled mercilessly on my nipples and looked deep into his steady silver eyes. With each touch, the pain and stimulation echoed down to join the tremors quaking over my belly. I could almost feel the vibration of Master's voice as he said, "Tell me."

"I-I have to go, sir." My hand shook as I held the nozzle between my tightly clenched butt cheeks. Another wave rolled over me. I sobbed as I fought to keep from leaking. "My rectum feels like it's ready to explode. I can feel the water all the way across the top of my colon. I c-can taste the soap." I glanced up. The bag was hanging almost flat. "I'm afraid to open the clamp again, sir." I dutifully pulled on my nipple. The stimulation was almost more than I could bear. "Please, sir!" I wailed. "I have to go!"

"Enough!"

My head snapped up at the anger in his voice. I panted, tugging on my nipple as I leaned over groaning.

"Your theatrics displease me. Display yourself properly!"

I sobbed, carefully straightening, horrified at having displeased the master I loved so dearly.

"Head up, shoulders back! You know what to do if you need to stop. If you are not stopping, open that clamp!"

I did. The spasms were held at bay for a moment when my hands left my nipple. I kneaded deeply and desperately, trying to open myself.

"Tell me!" he snapped.

"I have to go!" I wailed, massaging deeply into my belly. "I can hardly hold it, sir." I cried out loudly as another spasm rolled over me. "The soap is so nasty, sir. My asshole itches and it burns and my whole tummy is cramping!"

"And your cunt?" he snarled.

I slid my hand down from my belly. Even in the shower, my labia were slick and hot. "My pussy's so wet, sir!" I shuddered as pure, vicious pleasure washed through me. "I'm embarrassed and I feel so dirty standing here in front of you with an enema in my bottom. I'm so afraid I'm going to have an accident. The cramps hurt, and the water is pressing so hard on my pussy that I'm almost coming. Sir!"

"Stop." The order was mercifully quick. I closed the valve, staring in desperate relief at the flattened bag hanging over me. I rubbed frantically on my clit, so horny I could hardly stand it. As another wave rolled over me, I looked deeply into Don's eyes, drawing on his strength.

"Do you like that, love?" His eyes glittered like diamonds. "Does my pretty little pussy girl like standing in the shower with a soapy enema filling her ass while she fingers her clit?"

"Yes, Master," I sobbed. The wave was rising in me, pressing up from my cunt. "I'm going to come, sir. I'm afraid I won't be able to hold my enema in while I come. Oh, sir!" My eyes filled again at the thought of what might happen.

His lips curved in a cruel smile. "Remove the nozzle, slut, but do not release your enema, and do not come."

I slid the nozzle slowly through my sensitized ass lips, my tear-filled eyes locked to his as I willed myself to control the spasms shuddering through me. My fingers rubbed my clit in a fury as bands of excruciating pleasure and pain tightened across my belly and butt and cunt and the cramps once more savaged me. This time they didn't stop, though. They pulled tighter, pressing deep into my cunt until I was shaking so hard I could hardly stand.

"Now," he said quietly.

The orgasm exploded through me. As my cunt contracted in waves of pleasure, pussy juice squirted onto my wrist. With my eyes locked onto Don's, I leaned against the wall, shaking as I rubbed my pussy and tugged on the screaming pain that was my nipples and fought to hold my enema. I came until I was so far beyond shame and orgasm that all I could do was look into my Master's eyes and offer him my pain and my humiliation and my love.

At his whispered, "Go!" I dashed for the toilet. I barely made it, and I stayed there for a very long time.

Later on, at his direction, I gave myself a quick plain-water rinse-out and took another quick shower. When I was finished, I wrapped my hair in a towel and knelt at his feet with my head in his lap. He slowly moved his wrist back and forth over me, stroking my face.

"You are exquisite, my love," he said quietly. "Before," he paused and took a deep breath. "Before, I would not have realized how much of arousal is only in the brain. Thank you."

"You're welcome, sir," I whispered, enjoying the peace and comfort of his touch after the intensity of our still unbelievable play. We sat there quietly for a long while, then he said softly, "Did you enjoy yourself, my sweet?"

I could hear the laughter in his voice. I smiled up at him, kissing his cock in homage. "It was wonderful, sir. It was awful and humiliating and degrading and the cramps hurt something fierce." I blushed happily. "I loved it, sir. And I love you!"

We were both still smiling as I wheeled him into the bedroom. I helped him slide into bed and onto the hospital pad, and yawning happily, I stripped him down to his T-shirt. I carried in the supplies for his bedtime ritual, but as I was pulling on my gloves, he stopped me. My eyes widened as he ordered me to lean over him. He gave each nipple a single slow, sucking kiss. The pain was so excruciating tears stung my eyes. Then his breath whispered cool and soft over my skin.

"Let your sore nipples remind you that I will always honor your service, my love." He licked his lips lecherously at me. "Now tend to me, wench. Before you fall asleep."

Laughing, I moved his legs apart and opened the jar.

The Very First Time
by Brooke Carter

"The Very First Time" describes the initial submission of a young woman, experiencing for the first time the overwhelming love of a Master. The dance of seduction between submissives and dominants is deliciously described, more intensely than that in most "vanilla" relationships.

My Master took me last night: tenderly, brutally, gently, violently. It was as if i was being taken for the very first time—because i was.

Master and i had been corresponding by e-mail for several months. It began with us trading fantasies; his involved dominating a woman who looked very much like me. mine were all about being owned by an older man who looked very much like him.

By the time we agreed to meet, i knew i would become his.

i wore a very tight skirt and a very sexy pair of thong panties to our date. my sweater, also, was tight, and i wore a push-up bra that made me look a cup size bigger than i was. i was afraid Master wouldn't find me as exciting in person as he did online, but the moment i saw him, i knew i wanted him in real life even more than in fantasy. He is just over six feet, ten years older than me, gray at the temples, and heavily built. His eyes are a piercing steel gray and i could feel them looking right through my clothes. i knew he was thinking of me naked.

Still, i didn't know if he wanted me. We went out to dinner, and the whole time i was wondering if he wanted to have me. He ordered for both of us. Our conversation was light, never hinting at what i hoped we were both thinking. i was praying he would still be interested in me when the date was over.

When we'd finished dessert, he suggested we go back to his place and he show me his dungeon.

The second we were in the car, he was all over me. i melted into his arms, letting him kiss me deeply, moaning softly as he put his hands under my sweater and touched my breasts. He ran his fingers up my thighs and i shivered with excitement. He touched my pussy and i almost came. i was so wet i was more than a little embarrassed. i didn't want Master to think i was too much of a slut. But i couldn't help it: i wanted him.

His house was well-ordered, clean, neat. As soon as we were in the door, he grabbed me and put his arms around me. He kissed me again, then stepped back and told me to undress. i pulled my sweater over my head and then unzipped my skirt. i slid it down and stepped out of it. i wore a white garter belt, white stockings, and a matching bra and thong panties. i asked Master if he wanted me to take off my bra and panties, and he said the way i was would do for now.

"But soon," he assured me, "you'll be very naked."

He led me into the living room and offered me a glass of wine. We sat on the couch and sipped wine and resumed our dinner conversation, about work, traveling, food . . . not talking at all about what he wanted to do to me, and what i wanted him to do to me. But i was aware, the whole time, that i was in just my bra and panties, garter belt, and stockings. Nothing but my underwear. Master remained fully clothed. i was very aware that my nipples were standing out through the thin satin of my bra. i was very aware that my face was blushing very red.

Soon the Master's questions moved from casual topics to my previous relationships. He asked me to tell him what it was like when i lost my virginity. i told him how my first boyfriend and i had made love in the backseat of his car and I'd had an orgasm on his cock. He asked me if i'd let that boyfriend fuck me in the ass. i told him yes. He asked me if i thought that was a slutty thing to do. i said i did, and my clit gave a little surge of arousal as i admitted it. Did i like that, Master wanted to know.

"Yes," i said. "i like it very much."

Master asked me how many men i'd slept with. i told him. He

asked me how many men i'd given head. i told him that as well. He asked me how many men's cocks i'd touched. i told him that.

Each time my face blushed deeper and my nipples hardened more. i could feel my clitoris hardening, too, and my pussy getting very wet. Master had already asked me all these questions online, but telling him in person was having a new effect on me.

Then he asked me how many men i'd let have my ass, in addition to my first boyfriend.

"Just two, Master," i told him.

"By the time you leave in the morning," he said, "it will have been three."

my breath came short.

"Yes, Master."

He asked me how many girls i'd kissed, how many girls i'd gone down on, how many girls had gone down on me. Each time i told him, feeling my arousal mount. By the time he was ready to take me, i was so turned on i almost couldn't stand it. Master stood up and told me he was going to take me into the dungeon now.

Master led me down the stairs into his basement. There was a big leather-covered bed with eyebolts on it and a big X-shaped cross on one end of the frame. There was also a leather-covered sofa, and a large rack of toys. Master showed me each toy, describing how it was going to feel on my body.

After he'd shown me everything, he sat on the sofa and told me: "If you think you're in over your head, I'd be happy to drive you home. Otherwise, get on your knees and suck my cock."

i was on my knees before i knew it. my face was in his crotch. i unbuckled his belt and took out Master's cock and took it into my mouth, shivering with how delicious it tasted. i whimpered as i sucked him, and when he came i swallowed it all, wishing for more.

"You've used up all my come," he said. "i can't fuck you. So i have nothing to do but punish you."

i blushed and looked down at his softened cock. "Yes, Master," i said.

Master strapped me to the St. Andrew's cross and sliced my thong panties and bra off with a knife. Then he laid out several of the toys in front of me on the bed so i could see what he had in store for me.

He started with a paddling, making me writhe and moan on the cross. i pulled against the restraints and begged for mercy, becoming more and more turned on as i did. Master switched to a flogger and left hot strings of agony across my back and ass and thighs. He finished me with the cane, leaving parallel lines from the top of my buttocks to the bottom.

When he took me down, i could feel his cock, hard against me. He laid me on the bed facedown and fastened my restraints, wrists and ankles, each to a corner of the bed. He took off all his clothes and i moaned as he climbed on top of me.

Master entered me from behind and i came almost instantly. He fucked me slow and hard and i thanked him over and over again as he took me. When he eased his cock out of my pussy and i felt him smearing lubricant on my asshole, i knew it was time for him to take me in the way i most feared.

But as he teased open my asshole with his fingers, i began to want it more and more. When i felt his cockhead nudging open my back door, i moaned and begged him for it. He slid into my anus and fucked me gently until he came deep inside my ass. Just before he came, i did, too—the first time I'd ever had the experience of coming with my lover's cock in my ass. i thrashed and pulled against the restraints, moaning.

Master unfastened my restraints and drew a blanket over both of us. He curled up next to me and tucked a pillow under my head. We both dropped off to sleep.

When i awakened, i found Master looking into my eyes. i asked him if he would like his slave to make him breakfast.

"Not before you go upstairs to the computer," he said. "And write down everything that happened last night. Make sure you describe how much it turned you on."

my pussy gave a little pulse as i thought about writing down the events of last night, the most delicious fantasy i'd ever lived.

"Yes, Master," i told him.

And so i did.

Symphony of Strain
by Debra Hyde

Debra Hyde is a regularly published erotic writer. Recently, her work has appeared in *Best of the Best Meat Erotica; Ripe Fruit: Erotica for Well-Seasoned Lovers;* and *Body Check: Erotic Lesbian Sports Stories.* Hyde runs *Pursed Lips* (www.pursedlips. com), a weblog and personal site that focuses on erotica and general sexuality, and writes regularly online for Heather Corrinna's *Scarlet Letters* (www.scarletletters.com) and the *Yesportal* (www.yesportal.com).

Hyde says of "Symphony of Strain": "Some people consider punishment play fake and shallow, but to me, it's a game of creativity wrapped in ritual. It's an ingenious way to structure correction without hurting the psyche. The body gets delightfully battered and bruised, the mind comes away thinking more conscientiously, and it wipes clean the slate. Apologizes and forgiveness are rendered in full. Even better, punishment play has the added pleasure of getting me wet and making me ready. For whatever comes my way."

He isn't one for ambience, my Master. When I enter his domain, I won't find candles flickering near the window, their scent wafting in the air. I won't find a roaring fire or a rug of soft, warm fur. Instead, I find austerity. His books, his chair, his desk, his stereo system, and little else. Sometimes a card table, if he had bridge guests over. Sometimes pieces of ephemera scattered about if he's been working on his collection of antique paper goods. These are his passions and I'm simply one among several things that delight him. At least I rank among the best of his possessions.

When I approach him, I know what signs to look for. It's not just his quiet continence I spy out, but physical evidence: His desk chair pulled to the middle of the room, ropes and cuffs adorning it. Maybe his old umbrella holder stuffed full of canes or maybe a selection of whips, floggers, and quirts tossed carelessly on the floor. A blindfold if I'm lucky, a hood if I'm not. Or worse—nothing if he wants me to witness my own suffering.

But music is the real cue to his intentions, his mood. If the strains of Tchaikovsky or Mozart issue from the stereo, he intends to toy with me, a cat to my mouse. I'll quiver like caught prey and I know he'll play hard. He'll push me, then fuck me and be done with it. If it's Ravel or Debussy, he's filled with wicked lust and he'll push my face to his erection, demanding my deep, undivided attention until he's satisfied. But if I hear Bruckner, then I'm in trouble.

Bruckner. That's punishment music.

Master is a man of predictable tastes and habits. You might think that would make him boring, but given that some of his tastes and habits make me wet and aroused, I'd say boring is the wrong adjective. Yet how can a man with such routine habits be so inscrutable? I lack the answer. In fact, I leave it to the gods to decide. It'll take a whole pantheon of them to puzzle a solution to that answer.

This day, I am to knock before entering. I'm to enter, undress, and kneel before him. I'm to bow to the ground, forehead touching the cold linoleum, hands palm down. I'm to remain still until he calls me to him.

I wonder and worry about many things as I enter his house and make my way to his study. But mostly I hope my knees will hold out against the hard, unforgiving floor. Sometimes, the silliest thoughts nag you the most when you're walking into the unknown.

His voice answers my knock but it is aurally poker-faced, betraying nothing. I have no clue what his intentions are and it's unsettling. As I enter the room, he has his face in a book and doesn't even cast a glance my way. Quietly, I shut the door and proceed to undress, right where I stand. Methodically, I shed my jacket, then my blouse, my slacks, shoes, and socks. I have no undergarments to remove. They are deemed taboo, they're so inconvenient.

I follow my given directions and stretch out before Master. The floor is cool and my skin shivers lightly in goose bumps. My nipples grow tight, hard enough that a pulse throbs once, then twice from between my legs. Already, I'm aroused.

But I discover that his disregard for me was so unnerving that I failed to scan the room for clues. I didn't notice how the chair was stationed, what implements were visible. I didn't even steal a glance to see if he watched me undress or ogled my nakedness.

And there's no music. The room is silent. I don't know what to make of it. My shivers turn to quivering. I am anticipation, personified.

It isn't all that long before I hear Master put down his book. Usually, he would reach for me at this point and draw me into his arms. He'd kiss me and caress me. He'd grope and stroke my breasts, suck each nipple to his satisfaction. Typically, I'd be able to sense his cock twitch and rise to erection as we embrace.

But not this time. This time, Master rises and walks past me. As if I'm not even there.

Wood scrapes against the floor—he's dragging his desk chair out. A door opens—one of the cupboard doors below his library bookcases where he keeps the paraphernalia of our perverted play. I hear rope being worked, metals clips going into place, the dull thwap of leather hitting the ground. Master readies for play. But what temperament of play? Hard and fast or slow and luscious? I haven't a clue.

Until he leans over me, grabs me by the hair, and drags me to my feet. Startled, I fail to hear him come alongside me. My breath catches in my throat as I awkwardly scramble up from the floor. By the time I make it to my feet, the catch in my throat lets go. I am panting.

Getting to my feet is strenuous enough that I don't see the blindfold coming. It's over my eyes in an instant. I react with a quick gasp of surprise.

Master pulls me forward. I feel the chair's seat at my knees.

"Climb up."

His first words to me are demanding, insistent. Compliance is my natural response. I climb up onto a chair without hesitation.

Master cuffs my wrists, my ankles. He pulls my arms over the back of the chair, tying them so they're stretched down toward the ground. He pulls each leg as far apart as the seat of the chair permits, as close to each leg of the chair as he can get them. My chin rests on the back of the chair. I am so severely stretched to the four corners of the earth that I wonder how I'll maintain the position.

Silence follows, a silence in which I contemplate the two words he has granted me. "Climb up." Like his library, they are austere. Like the position he's placed me in, they are severe and taxing. Yet they tell me nothing else.

But what comes next does: Bruckner. In all its long, overbearing, indulgent glory.

If you've never heard a Bruckner symphony, let me describe it this way: It is the taffy of classical orchestral music. The themes of his symphonies are made remarkable only by the long-windedness of his expository passages, passages that go on and on forever. His symphonies typically last more than an hour, thick, tedious things that they are.

And I get wet every time I hear them.

Of course, other things figure into my arousal than the music. My scalp burns from Master's grip. My muscles strain from the position into which I'm bound. My body acutely senses every fluctuation in temperature—every draft that seeps in from the windows, that radiates up from the floor, even those Master makes as he circles me.

Yes, he's circling me; his scent moves with him. It fades when he's behind me, grows stronger when he comes alongside me, overwhelms me when he's right in front of me. He's scrutinizing me and I can only imagine how I look to him. His every bondage fantasy, made flesh. Quivering flesh that awaits its due.

I am exposed as well. With my legs forced apart and my cunt ready and able, I must look vulnerable. I *know* I look vulnerable. I can hear Master's breathing and it's that deep, heightened rhythm that I hear when his hand is around my cunt and I'm near orgasm. He's every bit as aroused as I am.

Except he's in no hurry to finish things. His self-control is amazing.

"I gave you a chore to do some time ago," he tells me now. Words to initiate punishment. Often, they accompany the sounds of Bruckner.

"Do you remember what it was?"

My mind races. I remember buying him choice fruits. Washing the lengths of fabric he sometimes uses to gag me with. Renewing his magazine subscriptions. Washing his car windows.

As I think, Master's hands wander over me. They cup my breasts and knead them. They play with my nipples. They caress my body, find their way to the cleft of my ass, to the round, bountiful flesh that surrounds it. One hand finds it way to my cunt. Fingers caress my labia, teasing them lightly. It feels delicious.

Then a finger unceremoniously forces its way into me. I gasp because I'm not as wet as I thought I was and there's no tenderness involved.

The sensations make me delirious. I can't think straight.

"Do you remember?" he repeats. His voice is still patient. It won't stay that way. Especially if I can't lay my finger on where I went wrong this week.

Transgressions are always simple things in Master's book. Like forgetting to hang the toilet paper or failing to throw out the junk mail. You know, all those little things you're supposed to do, day in and day out, but are so easy to forget. And my lapses into laziness guarantee the occasional reminder via punishment.

But the little things are also safe and nonthreatening. They rarely assault one's adequacy while reinforcing the idea of conscientious behavior. They encourage a good girl's vigilance, yet they're emotionally safe. Yet they're specter enough to make punishment thrilling and even a tad frightening.

Like now. My mind scrambles to figure out where I failed. I'm coming up empty.

Master speaks. "Let me give you a little reminder."

I hear something jangle. It's metallic. I feel Master grab a nipple and, if his pinch wasn't enough, something even stronger seized it.

Clamps! But the teeth burn gently, evenly. It's a mild clamp, one Master knows I can tolerate for some time. A clamp takes the other nipple.

But now Master raises the stakes: He's pinching my labia the same way and suddenly the same burn takes me there. And on the other labia. Master lets the chain that connects the clamps dangle freely.

You might think clamps would hurt there, but it feels too good to hurt. In fact, with gravity doing its job, with the weight of the chains tugging on my nipples and lips, my cunt throbs its approval.

"How many clamps are attached to you?"

I swallow before I speak. "Four, Sir."

"Can you think of anything associated with four that you failed to do?"

I think "four days" but I hadn't procrastinated about anything over four days. Four hours? No. Four items? I think of all the things I did for Master that week that might be grouped by four, all the while my cunt grows slick from the weighted delights. Then it hits me—the dry cleaning! I'd taken three of his sweaters in for winterizing and forgot to take a suit jacket with them. I had to make a second trip to correct my mistake.

"The dry cleaning, Sir."

"Very good! You remembered. I'm pleased."

I thank Master but I'm groaning as I speak. He plays with the chains, knowing how it'll affect me.

"Do you remember the estimated cost of the dry cleaning?"

I moan. I can't help it; those clamps feel so good. My body's screaming, "Fuck me!" while I try to do the math.

"Thirty-seven fifty," I manage.

"So thirty-eight strokes, then," Master says.

I nod. Remembering the seventy-five strokes I took for an overdue library-book fine, I know better than to resist. Master begins to tap the cane across my ass. He's warming me up. I hope he'll prepare me enough that I'll be able to endure the real strokes when they come.

When the cane strikes, it sings. It sings as it arcs toward my body and when it meets my skin. It even resonates as its impact travels into muscle. Silent overtones.

I, on the other hand, caterwaul. Without decorum or sensitivity. I have no musicianship, compared to the cane.

Master lays the cane to my ass in measured strikes, just enough to allow me to process each stroke. The impact, the sting, the deepening burn, the fade; each step takes me further from the pain of the current stroke and closer to that of the next. I hope Master will be kind and alternate the strokes, one for each butt cheek. That way, one spot can cool before it's tried again. He counts each stroke and picks up the pace as he nears thirty. Already, it's difficult and we have so far to go.

"Thirty."

He doesn't raise his voice when he calls out the number. He lets the cane do that. It hammers into me, harder than all the preceding strokes. I yelp and lurch, it hurts so much. But I know what this means: He intends to accent every tenth stroke, right down to zero, as a mark of progress. As a mark of punishment.

Master stops being generous. He no longer alternates from cheek to cheek. Now he lays them straight across my ass. Some hit tenderly, some oh-so-just-right, others in sheer agony. I accept, struggle, and scream accordingly.

But something else happens as stroke twenty nears: I begin to notice how good the clamps feel. They tug, pulling with pressure that's intensely superb. My nipples ache lusciously and my labia feel swollen. I imagine my cunt wide open, beckoning Master far more eloquently than I could ever voice.

When stroke twenty arrives, I bellow in pain, but I'm so aroused that I'm throbbing inside. My cunt clutches, wanting cock to grab hold of, but it gets nothing. Ignored, it aches. Desire builds with every stroke, no matter how gentle or brutal each might be. By the time the tenth stroke hits me, my body can resist no more—I come. I growl as I feel myself peak, as I feel myself dissolve into throes of release.

It's hard to feel my cunt clutch in contractions, though; Master keeps the cane at my ass, one stroke after another. I may have climaxed, but Bruckner's Eighth hasn't and Master times his strokes to its capitulation, not mine.

Finally, the last stroke. I expect an extra stroke for zero, remembering that zero's a number, too. But the null stroke is anything but void. I hear the zipper of Master's pants and his cock delivers the last stroke. He pushes into me. I'm so wet he encounters little resistance. It takes my breath away.

Penetrated, I melt at the feel of Master fucking me. He feels large, thick, and every stroke pulls at my weighted lips, lips so alive with sensation, it's as if every stroke sets a million nerve endings sputtering. Around us, the music billows, growing grander and more majestic by the second.

I can feel Master shuddering as he fucks me. I feel splendid to him, almost more than he can stand. I love it and I hope he uses me selfishly, without regard for making it last or making it mutual.

Sometimes, it's best when I'm fucked at my own expense.

But the sensations I feel are astounding. They're strong, incredible and they course throughout my body. I'm overstimulated and before I know it, I'm coming again, throbbing so deeply I feel a sudden wetness descend from inside me. Not quite a gush, but enough to feel like a "let down" of liquid, much like milk lets down from the breast.

Master feels it as well and it propels him into his own orgasm. Right on the trail of my orgasm, his commences, flooding me with his fluid. His bullish groan swelling up from behind me. Swift and powerful, he conquers me. Then he collapses on me.

It's some minutes before Master stirs. Sated, his cock slips from me and then he rights himself. He pulls away from me and begins to release me. The clips burn as they're removed, and my limbs regain a small measure of freedom as the ropes fall away from the cuffs, blindfold from my face. Slowly, I straighten myself and flex various body parts. My eyes adjust to seeing again.

I hear Master's zipper again, then his voice. "When you're able, get dressed."

Get dressed. No cuddling in afterglow, it would seem. I try not to pout visibly.

In the course of dressing, Bruckner ends. I realize that Master hadn't subjected me to the entire symphony. I'd endured only the first movement. As I reach for my blouse, I wonder if the rest still awaits me.

"No top," Master informs me. "Just your jacket."

For a second, his command paralyzes me. He wants me to go somewhere. Publicly. Sans blouse. Reluctantly, I obey.

"What would you have me do?"

"Why, go get the dry cleaning, of course."

If I weren't so addled by a cane, an orgasm, and a fuck, I would've seen that coming. As it is, I blush demurely and excuse myself. I'm floating so high from the scene that I'm good for little else.

My ass, red and worn, burns delightfully as I drive to the dry cleaner. As I pay for our goods, I wonder if I look as stoned as I feel. I wonder if I smell like sex. But transaction complete, I return home.

There, Master waits for me, sitting in his chair. His pants are open, his cock exposed. It's semierect and waiting for me. And the stereo is playing Ravel—beautiful, sensuous Ravel! Music to my ears!

As I kneel before Master's cock and open my mouth, it would seem that Ravel isn't music for just my ears. My cunt throbs, measure for measure and ready for more.

The Ring
by Melody Perry

Another pseudonymous tale of ownership, "The Ring" explores the idea of being marked with a piercing that denotes submission. One of this editor's favorite fantasies, a permanent piercing can be a powerful symbol of relinquishing control.

Master makes me wear it all the time. It reminds me that I belong to him—not that I'd ever forget. But it's very, very important to him that it be at the forefront of my mind, always.

I wear it every day. When I'm at work, having some serious business meeting, playing the part of the manager, I may cross my legs and feel the firm press of metal nestled at the top of my pussy lips. When I use the bathroom throughout the day, I have to touch it, caress it, remember why it's there. When I'm driving, I may press my thighs together and feel it, feel the tingle that comes when I receive any pressure at all on my crotch. When I walk in the door, I'm ready for him. I'm always wet.

If Master's home from work already, I go over to him. I lift my skirt and show him that I'm not wearing any underwear, as he has forbade me to do. I'm also not allowed to wear pants; my pussy must be exposed, always. So I can lift my skirt and show him the ring in my clit, show him that I remember I'm his.

Then I take off my clothes and *make* myself his.

When he fucks me, unless my wrists are bound, I must touch the ring in my clit. That's his steadfast rule: If his cock is inside me, my hand is on my ring, rubbing. When he enters me from behind I rub my pierced clit as he fucks me. When he spreads me out on the bed and fucks me, I tuck my hand between us and rub my pierced clit, feeling the shaft of his cock as it slides in and out of me. When he ties me up and fucks me, I must beg to touch my clit—and I do. I beg in earnest, because I want so badly to come.

If my pussy satisfies him, he'll untie one of my hands and let me touch my clit. If not, he might torture me a little more, making me beg for it until I almost can't stand it. Or if he's feeling particularly wicked he might touch my clit himself, teasing me until I'm almost ready to come—and then pulling away, leaving me gasping, wanting.

But Master's so good to me. He always lets me touch it. Eventually.

When we're together, if he's not fucking me, I must ask permission to touch it. I am naked when we're at home, so when we're watching TV, eating dinner, relaxing, I must ask—sometimes beg—to be allowed to touch my clit. Other times, he tells me to do it. I never say no. Even when we're in public.

Once he took me to a bar and found me a place in a far corner. He told me to touch my clit. It was hard to ease my hand down the waistband of my skirt without anyone seeing, but I managed it. I touched the ring in my clit, looking around as I slid my lower body as far as I could under the table. People were milling around, drinking, dancing, talking, laughing. Master sat across the table from me and sipped his drink. I came with all those people around. Master didn't tell me to stop. I asked him if I could. He said no. I came again. Master still didn't let me stop touching my clit. People were starting to look. I kept touching my clit, stroking the ring, rubbing it up and down. My face was moist with sweat and very hot. I came again. People were really looking now; some of them might even have figured out what I was doing. I begged Master to let me stop. He didn't. I came again and the tears flooded down my face. Still he didn't let me stop, even after I begged, sobbing. Until I came one last time. Then he relented and allowed me to snuggle up against him, whispering "Thank you, thank you, thank you, thank you." My whole lower body hurt for days. But every time I thought about it, I whispered, "Thank you."

The ring in my clit is for Master's pleasure, not mine. Every orgasm I have is offered to him, a promise that I'll love him forever. A promise that I'll always belong to him.

Lately he's had a look in his eye. A savage look. A nasty look. It makes me wet when I see it; incredibly wet. I know he has more things in store for me.

The other day I came home from work to find Master taking a nap. I took off all my clothes and went into the living room.

There was a business card from a tattoo and piercing parlor, with a time and a date written on it.

Now I knew what that look in Master's eyes meant.

And it made me wetter than ever.

At the bottom of the card it said NIPPLE PIERCINGS A SPECIALTY.

I could feel them harden as the card fluttered to the floor.

Competition
by Tanya Turner

Tanya Turner is a newcomer to writing but a longtime flirt, tease, and all-around kinky gal. She says she enjoys staying up all night and getting into trouble whenever possible. Of this story, she writes: " 'Competition' was inspired by a few things, mostly my love for dirty talking and being 'punished,' which I put in quotes because being spanked is actually anything but a punishment for me. It was also inspired by once telling a lie to a boyfriend about where I'd been and then being such a poor liar that I forgot that I'd lied, blowing my whole cover. Also, for me (and I know this isn't true of everyone), S and M is intricately connected to sex and, if it's done right, turns me on and gets me wet. I love getting fucked in some way after bottoming to a partner, and I wanted to get that across in the story."

"Where have you been?"

Even though it's close to 4:00 A.M., my boyfriend, my Top, looks asleep in our bed as I sneak into the house and change into my pajamas. But then I find that he's awake, and looking very alert.

"You know, out. I went to a bar with Janet and we had a few drinks, she got to telling one of her stories, and we both lost track of time."

"That's it?" There's an edge in his voice as he asks me, as if he doesn't suspect but *knows* I'm leaving something out. I know I'm busted. How could he possibly know that mixed in with the mixed drinks and girl talk was some minor flirtation? Could he possibly know about the hot, tanned, muscular surfer guy who chatted us up and then took things one step further, giving us sensual backrubs, feeling us up in front of the entire bar, raking his fingernails over the back of my neck, pressing me very tightly against him when he said good-bye, so tightly I could feel his very hard cock pressing into me through our clothes? He couldn't know about it, and yet he seemed to.

"Well, yeah, mostly. You know."

"No, Caroline, I don't seem to know." He's now tapping his foot impatiently, waiting for me to 'fess up.

"Well, there was this guy there, he was talking to us on and off during the night, and then later right before we left he gave us both backrubs and was just flirting with us a little."

"Really? And did you flirt back with him? You know what, don't even answer that. Finish taking the rest of your clothes off and then go stand against the wall."

Suddenly, I'm no longer tired. Despite my guilty conscience, or perhaps because of it, I feel a shiver of arousal and excitement run through me at his words. I throw the last of my clothes on the floor and quickly stand against the wall, in "my spot," as we've dubbed this particular location. I raise my hands above my head before he has to tell me, hoping to mitigate his anger even a little.

He walks over to me and pinches my back, starting at the top of my neck and working his way down my shoulder blades and beyond. He grabs a small amount of skin and pinches, over and over again, before raising his hand and slapping me on one shoulder and then the next. Then his big, rough hands squeeze my back, but not in the kind of dreamy, sensual way one gives a massage. No, this gesture has something else in mind. His touch is rough, invasive. "I knew you were up to something, Caroline, coming home this late when you said you'd be back at midnight. I tried to sleep but I couldn't, waiting to see what tale you'd tell me. I'm mad, but I'll get over it, but I want you to remember one thing. I'm the only one who matters, and I'm the only one who can really treat you the way you need to be treated." He pulls my head back by my hair, tugging a few times to make sure I'm listening and that I understand. "Whoever that guy was, that nobody, he can't do for you what I'm going to do. He couldn't even come close."

He brings his arms around me, cupping my breasts. More shivers pass through me at his touch and the memory of the nameless bar Romeo, who also cupped my breasts, holding their weight in his hands, not caring about the spectacle we were making. Somehow it seems like Joe is mimicking our bar antics, even though I know that's pretty much impossible. Now he squeezes my nipples, hard, pinching them over and over and then switching tactics, twisting them and pulling them away from me. The pain echoes throughout my chest, sending heat in waves up and down my body. "Did he do this to you, huh? Did he know how you like to have your nipples played with? Did he know how much pain you can really take? I bet he didn't, I bet he thought you were a nice girl, and he'd score by just being young and cute and buying you a drink or two. But you need more than that, don't you? Don't you?" As he says this he presses against me, smashing me into the wall. I can feel his cock through his boxers as it presses insistently against my ass. My now very hard nipples are pressing painfully into the wall.

Then he moves back and I close my eyes instinctively, no blindfold needed. I don't want to know what he has in store for me, and I'll find out soon enough. I sense him moving around, but in a flash he's back, and he tells me to put my hands up on the wall and to stick my ass out. At his words, my cunt tightens in anticipation. Then I feel the first blow, hitting my ass in the most exquisitely painful way. Without seeing, I know that he's using our special paddle, the one he presented to me on our one-year anniversary, with the word BAD engraved into it. If he hits me just right, the word will be faintly visible on my skin for a moment, but we're usually too worked up for that. Now he hits me over and over, marking my ass not with words but with a reddening all over. I push my ass out further, even though I'm not supposed to; he'll tell me if he wants me to move, but I can't help it. The paddling is too addictive, and each whack makes my cunt feel truly alive. Nothing else gets me as wet as this, nothing. I push my ass out a little more, wanting him to hit me harder, but at this next show of impudence, he stops and turns me around. With hardly a pause, he takes the paddle to my sensitive nipples, slapping lightly at first, occasionally hitting the sides of my breasts before moving back to my nipples.

The pain is intense, each blow causing me to suck in my breath and wonder if I can withstand it, even though I know I'd be heartbroken if he stopped. I open my mouth to make a sound, to somehow tell him how impossibly wet and aching he's making me, but then I realize I don't have to. He already knows; he's got making me insane with desire down to a science. His eyes roam up and down my body, weighing, measuring, assessing, with the cool, calm eye of a jewelry appraiser. Only his cock, visibly hard beneath his boxers, betrays his own arousal. He pauses for a moment, then leans forward, his mouth hovering in front of my reddened breasts. His tongue darts out and connects with a nipple, so wet and tender I almost cry. My nipples are somewhere between hard and soft, trying to adjust to his actions. He licks and sucks and lulls my nipple into submission, before bringing his teeth down and biting, hard. I gasp as I feel the bite's pain shoot straight to my cunt. He holds my nipple between his teeth, flicking his tongue back and forth, faster and faster until I have to clamp a hand on his shoulder to stay standing. He gives the other nipples the same treatment, and I again almost collapse.

Then, I know that we're almost there, we're almost ready for the finale. He crouches down so his face is in front of my pussy, so wet with my desire that my juices are starting to drip down my thighs, slow, tickling trickles that remind me what a slut I truly am. He pauses, staring, for what feels like forever but is probably only a minute. I want to squat forward, bring my cunt right up to his face, force him to fill me with his tongue, or his fingers, or his cock, anything to ease the ache that has utterly consumed my pussy. But I don't. I stay still, waiting for him to decide what will happen next. He nudges my legs farther apart, sliding my ankles to where he wants them. I'm leaning against the wall for necessary support, my legs spread as wide as I can stand it. He runs a knuckle over my pussy, as if to test me, even though it's totally clear that I'm more than ready. Then he slaps me, his hand hitting my cunt from underneath, rapid hard smacks that land on my pussy lips and make me scream. He doesn't let up, doesn't even acknowledge my yell, just keeps hitting me there, harder and harder. If only he'd shove a few fingers up my cunt while he does it, but he's not ready for that yet. He keeps up his pace and I bang my hand against the wall in frustration. It's too much, and not enough, all at once. Then he reaches for the paddle again and taps it against my clit—tap, tap, tap. My clit responds in kind, getting harder, bigger, eager for more. He keeps going, faster and faster, occasionally slapping the leather paddle against my inner thigh, hard, just because. I've been watching as he does this but I can't take it anymore, and close my eyes. He keeps going, spanking my clit and my pussy until the entire area is nothing more than a raging storm of heat and pain. Each blow is like adding another log to the fire, building and building until I can barely distinguish them anymore. Finally, after a series of particularly painful hits that have my nails scraping the wall, he stops.

I think now's when he's finally going to fuck me, I'm finally going to be rewarded for taking all of this, for the redness that blares my neediness across my skin. I know he's hard and even though my pussy really does feel like it's on fire, I still want him to fuck me, even more than I did before.

But he looks me right in the eye for a moment, then walks to the bed and gets in, settling onto his side and shutting his eyes. I stand there in disbelief, staring at him. When I don't follow him into bed, he turns around. "I just wanted to show you, and that no-good barfly, that there's no real competition between us. Anything he can do, I can do so, so much better, and you better not forget that next time, Caroline. I know he didn't fuck you, I would've sensed that the minute you came in. If he had, then I would have too, hard and deep and rough the way you like it, pinned against the wall. But since he didn't fuck you, I'm not going to either. I think I've proven myself already. Now get in bed, don't you know what time it is?" he scoffs at me. My body trembling, I turn off the lights and get into bed, hoping for sleep to dull the sharp, stinging ache between my legs. Maybe he'll want to fuck me in the morning. I certainly hope so.

Lucky
by Elle McCaul

Elle McCaul writes historical romance novels for several differ-
ent publishers. Her erotic short stories have appeared in
Naughty Stories from A to Z (Pretty Things Press) and *Sweet
Life 2: More Erotic Fantasies for Couples* (Cleis).

McCaul writes of "Lucky": "Ask me to name a few of my favorite male celebrities, and you'll soon get an idea of my ideal
man. The father (albeit ghostly) on *Six Feet Under*. Tommy Lee
Jones. Mick Jagger. Gene Hackman. Not one of them is under
fifty. So sue me. I have a thing for older guys. They're the only
ones who fulfill my need to play the role of the misbehaving
bratty lover. They know how to handle imps like me—which is
exactly what happens to the lead in my favorite story I've ever
written: 'Lucky.'"

It's only eight o'clock in the morning, and already I'm making goo-
goo eyes at the older man sitting across from me at the chrome-
topped diner counter. He's distinguished-looking, with silver-white
hair combed back off his head and the air of a rebel around him, even
if he has probably outlived most of the rebels of his generation.
There's a certain movie-star style to the way he moves, a self-
assuredness that I find incredibly attractive. He's like Gene Hackman
in *The Firm*, or Paul Newman in *The Color of Money*. (Sure, matinee
idol Tom Cruise was in both of those flicks, but I've never gone for
guys my age. I always crave a man who has seen the world, who has
the real-life experiences to know how to take care of a troublemaking
minx like me. Because I do like to make trouble. Everywhere I go.)

After enduring several minutes of my teasing glances, he walks to
my table and pulls out the red vinyl chair opposite from where I'm

sitting. This restaurant is one of my all-time favorites. Not an up-dated version of a fifties diner, but an actual diner from the fifties. The sparkly red chairs are now considered vintage. The menu is filled with real, hearty American food—big portions, blue-plate specials. The man fits easily into the surroundings. Even without a verbal invi-tation, he makes himself comfortable at my table, stares at me, and waits.

"You're very forward," I say, my lips pursed coyly.

"No," he disagrees, and I catch the edge of dark humor in his voice, see the crinkles around his intense green eyes from years of smiling. "It's you, naughty girl. You're the one who made the first move. That's not appropriate behavior at all."

"Oh, really?" I ask, knowing that I sound exactly like the smarty-pants brat I am, but unable to change my tone. "In your world, I'll bet girls are expected to be sweet and shy and demure, right? So who makes up these rules? Do you?"

He won't rise to the challenge in my voice. He sits there patiently for a moment, then lifts my heavy white porcelain coffee cup and has a sip of the hot liquid as if he has all the time in the world. I get the feeling that he's not going to speak again until I behave myself. But I won't apologize, and he can't make me.

"A girl who comes on strong seems desperate," he says, finally. "You don't want to appear desperate, do you?"

I run my fingers through my short black hair, pushing it off my face. I hold his gaze, telling him my response with my expression alone. No, I don't want to appear desperate—but there's no man around who would think I was. Looking away, I catch my reflection in the polished silver mirror behind the counter. I've got smoldering dark eyes, full red lips, the rarest pale skin. My hair is glossy and thick, cut in a boy's style with a lock that falls intentionally in front of my eyes. As I reach to push my hair away again, he shakes his head once and does it for me. The brush of his warm fingers against my skin makes me tremble.

Still, he's lucky to be sitting across from me, and I tell him so.

"Lucky," he repeats. "You think I'm lucky?" He almost laughs at the ridiculous quality of the question, and then he reaches into his pocket for his battered leather wallet and sets down enough cash to cover my meal. I watch him, mesmerized, as he stands and reaches for me, not helping me by the hand, but solidly grabbing me by the wrist in his firm, powerful grip.

"What do you think you're doing?" I ask, and now there's a vicious sneer in my voice, a hard-edged timbre that I can't shake. Even *I* want to give myself a smarting smack across the face for that tone of voice.

"This way," he says, pulling me after him. I only have time to grab my cinnamon-brown leather hobo bag, and then he leads me from TJ's 24-Hour Diner, out the back way to the gravel parking lot. The gray slivers of stone and rock crush under his heavy footsteps. "Lucky," he repeats again, practically spitting out the word, "do you believe for a second that I'm lucky to be the daddy to a bad girl like you? The games you play. The way you misbehave. Girl, do you honestly think I'm lucky?"

My heart is pounding so hard that I find it difficult to breathe. We've played out versions of this scenario in our bedroom before. James is always in charge when we fuck. He's been my master, and he's been my "Sir"—as in "Yes, Sir," and "No, Sir"—but he's never been my daddy before. That's the one taboo—the *last* taboo—left for us to cross. Now, my pussy spasms with urgency as he drags me toward his car.

"Misbehaving," he sighs, "just asking for a spanking. *Asking* for it with those dirty looks of yours." He glances skyward dramatically as he poses a question to the heavens, "And she thinks I'm lucky?"

Then the back door of his huge American car is open, and he has me over his lap across the deep blue backseat. My short, red-and-black-plaid schoolgirl skirt is hiked up in the back, my white cotton panties are tight on my ass. He strokes me once, twice, before he lets his firm hand connect fiercely with my panty-clad bottom. "Such a tease," he says, "and so fucking forward."

He doesn't swear very often, and I stiffen when I hear the obscenity because I know what that means. It means I've pushed him to his limits, and I'm in for a long, blistering-hot session over his sturdy lap. My bottom is going to be red and raw when he's finished. I recall from experience just how much heat he can bring to my nether regions. James knows how to do it. He concentrates on spreading out the blows evenly—punishing the whole of my ass so that it's hot and throbbing when he's done. Spankings from James last much longer than the actual time of discipline. I feel the aftereffects for hours—sometimes days.

Not caring at all that someone might see us, he slides my panties down past my lean thighs and begins to truly spank my ripe, round ass. His calloused hand connects firmly with my bare bottom, and I can tell that he's not holding back. My ass quivers with the blows, and I close my eyes tight and try to absorb every sensation. Although each spank stings, I raise my hips upward to meet his hand, and I kick my heels out when his palm meets my blushing ass cheeks.

As he punishes me, I think about our first time together—me standing outside of the hair salon where I work, catching a quick smoke break between clients. I had long sapphire-blue cornrows back then, and an attitude that was as wildly willful as my hair color. The day we met, I was wearing my favorite pair of skintight shiny black-leather pants and a long-sleeved metallic silver sweater with no bra beneath. My nipples were cold and hard from the chill in the air, but I refused to go into the salon for warmth until I'd finished the butt.

When he saw me standing there, he pulled the huge red Cadillac into the space in front of me and got out. Without a word, he walked to my side, then stood looking me up and down. When you live in the city, you learn how to deal with strangers. Without a thought, I adopted my best go-fuck-yourself expression, and I stood erect, readying myself for anything. But I wasn't ready for what he did. Gently, he reached for the cigarette from between my lips, and then crushed it out onto the cracked gray sidewalk.

"You're killing yourself with those," he said. "Someone ought to be looking out for you."

"Someone," I snarled. "Someone like you?" My hand was already on my half-empty Marlboro Reds, fingers ready to pluck the next fag from the pack.

He smiled, as if he could read my every thought with perfect ease. "You need a little authority in your life, don't you, bad girl? You need someone to take care of you." He was so close to me, and I thought I saw dark promises in his eyes. The way they gleamed with a hidden knowledge, as if he understood me. My clothes had suddenly felt far too restrictive. All of my cocky, hardcore confidence had disappeared, and I looked down at the ground, stammering something incoherent. He'd transformed me from savage to servile in seconds.

"No," he said, tilting my head upward. "You don't look away from me. Not when I'm talking to you. Not unless you want to feel the kiss of my leather belt against your naked skin." That's all it took. Dinner at a fancy restaurant that night after work and a spanking back at his home afterward. He made sure my ass was warm and red all over before fucking me. Made sure that I was on the verge of tears before sliding his cock between my legs.

I quit smoking that week, but I retained enough attitude to ensure that I was in for many more spankings, both planned and unplanned. Yet although he's continually given me what I crave, we'd never played like this before. He'd punished me, yes, in public and at home. But it had taken me curling up in bed next to him, and whispering my most secret fantasies to bring us to this erotic point.

"I need—" I'd started.

"What do you need, baby doll?"

"I need a father figure—" I murmured, blushing, hoping he'd figure out exactly what I was asking for. I shouldn't have doubted him for a second. James seems to read my desires before I fully understand them.

Now, his hand smacks fiercely against my bare skin and I cry out, even though I'm not anywhere close to my pain threshold yet. It takes a lot to make real tears come. But I am close to my pleasure threshold. And so is he. I feel the insistent pressure of his cock straining up at me from underneath. I think about all the careful choreographing that went into this morning's encounter. We drove separately: him arriving first; me coming in late and sitting across the room, ordering my standard breakfast fare of black coffee and well-buttered wheat toast. The flirtatious looks that I sent him were pure concoction on my part, an impish way that I tested his will.

Now, I'm a bad little girl and daddy's punishing me.

As he does, he taunts me with his words, knowing exactly how much I get off by the way he talks to me. "What did you think would happen to you?" he asks.

I say nothing, because that will win me extra-heated spanks.

"When you act like a royal brat, you get treated like a brat," he continues. "And in my book, your behavior requires the sternest form of punishment."

"Your book," I repeat, my head turned to face the rear of the car. My cheek rests on the smooth seat, and I breathe in the smell of well-cared-for leather. I know I should just bite down on my full bottom lip to keep silent, but for some reason, I can't. I want to talk, want to bring down his wrath upon me. For every stroke of his hand on my ass, my pussy will flood over with an undeniable pleasure. "Your book," I say again. "Did you write that, too?" I ask. "Along with all those other chauvinistic rules."

"Oh, baby girl," James sighs, as if deeply saddened by my sorry state. "You really do need it today, don't you? You're craving a punishment that you'll be able to remember later. When you walk. When you try to sit down. Whenever you move."

My pussy clenches at his words, and I kick out again, just to see what he'll do. "Girl," Daddy says, "don't make me take off my belt."

Oh, I will—and he knows I will. I'll make him take it off. Make my daddy put me over the seat and punish me with his oily black-leather belt. I'll make him spank me until my skin is a hot, rosy blush. And then I'll make him fuck me. Because I know my daddy understands. He'll make it all better with a few steady caresses, and then he'll push me up, so that I can sit on his cock, and he'll bounce me to the outer limits of pleasure that erase every wash of pain.

But in order to get there, I have to push him just a little bit further.

"You think you can make me cry—" I dare, and that's all it takes. James is instantly in motion, pushing me roughly onto the seat. He stands next to the car looking in at me as he slides his belt free from the loops. My heart thrums at an insane speed as I watch every move.

Still without a care that people might see us, he hauls me over the back end of his car and begins to wield the belt with the graceful finesse of a true sadist. He knows how to hit the mark, how to make me shift from one foot to the other. When he admonishes me, I realize that I'm honestly trying to stay in place for him, but unable. Pain blooms with each stripe of the belt. The sensation spreads throughout my body, radiating. Images before me seem clearer, as if suddenly the world has come into sharp focus: the smooth lines of the Cadillac, the rough gray gravel beneath my feet, the ruby red neon sign of TJ's. Pain is clarifying. James knows.

He makes sure to land the belt on the roundest part of my ass, striping me there. Then he lines up the next stroke above and the next stroke below. I hold onto the car, searching for purchase. I lower my head and grit my teeth. And I feel the tears start to fall, heavy drops that splatter on the rocks and on my polished patent-leather high-heeled Mary Janes.

The rest of this was just a game. The teasing. The misbehavior. Tolerating the pain of the hand-spanking . . . but this is real.

"Your ass will be on fire when I'm done," my daddy says, "so don't bother squirming. I'm not going to stop until I know you're truly done."

I try to tell myself to give in. To let it all just happen, wash over me, wash through me. But because I'm a defiant one, all the way to the core, I feel myself start to stand upright, and James is right on me, pushing me back over the car. Holding me in place while he lands the last few sizzling strokes. And then he's behind me, his pants open, his cock out, and he's fucking me against the rear of his car. I feel how hard he is, feel how aroused he is when he reaches one hand up under my white blouse to stroke my breasts.

"You need to be a good girl," he hisses, mouth against my ear as he drives his cock on home. "You need to behave for Daddy." I sigh and close my eyes, feeling the wealth of bliss start to unravel within me. Filaments of pure white-hot pleasure slip through my body, and I half-sob, half-sigh as I sense the climax emerging.

I called him lucky. But maybe I was wrong.

Maybe it's me who's the lucky one after all.

Without Mercy
by Erica Dumas

Erica Dumas is another favorite of mine, a writer who always pushes the edges of consensuality and surrender in her fiction. A submissive woman in real life, Dumas has written for many publications including the *Sweet Life* series and *Necromantic* (www.necromantic.com). A straightforward tale of negotiated "rape," "Without Mercy" describes what is a powerful erotic fantasy for many submissive women.

You promised to take me without mercy. I begged you for it, and now you're going to do it. And I'm scared. I'm so incredibly scared. I'm scared of giving in, I'm scared of resisting. I want it, and I've wanted it forever. But I'm scared.

You come up behind me and slip your arms around me, pressing the tip of the knife into my throat. I gasp and you say "Don't scream." Then you growl into my ear, "Or I'll make you very sorry." Immediately my pussy floods with juice. You run the knife down my throat, the tip just barely touching me, and I moan softly in fear. You tease my lips open with the tip of it and I taste the sharp metal.

"Please," I whimper. "Please, no!"

You slide the knife deep into my mouth and I'm too scared to say anything. You take the knife out of my mouth and a long string of my saliva follows it. It glosses my chin as you close the knife and put it in your pocket.

"I don't really need, this, do I?" you whisper. "You know you can't stop me."

"Please," I moan. "Please don't rape me."

It sends a charge through my body, that word: *rape*. It makes my clit swell and throb hard against my panties. It makes my cunt clench even tighter. It makes me want you. But it makes me scared: the greatest terror a woman can know, and you're going to do it to me. Because I begged for it. Because I made you promise.

I say it again. "Please don't rape me," and my cunt aches, pain seizing my clit as it hardens so much my panties dig into it.

"That's exactly what I'm going to do," you whisper. "Rape you."

And I know it's true.

You force me hard into the bed and put your knee in the small of my back, holding me down as you tie my wrists behind me with rope.

"Please," I beg. "Please don't do this."

You ignore me and pull up my skirt. My panties are skimpy, small. I hear the knife again and in an instant you've slit them, pulling them out from between my legs so quickly that I feel the heat on my clit—panty-burn. I gasp and push my ass into the air involuntarily. You hold me down.

"That's it," you growl as you stuff my shredded panties into my mouth. "Push your ass up for me. Beg for it."

I hear your zipper coming open. I feel the hard length of your cock slide against my ass, pressing between my cheeks. You mount me, forcing my legs open with your knees. I try to resist but you grab my hair, shove my face into the pillow, and *force* them. So rough I'm afraid I'll pull a muscle, but I don't care. I struggle, but it's no use. Your hard, bunched thigh muscles push my legs wide open as I squirm.

Your hands go under my shirt and cup my breasts as you lower your body onto mine, the head of your cock pressing between my swollen lips. I gasp—now is the moment. Now is the moment I'd dreamed of. When my rape is inevitable, and when you realize I'm wet.

Not just wet: gushing.

You shove into me hard, so hard it would make me scream if I wasn't so desperately ready for it. I feel your cock going into me all the way, hitting my cervix with a rough push. But I don't scream. I don't scream at all: Instead, I moan, the sound muffled by my wet, ruined panties.

I can't stop myself. I lift my ass to take you.

You pump into me, my pussy so tight around your cock, its blood vessels swollen with desire. I know I'm going to come and I fight it, more determined than I've ever been not to come—knowing that I don't have a choice. You fuck me hard, rough—without mercy. You slam into me, your hipbones striking my ass with each thrust. Your cock hitting the back of my pussy so hard that little shudders of pain go through my body with each surge of pleasure.

"No," I beg, what's left of my underwear hanging half out of my mouth. "No, no, no, no, no . . ." I say it over and over again, the word I've dreamed of, the litany I've fantasized about being able to say and know it will be absolutely ineffectual. And it is: It only makes you fuck me harder. But as I say it, over and over again: "No, no, no, no, no," it transforms—it no longer means "Don't rape me." It doesn't even mean "Don't fuck me." It means please, God, please, please, please, oh please don't make me come.

And that's when I do come, uncontrollably, my whole body shuddering, my pussy contracting around your pounding cock—the moment when I start to scream, loudest of all: "No! No! No! No! No!" I want to howl it: "Don't make me come, don't make me come," but I can't—I'm so far beyond words I couldn't say anything except "No." So I scream it, over and over again, at the top of my lungs, not even caring if the neighbors call the cops. I scream it and thrash under you, struggling against the ropes that bind my wrists, fighting against the weight of your knees forcing my legs wide open. Resisting the pulse of your cock into me, making me come.

"Please," I whimper, as my orgasm trembles to a close. "Please, no, no, no, no . . ." It now means "Don't let me have just come. Please don't let me have just come." And that only makes me come harder, and whether it's a second orgasm or a resurgence of the first, I don't know. Sobs wrack my body as it explodes through me, and I hear you groaning, too, a bestial, violent sound, as you burst inside me and pump me full of your come. I struggle to stop pumping my ass with yours, fight to prevent my body from begging it. But it's no use. I've been savaged, subdued, overwhelmed. I've been forced by my own desire. I've been taken, without mercy.

But mercy is so overrated. And your cock is the greatest mercy of all.

MASTER

MASTER

30 SPANKING TALES
FROM THE TOP

edited by N. T. Morley

HEAT
NEW YORK, NY

THE BERKLEY PUBLISHING GROUP
Published by the Penguin Group
Penguin Group (USA) Inc.
375 Hudson Street, New York, New York 10014, USA
Penguin Group (Canada), 90 Eglinton Avenue East, Suite 700, Toronto, Ontario M4P 2Y3, Canada
(a division of Pearson Penguin Canada Inc.)
Penguin Books Ltd., 80 Strand, London WC2R 0RL, England
Penguin Group Ireland, 25 St. Stephen's Green, Dublin 2, Ireland (a division of Penguin Books Ltd.)
Penguin Group (Australia), 250 Camberwell Road, Camberwell, Victoria 3124, Australia
(a division of Pearson Australia Group Pty. Ltd.)
Penguin Books India Pvt. Ltd., 11 Community Centre, Panchsheel Park, New Delhi—110 017, India
Penguin Group (NZ), 67 Apollo Drive, Rosedale, North Shore 0632, New Zealand
(a division of Pearson New Zealand Ltd.)
Penguin Books (South Africa) (Pty.) Ltd., 24 Sturdee Avenue, Rosebank, Johannesburg 2196,
South Africa

Penguin Books Ltd., Registered Offices: 80 Strand, London WC2R 0RL, England

This is a work of fiction. Names, characters, places, and incidents either are the product of the author's imagination or are used fictitiously, and any resemblance to actual persons, living or dead, business establishments, events, or locales is entirely coincidental. The publisher does not have any control over and does not assume any responsibility for author or third-party websites or their content.

Published by arrangement with Bookspan.
Master copyright © 2004 by N. T. Morley.
Master/Slave copyright © 2004 by N. T. Morley.
Interior text design by Stacy Irwin.

"Good Fortune" first appeared on goodvibes.com. It is copyright © 2003 by Scott Wallace and is reprinted by permission from the author.
"Attraction" first appeared in *Torn Shapes of Desire*, published by Intangible Assets Manufacturing. It is copyright © 1997 by Mary Anne Mohanraj and is reprinted by permission of the author.
The remaining stories in this collection are copyright © 2004 by their respective authors. They are used by permission.

PRINTING HISTORY
Venus Book Club hardcover edition / 2004
Heat trade paperback edition / July 2005

Library of Congress Cataloging-in-Publication Data

Master/slave / edited by N. T. Morley.
    p. cm.
    Originally published by Venus Book Club (Garden City, N.Y.) as two separate works:
Master (2004) and Slave (2004), but here combined into one.
    ISBN 0-425-20269-0
    1. Sadomasochism—Fiction. 2. Erotic stories, American. I. Morley, N. T. II. Master III. Slave.
PS648.S24M37 2005
813'01083538'090511—dc22
                                        2005040425

CONTENTS

Introduction
by N. T. Morley

In bringing together these stories, I realized how often erotica is told from the point of view of a submissive woman surrendering to a dominant man. But what about that man—who is he? Is he a cruel, heartless exploiter, using his "victim" to satisfy his own needs? Is he a tender lover, giving his woman exactly what she most desires even though she must be tied up, shackled, bound, collared, and humiliated to be able to receive it? Or is he, simply, a man with needs like other men—needs so intense that he's willing to torment, restrain, and abuse the object of his affection in order to satisfy them?

The answer is that he is all those things, and more. The stories in *MASTER* are told in the voices of dominant men taking power over women—power willingly given, but power nonetheless. There is an old Christian adage that says "the most powerful position is on your knees," and the women in *MASTER* have discovered that fact to be true—they kneel in prayer to their dominant Masters, worshipping the pleasures these men so forcefully provide. But as profound as it can be to give up power, the male characters in this book make it quite clear that standing above a kneeling supplicant is a place of intense pleasure, as well.

The men in *MASTER* are not macho stereotypes or muscle-bound action heroes; rather, they are men who have learned that their pleasure comes from giving submissive women what they most desire—the chance to submit, to surrender, to experience release from all responsibility. They are controlling bastards, at times; they are sometimes callous, cruel, and arrogant, nasty and brutish. They're masculine archetypes, the in-control men that other men both envy and resent. But as you will understand as you read these stories, there is one trait they share that your average Joe does not possess: As cruelly as they may treat their women, they never, ever take them for granted.

In the outside world, men who mistreat women are regarded by thinking people as a certain kind of criminal. In the bedroom, however, when a woman has whispered her darkest secrets into his ear,

her breath warm against his flesh, when she has admitted to him her most taboo desires and, in so doing, given him the most profound gift a woman can give a man—when she has *asked* him to become the bastard she so desperately wants him to be—he becomes a kind of god. Like the ordinary man who, in times of trouble or war or strife, must become a hero because that is what is needed, he takes on the responsibility of being the icon above reproach, the deity whom his lover will worship. It is a profound responsibility, and one not lightly accepted by any but the reckless. And in taking that responsibility, he offers his girl the kind of gift that only a certain kind of man can give. Whether he's Daddy, Master, Lord, Sir, or any number of expletives a willingly bound woman may wish to heap upon him as he savages her, he has become more than man. Perhaps, even, more than human.

I should note that, as in the companion volume *slave*, I speak of the bedroom only as a figure of speech. The men in *MASTER* do not constrain their deliciously brutish behaviors to the sleeping chamber. Quite the contrary: These Masters bring women to their knees in restaurants, nightclubs, living rooms, fetish clubs, dressing rooms, and warehouses equipped with pulleys and chains. They place those supple leather restraints around the wrists of their willing submissives on rooftops, dive bars, and offices. They strip their eager victims bare in public restrooms, public transportation—even in alleys and on street corners. There are no doors on the bedrooms here, no rule that says a woman's submissive journey will begin in polite supplication before a four-poster bed. Rather, a woman who submits to these men, who lowers herself to her knees before them or sinks into their arms knows that nowhere is she safe—and nowhere could she be safer.

MASTER is a book of stories about men who love women more than ordinary men could ever dream of doing. Whether you see yourself in the motorcycle boots of the narrators or the fuck-me pumps of their slaves, I hope you enjoy these adventures as much as I have.

—N. T. Morley
San Francisco, Summer 2003

Good Fortune
by Scott Wallace

Newcomer **Scott Wallace**'s short fiction has appeared in the anthology *Sweet Life 2* and on websites like Goodvibes.com. About "Good Fortune," Wallace says "I love the idea of public sex, especially when it's semi-consensual. 'Good Fortune' came about when my girlfriend bought me some Flirty Fortunes as a gift; they're fortune cookies with filthy sayings on them. Naturally, I thought of a fantasy where a very willing young woman was seduced by a very personalized incarnation of such novelties. I think the result gets at what is sexiest to me about being dominant over my girlfriend in real life—that she slowly gives up control, becoming more and more turned-on, until she's so excited she'd do almost anything, including stripping in public and having sex anywhere I tell her to. I won't say we acted out this exact scene, but one very similar to it did happen shortly after she gave me the gift. Both of us remember that evening fondly."

"I'm famished," said Ivy as Adam pulled her chair out for her.

"I'm glad," said Adam, taking his own seat. "This is the best Chinese restaurant in town. I recommend the Peking duck."

Ivy looked around, plainly impressed by the lavish surroundings. Shoji screens with images of swans, sunrises, clouds, and bamboo trees were scattered around the restaurant, suffusing it with a gentle, soothing light. The scent of finely prepared Chinese delicacies was intoxicating. The waiter, clad in a white tuxedo, approached with their menus.

"Something to drink for the lady?" he asked.

"House red?" said Ivy, peering over the menu.

"The same for me," said Adam.

"Very good," said the waiter, and placed a tray in front of Ivy. The tray held a single fortune cookie.

Ivy looked up at the waiter, but he had vanished around the twists and turns of the shoji screens. "What's this?" she asked, picking up the fortune cookie and peering quizzically at Adam.

"I don't know," said Adam innocently. "You'd better open it."

"How did he know I love fortune cookies?"

"Ancient Chinese secret," said Adam. "Open the cookie."

Ivy cracked open the fortune cookie and began eating it, savoring the crisp, sweet morsels.

"You're not reading the fortune," said Adam.

"It's an old superstition I have," said Ivy. "You can't read the fortune until after you've eaten the cookie."

"Good thing you like fortune cookies."

"But I usually don't eat them at the start of a meal." Ivy munched the last bits of cookie and unfurled the tiny white slip of paper. She turned several shades of pink, then red. She looked up at Adam and then back down again. Her date was smiling enigmatically.

"Well?" he asked.

"Well what?" said Ivy meekly, too embarrassed to look her date in the eye.

"Well?" said Adam.

Ivy was dressed in a little white cocktail number that, Adam thought, looked incredible on her. It was skimpy in all the right places, cut just low enough to display a hint of cleavage and a fetching swell where Ivy's slim breasts tented the material. He could see the spray of pale lace at the neckline where her bra peeked over. As Adam watched, Ivy's nipples grew visible through her thin dress.

Ivy looked up at Adam, blushing more fiercely than ever. She looked down again, embarrassed, then up again, locking eyes with him. Her nipples became still more visible, and Adam couldn't resist a glance at them, even as Ivy was watching. He and Ivy hadn't slept together yet, though it was pretty clear they were going to. Imagining the sight of those small pink nipples, taunting himself with the

thought of their taste and feel against his tongue, brought Adam's cock to full mast in his silk Armani suit pants.

Ivy's pale cleavage blushed as red as her face, and she clutched the tiny slip of paper like a waif with a $100 bill.

"Well?" repeated Adam.

Ivy unclenched her hand and looked down at the sweaty slip of paper.

It said, TAKE OFF YOUR PANTIES.

"Well," said Adam, and this time it wasn't a question.

Her face hot, her breath coming short, Ivy looked around the restaurant and shifted in her seat, nudging herself closer to the table. They were in the middle of the room, and while the shoji screens presented some cover, they were nowhere near a wall.

Ivy's hands crept up her thighs, lifting the hem of her skirt up above the lace tops of her white stockings. She felt so wicked for having put her white lace thong on over her garters—but she'd imagined that tonight was the night she and Adam would finally sleep together, and she wanted to impress him with her worldly knowledge and brazen sexiness.

That had certainly backfired. Now Adam was watching her blush, a smile on his face, plainly enjoying the way in which he'd embarrassed her.

But Ivy was enjoying it too. Her nipples were so hard they hurt. Her stomach was doing flip-flops. She knew when she took off her panties they would be wet.

She eased her hands up under her dress and pulled down the thin white satin of her thong. She looked around nervously, but no one seemed to be noticing her. She eased her panties down her thighs, hoping that the tablecloth would provide enough cover for her. She brought her panties down past her knees, over her calves, and then dropped them to the floor. She lifted one high-heeled shoe and then the other, and bent down as if picking up a dropped fork. She tucked the panties in her handbag, and zeroed her gaze back in on Adam, who was smiling.

But not before she had noticed that her thong was, indeed, soaked through.

"May I take your order?" asked the waiter as he set down their wine.

"Oh," said Ivy. "I haven't even had a chance to look at the menu. Can . . . can we have a minute?"

"Certainly," said the waiter, as he deposited another tray in front of the blushing Ivy.

Ivy looked at Adam, her clit throbbing painfully between her tightly clenched thighs. So aware was she of her lack of underwear that every time she shifted in her chair she felt a surge of arousal.

Adam nodded toward the fortune cookie.

Ivy broke it open, staring into Adam's dark eyes as she ate the cookie in small pieces, savoring the sickly sweet, crunchy crumbs. She clutched the second fortune desperately, afraid to look.

"Read it," said Adam.

Ivy opened her palm, finding the second fortune soaked with her sweat. She read it, unable to stifle the tiny moan that escaped her lips. Her eyes seemed to cross and her head began spinning.

"Read it," said Adam softly. "Out loud."

"It says . . ." she began, and stopped, her throat tight. Ivy took a deep breath, then looked into Adam's eyes. Her face pinkened further and she swallowed. Her mouth felt sticky with the sweet of the fortune cookie. Her pussy throbbed as she tried to find her voice, the filthy sentence grasping her even as she longed to say it.

"It says . . ." she started, and couldn't go on.

Finally, she leaned across the table, bringing her face close to Adam's, and he leaned close as well.

Ivy whispered: "It says: FINGER YOUR PUSSY AND TELL ME HOW WET YOU ARE."

"Then you'd better do that," said Adam.

Glancing around, Ivy nervously let her thighs slip a few inches apart. Snuggling her hand gently under her skirt, she touched her cunt and felt a sudden flush of excitement as its juices dribbled onto the tips of her fingers. She removed her hand and leaned close again.

Adam looked at her and shook his head.

"It said, 'finger,' not 'touch,'" he told Ivy, and her clit gave a surge.

Her eyes roving the restaurant to make sure no one was watching, Ivy drew her hand back up her thigh. She snuck it under her skirt

and pressed it firmly against her sex, spreading her thighs to gain access. She put one finger in and gasped, feeling like she was going to pass out.

She leaned very close to Adam and said, "I'm very wet."

"How wet?" asked Adam.

"Incredibly wet," whispered Ivy.

"Wet enough to get fucked?"

"More than that," she blushed, her voice soft and husky with desire.

"Enjoying your wine?" asked the waiter, his smile tantalizing as he stood beside them with a pad ready and a tray tucked to one side.

"Oh, God," said Ivy, before she could silence herself. Her eyes were riveted on the new tray in the waiter's hand with its single fortune cookie.

"I think we'll have the Peking duck," said Adam. "And we'll start with an order of pot stickers, some egg rolls, and the hot and sour soup."

"Very good," said the waiter, jotting the order down. He placed the tray before Ivy and left.

Ivy looked at Adam, hunger in her gaze, her hand shaking.

"Read it," said Adam, standing up. "I'm going to use the restroom."

Ivy cracked open the cookie and ate one crumb, then another, savoring each morsel as she stared at the white slip of paper without reading it. Finally, she let the fragments of fortune cookie fall to the white tablecloth and read the fortune without finishing the cookie.

She took a deep, slow breath, shifting nervously in her seat.

The fortune said: YOU WILL HAVE SEX WITH A HANDSOME STRANGER IN A CHINESE RESTAURANT'S MEN'S ROOM.

Ivy stood up, her knees shaking. She left her purse, panties and all, tucked under the table. She walked on unsteady legs toward the back of the restaurant, picking up speed with each table she passed.

By the time she reached the long corridor that led to the restrooms, she was practically sprinting.

Adam was waiting for her with the light turned off. As she slipped into the men's room, he grabbed her and pulled her deeper into the jasmine-scented darkness, slamming her against the door so that her behind forced it shut as Adam crushed her to the door with his

weight. A moan escaped Ivy's lips in the instant before he kissed her, his tongue swabbing the fortune-cookie sweetness out of her mouth and replacing it with his salt-wine taste. He gently pushed her legs apart and drew his fingers up her slit, feeling for himself how wet she was. Ivy regained her senses and began to claw hungrily at Adam's belt, her hands shaking so bad it took her three tries to get his zipper down. By then, Adam had unzipped the back of her dress and pulled it forward. She shrugged it over her shoulder and down her arms. She took Adam's cock into her hands and stroked it hungrily as he unclasped her bra and brought his mouth first to one hard nipple, then to the other, suckling them. Ivy dropped to her knees, Adam's tongue leaving a slick trail up her neck. She took his cock in her mouth and sucked hungrily, moaning low in her throat as her lips slid up and down the shaft.

Adam leaned hard against the door, his hands caressing her face as she sucked him. She looked up at him but she could see absolutely nothing—just darkness. Adam took her shoulders and lifted her up. Her tongue lolled out as his cock slipped out of her mouth. Adam took firm hold of her and turned her around, pushing her gently forward into blackness. Her dress went sliding over her shoulders, past her hips and down her slim legs. She stepped out of it, not even caring that it was now on the restroom floor. She shrugged off her bra and Adam eased her against the sink, bending her over. Her breasts pushed against the cold porcelain and she gasped. Ivy let him spread her legs wide. His cock, still moist with her spittle, nudged open her pussy lips.

Ivy stifled a moan of pleasure as Adam entered her. She gripped the sink and stifled another moan, this one with much greater difficulty, as he pushed all the way into her and reached under to stroke her clit. Then she couldn't stifle her moans at all—they were erupting, uncontrolled, from her wide-open mouth, as Adam fucked her deep and rubbed her clit quickly. She came almost right away, and began pushing herself back onto Adam's cock even as his other hand caressed her nipples and covered her small breasts. Soon she knew she was going to come again, and she reached her second climax just as Adam bit the back of her neck, hard, almost as hard as she liked it, making her squeal with hunger as he pumped into her. Ivy gripped

the porcelain sink, her ass raised high and her legs spread to take Adam's thrusting cock as he sighed warmly into her ear, emptying his cock deep into her clenching, hungry cunt.

When he drew his cock back out of her, soft now, Ivy trembled hard against the sink. Adam helped her back into her dress in the dark, not bothering with her bra, which he tucked into the pocket of his suit jacket. He guided Ivy to the door and she slipped out into the restaurant, hair mussed, face pink. Her pussy felt wet and filled as she walked back to the table and sat down, her head swirling.

The appetizers and soup were waiting. The waiter had swept away the fragments of her last, unfinished cookie, along with the three slips of paper.

Adam joined her a moment later.

"Eat up," he said. "You said you were famished."

"I . . . I don't seem to be hungry anymore," said Ivy, her voice hoarse from moaning. She looked up at Adam and smiled sheepishly.

Adam's dark eyes seized her, and his own mouth twitched in a wicked smile.

"Those fortune cookies can be filling," said Adam.

Ivy took a deep breath, closed her eyes and sighed.

"Yes," she said. "They certainly can."

Beg Me
by Alison Tyler

Alison Tyler is undeniably a naughty girl. With best friend
Dante Davidson, she is the coeditor of the bestselling collection
of short stories *Bondage on a Budget*. Her short stories have appeared in several anthologies, including *Erotic Travel Tales 1*
and *2, Sweet Life 1* and *2, Wicked Words 4, 5, 6, & 8, Best
Women's Erotica 2002* and *2003, Guilty Pleasures,* and *Sex Toy
Tales*. With Thomas S. Roche she is the coauthor of *His & Hers,*
both from Pretty Things Press.

Longtime fans will know that Tyler is superb at evoking the
eroticism in the mind and body of a submissive woman, whether
she's experiencing a well-deserved spanking, a bondage adventure, or a sensuous, vanilla seduction. Tyler also writes some of
the hottest lesbian scenes I've ever read, understanding and com-
municating the very essence of erotic femininity. Here, however,
Tyler offers us a rare treat: She breaks form and writes from the
point of view of a dominant man. Tyler says of "Beg Me": "Truly
getting into a character's skin is an almost indescribable sensation. For me, when a story works, it's as if I'm falling. Like those
dreams everyone has in which the ground fades away, and you're
left free-floating in space. Finding a character's voice has the
same effect on me. My real self fades into nothing, and I free-fall
into the character. That's what happened with 'Beg Me'. When I
finished writing it, it was as if there was nothing left of me at all."

White.

Her skin is so white that I can't stare at it for too long. Instead, I
look down at the sandy-beige carpet beneath my feet, studying an
empty circular space directly in front of me. I see the heavy work

boots I'm wearing, the faded 501s. Then I move my gaze to my reflection in the mirror. I'm tall and strong, with dark eyes and a darker goatee. I don't have piercings or tattoos. No additional adornments. If you look into my eyes, you understand who I am.

With Dana, it's different. I don't need to look into her eyes, only at her body. But I hold off for a moment. I make myself wait, looking down at the carpet instead, and I listen to her ragged breathing as she tries to control herself, as she tries not to fight against the binds that hold her.

But then, because I can't help it, I look back at her. I am captivated.

Her flesh is pure, waiting for me. Waiting for the mark of my crop to color it, to decorate it, to adorn it, to finish it. She is untouched. She is waiting. She is mine.

This is our regular routine. Dana is punished often in our relationship. Because she needs it. Because she wants it. We have set rules, certain days that she is whipped with my belt, certain days that she is caned. This goes without saying. As soon as we were in a true relationship, I put her on a schedule of discipline that we could both agree on and look forward to. I'm like that in all parts of my life. Regulated. Serious. In control.

Of course, she is often punished on other days, either because she is bad or because she is good. I am telling you this only because I want you to understand the most important part—I am not a cruel person. Not entirely. Dana is punished because she knows deep inside herself that she deserves it.

And I punish her because I like to.

Though, sometimes, like right now, her beauty startles me. It makes it difficult for me to jump into a scene, to lay into her right away. Pain is what she wants, and what she'll get. But sometimes the innocence of her naked body gives me pause. It makes me want to climb right on the bed next to her and press my lips to her ear, whispering, "Why do you need it so rough? Why do you need so much darkness?"

But then I look into my own black heart and I try, unsuccessfully, to answer those same questions. And all I ever come up with is: because. I need to inflict pain because it is how I show love. I need it rough because it's the only way I can feel anything. I need darkness because I am afraid of the light.

Not her light, though. Not the pure whiteness of her skin. That doesn't frighten me at all—it excites me. A bare canvas waiting for the stroke of my brush.

I pace, flicking the fine bone handle of the weapon against my hand, letting her hear the noise as it smacks against my weathered palm. She twitches at the noise, tries to turn her head to watch me, to place me in the room, but she can't. She's tied fast and hard to the bed. She can't move at all.

"Please, Master," she whispers, "don't . . ."

I roam, nearly dancing in my steps, back and forth, closer to the bed, then away again, near enough that I can smell the heat on her, and then back to the wall, where I lean against the smooth, wood paneling and watch her.

Just the look of her body, so carefully tied, is enough for me. At least for the moment. Just the scene before my eyes, the way she works so desperately to control herself, to contain herself, makes me sweat. I'll make her pay for this, for having such an effect on me. She will pay.

But still, I have to admit it: what a show. What a brilliant fuckin' show. She can't really move, but she can tense and release those long muscles in her thighs and her back and her ass, the cut throbbing muscles that betray her. She wants this. She aches for this. And the longer we wait, the more chance there is that she'll beg me to give her what she needs. What she craves.

I want her to beg.

Her wrists are fastened with thick leather straps, bands that I bought on my last trip abroad. Crafted of well-tooled leather, they are imprinted with designs: curling waves, two-toned diamonds, ridged zigzags. The leather was worked well by the tall Italian boy I bought it from. I can see him still, in his tiny workshop near the bridge, bending over the table and pounding on the hide until his sweat dripped onto the skins, until he became part of his craft.

Now these bands capture her finely boned wrists securely—I made sure the silver buckles fit tightly, digging into her flesh—and as her sweat mingles with his on the inside of the leather, she, too, becomes one with the art.

(Beg me.)

For this is art, modern art. No one in the fringe world would dispute me on this one. Dana, my lover, my whore, is a show all to herself. Her translucent skin bruises so easily, and I have to watch myself and take it slow. That is a lesson in patience. But her greatest features—as far as the sick and twisted Doms are concerned—are the bruises on her soul. She needs everything that I need to give her. We are the perfect opposites, and I will make her pay for that fact. I will torment her.

(Beg me.)

I let the crop handle hit my palm again, and watch as she flinches, as she tries to toss her light brown hair out of her eyes. She wants to see—it would be less frightening to her if she could see—so I use the other end of my weapon to lift her curls from her face, and I let just the very edge of the crop brush her pale cherry lips. Automatically, she opens her mouth, ready to suck.

I have trained her well.

"You want to watch," I say, a statement, not a question. "Want to watch as I beat you, don't you? It makes it easier if you know when the next blow is gonna come, when the pain is gonna start." This is different with each slave. Some need to watch, they need to see the arc as a master's arm swings up and then cuts down hard. They need to know it's coming. Others think it's better the other way, they want their eyes closed—it can be so safe behind closed lids. (If I don't watch, then it's not real.) It's up to a true dominant to discover what the slave needs, wants, deserves. Often these are not one and the same.

(Beg me.)

Her silver-gray eyes open and close, the thin silky skin of her eyelids unable to shield her from my power. From my rage. She swallows hard. I watch her throat contract—watch her mouth work for the spit to pry her tongue from the roof of her mouth. She's having a difficult time with this. No matter how many times we go over this lesson, it doesn't seem to get any easier for her.

Another swallow before she is able to speak. I lean forward and press my hand against her throat, press a little too firmly for comfort. This helps her, as pain always does. This helps her to release.

"Yes," she whispers, and I feel her words on the tips of my fingers. "I want to watch."

I stare into her eyes, let her try and read the message I'm sending her. I test her with my glare, and am proud enough when she gets it, when she closes her light eyes, bites her lip, and prepares herself for the first blow.

"This isn't about what you want," I remind her, moving again, so that now I'm on her right side, out of her line of vision. "This is not about what you want at all."

I raise my arm and bring it down once, hard, catching her across the tops of both thighs, digging into her soft skin, driving her down into the mattress. Her moan is exceptional, musical, a low, hungry growl that tells me I've already reached the door to that secret place inside her where she doesn't like to go. Where there is only fear and endless desire—waves of burning desire that she needs my help to find. To ride. To crest.

"This is about what you need."

Then we wait. I can wait as long as it takes, as long as she requires. I stare at the welt as it blossoms on her skin, stare as the true color emerges, in the same, magical way that a Polaroid develops. The lovely purplish line against her skin seems to throb in the dim light of the room, to glow with the tangible heat of her pain.

(Beg me.)

Her breathing is desperate now as she tries to control herself, as she tries to return to the stable center where she functions day-to-day. But it's gone. There is no stable center. In this world, in this scene, there is nothing but slip-sliding chaos, nothing but heat and fire. Sex and sin. Confusion.

How white her skin looks in contrast to that one, lone stripe. I step back, making enough noise with my feet on the floor that she is aware of the next blow a second before it catches her. This time she tightens up, freezing her muscles, and I admonish her for it. She knows what a mistake that is—it hurts so much more when you tense.

"You must really need the pain tonight, darling," I say to her, not without compassion. I am her dominant, her master, but I am also her lover. Even if I show my love in a unique way. "Tightening like that makes it burn so much longer. Makes it hurt so much worse."

She's not listening to me, though. She's consumed by the throb-

bing, excruciating line of hurt riding just a few inches above the first one. But, other than a dark moan, a panting moan, she is quiet. It takes a lot to make my lover cry.

(Beg me.)

I move to the other side of the bed, but then, having second thoughts, I climb onto the mattress, next to her, and I press the cane into the line of the first welt. Intensifying the feeling for her. Denying her the relief, denying her the ability to adjust to the pain. She doesn't want relief, my Dana. And more than that—she doesn't deserve it.

(Beg me.)

She cries at the feel, cries harder, louder, as I roll the weapon against her skin and lay it flat into the second stripe. She knows that I will make this punishment last. She knows that I can continue tormenting her, torturing her, until the night is over and the first red rays of dawn pour through the window. That's the most frightening moment for her, when she realizes that even though the midnight hour is far behind her, we are still entrenched in our roles.

Morning doesn't necessarily end a scene. And how scary is that? How terrifying is that? Morning comes, but the nightmare isn't over.

(Beg me.)

From this close point, I bring the crop up and down on her a third time. So hard that I shake the bed. Ah, darling, I want to tell her. Why not give in? Why not make it easier on yourself? I know the answer, though, without verbalizing the question. She doesn't want it easier. Not my Dana. Not my naughty girl.

"Count," I tell her now, already well-steeped in the game, the sweat rising in sparkling tingles along the back of my neck. "We're going to start with a dozen, and I want you to count each blow for me."

Her voice is a choked sob, so low that I have to press my lips against her mouth to hear her. She says, "Yes, Master," exactly as she should. She says, "Thank you, Master," and her lips form the pucker of a kiss as she tries to show me how grateful she is. I don't let her. I don't let her kiss my fingers, kiss my crop. That will come later, when she is nothing more than a sobbing heap. Then I will let her thank me. Now, she doesn't know what she's thanking me for. The future is held out before her like an unwrapped present.

The cane comes up and down on her and she counts. There are

no tears. She can take it. She can take exactly what I tell her she can take. How lovely it is to see those welts on her skin. This isn't a game. This isn't about power or control. This is about giving someone what they need and taking what you need and together, somehow, making it all right. Because somehow it's possible: everything that's wrong and dirty and sinful and impure, somehow, sometimes, you can make it all right.

And, thinking this, I meet my gaze in the mirror over the bed. My eyes are still hungry, but the need is almost filled. Thinking this, I stand back from her, and I lift the cane, and we start again.

The First Time She Kneels
by Anonymous

The author of "The First Time She Kneels" says he wants to remain anonymous because every word of the story is true. "As a lifestyle dominant, I've discovered that certain generalizing attitudes about women are incompatible with political correctness—but incredibly hot. Dominance has never been about punishment for me, but about sex—about totally owning that woman's sexuality, teaching her how to please me without concern for politeness, without concern for her feelings or her ego. A woman who is willing to give up that ego and learn from scratch how to please me—that is the greatest pleasure I've ever experienced."

The first time she kneels with her hands behind her back and her mouth open, beckoning, hungry to be fucked: That's a critical moment. The uncontrolled hunger she feels in that instant, before she is taken orally for the first time, is the most important aspect of a female slave. If that hunger is not overwhelming, if it does not threaten to consume her, she has not yet achieved the proper need for submission. If, as she kneels before her master and watches him take out his cock, she nurtures even the faintest belief that she might have been born to do anything other than kneel and suck it, then she is not yet blessed with the knowledge of her place as a true submissive.

There is no act more dominant, and more dominating, than receiving a blowjob, just as there is no act more submissive than properly giving one. I say this from years of experience with many submissives, knowing that for the ones I am drawn to, there is no act that more completely displays their submission than taking a master's cock in their mouths: tasting him, swallowing him, pleasuring

him, and accepting his come. And—there can be no exception, for my submissives—swallowing every last drop.

Most girls have spent their lives giving halfhearted blowjobs. The first type of woman gives head to avoid going all the way, the second type because she thought her boyfriends wanted it. The third type of woman genuinely enjoys sucking cock, but she's never had the benefit of having specific instruction—after all, men are usually reluctant to give feedback, as if a blowjob is such a kind gift from a woman that to criticize would be to jeopardize future blowjobs.

All of these women, I can work with.

A woman who has offered oral sex merely to avoid the risk of pregnancy or preserve her sought-after virtue—she can be shown the importance of offering the perfect blowjob, because her conditioning is such that the avoidance of punishment will be a familiar motivator in gaining oral skills. Though my punishment is much more swift, direct, and harsh than simply pressuring her for sex. It is also more effective, and a woman for whom blowjobs have been a tool of virtue and protection will soon be a skilled cocksucker, knowing that providing oral sex for me will prevent her from suffering physical pain, isolation, or both—whatever is most abhorrent to that particular submissive.

A woman who gives head to her boyfriend because she thinks he expects it—she is also someone I can work with. She imagines that men consider blowjobs their birthright, and therefore she provides, whether for the convenience of avoiding argument or because she wishes to please her man, it doesn't really matter. Because some part of her believes that blowjobs are a man's birthright, and therefore her reluctance can be converted into unthinking, blind willingness to perform her duty when a hard cock is shoved into her face. Such a woman can learn that oral sex is her duty, that providing a satisfactory blowjob is the most important skill she can learn to establish her worth in the universe. That small part of her that believes that men are owed blowjobs can be nurtured, rewarded, and expanded until it dominates her whole mind whenever she lowers herself to her knees before a hard male organ.

The third kind of woman—the kind who likes giving head, but has never learned to do it properly—is more difficult to work with.

Often she believes she is an accomplished cocksucker, having received insincere but sufficiently convincing praise from the unfortunate men who have received her attentions over the years. Her self-esteem requires her to believe that she is a skilled fellator, and it is a very delicate matter to encourage her to unlearn this. If her ego prevents her from accepting the truth when I inform her that her cocksucking skills are unacceptable, she may be so injured as to resist further training. It takes quite a bit of work to guide these women into deep enough submission so that they can abandon all they know about sucking cock and be trained from the throat up.

There is a fourth kind of woman, however, and she is the one I most treasure. This is the woman for whom cocksucking is not a form of sex, but a form of worship. I am her God, merely by virtue of my having a hard cock which I put in her face. There is no reciprocation expected, no spankings or punishments or attentions desired as reward for a good blowjob. The blowjob, for her, is more than a reward in itself. It is her whole world. She lives to get down on her knees and lavish affection on a male organ, to service it until it fills her mouth with the pungent testimony to her place in the universe. There is no ego involved; she does not worry about whether she is a good cocksucker, for there is no conscious thought involved. Only overwhelming, undying love for cock, the kind of love that will drive a woman deeper and deeper into submission, accepting every manner of instruction and criticism. Every shortcoming in her cocksucking skills becomes a spiritual lesson, and she learns with great eagerness. At no point does she resist my instruction and imagine that another man might think her most mediocre blowjobs were fantastic. Rather, she accepts without thought the knowledge that she can never, ever, be a good enough cocksucker to satisfy her God, and the only way to aspire to such satisfactory status is to do it as often as possible—not just frequently, but constantly. Without provision for her own needs, except her one central need: the need to suck cock.

This is the kind of woman Lisa proved to be. I was lucky enough to meet her at a London fetish ball; I was visiting from the States and had come stag. Lisa's date, a French magazine publisher, had gotten exceedingly drunk and gone off to drool over a bitchy German dominatrix.

To look at her, Lisa was not the most beautiful woman in the

world. Rather bookish and plain of face, her body was boyish even in the tight confines of a PVC corset, garters, high boots, and a G-string. Her short, mousy-brown hair accented that appearance. But her plain face was graced by something that made me seize upon her as the answer to all my prayers. Her mouth was beautiful. Wide and full, it would have appeared too big for her face, to some eyes. To me, it was breathtaking. Her lips were full and pouty, giving her what is sometimes called, uncharitably, a "horsey" look. But I saw none of that. I saw only the most beautiful mouth, a mouth that seemed to exude a quivering need so intense that I suspected right off that she belonged to the third type of woman: the woman who considers herself an accomplished cocksucker, whether she is or not. Though I've said these are difficult women to deal with, I was eager to do that work with Lisa because of her beautiful mouth. I discerned from casual conversation that she was submissive to this magazine editor, and he expected her to be monogamous with him despite the fact that he played around on her. He had treated her rudely of late, however, and it did not take much convincing to get Lisa back to my hotel room. An hour's flirtation, a few drinks, a deep kiss, and a whispered promise of a four-poster bed, and we were off.

Her corset was thoughtfully fitted with buckles, and as I roughly forced her up against the hotel room door the second I had it closed, I pulled them open as I kissed her deep, my tongue savaging her mouth. She melted into me as I exposed her slender breasts with their pierced nipples. I could already tell she was a delicious submissive, but there were many tests to put her through before I decided what kind of woman she was.

When I slid my hand down the front of her PVC G-string, I found she was extremely wet. I saw no reason to wait.

Grasping her hair, I listened to Lisa gasp as I pushed her down onto her knees. Leaning against the wall, I was pleasantly surprised that she showed no reluctance, no expectation of long, chaste sensation-play before she put out. Rather, she went right for the zipper of my leather pants, almost ripping my jockstrap as she pulled my cock out.

The second her mouth descended over my cock, I knew she was the one.

It's impossible to describe the attentions of a woman who lives for no other reason than to suck cock. There was something so profound about the hunger with which Lisa devoured my hard shaft, that I felt immediately I was in the presence of greatness. I moaned soft encouragements as I leaned over her, forcing her back until her head was wedged between my cock and the hotel room door. She did not hesitate, did not seek to find a more comfortable position. Rather, she was absolutely and totally focused on sucking my cock. The only movement she made came when I started to move my hips, fucking her face. She adjusted the angle of her neck in order to straighten it, so my cock could slide, unhindered and without the slightest hint of a gag reflex, down Lisa's throat.

She didn't stop to tell me I could come in her mouth. Her arms remained around my thighs, her hands gripping my ass like she would never dream of letting me get away. She even seemed to encourage me to fuck her face harder, to pound her as if I were fucking her pussy. I knew her throat would be red and raw tomorrow, but I didn't care. That seemed to be exactly what Lisa wanted.

I gave her the warning that is customary and polite during your first session with a new submissive—the groan that told her I was going to come. Her only action, then, was to slide her lips down far enough that she could receive my streams on her tongue, filling her mouth with my cream. Not a drop leaked out of that broad, inviting mouth. Her throat muscles worked as she swallowed in tiny spasms, trying to save every hint of taste.

When I pulled out of Lisa's mouth, she was panting. Her huge eyes looked up at me, bright with promise. We'd never turned on the lights in the hotel room, so her face and upper body were the only parts of her illuminated; I could see her small, pierced breasts and the lush curve of her slender throat, which just a moment before I'd fucked. I could see the beauty in her face as she looked up at me. And in that moment, there was no question in my mind that this was the one.

Lisa was the fourth kind of woman, without a doubt.

Because as she knelt there, her lips parted, her breath coming short, I saw one thing in her face.

Hunger.

Hunger for more.

If I'd gotten hard right then, she would have sucked me all over again. Without care to her raw and raped throat, without concern for her jaw muscles. With concern for nothing but the simple fact that there was a hard cock in her face.

As it was, Lisa had to wait fifteen minutes before she got me hard again with her mouth—record time for me. By then, we were on the king-sized hotel bed, her laying sprawled across it with her face in my lap as she hungrily sought to make me hard and then whimpered with delight when she succeeded.

That second time, I didn't limit myself to her mouth. I also explored that tight pussy of hers, tight because it rarely got enough attention—so determined was Lisa to give head at every opportunity. She still sucked me until I came in her mouth, but this time my cock was slick and tangy with her juices, a fact that didn't dissuade her the slightest bit.

There have been many more blowjobs from Lisa since then, and each one holds the promise of a million to come, as her hunger grows. For Lisa, every inch of cock slid into her mouth and down her throat makes her want more, more—more.

Lisa is definitely the fourth kind of woman.

The finest specimen I've ever had.

Attraction
by Mary Anne Mohanraj

One of erotica's brightest lights, **Mary Anne Mohanraj** is known as the author of *Torn Shapes of Desire, Kathryn in the City,* and *The Classics Professor.* She also edited the very popular erotica collections *Aqua Erotica* and *Wet.* Her writing has appeared in a wide variety of anthologies and magazines, including *Herotica 6, Best American Erotica 1999,* and *Best Women's Erotica 2000* and *2001.*

Mohanraj also founded the erotic webzine *Clean Sheets* (www.cleansheets.com) and serves as editor-in-chief for the Hugo-nominated speculative fiction webzine *Strange Horizons* (www.strangehorizons.com). She is currently a doctoral student in Fiction and Literature at the University of Utah. She has received the Scowcroft Prize for Fiction, a Neff fellowship in English, and currently holds a Steffenson-Canon fellowship in the Humanities. She can be found at www.mamohanraj.com.

Of her contribution to *MASTER,* Mohanraj writes: "I must admit that this is thinly disguised nonfiction, stolen from my college days at the University of Chicago. The restaurant in the story is the Medici, the large room found later is actually on the top floor of Eckart, what used to be known as the Barn. Even the first initials of the characters' names match their originals. I'm just lucky that they were kind enough to let me tell a small part of their story."

The collar was hard to miss against her pale skin, sharp against the soft curve of Belinda's throat. I imagined I could see her pulse racing under the studded black leather, unlikely as that was in dinner candlelight.

I'd never seen her look so beautiful.

It wasn't a romantic place where the four of us had gathered—just a student hangout with good burgers and mediocre pizza. Mark and I had only dessert, the raspberry soda of the Himbeersaft spilling out onto my fingers as I resisted asking her to lick them clean. We'd ordered Thai earlier, before coming to meet Belinda and this new man, this stranger. Not a stranger to her, of course—not quite. They'd known each other for months over the Net, and in some ways Geoff knew her better than I, who'd only known her for a few months, or even Mark, who usually shared his bed with her. Though they'd never met in the flesh before that night, it was clear that Belinda's heart was in her throat, and Geoff's eyes were oddly knowing as he watched her.

A master has to know his slave.

He made me uneasy. Some feminist instinct prickled my skin when she waited for his nod, when she lowered her eyes in shame at some minor disobedience. There was a power in those dark eyes, those overlarge hands. And though a part of me wanted to rescue Belinda, who clearly didn't want rescuing, a part of me was perhaps . . . jealous?

There are times when independence is not desirable.

Mark's arm was warm around me as we sat facing them in the wooden booth, dinner over, nobody quite ready to take those first steps out into the warm night. Belinda was, perhaps, having second thoughts about her role as slave with this man, I wondered whether he'd think himself capable of mastering me, and Mark, perhaps, pondered whether he'd sleep alone that night. I don't know what Geoff was thinking.

I wondered if he thought at all.

As we left the restaurant to meet some friends, we slid from our pairings. Belinda's breast felt soft against my face as I held her back, letting the men walk forward. "Are you all right? Do you know your safeword?" My questions served to assuage a very real anxiety . . . and sate an overwhelming curiosity. She laughed, huge eyes smiling, and hugged me close. I wish I could remember what she said that made me kiss her then. I didn't know whether I wanted to let her go . . . and wasn't sure what he would do if I didn't.

The night was very dark, and his eyes disappeared into it.

Later, I turned from laughing in a well-lit room with an old lover to see Belinda kneeling on the table, legs spread, arms locked behind her head, sweet breasts outthrust. I caught my breath, and Geoff turned toward me. Smiling, he asked if I'd like to kiss her. I answered that *I* didn't need his permission . . . and slid across the polished wooden table to kiss her deeply, caressing a breast and feeling an inaudible moan in that pale, bound throat before releasing her. The crowded room seemed oddly still, and a mixture of desire and shame rose in me as I slid back into Mark's ready arms. She still knelt there, softly smiling. Somehow that made it almost all right. But even if she'd been crying, I don't know if I would have stopped.

There is something infinitely desirable in helplessness.

And in power. He continued to tease me—perhaps unknowingly—though I doubt it. Geoff seemed oddly aware of his surroundings. Maybe that's a necessary quality in a good top. How can you surrender all thought, all judgment, if you aren't sure that someone is making trustworthy decisions for you? Though he concentrated on Belinda, the one he'd come to see, he spared a little time to verbally spar with me through the evening, on the bus ride home, and over the next hour or two as we headed slowly, inexorably to bed.

Sometimes you don't want to make choices.

I don't know whether it was fear or desire that kept me in Mark's arms that night, who surrendered his room to them while we took the almost too-narrow couch. Later, lacking a condom, I mastered my embarrassment and knocked on their door. I heard a pause, rustlings, and then, "Come in." She was beautiful, bent naked on one knee before him, her silk hair falling down to shield a flushed face. He was fully dressed, a wide-stranded whip in his hand.

He requested a kiss in payment for the condom.

It was . . . more than nice. He pulled away before I did, and I wonder now what would have happened if I'd pushed him on it, running my hands across that well-muscled chest, pressing my hot body against his. Would he have taken me then and there? With her kneeling and watching us, and Mark waiting out in the other room? Or would he have laughed and pushed me away, sending me back to Mark like a small child reaching for something too dangerous?

Uncertainty can be an aphrodisiac.

I couldn't let him make that choice, of course, and quickly slipped out the door and back down the darkened hallway. And Mark was waiting, sweet Mark, and the strength in his arms was appealing. We heard her moans and the slap of the whip down the length of the hall, despite closed doors. An effort of will not to run back . . . to rescue her? To join her?

A muffled scream.

And suddenly I couldn't wait any longer, and we were tearing off clothes far more quickly than I had originally planned, sinking deep into each other and the heat of that first summer night as Belinda's pleasure and pain echoed in the long halls. I couldn't remember the last time I'd been so hungry . . . and who can tell how much of it was Mark stretched out beneath me, and how much was the crack of Geoffrey's whip, leaving long red stripes on Belinda's pale skin . . .

Attraction is composed of desire and danger.

Carolina Rose
by Thomas S. Roche

Thomas S. Roche is one of the best-known names in erotica, and is also an accomplished writer and editor of crime and horror fiction. Responsible for the challenging and edgy *Noirotica* series, Roche has also written more than two hundred published short stories and a wide range of articles on sexual health and pleasure, vintage noir fiction, horror movies, Goth and classical music, freak culture, and rock 'n' roll.

Says Roche: "In 'Carolina Rose,' I wanted to play with the idea of a dominant/submissive relationship so great it transcended death. Most ghost stories are about traumatic experiences that bind a spirit to this world—but isn't it just as likely that one would be bound by the ultimate experience, that of total and willing submission? That's the long version, but mostly I just wanted to write a fun, slightly creepy erotic ghost story, like Charles Addams or Edward Gorey with a hard-on. The story is also a kind of wish fulfillment; as a horny narcissist, I do fantasize about spending a night in a mansion where even the ghosts are there to serve me."

My host chuckled, puffing on his Cuban cigar. "Of course, she wasn't the ordinary kind of slave girl."

"Excuse me?" I tasted my own cigar, chasing its mellow bite with the sweetness of brandy. "What exactly is the ordinary kind of slave girl?"

Atchison smiled. "Well, don't forget, son. You're in the Carolinas. The ordinary kind of slave girl . . . well, you know what that means. But ironically enough, Colonel Greene was an abolitionist."

"You're joking," I said. "And yet he had slaves?"

"Not colored—" Atchison quickly saw my automatic, conditioned, private-college response to that word, and he chuckled. "Forgive me, my Yankee friend. Colonel Greene kept no slaves of color. His slaves were of the same pasty-gray, off-pink variety that you can see flaunting their piercings at any hip-enough club in one of your esteemed Union capitals today." As he spoke, Atchison's drawl had grown from its normal lilt to a molasses-thick crawl, culminating in his referring to my hometown as part of a different country. He was, if you'll forgive me, yanking my chain.

"Oh, pardon me, my slaves," drawled Atchison. "The same type you and I might enjoy to this very day. It came out after his death that he did have quite a harem of slave girls. White ones. Europeans, even. And all . . . quite willing."

"Did his wife object?"

"She died quite young, and Colonel Greene swore never to remarry. He spent his later life as a bachelor, but secretly kept a stable of young maids who served him quite faithfully. Not unlike you or me." Atchison smiled cruelly. "Oh, excuse me, make that just me."

"You don't say," I growled. Atchison enjoyed teasing me; he was aware that my most recent live-in submissive, a graduate student named Paulette, had turned out to be an entirely top-from-the-bottom type who, two weeks before, had left me for a millionaire who'd agreed to pay for her tit job. Though Atchison and I had only met this evening, we had corresponded for some time over the Internet, sharing our opinions, tricks, and experiences in the subjugation of willing young females. I had told him the story of Paulette's betrayal, and while he expressed sympathies—he, too, had recently lost two of his live-in submissives—there was, understandably, the kind of alpha-male competition that leads masculine tops like us to revel in each others' poor fortunes with women.

When I had mentioned that I would be traveling to Atlanta on business, Atchison insisted that I rent a car and come visit him at his mansion. Though he was currently bereft of live-in servants after his recent ill fortune, he would appreciate a chance to share a brandy in person with a fellow Master.

Atchison continued: "After it was discovered just why Greene was such a recluse, it was, of course, hushed up by the local authorities.

Apparently it was quite a stable of fetching whores, you see. The old man seemed to have some sort of charm. During his life he tempted many young women into his employ, and this being the South, it was kept quiet, written off as one of those Southern peculiarities."

"And one of his slave girls haunts the house?"

"Tsk tsk," said Atchison. "You Yanks seem to think everything needs to be rushed. Indulge a new friend, will you, and let me tell you the story in my own time? Though the Colonel was an abolitionist, he did feel obligated to fight for his people in the Civil War. He was killed in battle, and following the terms of his will, this mansion was sealed up for a dozen years before it could be sold. He died childless, so his entire fortune was left to his employees. All of them girls between eighteen and twenty-five," he added with a wink. "Quite a tempting stable, wouldn't you say? And, suspiciously enough, none of them was of the servant's class—they were all aristocratic chippies who had run away to join the Colonel's household at the cost of being disowned by their families. Each of them took the Colonel's endowment, if you'll forgive the pun, and went off to make lives for themselves, no doubt marrying well and never telling their husbands about their years of willing submission at the hands of the famed Colonel Greene. There was, however, one girl named Rose, who refused to leave."

"And of course she was the prettiest of them all?" I asked.

"So the story goes," said Atchison. "There's a picture of her there in the hall. I found it in the basement when I bought the place. It was devilishly expensive to have restored, but I figured it was worth it, for such a stunning specimen. You can see the photo, if you like. It's right there."

"Is she naked?"

"Afraid not," said Atchison.

I shrugged. "I'll stick to the Internet."

Atchison frowned. "Apparently, young Rose was madly devoted to Colonel Greene," said Atchison. "She remained in the mansion, maintaining it. She stayed here all alone. One day the gardeners found her. She had taken her own life with the Colonel's revolver."

"Good God," I said. "How tragic."

"The terms of Colonel Greene's will were that any servant still

working here at the end of the twelve years would have the right to be buried on the grounds, as well as inherit the money gained from the sale of the estate. Of course, there wasn't anybody to sell it, so the state took over the sale—and the buyers picked it up at auction for a steal. They must have known what a good deal they got; they had pity on the poor girl and buried her out back, next to Colonel Greene. You can see the plot from the window, if you like."

I walked to the window and peered out. Sure enough, on a nearby hill, illuminated by the light of the moon, were two gravestones side by side.

"For years visitors said they saw her," Atchison told me. "It seems she still wanders the hallways, forever mourning her dear Colonel's death."

I stared at Atchison, the look on my face telling him just what I thought of his story. He burst out laughing, slapping his knee.

"Had you going there, didn't I? Of course, that's the story, but it's all bullshit. I've been living here two years, and I've never seen a thing." He dabbed at his eye with a napkin, his fit of laughter having brought him to tears. "I must say, I wouldn't mind if I did—I could use a blowjob from a spectral slave girl! Especially since the last two left."

I shook my head and put down my brandy. "Perhaps you could have one of your real slave girls show me to my room? It's getting quite late, and your ghost story's left me peaked."

"Now, now, you know we don't have slave girls here," said Atchison, winking at me. "They're paid servants, and they've all gone home. I already told you, Monique and Kelly both left me, or you'd be welcome to try both of them out. In fact, I dare say I feel bad about not being able to offer you proper hospitality. Since my bad luck, the slave girls only show up for special occasions, like the party next week. Surely you'll stay for that, won't you?"

"I'm afraid I have to be back in Atlanta for a business meeting."

"Slave girls galore," smiled Atchison. "All the fetish celebrities will be here. They come from New Orleans, New York, L.A. . . . in fact, I understand that a number of particularly attractive bondage models will be visiting. You've seen the most recent *Playboy*?"

"Don't taunt me," I sighed.

"Well, I'm hoping I will have a live-in by the end of the party. Perhaps two or three, if fate smiles."

"You'll have to invite me back, then."

Atchison chuckled. "Forget it. You're staying."

I yawned. "I'll think about it," I said, just to shut him up. "Now, my room?"

"Yes, of course," he said, and led me upstairs.

I'm not the kind of man who believes in ghost stories. They're garbage, the kind of comfort sought by the superstitious and the weak-minded. But I wasn't able to sleep, because the long trip had left me horny. So had my weeks of being single, without a submissive's pretty backside to warm, spank, or fervently plough. I found myself thinking about what it must have been like for Colonel Greene, a wealthy eccentric with a talent for tempting young girls into his employ. Rather than wrestling with the vagaries of relationships and the negotiations of consensual power exchange with overeducated Harvard girls who consider sexual submission not only their birthright but a particular blow of feminism against male oppression—provided the "Master" does exactly as he's told—the Colonel kept his stable fully stocked with aristocratic young things seeking escape from their own class, dreaming of life on their knees with his dick in their mouths. Was it a simpler time, women's expectations easier to fulfill? Who knows? Regardless, in the tradition of the best Southern aristocrats, the Colonel had indulged his own peculiarities and become terrifyingly excellent at them. A lucky man, surely, not unlike Atchison. I had to admit, I envied them both.

I also found myself wondering what it might be like at the fetish ball. Atchison had promised celebrities from all over, engaging their darker impulses in leather, rubber, vinyl, and lace.

My cock grew hard against the soft sheets. I always sleep in the nude, and I'm not averse to satisfying myself. I lay there toying with the possibility of jerking myself off, wishing there was one of the Colonel's slave girls to keep me company.

I heard a footstep, and sat up in bed, suddenly wide awake.

She was there, at the foot of my bed. One of Atchison's paid ser-

vants? Or one of his errant slave girls, returned with a front-door key Atchison never repossessed? Whoever she was, the girl wore a traditional maid's outfit, a little shorter in the skirt and tighter in the bosom than most you might see. She was young and slim and beautiful. Her long blonde hair was tied in a bun. She was a wisp of a girl, barely five feet tall and clearly no older than her early twenties. Her lips were full and inviting.

"I would be happy to help you with that, Sir."

"How did you get in here?"

"You were quite distracted," said the serving girl. "You didn't hear me come in. Will you allow me to help you with that, Sir? I would be happy to do so."

I looked her up and down, admiring the way her pert little form filled out the too-tight maid's outfit.

"All right," I said.

She walked to the side of the bed and bent over slightly, showing me the swell of her hips and the creamy silk of her upper thighs.

"Unfasten me, please, Sir?"

The outfit had a curious, old-fashioned clasp, kind of like what used to be called a frog clasp. I undid it and the servant pulled the outfit over her shoulders, then wriggled it down to the slender swell of her hips. It fell to the ground like a pool of midnight.

She was naked underneath—no stockings, panties, slip, or brassiere. When she turned to face me, I saw that she was shaved.

She reached behind her and pulled the pin out of her hair, fluffing it so the pristine bun fell down, shimmering and pale, around her shoulders. Her breasts were small but exquisitely formed, and they were deliciously accented by the wisps of gold that swayed around them in the breeze of the old mansion. Her nipples were very hard.

I peeled back the covers, showing her my hard-on and the full length of my naked body. She crawled into bed with me and I pulled the covers over both of us, feeling the chill of her white flesh as she cuddled against me.

Her lips, too, were cold, and as her tongue traced paths along mine I ran my fingers over the firm flesh of her buttocks. "Poor circulation," she whispered. "I'm going to catch my death of cold one of these days." I slipped my fingers between her legs, tracing a path

down her slit, finding it more than moist. She rubbed her belly against my cock, reaching down to curve her fingers around the shaft. She cooed in delight as she felt its size and thickness. She slipped under the covers and, quite buried in the warmth and smell of me, began to do her work.

I moaned softly as the servant's mouth slid up and down my cock. Her fingers tickled my balls and I ran my hands through her hair. She was an expert, that much was clear; she could have brought me off in moments. But I held back, exercising every ounce of control I could to keep from ending this lovely tryst too soon.

Her mouth came off of my cock and I heard her muffled voice from deep under the covers.

"Would you like to fuck me," she asked. "Or would you prefer to come in my mouth? I'm happy to swallow, of course, Sir. In fact, I quite like it."

"You're not getting off that easy," I told her. "Climb up here and let me fuck you."

"Of course, Sir, it is quite possible for you to fuck me and then come in my mouth. If you'd like that, Sir, that is."

"I'll decide later. Just get up here and fuck me."

She slid up my body and spread her legs, working her slit against my shaft. She didn't reach down to guide it; it was as if her cunt was so hungry for me that it all but slurped me up. She moaned softly and whimpered into my ear as her hips pumped my cock deep into her pussy. My own hips rose to meet her thrusts, and I drove into her powerfully, feeling my cock striking the back of her cunt, touching her cervix. Rather than shying away, however, she begged for more, slamming herself down onto me so that I fucked her with what many women would consider painful force. The servant girl couldn't get enough, though.

"You can take me all ways," she whispered. "I'm quite well trained to take it in the ass."

I looked up into her pretty face and thought about the delights of corrupting that pert, well-trained behind. I smiled.

"Yes, I think I should like that very much," I said.

"How would you like me, Sir? Fucking me doggy style is usually easiest. But if we remain laying here and I turn over, it's often more

difficult for me to take. Would you like that, Sir? If it hurt just a little bit?"

I kissed her lips, and felt her nipples hard against my chest.

"Yes," I told her. "I'd like it very much if it hurt you."

She slid her body off of mine and rolled over, sitting in my lap and lifting her hips so she could place the head of my cock between her cheeks. I could feel the tightness of her asshole resisting my entrance, the position making it tighter than usual.

She hesitated, hovering with my cockhead at the entrance to her back door.

"If you want me to enjoy it, Sir," she whispered. "Please be gentle."

"And if I don't want you to enjoy it?"

"Then do as you wish," she whispered, and arched her back so she could kiss me on the lips.

I wasn't gentle at all. Rather, I read the subtext of her reluctance and drove into her ass with the fiercest of thrusts, drawing a loud wail from her lips. She pushed herself against me as I curved my hands around her naked body and held her hips still, pounding up into her ass so that her whole nude form spasmed. She moaned, thrashed, and spread her legs very wide. Her hand hovered over her moist pussy, hungrily seeking to rub her clit. But she was well trained; she asked permission first.

"Please, Sir," she whimpered, her voice rendered staccato by the rhythmic thrusts I was giving her. "I'm so very close to coming. Please, Sir, may I touch myself?"

"Not a chance," I said, grabbing her wrist and pulling it away. She groaned in torment, and her thrusts onto my cock became harder, rougher, meeting each of my violent stabs into her as she wailed in discomfort and mounting arousal. When she was quite lost in the sensations, I brought my hand to her pussy and began to rub her clit, firmly, matching each thrust into her ass with a stroke on her clitoris.

I would have come inside her even if she didn't reach her orgasm—after all, it gives me great pleasure to leave a submissive hungry and wanting, knowing her place in the world is not to feel her own pleasure but to provide the pleasure of others. But this girl was a

peach, and with a cock in her ass and a hand on her clit I had the feeling she couldn't have avoided coming for the world.

"Oh God, Sir," she whimpered. "I'm coming, oh, I'm coming, thank you, thank you Sir oh God!"

She moaned and gripped my arms tightly as she pounded onto me, fucking my cock deep into her ass. When I came myself she seemed to be eager for it, begging me to fill her. Her delicious body wriggled against mine until her tight back door had milked the last come from my shaft.

My hands came to rest on her tits, gently stroking them as I sank into the arms of Morpheus. She laid on top of me as her ass leaked the copious load of come I had just given it, the wetness dribbling over my balls and onto the sheets. The servant girl whispered softly in my ear as I drifted off: "Thank you, Sir, thank you for fucking me. Your cock is delicious. Thank you, Sir, thank you so much."

"What is your name?" I mumbled, just before sleep claimed me.

I never heard her answer.

When I awakened in the morning, bright gray rain-light poured through the windows. The servant girl was gone.

The evidence was clear, though; I could smell the musk of her pussy and ass on my cock, the thick flow of her juices soaked into the sheets. Her maid's dress was gone, but her hairpin lay discarded on the nightstand.

I rose and put on my robe. I left the room to find Atchison.

I stalked the top floor of the mansion, knocking on each bedroom. When I received no response, I opened the doors and found each bed pristine, untouched. Including the servant's quarters.

I proceeded to the lower level and found much the same story. My own glass of brandy and well-smoked cigar on the coffee table. Atchison's nowhere in sight.

No servants, either. A perfectly maintained mansion, without servants.

I laughed. Some practical joke played by Atchison, I thought. That devilish bastard thinks he'll spook me.

I sank into the softness of the silk divan; it creaked dangerously and collapsed, a plume of dust shooting up from it.

I jumped up, looking around. Everything was dustier than I remembered.

I recalled what Atchison had told me. There was a picture of Rose in the hallway. Rose, the servant girl who haunted the mansion.

I expected it; Atchison's hoax required this detail. No doubt he's a master with Photoshop, a genius with a digital camera.

The girl was there, the girl I had made love to the previous night. Clad in her maid's outfit, in a sepia-toned photograph that might have been taken as early as 1860.

That, I expected. But Atchison's one admirable detail still haunts me. The servant—Rose—was sitting on the lap of an older man, one with a white beard and suit. He looked like Colonel fucking Sanders with a leather daddy complex and a hard-on. The snow-white beard obscured much of his face, but there was no mistaking it: It was Atchison.

You might think I should avoid a man who would play tricks like that. And I have, for the last six days. I returned to Atlanta and did no further checking up on Atchison, didn't return his e-mails asking me how I enjoyed Rose, if I was indeed as rough as he'd promised her I would be. And I didn't answer his impassioned reminder that he was expecting me at his annual fetish ball on Saturday night.

Do you have any idea what a full-fare ticket to Charlotte costs on such short notice?

Clearly Atchison's online account of how he came by his money—as a designer and investor in the earliest phase of the computer revolution—isn't wholly accurate. I suspect that Colonel Greene is more than a piece of regional history to him. I suspect that somewhere in Atchison's forebears is the white-bearded Southern monarch who left a broken-hearted slave girl sobbing with a Civil War revolver to her head and a need to serve that even death couldn't eliminate. I suspect Atchison has the Colonel's blood pumping through his veins, one way or another.

But at the fetish ball, I'll be occupied with other things, so I doubt I'll have a chance to ask him.

What I'll find there, I can't say. A mansion full of ghostly serving girls and long-dead aristocrats with a penchant for kinky sex games? Or an old-money prankster with an eye for detail and a bevy of well-paid whores on his payroll?

One thing I do know: It's what drove me back to the mansion.

I looked up a portrait of Colonel Greene. It was available online, in archived copies of the county register.

Family resemblances can be more than a little haunting.

Joey's First Spanking
by Paul Cummings

Paul Cummings is the pseudonym of a professional man who engages in BDSM privately and writes erotica under various names. "The idea of discovering a spouse doing naughty things is incredibly hot to me," he writes. "As is the idea of taking that ill-gotten knowledge and giving her *exactly* what she wants, whether she wants it or not. This story of a first-time spanking is exactly what gets my hard drive running."

I first spanked Joey when she'd done nothing wrong. Other husbands might consider this a grave transgression, but I'm not inclined toward such judgments. Joey, however, has a tendency to feel guilty about things. So I knew that a spanking was well deserved, and I resolved to give her one.

I'd long noticed the way my wife wiggled her butt when she knew I was looking at it. Her ass was her most glorious asset, full and pretty and perfectly firm.

Joey and I had a healthy sex life, but lately I'd had the sense that something was missing. Just past our second anniversary we'd started to lose that newlywed charge. Whereas we used to make love every day, it had become typical for us to go a whole week without a session of fucking.

It wasn't until I happened across a story she'd left on the hard drive of our computer that I knew that a good spanking was what my wife needed.

The filename was "Spanking Monique," and it was a lengthy recitation of a squirming young girl's experiences being spanked by her husband. That, in itself, would have inspired me to put Joey over my knee. But what clinched the deal was that my wife had done a

search-and-replace, writing her own name into what I can only assume was once poor Monique's. Joey put her ass in the air, moaning. Joey felt her master's hand striking her bare bottom and sending shivers of pleasure through her. Joey had always wanted to be spanked, but felt much too guilty about it to confess that fact to her husband.

Joey hadn't brought up any dissatisfaction with the frequency of our lovemaking, but I suspected that its relative rarity left room for old behaviors and fantasies to assert themselves. Perhaps she'd fantasized about being spanked her whole life, and now, as things slowed down between us, Joey's fond fantasies were dominating her mind again. I had noticed her going on the Internet more often; I had suspected she was looking at porn, but hadn't suspected she would be so bold as to beg me to spank her. Why else would she "forget" to delete the product of her illicit surfing?

I had never spanked a girl, but I resolved to spank the bejeezus out of my wife. I know that trust and communication are critical between a man and his wife, but so is the deception and intrigue that comes from planning a sexual coup, whether it's a surprise weekend in the Bahamas or an ass-reddening session over my knee.

I downloaded a program called "SpyWare" that allowed me to secretly track Joey's every keystroke online. I then found excuses to work late, leaving my wife with long evenings to cruise the Internet. Each night when I returned home, I would find her hunched over the computer, "working late" herself. She became even more responsive to my amorous attentions than she had been in the early days of our marriage. I would come home late and fuck her silly, finding her achingly wet and ready for me. As I fucked her, I would try to suss what she was dreaming of—herself, over a master's knee, ass in the air, squirming?

I started fucking her from behind, running my fingertips gently over her ass as I pounded into her more and more roughly. She went crazy when I did that. It would have been a small matter to draw my hand back and plant an exploratory love tap on her behind, but I wanted to save it. The first time Joey found herself spanked by me, I wanted her to get everything she'd ever dreamed of.

After she'd gone to sleep, exhausted by our stern fucking, I would

sneak into the home office we shared, and trace my wife's explorations through spanking erotica web pages, instructional sites, and, most commonly, chat rooms. I felt no jealousy as I relived her sessions with dominant men online; I did feel a touch of guilt, but I resolved to make good on every promise her online lovers made.

More importantly, though, I followed the instructional sites, learning every nuance it was possible to know about giving a willing girl a spanking.

It was only a week before I was ready to make my move.

We'd made love every night since I'd discovered her illicit online adventures, our fucking gradually becoming rougher as I got in the habit of taking her from behind so her beautiful ass was exposed to me. Now, I was ready.

When I returned home late, Joey was even more aroused than usual. She must have had an unusually good session of being spanked online.

Joey started by sucking me right on the living room couch. She was wearing a T-shirt and sweats, her full breasts showing through the thin cotton of her top, her ass beautiful in the tight sweats. Joey is an accomplished cocksucker, and soon I was very close to coming in her mouth. But that was out of the question.

"Take off your clothes," I told her.

Joey stood up and whisked her T-shirt over her head. Her breasts were pink and flushed with excitement. She pulled down her sweats and I saw that she wasn't wearing anything underneath.

"Come over here," I said. "Get on top of me."

Joey went to straddle me, to sit down on my hard cock. She never made it. Before she could settle into place, I'd grabbed her arm and turned her over my lap. She gasped in surprise as I held her down, her belly against my hard cock, still moist with her spit. Joey began to giggle.

"What are you doing?" she asked me.

I brought my hand down hard on her ass, and she yelped.

"Be quiet, Joey," I told her. "I know all about it. I know everything you've been doing online. I know about the chat rooms, the porn, the stories. I know everything."

"But I—" she began.

I brought my hand down hard on her naked ass again, making her squirm. I wrestled her more fully into my lap, spanking her again and again. The fight went out of her and she remained sprawled across my lap, moaning softly. Her ass began to rise high in the air.

"If I've violated some sort of trust," I said, "then I apologize. But I think you know as well as I do that for this marriage to succeed, you need to be kept in line."

"Yes," she sighed, and I spanked her hard enough to make her gasp again.

"Yes, what?" I growled.

Joey's voice was low as she answered. "Yes, Master."

"That's right," I said, my hand coming down as I started to administer a rhythmic spanking as I spoke to her. "I'm your husband and your Master. Am I your master, Joey?"

Joey's ass was wriggling back and forth as I spanked her right on her sweet spot, as I'd read about so many times in the week since I discovered her proclivity. "Yes," she moaned.

I spanked her harder than ever, so hard she whimpered in pain.

"Yes, what?"

"Yes, Master," she said.

"I can't have my little slave whoring herself around on the Internet, can I?"

"No," said Joey, and I whacked her so hard she lifted herself off of my lap, her mouth open in a soundless wail of pain.

"No, what?"

"No, Master," she gasped.

"At least, not without my guidance," I said.

Joey's eyes turned toward me, and I would have sworn they were filled with the warmest love I'd ever seen in them. I grasped Joey by the hair, pushed her face down into the sofa, and began to spank her again.

"As soon as I've taught you tonight's lesson, Joey, you and I are going to go online. Together. Would you like that, Joey?"

Another moan escaped Joey's lips, her ass lifting as she pushed onto my hand. "Yes, Master," she said.

"From now on, I watch everything you do online, and you share

it with me. What's more, you're going to be punished for being a little slut. Which doesn't mean you're going to stop," I said. My hand met Joey's sweet spot in a steady, building rhythm, and her whole body was pink with excitement. I had read about this moment, but had never dreamed it would happen the first time I spanked my wife.

Her breathing had changed as I spanked her. She was whispering "Yes, Master, yes, Master, yes, Master" over and over again as I landed rhythmic blows on her ass. It was bright red now, bearing the marks of my hand. Joey began to shudder all over.

"Are you going to come, Joey?"

"Yes, Master," she gasped.

I paused the spanking and caressed her red-hot ass. "Beg for permission."

"Please, Master," she whimpered. "Please, may I come? Please, Master?"

"Only if you promise to never come again without asking permission."

Joey's nude body shivered all over, and she sighed.

"Yes, Master. I promise."

I brought my hand down on her ass again, and she came on the second stroke. Great heaving sobs of release escaped her lips, and as she came she moaned "Thank you, thank you, thank you, Master!" The moment she finished coming she reached under her body and wrapped her hand around my cock. I was so turned on from administering this spanking that it only took a few strokes of her hand before I came all over her belly, and Joey moaned softly as my warm fluid covered her stomach and tits. "Thank you, Master, thank you, thank you for coming on me."

Joey looked up at me, her eyes warm and satisfied. Clearly, if I wasn't yet a well-trained master, my wife would soon get me there.

But Joey was already a well-trained slave, conditioned to respond with obedience and love when I dominated her.

I smiled as I looked down into Joey's face and listened to her coo: "Thank you, Master, thank you. I'll do anything for you, Master. Anything at all."

"Anything?" I asked her.

She nodded fervently. "Anything, Master. Anything at all."

A well-trained slave, indeed. I would have to send a thank you to all the men she'd chatted with online.

Better yet, I'd let Joey thank them. In person.

The Man With the Leash
by Lizbeth Dusseau

Lizbeth Dusseau writes: "Some years ago, while doing some investigative research at a 'vanilla' sex club, my husband and I observed a remarkable scene of sexual submission. After the many BDSM-related experiences I have witnessed or been involved with since, this amazing incident, which I recount here, remains one of the most stunning examples of true dominance and submission that I have ever witnessed."

He moved with urgent purpose through the smoky nightclub, leaving a wake of mystery and wonder, dropping hints of the unusual scene about to knock this vanilla sex club on its ear. Though he dressed simply, in pressed slacks and starched open-collared shirt, his mannerisms made one think of arrogant executives: the chiseled jaw, the darting eyes, the shameless ego. Jaws dropped—at least figuratively—as his girl, a surrendering plain-faced brunette, moved behind him, collared and tethered to a leash, exhibiting a behavioral abnormality rarely seen in any world but theirs.

In charge for one astounding hour, the man had his stage, his audience in rapt attention, and his actress under his command. While he aimed for a particular end, an explicit need only he understood, she was the embodiment of sensuous resignation, diverting her eyes, except when he demanded that she look directly at him. She was dressed as simply as the man who held the leash, wearing a slim black skirt, a dark T-shirt that buttoned up the front, and black, leather boots that fit tight around her ankles. Her brunette hair was blunt cut and shoulder length. And while flat-chested, her hard nipples strained the fabric of her shirt, revealing a basic, almost boyish beauty in her

simple look. Her passive face would be hard to remember, difficult to pick out in a crowd, but her aura was not likely forgotten by anyone in the club that night, as garish overstatement gave way to an exhibition of unpretentious surrender.

The pair moved effortlessly through the crowd toward the center of the main lounge, where the atmosphere of erotic expectation was thick and unsettling. Those present were primed for sex and a night of hedonistic abandon, yet their sexual anticipation hid behind casual postures, teasing glances, and nervous negotiations that would eventually becomes less timid and more direct as the night wore on. Liquor did a lot to loosen inhibitions in this sex club, but the startling pair would do the same with their exhibition alone.

Indifferent to the bodies milling around him, the man with the leash shoved his collared chattel forward to a tiny dance stage and whispered in her ear commands only she could hear. Dropping the tether, he backed off and, along with a crowd of growing admirers, watched as she lifted her shirt and mindlessly massaged her tiny tits. Her eyes never strayed from a spot at his feet, as she pulled her nipples brutally and bit her lip when the pain darted downward to her groin.

"Move on," he prompted her, with some impatience.

On cue, she lifted her skirt, exhibiting thick tan legs and a bare shaved pussy, already glossy with a layer of moisture.

Then, as if her performance was not enough, the man moved in close, whispering again. The girl immediately dropped to her hands and knees as he stepped back and focused critically on every exacting move she made, and nothing else—as if the two were alone in the room and the rest of the world had disappeared, and there were not thirty pairs of eyes watching in horrific wonder. He watched her as she raised her skirt above her tight ass, as she massaged the cheeks with her hand and ran her fingers down the crevice, drawing the wetness from her pussy toward the tight rosette of her anus. She tucked her chin to her chest, hiding her face, along with the lust in her eyes and her parted, panting, sensuous lips. Faceless, she was her body and nothing more—his body to command.

Her willingness advanced his plan. Inspired, he crouched beside

her, picked up the leash and held it in his fist. While she continued her play, he jerked the chain, annoyingly tugging at the collar and her neck. Tiny, sensuous gasps escaped her lips, but she dared not utter a word of protest. Burying his free hand in her hair, he grabbed the brown locks and twisted them inside his gripping fingers.

"Tell me you want more," he whispered, so that only she and those close by could hear.

"More," she instantly answered in a soft, pleading shudder.

"Tell me 'harder,'" he insisted.

"Harder, sir," she answered.

He sneered derisively, dismissively, "I should just leave you here and let them take your sorry ass." Giving her head one last brutal shake, he then let go, pushed off, and rose to his feet. He hung on to the leash with his one hand and tugged. "This way." Pulling her from one subservient act to the next, he led her toward the tables where a dazzling blonde in a pink silk slip sipped a rum and Coke.

"Do you mind?" he asked the woman.

The blonde looked up at him, amazed but clearly intrigued. Then with a mischievous smile, she nodded and raised the slip to her knees, opening her thighs in welcome.

"Please her," the man with the leash crisply ordered his brunette.

The girl moved with caution but deliberately, stopping inside the V of the blonde's legs. Rising to her knees, she ran her palms along the silk-covered thighs and the curve of the tart's lush hips, and upward to her breasts, where she lovingly grasped both and gently kneaded the plush cushions she found inside her hands.

"That's what real tits should feel like." The man above her chided her own inadequate equipment.

A tremor of regret passed across the brunette's face as she heard him speak, yet she continued to pleasure the lovely blonde, scooting further inside the woman's legs. Drawing the heavy breasts from inside the silk, she suckled the abundant flesh with parted lips, then wetted the pretty nipples with her tongue and blew warm air to make them knot as tightly as her own small buds.

"Oh, honey, you can do that more," the woman purred, while reaching out to gratefully stroke the brunette's hair. Her eyes glim-

mered darkly. "And lower," she urged in a voice simmering and erotic.

The girl hesitated just long enough for the man in command to give the leash an impatient tug. Continuing now with determination, her hands caressed their way down the pink silk until they moved inside and underneath. As if she were opening a Valentine gift, the brunette carefully pulled up the slip, uncovering a plush snatch of pale pink skin and a neatly trimmed triangle of wispy blonde curls. Her head moved down into the redolent valley, with her lips and tongue leading her again. While holding the outer labia open with her fingers, she explored with her mouth until, with sudden and urgent abandon, she began frantically flicking the hood of the blonde's blood-swollen clit.

It would seem that a hundred soft sighs were heard in hushed sequence around the humid, smoky room. No one dared move but the girl on the floor, whose head bobbed lithely on the pink crotch, and the woman who owned that crotch, whose languid body responded in undulating orgasmic swells.

"Ah, yesssss," she softly hissed, as her head fell back against the chair. When her trembling body started to climax, she grabbed the side of the chair with one hand and the brunette's hair with the other.

The girl hung on to the pink, cumming pussy despite the wildly erratic movements, her face glistening, smeared with female juices.

Once the woman's tremors subsided, she slumped back in the chair, almost fainting. Seeing her satisfied expression, the man with the leash jerked his girl back to him, reclaiming her complete attention. After pulling her to her feet, he led her toward the back of the club, as though he sought a more private location. Even so, a motivated crowd of voyeurs followed them, hoping the show would continue.

The couple now stood face to face and chest to chest, just inches apart. Although they were nearly the same height, his energy persisted in towering over her, nearly consuming her as if she was a part of him, little more than an extension of his unyielding will, a playground for his schemes. No different than the scene before, their private conversation became a public show. That was what he wanted.

"What do you deserve?" he asked, his sharp eyes riveted on her scared ones.

"Nothing," she answered.

He let go of the leash and grabbed her neck, clutching it with a claw-like grip. His other hand reached for the top of her shirt and with an abruptness that stunned the audience and his chattel, he ripped the two sides open. She swooned with awe and fright. He then laid her down on an empty lounge table and began to fiercely pinch her nipples. Her eyes remained closed, but the pain registered on her face.

The man leaned in, hissing in her ear. "Play with your pussy till you come."

While he continued to squeeze her nipples, the brunette reached for her crotch and began to roam the wet slit. Knowing exactly what to do to get off, her fingers massaged around the bud of her clitoris with painstaking precision. She performed with some urgency, sensing that the man in charge of her would not allow a leisurely masturbation.

In speechless wonder, the audience observed her slick shiny folds expand before their eyes, and watched her clitoris bloom and her vaginal muscles pulse in readiness as she worked herself to a climactic frenzy. The air in the room seemed to rise ten degrees, a force that fed off her lust. She strained as the man above her crushed and twisted her nipples between his fingers.

"Open your eyes," he whispered gruffly.

Her eyes fluttered wide, staring dazedly into his surly expression. He seemed to have climbed inside her head where he read her thoughts. He watched her jerk, struggling with the pain that by then was her constant stimulation. Whether that pain was welcome was not exactly clear. Nevertheless, it was endured, because that was what she did.

"Come, or I'll pull your hand away," he ordered in a seething tone.

She shook her head back and forth, her face wincing as if in protest. "Please," she begged.

"No, come now," he insisted, giving her nipples another angry squeeze. This last jarring pain seemed to have tripped a switch in her brain and body.

Her fingers flew, her body strained. She arched her back and every muscle went taut. Something wild swept through her, and yet the restraint was obvious. Whether the crowd made her shy or the man who mastered her every move restricted her pleasure by some unspoken rule, no one would know. The result was the same. The girl remained under his power, controlled even in her moment of rapture. She was left spent, but hardly satiated at the finish.

He gave the girl no time to recover. While her body still spasmed, he pulled her to her feet. His one hand moved to her crotch, diving into the liquid that bathed his fingers. He then raised his cum-soaked digits to her lips and without instruction, she licked them, one by one. Her eyes remained nearly closed, her dreamy reverie apparent. A moment later she slumped to her knees, bowing her head and hanging on to the man's legs in affectionate gratitude. She looked up, eyes beseeching him. She wanted inside his pants, a hope everyone shared. It only seemed right after everything else that happened that night.

But he pushed her off with a sweep of his hand.

"I should find one fat prick to take your ass and another to fill your mouth."

That would have worked too, the crowd would agree.

She languished with desire as she heard his rough words.

"But not tonight," he said, as he wound his hand through her hair and scowled. "You've already had more than you deserve."

That said, the performance ended. He dropped the leash in her lap and turned away, leaving the brunette to scramble to her feet and follow him to the front of the club. Her shirt was still unbuttoned, the tips of her small breasts just barely hidden inside the flimsy cotton. Still collared, leashed, and humbly acquiescent, she followed him into the desert night.

The air in the sex club buzzed as the simmering erotic heat began to boil. Randy spectators resumed their quest for sexual satisfaction and negotiations were swiftly made. Couples disappeared into private rooms while others fucked in the public lounges. No one quite understood what they had seen that night. Days later, some would doubt it

ever happened. But no one would forget. As the remembrance of that strange play between the yielding brunette and the man with the leash lingered on, it would continue to lure and beguile the voyeurs in that hour of mystery, causing them to wonder about themselves, what might be missing in their sexual passion, what hidden lust might lie dormant, waiting.

Zephyr
by Zach Addams

Zach Addams is the pseudonym of a well-known erotic writer who has done plenty of research at sex clubs. His work has appeared in the recent *Love Under Foot* and various other anthologies.

" 'Zephyr' was inspired by my experiences at various BDSM parties while on vacation in the San Francisco Bay Area," says Addams. "It's far from true, but all the characters—including my own, the narrator—are inspired by actual people I met. 'Zephyr' is still out there, checking coats at some private party, and I hope some day my lover and I get to play with her."

We arrive at the play party with you naked under your wool coat. I specifically insisted that you wear the wool, because I knew its prickly sensations would dominate your thoughts; by the time the cab pulled up to the party space, you would be painfully aware of your nakedness. Perhaps that isn't entirely accurate: You're not entirely naked. The two garments you wear are your knee-high boots with three-inch heels—and my collar. You always wear my collar to parties.

I pay for our entrance and we check our coats. When you slip yours off, I watch as the girl at coat check looks up and down, her eyes wide. I smile as I take off my coat. She recognizes the meaning of the collar and addresses her remarks to me.

"She has very nice breasts," says the coat-check girl. "And I love that she's shaved."

"Thank you," I say, only slightly disappointed that her eyes don't stray toward my skintight leathers, my form-fitting top. If her short black hair, nose ring, black spandex muscle shirt, and tight PVC hot

pants hadn't already tipped me off, perhaps the entwined women's symbols tattooed on her shoulder would have. Still, she smiles at me, and there's a hint of flirtation in that gaze, which makes me wonder. "I'm Zach," I tell her, extending my hand to shake hers.

"Zephyr," she says. "We both have names that start with Z." She doesn't ask your name; in this space, you're merely a topic of discussion, not a person, as marked by the tag on your collar: slave. Not "submissive," "play partner," "girlfriend," or "wife." When we walked through this door, you became nothing more than a commodity that belongs to me. "I'm only working until eleven," she says. It's just after ten. "Any chance you'd be interested in letting me play with her afterward?"

I look at you—not to gauge whether you're interested in playing with her, but to gauge whether this woman turns you on at all. Sometimes those things are so different. The former is utterly irrelevant when you're wearing my collar. The latter, however, makes all the difference in the world.

My gaze lingers over your breasts, aware that the room is much too warm to explain the hardness of your nipples. But I've another barometer in mind.

"Let's see," I say. "Bend over, Anya."

No one is waiting for their coat, so I feel free to take this liberty. You obediently bend over the coat-check counter, close to Zephyr.

"Spread your legs, Anya. Zephyr, perhaps you'd like to touch her breasts? Perhaps kiss her, even?"

"With pleasure," says Zephyr as you obey my command, spreading your legs. Zephyr begins to caress your tits as she kisses you, her thumbs playing with your hard nipples. You moan softly between deep kisses, Zephyr's tongue exploring you. I reach behind you and slip my hand between your spread legs, seeking your pussy.

It's not just wet. It's gushing.

"We should talk about this further," I tell her. "Anya, go fetch me a drink and wait for me."

"See you later," Zephyr says, her lips very close to yours, colored pink by the remnants of your burgundy lipstick.

You have some difficulty standing up, your legs clearly wobbly. You obediently walk down the hall toward the lounge area.

I smile at Zephyr. "Now, shall we talk about what you're going to do to my wife?"

Zephyr leans heavily on the counter, smiling. Her eyes burn as I look into them.

"Yes," she says. "I'm dying to hear your ideas."

It's a good twenty minutes later that I find you in the lounge area, obediently kneeling beside an armchair you've reserved for me. You hold a glass, the ice beginning to melt. After my heated negotiations with Zephyr, I'm thirsty, so I don't mind the watery taste of the drink. I sit in the armchair and sip it.

You know better than to ask me what Zephyr and I talked about. But I can see the anticipation, the nervousness in your eyes as you scan the scene. This early, people are mostly downstairs in the dungeon; it's only later, when they've exhausted themselves, that they'll be upstairs in the lounge.

It's not long before Zephyr comes out, carrying a play bag slung over her shoulder. Now that she's not behind the counter, I can see how truly gorgeous she looks with those skintight PVC shorts and spandex sleeveless crop-top showing off her slim, taut body. Though her breasts are small, the outline of her bust shows quite plainly through the too-tight shirt. She wears knee-high PVC lace-ups polished to gleam. Her boyish hair gives her a devilish, mischievous look.

She walks up to us and tucks her thumb and forefinger under your chin, lifting you to look at her.

"Ready to suffer?" she asks you.

"Yes, ma'am," you say softly.

I lead the way down into the well-furnished dungeon, where numerous scenes are being enacted on willing, bound submissives. Men and women both are stretched across racks, crosses, and platforms, being whipped, caned, and spanked. As we enter, the trio using the nearest St. Andrew's cross finishes up and Zephyr quickly grabs it, tossing her play bag at the foot. Just beyond the St. Andrew's cross there's a four-poster bed covered in rubber sheets that also, quite luckily, happens to be vacant. I toss my bag on that, knowing it will be

of much more use than the cross. It will give you a perfect view of what's to transpire on the bed.

"Now," Zephyr whispers as she takes you in her arms in front of the cross. "Let's get you situated."

Her kiss turns into a bite, making you gasp. She grasps your hair and pushes you to your knees, a position you take willingly. I occupy a corner nearby and watch.

"What do you do?" Zephyr asks you.

You lower yourself to her feet and begin to kiss her shined boots, using your tongue.

"You've trained her well, Zach," says Zephyr, as you lavish affection on her boots.

I shrug. "She's still got a problem with jealousy," I say. "She expects all the attention to be on her."

"Oh, really?" laughs Zephyr. "I know how to fix that," she says. "In fact, I've got the perfect idea."

"Me, too," I say, taking a sheet out of my play bag and spreading it out over the bed.

She grasps you by the shoulders and picks you up, guiding you to the St. Andrew's cross as she manhandles you by driving her knee into your crotch. You spread your legs obediently and she produces restraints from her bag to clip you spread-eagled to the cross.

The cross leans slightly forward, making the angle easier on you. But its maker has thoughtfully provided a vinyl-covered pad that can be slipped into place under your belly, forcing your ass out invitingly while taking any unexpected pressure off your wrists. Zephyr pushes the pad into place and fits a ball gag into your wide-open mouth. She runs her hand up and down the inside of your naked thighs. When her hand finds your pussy, she smiles.

"You were right, Zach," she says. "Anya's very, very wet. She probably can't wait to get fucked."

"She's always that way," I smile. "Though I dare say you've already had quite an effect on her."

"Flattery will get you everywhere," says Zephyr, and spanks your ass, bringing a gasp from your deep red lips. I sit on the side of the bed and watch as she reddens your ass with repeated blows of her open hand, creating a rhythmic noise that draws approving eyes from

all around the dungeon. You look quite fetching strapped to the cross like that, and I know that no matter what we do, we'll soon attract a crowd.

Zephyr presses a red handkerchief into your hand, knowing that you'll drop it if the scene gets to be too much. In the two years we've been together, however, you have yet to drop the hankie.

"Now, Anya," says Zephyr, leaning close to press her hips into your ass. "I've been asking myself, what is the very worst thing I could do to you? I've packed so many nasty things into my play bag. I mean, Zach here tells me he'll let me do whatever I want to you, and you can't say no. I've got lots of good ideas. I've got needles—I could pierce you up and down your back." She runs her fingers over your shoulder blades for emphasis, and you shiver. "Or maybe I could pierce your pussy and stitch it shut—do you think you'd like that, little Anya?" Her hand begins to stroke your cunt and I hear you moaning behind the gag. "Then again, perhaps just a good caning would be in order. I think a slave like you wouldn't even need any warm-up. How would you like to be caned right on your ass?"

She pinches your bare buttocks firmly. That brings the loudest muffled whimper yet from your lips, as you contemplate the pain I've inflicted on you with the cane—and the fact that the marks of our most recent session have just recently faded.

"But all those would hardly be torture, would they? A girl like you loves being hurt, doesn't she?" Zephyr's lips are close to your ear now, and I know you can feel her warm breath on you. I kick off my boots and lay back on the bed to watch. My cock is already hard in my leather pants.

"So I think I know what would be the very nastiest thing I could do to you," she said. "I've got the perfect tool to hurt you, Anya, and it's not in my little black bag."

Zephyr steps back from you, smiles, and walks around the cross to the bed.

She crawls onto the bed and lays on top of me, pressing her lips to mine.

I try hard not to watch you, for that will give away the game. But I know your eyes are wide, your face flushing hot with shame. My hands come to rest on Zephyr's tight ass, kneading her buttocks

through the PVC shorts. I reach under her as she kisses me and unbuckle her belt.

"Would you like that, Anya? Would you like that if I fucked your
husband right in front of you?" She giggles, a strangely girlish sound
coming from the boyish face. "No, what am I thinking? You'd hate
that. That's the whole point."

I slide my hands under Zephyr's shorts and begin to peel them
off her. They're very tight, but once they're over her ass they come
easily down her legs, revealing that she's wearing nothing underneath. She kisses me deeply and kicks the shorts off over her ankles.
Then she strips off her top and presses her small breasts into my face,
rubbing the hard nipples back and forth against my lips.

"Mmmm," she sighs. "I get so wet hurting girls like you, Anya.
And I know this is the worst thing I could possibly do to you. I'm going to love fucking your husband, Anya. And you're going to hate
watching it."

I glance over to you, seeing the moistness of your eyes, the difficulty with which you grip the red hankie. Now naked except for her
boots, Zephyr pulls open my shorts and takes my cock in her hand.
I've gotten a condom out of my pocket, and she tears it open and
starts to roll it down over my hard cock.

Your eyes are now locked in mine, and I can see the horror, the
dismay, the fear in them. But I know that when I turn my eyes away
from yours and lock them in Zephyr's, the horror must grow much
worse. With difficulty I focus entirely on her, looking into her eyes as
I kiss her deeply and she slowly rises over me, spreading her legs to
mount me.

Her cunt comes down firmly on my cock, sliding it easily in despite her pussy's tightness. She moans as she begins to slide up and
down on my cock. I glance as quickly as possible to the hankie, making sure it's still in place, and then return my eyes to Zephyr's as she
fucks me, her hips grinding as she moans, breathless.

"That's a nice cock," she sighs. "You're so lucky to have it, Anya.
Do you even know how lucky you are?"

Zephyr begins to fuck me more quickly. My hands rest on her
hips, following each of her movements. She reaches down and starts
to rub her clit. I know she's going to come. That's the critical part—

when I fuck you, I never allow you to come without asking. Zephyr plunges toward her orgasm, lifting herself perpendicular to me and pumping up and down so she can rub her clit more effectively.

I glance toward you again, and this time you catch me. Your eyes are no longer moist; I see the flush of sexual arousal reddening your breasts. Your ass, thrust back toward the crowd that has come to surround you a respectful five feet away, slowly grinds against the vinyl padding in time with Zephyr's cunt on my cock.

"Fuck," moans Zephyr. "I'm going to come!"

I hear you choke, a strangling sound, and immediately wonder if it's a sob or a gasp of excitement. But then Zephyr is coming, her eyes locked in mine, her slim body looking gorgeous as she fucks herself onto my cock, rubbing her clit and bringing herself off. Her cunt grips my shaft rhythmically, trying to milk me dry. She moans, coming to a halt as her pussy's spasms lessen around my cock.

She pulls off of me, slips off the condom, knots it, and tosses it into the trash can near the bed.

"Mmmm," she sighs. "A wonderful cock. And he didn't even come. Do you still need to come, Zach?"

I nod.

"Well, there's one pussy that hasn't been fucked yet. I think she needs it even worse than I did."

I get off the bed, my cock dangling hard out of my open leather pants. I grasp your hair and pull your head back so I can lock your eyes in mine as I press up behind you. Zephyr climbs back onto the bed and reaches under the cross, taking hold of my cock and guiding it into you.

You moan deep in your throat as I thrust into you. I can feel your pussy juicing around me, wetter than I've ever felt it. I fuck you rapidly, knowing that what will make you come is me taking you, heartlessly, pounding you uncontrollably.

But Zephyr's hand has lingered behind, thrust under the cross as she reaches through the footboard of the bed. She's rubbing your clit, just as she rubbed her own. Your moans, strangled and deep in your throat, make droplets of spittle ooze out around the edges of the ball gag, staining it deep red with your lipstick.

"Would you like to come, Anya?" asks Zephyr.

You nod, desperately, hungry for it. I realize you're holding back, still trying to obey my rule, still trying not to come without permission.

"If you want to come, drop the hankie," says Zephyr, and before she's even finished saying it you drop the hankie and shudder against me, violently resisting your climax.

"Can she come?" Zephyr asks me.

"Yes," I say. "In fact, I expect it."

I haven't even finished saying it when you come, your pussy gripping me just as Zephyr's did a moment ago. Your whole body pulls fiercely against the restraints bonding you to the cross, and Zephyr's hand follows your clit mercilessly as she drives you deep into an intense orgasm. You haven't finished coming yet when I do, my cock exploding inside you, shooting deep.

"Isn't that romantic?" coos Zephyr, as I unbuckle the ball gag. It lets you gasp for air and, more importantly, lets Zephyr place her fingers in your mouth, making you lick them clean of your juices.

When she's finished with that, she gets off the bed, snatches the red hankie, and places it back in your hand. Still nude except for her boots, she leans over her play bag and takes out a cane.

"Now that Zach's gotten what he wanted," says Zephyr. "I plan to take what I want."

I zip up my leather pants and lay down on the bed as the first blow of the cane hits you, making you scream. Your voice is so pretty now that the gag's been removed, and the sound of your pain is delicious. But within moments you're pressing back against your bonds, trying to present your ass more fully for Zephyr's blows. From the way she starts out slow, I know she's an expert, warming you up no matter what kind of mindfuck she laid on you earlier. Soon, I know, she'll have you writhing and perhaps coming again from the blows on your sweet spot. I want to see you come again, howling as the pain swirls through your naked body.

But for now, I'm content to watch.

Watch your eyes, locked in mine, forever unable to leave.

·   ·   ·

Some hours later, Zephyr drops by the bed, where you and I still lay, your naked body curled childlike in my arms.

She bends over and kisses me lightly on the lips. "Thanks for letting me play with her," she says. "And you."

"Perhaps we'll see you again sometime?"

"Certainly. After all, we have to keep her vigilant against her jealousy, don't we?"

Zephyr then looks into your eyes and smiles.

"May I?" she asks me.

I nod, and she kisses you, hungrily, passionately, telling me what I already knew: That her connection to me was only about you, that her passion resides where it always had—deep inside your cunt, not hers. My cock was nothing more than a convenient tool to hurt you, to make your pussy flood and your ass hunger for her cane. Her orgasm wasn't mine to give; it was yours, as you watched and wept and struggled against your jealousy.

You kiss Zephyr back passionately—perhaps telling her the same thing. Then again, you're much too complicated to fully understand. I've long ago given up trying, content to know that I know everything about you that I can. Content to know that I can still blow your mind.

"See you around," says Zephyr.

"Thank you," you tell her.

"Don't mention it."

You rest your head on my chest as the play party slowly clears out. It's almost time for cleanup, but I steal a few minutes now, watching Zephyr disappear up the spiral staircase into the world.

In the Belly
by Eroticus

Eroticus is the pseudonym for a writer who specializes in realizing fantasies, both on the web and in print. He also writes as Reese Gabriel, and under that name he contributed another story, "Atonement," to this volume. You can find Eroticus/Gabriel at pinkflamingo.com and chimerabooks.co.uk, as well as on redsrealm.net.

In "In the Belly," Eroticus/Gabriel plays with one of my own favorite and most taboo fantasies—I'll let you discover which one as you read the story. He says of this intense, edgy, and very sexy story: "Who wouldn't want to tame a superstar? To bring a sex goddess to her knees? Close your eyes and picture your favorite one, put her in the starring role, and sit back for the ride of your life. And the best part is, she wants it, all of it. The humiliation, the bondage . . . and that's just the beginning. Domination, you see, wears many masks, and as the characters of this story discover, the ultimate form of domination and branding is much, much simpler than whips or chains."

I'm in the belly of the whale. A has-been, never-was rocker, two stories below the blazing lights and amplifier stacks, negotiating vacant cinderblock corridors that seem to stretch forever; my world reduced to paint-chipped walls roofed by conduits and pipes, miles of them packed like intestines, while up above the sold-out crowd is screaming for an encore.

Seventy thousand plus, kicking and elbowing the womb of the entertainment behemoth, begging release as they chant her name.

Olivia.

She needs only the one, unless you're from some other galaxy.

"Long time no see, Ian. You're looking good."

I nod, having made it as far as her inner retinue. Three living steroid advertisements lined up across the hallway, barely ten feet from the Promised Land of Liv's dressing room. "Same here, Sean."

"He's all right," says the T-shirted, buzz-cut Sean to the newbies. "He knows her from way back."

The other two, a ponytailed Latino and a chunky Samoan with biceps that put my thighs to shame, eye me suspiciously, calculating if it's worth the ten-second effort it would take to bounce me out of the stadium like a superball.

"You used to fuck her?" asks the Samoan, pointing a finger the size of a banana.

I manage a wry smile. "We made music together, if that's what you mean."

The Samoan doesn't like the answer, but Sean's already vouched for me. A wall of muscle parts for me like the Red Sea, and I'm through the gauntlet, unscathed.

"Hey, Ian," Sean calls out, my hand already on the knob. "You know she's changed."

The worry on his face flashes for half a second and then it's gone; it's a weakness the big man can't afford.

"Just promise me, Sean, you got my back tonight, no matter what."

"Sure thing, Ian."

Inside I find a pair of barely legal teens on the green leather couch, toking up a storm and giggling over one of her magazine spreads. Boy groupies, if you can believe it. Olivia's new manager is for shit letting them back here. Supposedly she and her backup singers pick them out of the crowd now, just like their male counterparts.

I take a good look around, sizing up Olivia's new life. Nothing spells out of control quite like empty liquor bottles, overflowing trashcans, and a wardrobe-strewn floor. Not to mention a dildo the size of an elephant prick covered in yellowed, dried lubricant and nailed to the wall.

"Get the fuck out," I tell the dynamic duo, risking their puny, postpubescent wrath.

They look at me like I'm some kind of video-game character:

Funky Mister Hard-On Killer trying to keep them from their life's dream of getting it on with a superstar.

"Why don't you get the fuck out," one of them retorts, his beady eyes half hidden by a ridiculous ski cap.

"Yeah," snorts the other, his face outfitted with more rings and studs than a Vegas hooker. "Before we kick your ass—old man."

I unzip the leather jacket to reveal a well-toned if not very muscular chest. "Why don't you try me? I got scars older than you pups," I grin. "Plus," I chomp my teeth for good measure, "I'm a biter."

They take one look at each other and run. Hat Head runs comically into the dildo stuck on the wall as he tries to put as wide a berth between us as possible while Ring Face is looking like he's going to piss his pants. Sean is surely having a good chuckle right about now on the other side of the door. Personally, I am pumped as shit. Sure, it wasn't much, but these days I get a rush out of doing anything that doesn't involve a needle or crack pipe.

Twenty minutes and two encores later, she floats in, Sweet Miss O., wearing her fifteenth costume for the night—a silver micro-skirt, halter top, and go-go boots that do little to disguise her ample curves. She has silver nails, too, and eye shadow. The only thing lacking is moon-color mascara.

I'm waiting for her on the Argentinean leather sofa, which according to her contract, must be brand-new for each show and mint green to match her eyes. Liv takes one look at me and the shimmering face falls like a diver off a Hawaiian cliff. The crash occurs in record time: less than a nanosecond's morph from Postshow, Anticipatory Boy-Toy High to Unwanted Blast from the Past Low.

"Fuck," she stamps her Barbie-sized foot. "Fuck and double fuck." The hands go up in pure tribute to her half-Sicilian lineage. "I mean, Jesus, Ian . . . what the fuck? It's been how long?" She draws a cleansing breath, something she's probably borrowed from that bullshit guru the papers say she's into now. Predictably, the move does little to abate her dark mood. "Just get the fuck out," she decides, like I'm some kind of migraine you can pop a pill for. "Just, leave, before this gets any uglier. I mean it, Ian, I'll sic security on you, I swear to God."

"You're the third person to threaten me tonight," I note sardon-

ically. "Counting your two little friends. I hope you don't mind I sent them home for a fresh diaper change?"

A string of vituperatives follows. I'd almost forgotten how volatile Olivia could be when crossed or otherwise contradicted. I'd also forgotten how small she was in person. Barely 5'2". And so damned vulnerable. Like a china doll. When she wanted to be, at least.

"Just take it easy, Liv." I move to discreetly close the door and take the fuming wildcat in my arms, all in one smooth motion. Call it reflex. Something you don't forget, like riding a bike, or cutting a fresh line of coke.

"Let go of me," she screams. "You don't have the right. You fucking ran out on me, Ian! Did you forget that?"

I hold her by the upper arms, forcing eye contact. "It was rehab, Liv. Court ordered. Followed by jail. Not much choice on my part, was there?"

Olivia stomps on my boot with the pointed heel of her own. I hadn't seen that coming and it hurts like hell. The ensuing moment's distraction is all the time she needs to follow up with a knee to the groin.

The responsive sounds issuing from my mouth prove to be both unprintable and unpronounceable.

"Stupid prick," she sneers, despising the weakness implied by my doubled-over position. "Couldn't even wait to get famous before you got fucked-up on drugs, could you? You always were premature in everything you did."

You had to admire the girl's wit. "What about you?" I retrieve the empty plastic vodka bottle lying conveniently at my feet. "How long have you been looking at fame through the bottom of this?"

She wants to attack me again, but this time I'm ready.

"Let go of me," she squeals, as I pin her against the wall. "You drugged-out felon!"

We eye each other for a split second, snakes tied in a bag. My cock is hard as steel and I know if I check I'll find her slick and wet. This is how it's always been between us; for all the lovers, fans, and swooning billionaires at her beck and call, I was the only one who ever knew what the great and fabulous Olivia Denarius needed in bed. To be put

down and controlled, told what to do, and used like the commodified slut everyone already thought she was. Without asking, I take her mouth, drawing a drop of blood from the corner. Her teeth spar, but there is no real resistance.

When I finally let her go, she is panting.

"These are mine," I say, squeezing the heaving, unaugmented tits—the set of which has just recently been voted one of *Hot TV Tonight*'s Seven Natural Wonders of the World. "I own them, just like I own you. Why do you fight it so much? It's what you want."

Liv turns her head, eyes closed, away from me. The sentence comes out breathless and broken, not at all like her famous onstage belting. "I don't want to want you . . . anymore . . . not like this."

"Your body says different." I slide my hands down her bare skin, gripping tightly, thumbs pausing to tease the belly-button ring before hooking with finality into the waistband of the sequined skirt.

"It lies," she breathes, palms flat against the wall, so submissive I nearly explode in my jeans. I want it all; that lush mouth wrapped round my twisted prick, that dark brown beaver spread for me like *Play Gent* magazine wants it spread—to the tune of a half-million-dollar offer at last check. But I've got to pace myself—it's going to be a long night, and unlike those skater punks I chased out, I didn't have it in me to stick it to the auburn beauty five or six times before dawn.

"Tell me," I dare, worming a finger under her pathetic excuse for a skirt and into the tiny G-string. "Tell me you don't want this—that you don't still lay awake after all this time, thinking of me, craving me."

This last statement was a shot in the dark on my part, but there must be some shred of truth to it, because next thing I know she's opening for me like a can of sardines.

"Oh, baby," she whispers hotly, her hands all over me like a kid under the tree at Christmas. "Take me. I need you. Fuck me, Ian, right here on the floor . . . take me hard and nasty, give it to me like the little bitch I am. I wasn't there for you, baby. While you were hurting so bad, I fucked every guy in sight. The tabloids didn't tell the half of it. And the whole time I didn't visit or write you, Ian, not even once."

No shit.

I seize her hands by the wrists to keep her greedy little fingers out

of my crotch. "It's not going to be that easy this time, baby. You're going to have to earn it."

For want of anything better, I tear off Olivia's halter to use as a makeshift tie for her hands.

"What are you doing?" she gasps, eyes bugging over her suddenly bared breasts. "Have you lost your mind?"

"Nope," I say, spinning her around and working up a nice, simple slipknot. "Actually, I've found it. Finally."

"You're a maniac, that's what you are. I'm gonna call for help and they're gonna come in here and kick the living shit out of you!"

The international sex symbol continues to threaten viciously as I bend her over the arm of her precious green couch. It amazes me now to think how much she's called the shots in the past, how we both lived for so long in a world contrived almost entirely of her own moods. Me, writing songs to suit her and backing her up on guitar while she flew on half-winged fantasies that always needed picking up after. Always.

The little G-string snaps satisfyingly in my grip. Liv groans and then outright moans into the Argentinean leather as I give her three firm smacks with my cupped hand. As always, the spanking calms her, putting her in a place of receptivity.

"Tell me you don't want this," I say for the record. "And I'll walk away. But if I stay, I'm warning you, it's going to be different. Prison changes a man, Liv. Even chicken-shit minimum security. So does rehab—ever spent your night over a toilet bowl with the dry heaves, a black hole sitting on your chest so heavy it could swallow the whole fucking planet and you wish it would?"

My hand is still on her buttock. I can feel Liv twitching, the skin burning under my touch. Seconds pass, agonizing. I need the words and so does she.

"Don't," she says at last, her voice barely audible. "Don't . . . walk away."

I make her come once, a shivering, teasing little orgasm on my finger. Afterward, I make her lick it clean, and then, as a finishing touch, she laps her juices off the arm of the couch where she's oozed out. I take this time to explain something crucial between us; what I see as the difference, the razor's edge between before and now, past and fu-

ture; the old me stressed out and doped up in a vain effort to fuel her endless need for masochistic attention vs. the new me, calm and cool, smiling like the proverbial cat who chowed-down the canary.

"Do you want to fuck my mouth now?" she looks up at me, crouching on the floor, hands still tied behind her back, the eyes a near perfect match to the spit-polished leather.

"No." I take up a nice full wad of her sweat-soaked hair in my hand. "I want us to take a little ride now."

Here's where Sean's help is going to be invaluable. Removing the star of a sold-out coliseum venue with her hands tied and her torso stripped is not something law enforcement people—or any people for that matter—tend to look kindly on.

Granted, putting her in the trunk of the limo would eliminate the possibility of suspicious eyes on the outside, but I still had to get her to the garage, through a phalanx of after-show hangers-on.

Peeking my head out the door, I called for my old buddy, praying he was within earshot. He was, and within a moment he knew what I needed.

"There's a back way," said the ever-resourceful former wrestler, having assessed the situation with an expert eye. "I'll distract the other two guards, you can take her down the back hall and through the service crawlway."

"You'll never get away with this," warns Olivia, as I wipe away the thick makeup from her face. "I'll scream rape as soon as we get out there."

I can see the way she's eying the beefy Sean. "Rape" at his hands is exactly what the cunning little songstress wants. In fact, unless I was sorely mistaken, the other two goons had been hired for this very purpose. The one thing about Sean, of course, was that he remained faithful to his wife and daughter no matter what. This fact had always killed Olivia.

"Say one word," I tell her as I hold her chin, giving her a good full dose of my bottomless black eyes, "and I'll disappear again. Forever."

She hangs her head in a semblance of defeat, the long auburn rivulets falling over the perfect tits and stomach in a move designed to engender pure, mainlined pity. Need I tell you that I am not fooled? Five minutes later, we are on the verge of a clean getaway.

"You should have been an escape artist." I pat Sean's sizable shoulder as we prepare to part ways at the man-sized vent. "Or a burglar."

The bodyguard smiles thinly as he heaves off the heavy metal grate with ease. "I sent a limo round back," he informs me. "It'll meet you on the other side. You'll have to drive it yourself."

I thank him with a firm, manly handshake.

"Excuse me," Liv interrupts our display of male bonding. "But there is no way in hell I'm going in there."

"You are," I say of the coal-black tunnel that appears to have no end. "Unless you'd like me to use my belt on you."

"You wouldn't dare."

Actually, I intend worse for her. Much worse.

"Try me."

She gives an indignant huff, even as she relents. I have her follow me into the tunnel, untying her hands for the time being so she can hold onto my belt. She's scared, but won't say so. Using the duct is a matter of necessity, though to be perfectly frank, I'd have gone this way anyway, just to hear how humble and grateful she was going to be once we'd made it through without being eaten alive by rats or swallowed by land sharks. Fear and humiliation, of course, are aphrodisiacs and with a girl like Liv, you have to fight like hell to stay ahead of her hormones. Tonight, I aimed to tip the balance, forever. The way isn't nearly so long as I'd expected, though Liv's relief is palpable as we reach the dreary luminescence of the underground garage. I reattach her hands behind her back now, mostly for psychological effect.

"You'll be enjoying the scenic view," I gesture dramatically to the open trunk of the '00 Lincoln, black with gold trim.

"Please, Ian, don't put me in there. I'll be good, I swear."

I have to prevent her from going to her knees on the concrete to show me just how good she can be. Leave it to Olivia to try and call the shots, even at this stage.

"Nice try." I scoop her up in my arms, setting her gently on the plush carpeting lining the metal interior. "But you're going in, like it or not."

She looks at me, silent and on her side, unable to shield her tits or

thighs from my view. As an afterthought—my hands already poised to shut the trunk—I ask, "You're not going to mess with the wires are you, to signal for help or anything?"

Liv's million-dollar Lloyd's-of-London-insured eyes evade mine. "No," she replies, a storm of emotions swirling in their emerald depths. "I won't."

Praising my ingenuity and good luck, I hop behind the wheel and put the car in gear. I have everything ready in advance on the other end. A drummer buddy of mine who is currently on tour getting all the pussy he can handle (drummers get all the women, it's true) is loaning me the use of a deviously converted garage, where he and his fillies sometimes play.

Among the advantages of the place were cork walls to stifle screams and a really impressive pulley and hook system that allowed you to truss up a girl in pretty near any position you could think of.

And then there were the toys. Hanging from a rack on the wall, a seemingly endless variety of whips, scourges, and paddles. I can see the dread written all over Liv's face as I help her from the trunk and deposit her, standing, in full view of the place.

"There's no way you're going to use any of those on me," Olivia announces as I untie her hands.

"On the contrary, Liv. I'm going to make you beg for it."

I let her run to the door. It's locked, as is the smaller one to the house. "This is pointless," I say, interrupting her frantic banging. "No one will hear you, and there's no way you can escape."

She comes back to me, her attitude markedly changed. "Ian, please. I'll suck you like you've never had before," she bargains, her voice rising in pitch with each syllable. "Or my ass. Would you like anal? What about money? Shit, you can have points off my next album. That's worth what . . . millions, right?"

"Just take your clothes off," I tell her patiently, "and go back to the center of the room, hands over your head."

She looks again at the whips, hooks, and chains. "I'd never survive anything like that, Ian. You know how fragile I am—you know that better than anybody."

"I'm giving you till the count of three."

"I'm sorry, Ian . . . for everything I said tonight, for everything I've ever done."

"Your delays are costing you," I inform her, selecting a nice, easy-to-wield buggy whip. "An extra lash for every minute you keep me waiting."

The boots are coming off, though she keeps on talking, playing for a new angle. Will I really truss her up and beat her? Will I really take the game to that next level?

Correction, this is no longer a game. It's life and death for both of us.

The skirt is the last to go. Very slowly now, unblinking, Olivia follows the final command and raises her arms. A powerful, charged silence falls over the wickedly appointed garage as I approach, taking her hands and fixing them in steel. Every little sound, the clinking and scraping of metal, the raising of the winch, cuts through her stomach and mine. I swear she will orgasm just from the setup, from being raised to tiptoes on concrete, naked and defenseless, arms pulled tight, breasts taut, ass straining, and begging uncontrollably for what her heart fears so much.

"I—I have another show tomorrow," she reminds me weakly, as I gauge her readiness.

"I won't mark you anyplace people can see," I promise, flicking the tip of the riding crop over her nipples just hard enough to make her moan. "Except for one."

She looks at me, ecstasy and fear mixed with healthy female curiosity. "Wh—what do you mean?"

I run a hand over the taut, flat belly which I intend very soon to distend. "You're going off the pill," I tell her. "From now on you'll take my seed . . . unprotected."

Olivia's eyes dance with the secret joy that only I know is there. It's something we had spoken of once or twice long ago, before any of the colored lights and autograph hounds. Was it really so crazy? I wonder as I move behind her to whip her pert ass cheeks. We'd tried everything else—friendship, partnership, even bitter rivalry. Why not marriage? But not the sort that other people look for, with white satin and prenups and a house in the suburbs. Olivia is still a singer and

I'm a songwriter; not only that, she's a woman who needs a firm hand, while I need . . . and I pause here to relish the thought . . . to dominate, to wreak havoc on lovely white skin, to discomfit and bring to whimpers the mightiest sex goddess in the universe.

The crop hurts like nothing Olivia's ever known, nor have I myself felt anything so sweet and true, the sheer mastery, the sound and hiss of leather whistling in the air, the cracking as it finds its target, punishing, molding, welting. True to my promise, I make her beg first, the whip handle inserted judiciously and teasingly in her treacherous but most lovable cunt.

Afterward, I pause to relish my work. Could there be a finer sight? The resplendent jade-eyed goddess, ripe for the plucking, hanging and twitching, conformity brought to her humbled ass, the promise of bliss issuing from between sopping, defenseless thighs.

This, far more than the roar of the crowd, the lights of the arenas or the adulation of the masses, is foreplay. But I won't accept her surrender. Not just yet.

"Look at me," I demand, compelling Olivia to raise her lowered eyes.

She responds to the tip of the whip pressed under her chin; a beaten, marked woman. "W—why are you doing this?" Liv wants to know.

I delay my answer as I lick the salt from her left breast. Sweat clings to it as it does to every other part of her perfect, unblemished skin. She moans in response, as much to the realization of my newfound power over her body as to the sensation itself.

"Because, love," I tell her with the true and pointless logic of a rock and roll god, "I can."

She responds to my kiss, warm and open and wet, even as I grab her ass cheeks hard, kneading the hot wounded flesh.

"Pleasure and pain, Olivia, are mine to give."

She nods, breathless, her eyes conveying a hundred emotions that her slack, pouting lips can no longer convey.

"So too, freedom." I caress her praying fingertips down to the smooth, steel shackles. "And bondage."

My cock throbs as I see her shuddering; the implications are only now sinking in for her. This isn't just a passing thing, the result of

some bad drug trip. I really mean it. I intend to change everything between us.

"You'll wear this," I say, showing her the collar. "Whenever we're together."

The sight of the leather device, metal studded, induces fresh rebellion. "This little game has gone far enough," she replies, shaking bravely at the chains. "Let me go, now, before I make you very sorry."

I have to keep from laughing at her; such a pretty little thing, all attitude, on tiptoes, buck naked, whipped like a cur and still playing the part of the diva.

"But I'm not going to let you go," I explain pleasantly as I push back the layers of hair behind her neck to accommodate the collar more easily. "I'm going to take you, right over there on that mattress; we're going to share hot, unprotected sex, Olivia, just like I told you. As a matter of fact, when I unchain you in a couple of minutes, you are going to crawl over there on your hands and knees like a good little girl and lay down for me right in the middle on your back—legs wide apart."

She glances at the dirty mattress strewn in the corner of the garage. The smell of sex and stale liquor hang thick above the grimy, gray material. There are no sheets and at each corner you can plainly see the straps that have been attached by which one may restrain and freely fuck one's partner.

I can see the revulsion, the terror—and the arousal. She wants it, but she's going to fight me some more. Frankly, I'd be disappointed if she didn't.

"We could go to a hotel," she suggests in a voice that is kitten soft. "It would be a lot nicer there."

"I suppose it would," I shrug, pretending to play the game for the moment. She smiles a little, and I can see the deviance brewing—even now, she'd like to turn the tables. It would be a long way to any hotel, I promise you, and she'd find some way to see we never arrived.

"We can go anywhere you want, baby, play any game. How about the Imperial Arms? Remember the Alcazar Suite, with the Jacuzzi and the oriental columns? I could be your harem girl . . ."

"Hmm," I nod, giving her another moment to think she's winning. "That's true."

The smile grows.

"Then again," I fix the collar dramatically and irrevocably around her neck. "Given your new status, these accommodations probably suit you a lot better, don't you think? In fact," I massage her welted buttocks, "I've even been thinking about having you branded. Would you like that, my dear—having my name seared into your flesh?"

"You wouldn't dare," she says warily, her voice holding far less conviction than it would have an hour ago.

"I'm tired of debating, Olivia. I am releasing you and you will do as I told you or else I will whip you again—and this time, I assure you I will not be so conscientious as to where and how."

So that nothing is left to her imagination, I flick my fingers suggestively and painfully across her breasts—just one of many spots which on a woman may be effectively and enjoyably marked. I release her wrists now and hold her briefly by the waist, slowing but not preventing her fall.

I look down, deciding I like the sight of her at my feet very much. She seems momentarily stunned, so I administer a mild refresher with the crop to her deeply flushed and punished buttocks. "To the mattress," I remind the princess of pop.

Olivia knows I am serious now. Head down, she puts herself in position. The long, spun hair hangs to the floor. She is crawling like an animal—a fine-collared pet that is about to learn its place once and for all. I see her looking a bit woozy as she approaches the mattress. At the edge of it—the multiple scents assaulting her nostrils, no doubt—she stops.

"Please," she shakes her head, "I can't do this."

I go to her. "Yes," I assure her, pressing the back of her neck to the mattress with the sole of my boot. "You can."

Her cheek makes an indentation in the worn-out material. She balks at the sour taste of it in her mouth. "All right," she exclaims. "I get the point. Just let me up and I'll do what you say."

"Too late," I tell her, deciding to impose swift retribution for her disobedience. "I want you on your belly now; crawl to the center of the mattress on your stomach and lick it."

She does so, tears in her eyes.

"Now it has your scents, too, Liv. Your saliva. Your tears. Your come."

Her body is shaking; she's orgasming and I've not even touched her yet.

"We'll come back here every day," I tell her as I begin to undress. "Until you're pregnant. As long as it takes. And when you don't have my cock in you, you'll wear a chastity belt." I reach down and scoop at her opening from behind. She's drenched, of course. "Needless to say, I'll be your manager now. I'll handle all your contacts, and your money. You'll get an allowance from me. If you're good. We'll keep close tabs on your diet, as well. Regular meals, and a few treats, if you earn them." I slap the meat of her thigh. "Back up on all fours, now Olivia. It's time to practice making a baby."

She complies, offering no resistance as my naked cock sheaths itself in her gaping, silky wetness.

"This is mine," I grasp her hips, slamming myself hard to the hilt of the cunt that I now claim. "Do you understand?"

"Yes," she cries in fury, childish female rage simmering with desire.

I continue to pump her hard; she's obviously taking pleasure, but I want pain, too, and the psychological implications of her being taken, had, used. "It will be like this all the time, Olivia," I continue to push at her comfort zones. "We aren't just going to be husband and wife or parents together. We'll also be master and slave."

Olivia groans, throwing back her head.

"You can't come," I inform her. "Not without permission."

Liv's tiny fingers dig into the mattress. It is a futile gesture, the meaningless protest of a collared bitch.

"Your orgasms belong to me, Olivia. Along with everything else."

My words are pushing her over the brink. She won't be able to hold herself back for long—all the powers of hell will be inadequate for that task. Still, I intend to make her suffer as long as possible.

"Do you know how many times I masturbated, Olivia? Thinking of you in rehab? Seeing your goddamned videos on the television? Watching you fuck the camera, hump the audience?"

"I—I did what I was told . . . I never meant to—"

"Always the excuse, eh, my pretty, treacherous little slut?" My

hands are twisted in her hair. My seed is poised, my genetic code ready for its fateful invasion. "Now," I grunt. "Now, Olivia."

We explode together, I in crushing victory, her in crumbling defeat. I have never felt myself shoot so hard or so long into a female, and certainly never half so satisfying. There is indeed something to be said for owning one's woman.

"Turn over," I prod her.

She mumbles something incoherent from the spot where she has collapsed. I note with amusement that she is no longer too proud to lay her priceless flesh upon the pocked, flea-bitten surface.

"Turn over," I repeat more sternly, delivering a crack of my palm across her buttocks. "We don't want to lose any of those strong little swimmers of mine, do we?"

Olivia struggles to obey. She is weak as a lamb, and I oblige her with a gentle but decisive shove onto her back. "Knees up, legs apart," I command. She winces when I shove the pillow under her behind, but from everything I've read, the elevation of the womb is crucial at this point.

"Good," I nod, quite satisfied with the ease of her submission at this juncture. "Now put your hands over your head."

She obeys, and one by one, I secure them in the straps. Binding Olivia's wrists will contribute nothing toward my overarching goal, except that I enjoy seeing her in close confinement this way. In fact, just a few strokes of my cock and I could be hard again. Being the genius that I am, however, I have a more interesting idea.

"Might as well make your mouth useful," I reason, climbing on top of her face. Her last visible expression before being covered by my balls and ass is precious. Outrage and moral indignation, mixed with dark fascination and a level of raw sexual need I have never before seen in any human being.

"And don't you dare think about making me ejaculate between those pretty lips of yours," I steer her head onto my cock. "You'll have plenty of time for that, after we've achieved our objective."

The collared Olivia sputters in protest but has little option other than to receive me to the quick. Her show of dissatisfaction is short-lived. In a matter of seconds, in fact, her hips are undulating and her

pussy is once again simmering, which tells me she's more than accommodating the new position.

The blowjob is first-rate.

I have to hand it to her; Olivia is good at what she does. In record time, the sexy little mouth that has crooned ten consecutive number-one hits including, "Baby, Take Me," and "In Your Heart, In Your Bed," has managed to breathe new life into my flagging organ.

"Nice microphone work," I note, pulling myself out with a loud pop. "Now let's see if we can get a fresh load up in that fertile womb of yours."

Olivia's expression says it all; she is beyond reason, beyond protest and firmly launched into that realm of sheer female space known as absolute submission. I'm greeted with an immediate moan as soon as I reenter. She pulls impotently at her wrist straps then wraps her legs round my buttocks.

"Please," she begs, sounding like the most humble and well-behaved wench a man could ask for. "I beg to come . . . please, master?"

"No," I tell her, grabbing a monster orgasm for myself. "You may not."

Olivia closes her eyes. The waves pour over but do not overcome her. She resists the ultimate prize and in so doing gains another: that of utter subjugation to my will. When next she looks at me, I know that I have won. She is mine, by a bond brighter than gold, stronger than matrimony.

"Soon," I whisper, running my hands over her belly. "Soon."

My touch is like ice and fire, like a slow motion whip to her skin. She is gone, unable to move, and yet I tie down her ankles just the same.

"Don't be embarrassed about the drooling," I tell her, remembering her fastidiousness as I affix the rubber ball gag between rows of pearl white teeth. "It's unavoidable in your current predicament."

This last little indignity leads her to clench her fists. She is determined to hold something back, to maintain some scrap of pride and dignity. And yet we both know what will happen now, should I deign to touch her again, even once.

"Get some rest," I advise, as I head for the kitchen for something to eat. "I intend on shooting at least two more loads in before dawn."

As I turn out the lights, the last thing I see is the eyes; the Fabled Jeweled Eyes of Olivia—threatening, pleading, and manipulating all at once. I'm going to enjoy owning her, I decide, very much.

The C-Word
by Mickey Chase

Mickey Chase is a writer who loves to focus on BDSM and, in private life, adores nothing more than pushing a lover's boundaries. Chase says, " 'The C-Word' wasn't an actual scene, but it is based on my current submissive, mingled with a few other scenes I experienced.

"Dirty words are incredibly important to me in BDSM, and I definitely have had partners for whom certain words were totally taboo. For this lover, it was definitely the C-word—it made her nervous and nauseous just to hear it, though she never made it an absolute boundary or asked me not to use it. I guess I'm truly a sadist, because nothing turned me on more than saying it to her, or, as I learned her buttons better, making her say it. She slowly learned to identify the word with intense, powerful submission as she surrendered her reluctance to hear and say that word, and soon I'd taught her to whisper it, then moan it as she came. Now, it's one of her favorite erotic words. All I have to do is whisper it in her ear and she gets wet to the knees, horny and ready for me.

"It's useful to have such a simple method of control," he adds.

When Gina first knelt down before me, she had a piece of paper in her hand. It was a list. She had filled it out from a text download from an obscure Australian website. It was a list of terrible things I could do to her—bondage, punishment, torture, role-playing, humiliation. Ten pages long and single spaced, each activity marked with a YES, NO, or MAYBE.

All the spellings were Australian, which amused me to no end as

I sat on my sofa and ran my fingers through Gina's hair, her face resting in my lap. I smiled when I saw how many YES answers there were, and my cock began to get hard against Gina's cheek. Obediently, without being asked or given permission, she began to kiss my shaft through my pants. She looked up at me as if for permission, but I only looked at her with the faintest hint of a smile on my face, secretly pleased that she knew what to do when she felt her master's cock get hard. Blushing red, she unbuckled my belt, unzipped my pants, and took my cock in her mouth. She sucked me hungrily as I read through the remainder of the list, and the skill with which she serviced my rod told me one thing: This was a slave I would very much enjoy having.

She sucked me expertly, sensing when I got close to coming, slowing her pace so I didn't come in her mouth. But she kept sucking. She kept sliding her mouth up and down on my pole, teasing the head with her tongue, gently licking my balls and looking up at me even when I wasn't making eye contact. I was engrossed in her list, planning her thousand and one nights of savage torment, exulting in the many ways I would make her moan.

She was a strikingly adventurous bottom for a woman of twenty-eight; of the three masters she had experienced, I knew from our online conversations, Gina had found none who would take her as far as she wanted to go. She was the sort of submissive who dreamed of being extinguished by the torrent of her owner's lust, of being destroyed and then rebuilt in the most beautiful ways. Her list included many things I ached to do to her. It included many YES answers that seemed almost beyond the pale of safe, sane, and consensual play. No wonder the list was Australian—she must have scoured the web to find one that went this far.

At the bottom, after the last circled YES, was a series of lists to determine which sexual words the submissive found arousing. There were a lot of exclamation points after Gina's circled words in the YES category. But there was one notable exception, perhaps because they don't use it in Australia.

Gina had made a handwritten note at the bottom.

"Never, ever use the C-word," she'd scrawled.

· · ·

I'm a respectful top, of course. But I enjoy pushing boundaries. That one, however, was sacrosanct—it was a "never." Gina and I played regularly for a year, the agreed-upon period of servitude. I respected Gina's NOS—every one of them made me rather nauseous. A few of Gina's MAYBES also made me nauseous, but I can never resist a challenge. By the end of the year contract, each one of her MAYBES had turned into a YES. Each one of her YESES had become a THANK YOU, MASTER. And the MAYBES that pushed my own personal boundaries had become a constant source of erotic charge between us, expanding my own repertoire exponentially.

I never teased or challenged her about her NO answers. I never pushed them, never violated that trust.

But that one single NO nagged at me, making me hard whenever I thought of it. When we played, I would often be screaming that word in my head, a smile on my lips as Gina moaned and cooed and orgasmed, never knowing what horrible, forbidden word was echoing in my brain. And I never, ever said it.

At the end of the year, I ceremoniously dissolved her servitude with the removal of her black leather collar. Gina petitioned me to allow her to serve for another year.

I told her a year was out of the question. It was marriage or nothing. I'd already bought the ring—a glittering custom-made white gold ring with a tiny diamond. It didn't go on her finger, though. It went through her clit, at the skyward terminus of those luscious lips, hovering above that tempting snatch that would do anything—anything—for its master, except be called what, to me, it was. She accepted, and I inserted the ring into her clit, then fucked her silly as I had a hundred times and planned to a thousand more.

We decided to have a white wedding, even though we'd be married at the justice of the peace—because this was the one time other than Halloween, Gina knew, that she could get away with wearing a wedding dress in public.

In anticipation of our new contract, I gave her a new form to fill out. It was similar to the original form, but I'd expanded the MAYBES to STRONG MAYBES and WEAK MAYBES and PROBABLY NOTS. There were a number of additions that had presented themselves during Gina's year of servitude. There was also an expanded dirty word list,

some of the obscure Australianisms (which I had, quite thoughtfully, used repeatedly, punishing each of her giggles severely) replaced with words I knew she'd say "Yes" to.

And one I knew Gina would mark as off-limits.

Or at the very least, a PROBABLY NOT.

I can't say why I did it; I guess I was hoping to push that final boundary. I wanted to hear her say the word, beg for it to be said to her.

And it was the one surprise I found on the new version of Gina's list.

The C-word was marked as a STRONG MAYBE.

Clearly, my fiancée had changed as much as I had in the year we'd spent together.

Two hours after our wedding, I had her lashed to the X-shaped cross in my basement still wearing the virginal lingerie that had gone under her wedding dress. The shimmering white panties were tugged down so the top of her rear furrow showed itself above their waistband; the garters descending from her white corset looked fetching spread wide as she leaned heavily against the cross and wrestled against her bonds. Her pale thighs were crisscrossed with the marks of my cane. Gina was moaning in rapture and bridal surrender.

Pressed up behind her, I was hard as a rock. I reached around between her and the cross. I slid my hand down into her white panties and felt it—that thing I'd never been able to call what I wanted to. I knew tonight, our wedding night, I would hear it from my wife's lips.

My fingers slid in, finding her wet. I whispered in her ear.

"What am I fucking?" I asked her.

"My pussy, Master," she sighed.

I took my hand away, stepped back and lifted the cane. She yelped as I left another angry mark of fire across her upper thigh.

Back again, I grabbed her panties and pulled them down. Her crotch was shaved, as I liked it. I pressed more firmly between her lips, fingerfucking her. When she moaned, I slid out and spanked her lightly with my open hand, striking her clit. Light blows on her clit always makes Gina come right away. When she was on the very edge, I stopped and held my hand at the ready.

"What do you call it, slave?" I asked her. "What do you call this hole I fuck?"

"My . . . my snatch, Master," she gasped. "Please . . ."

I stepped back, and this time Gina twisted in the bonds as I left another stripe across her thigh. She moaned, gripping the polished wood of the cross, smooth as her snatch.

When I put my arms around her again, there was a knife in my hand. She gasped in surprise as I drew it down her body. It cut easily through the sides of her panties, and I drew the shreds hard up from between her legs, abrading her clit. Then I spanked it again, this time with the knife in her mouth.

"What do you call it?" I asked, and eased the knife out.

"My slit, Master," she whimpered. "Please don't make me—"

I stepped back; the cane was in my hand, and this time I had Gina's whole delicious ass to work with. The stripes grew as she moaned and twisted, and I could tell she was soaring from endorphins. At first I thought she was sobbing. Then I realized she was giggling—rapturous, euphoric—and her giggles turned briefly to a choking sob before she sighed.

"I knew it would come to this," she moaned. "I knew you'd make me say it."

I pressed up behind her, kissing her neck. "That's what STRONG MAYBE means, slave."

"Yes, Master," she said. "But I won't say it."

She sounded serious. I waited to hear her safeword, but it didn't come.

"So be it," I said, and stepped back, raising the cane.

A wonderful thing happens when I cane Gina beyond a certain point. Past the endorphins, past the sobbing, past the moans, she gets ready to come in a way that is so rife with surrender and ecstasy that I almost come in my pants. When I knew she was on the very, very edge of climax, I could take it no more.

"Tell me what it is!" I shouted.

"My hole, Master," she whimpered. "My slit, my snatch, my pussy, my coochie, my—"

I had the panic snaps undone in an instant. I'd given up. I could feel the fear in Gina's body; perhaps her safeword was on her lips, but

she didn't utter it. Instead, she let me wrestle her over the edge of the four-poster bed, bending her so hard her feet lifted off the ground and she hung there, dangling. When I forced her thighs wide and entered her in a single violent thrust, she came.

She was still coming, soaring on her orgasm as I pounded my cock into her, seeking my own climax, my body striking the sizzling welts of her recent caning.

"What is it?" I shouted. "What am I fucking, slave?"

"My slit!" she moaned.

"What is it?"

"My pussy," she whimpered.

I lifted her fully onto the bed, climbing on without ever letting my cock out of her body. I angled up and fucked her so hard she screamed. I wasn't sure she'd finished coming, but when she came again, I knew. Gina often comes more than once, but rarely so soon. I grabbed her hair and turned her head to the side, pressing her face into the pillow as I growled.

"What is it?"

"My . . . my . . ." she couldn't speak, so overcome was she with her rapid-fire orgasms.

I pulled my cock out of her, held it at her very entrance.

My eyes were moist with tears as I looked at her pink face, feeling her under me, her ass raised in the air as I fucked her from behind. I waited, feeling her rock slightly against me, the spasms of her climax still rumbling through her.

"Say it, slave," I whispered. "Please."

"My cunt, master," she sighed. "My fucking cunt."

"What am I fucking, Gina?"

"My cunt," she moaned, over and over again. "My cunt, my cunt, my cunt, my cunt, my cunt—"

She had pushed me to the edge, as she so loved to, as I so loved, and my anger, so often denied, brimmed out as I pounded her violently. "And what are you, Gina?"

"Cunt, cunt, cunt, cunt, cunt—"

I grabbed her hair. My face against hers, I growled at her. "What are you?"

"I'm a cunt," she breathed.

"That's right," I snapped. "You're a fucking cunt!"

"I'm a cunt."

"You're a cunt!"

"Yes, Master, I'm a cunt!"

I pounded into her with newfound fierceness and before I left my seed in her, Gina came again, one final time, moaning, twisting, and gripping the bed, clawing at the sheets with the panic snaps rattling like jewelry from her leather-shrouded wrists.

We rarely sleep in the basement; it's a kind of sacred place reserved for obscenities. This time, though, I was too exhausted to move. When I finally awakened, deep into the morning, Gina knelt beside the bed with a tray of food for me.

"This cunt offers you food, Master," she said.

I reached out and took an apple. Regarding my shadow in its polished surface, I smiled.

"You were topping from the bottom again," I told Gina.

"I know, Master," she said. "This cunt knows you'll have to punish her."

I sighed. "Why did you mark it as a NO?"

"Because this cunt couldn't bear to hear it, Master."

"And why did it become a MAYBE?"

"I . . . I knew you wanted to say it, Master."

"How did you know?"

Gina shrugged.

"This cunt doesn't know how she knew, Master."

"And why did you finally say it?"

"This cunt doesn't know that, either, Master. This cunt just said it."

"You wanted to say it."

Gina took a deep breath. "In a way, Master. Yes. This cunt wanted to say it."

"You're asking for another caning, Gina."

"This cunt knows that," she smiled. "Master."

"You're asking for more than a caning," I said. "You're asking for a new name."

Gina lowered her head.

"Come to bed, cunt."

"Yes, Master," she said.

My cunt set the tray down on the nightstand and crawled into bed, naked.

Fear of Heights
by Michael Hubbard

Michael Hubbard is a BDSM player who writes technical documents for a living and has just recently started writing erotica. This is his first published story, and he says he's at least as proud of it as he is of any software documentation he's ever written, though he admits writing erotica doesn't pay as well!

"Fear of Heights," in a sense, is an exploration of what is sometimes called "terror play." In it, a submissive's fears and phobias are explored and conquered by turning them into a fetish, using the erotic charge of fear to heighten sexual response. Most BDSM relies on some kind of fear for its power— but here, it's explicitly central.

While this kind of play is not for everyone, the loving context of the "terror" scene in "Fear of Heights" makes it the sort of thing that most of us, including me, can certainly appreciate as a delightfully taboo turn-on. In fact, I for one find it rather sweet—as well as hot!

I could feel Amy quivering against me. The elevator hummed softly, passing floor after floor. I slipped my hand under her top and felt her nipples, hard. I put my hand under her skirt and found her wet.

But she was shaking.

This early on a Saturday, there was no one headed up to the observation deck, and none of the office workers in the building were working, either. We were alone, and as the modern elevator whisked us past the tenth floor, the twentieth floor, the thirtieth, I felt her shaking more, her breath coming faster.

"Are you all right?" I asked.

Amy shook her head. "No," she said. "I don't think I can make it."

I chuckled.

"That's not our agreement," I said.

Amy took a deep breath and nodded.

"Yes, Master," she said.

We passed the fiftieth floor and neared the observation deck. She put her arms around me and begged me to hold her close.

The elevator doors opened on the giant garden.

"Good morning," said the attendant.

I took Amy's hand and turned her around. She shook, her face white with fear.

"Please," she begged.

"Go," I told her.

"Good morning," repeated the attendant. "That will be four dollars each."

I frog-marched her out of the elevator. I handed the uniformed attendant a ten and pressed her on past his podium.

"Is she all right?"

"She's a little nervous about heights," I said. "She'll be fine."

Amy shook against me as I forced her out onto the observation deck. There were blooming flowers all over near the elevator, but I pushed her toward the edge, where there would be two things we wanted: a railing she could hold onto as I pushed her out to look over, to see the ground sixty stories below.

And high hedges, to hide what we were doing from the attendant.

"Please," she begged.

"Come on," I told her. She became more and more difficult to push forward as we got closer to the edge. I turned her and spun her up against a nearby ivy-covered hedge, pushing her into the sharp branches. I reached under her skirt and felt her bare pussy, dripping.

"Right here," she whispered. "Can't you do it right here?"

"No," I said. "On the edge," I told her. "On the railing."

She moaned as I pulled her away from the hedge, her low-cut blouse revealing the scratches the bushes had left on her cleavage. I forced her to the edge of the building and pushed her up against the railing, my arms around her.

"Look over," I said.

Her eyes were clamped shut.

"Look over," I told Amy, snaking my fingers through her hair and pushing her forward, bending her over the railing.

"Oh, God," she said, her eyes still shut.

I reached down and yanked her skirt up, revealing her bare ass and her naked, smooth-shaved pussy, unencumbered by panties.

"Spread your legs," I told her.

She spread them, parting her thighs wide to reveal her open cunt. She leaned forward, gripping the railing. Her eyes were still closed.

I took my cock out and put it at the entrance to Amy's cunt. I reached under her and began to stroke her clit with one hand, while I put the other hand up her blouse and started playing with her nipples.

"Open them," I said. "Open them or I won't fuck you."

"No," she whispered. "I can't."

"Open them or I'll throw you off."

A gasp choked in her throat, almost a sob. Her eyes popped open and she stared over the edge. In that instant I entered her, thrusting into her so hard that she lifted off her feet. She opened her mouth to scream, but nothing came out. I fucked her harder, slamming her into the railing. She shut her eyes again.

"Open them," I said. "Open them or else."

Moaning, she opened her eyes, looking down into the gaping maw of the city. I worked on her clit rhythmically, feeling the intense arousal her fear had brought. I pounded into her steadily, letting go of her breasts so I could bring my other hand around her, lick my thumb, and slide it into her tight asshole.

"Oh God," she moaned. "I'm going to—"

"Yes," I said. "Do it now."

"Please . . . please don't let go of me," she choked.

"I won't," I said, and she groaned, coming on my cock as I fucked into her. I thrust my thumb deeper into her ass, grasping her hair just as she came and pushing her face forward over the railing. She stared into nothingness, great heaving sobs of liberation coming from her lungs. By the time I came, she was slumped against the railing, leaning far over.

"Th—thank you," she moaned softly.

"Thank you, what?" I asked her.

"Thank you, Master."

I let her down off the railing and pulled her skirt down. I zipped up my pants and put my arms around her, cradling her as she leaned against the railing.

She was staring down, the last thing I expected. Underneath us there was a great wide mesh of steel, designed to deter jumpers. But for someone like Amy, terrified of heights, that mesh was no comfort at all. All she could see was the huge distance between her and the ground, and it terrified her.

But for someone like Amy, fear was an aphrodisiac. She'd never before come as fast as she had today. And she'd never before leaned like this against a railing, looking out into the empty space.

Lucky thing, too, because on Monday she had to start working on the fifty-fifth floor of this very building.

"Think you're ready?" I asked her.

She snuggled more deeply into my grasp.

"I don't know," she said. "I think maybe I need some more therapy."

Master Plan
by Debra Hyde

Debra Hyde is a regularly published erotica writer. Recently, her work appeared in *Best of the Best Meat Erotica; Ripe Fruit: Erotica for Well-Seasoned Lovers;* and *Body Check: Erotic Lesbian Sports Stories.* Hyde is routinely published in *Prometheus* magazine. She runs *Pursed Lips* (www.pursedlips.com), a weblog and personal site that focuses on erotica and general sexuality, and writes regularly online for Heather Corrinna's *Scarlet Letters* (www.scarletletters.com) and the *Yesportal* (www.yesportal.com).

She says of her contribution "Master Plan": "I've always been curious: What does a Master get from prodding his slave? Near as I can tell, it's a primal thing. Much like a cat playing with a doomed mouse, the imperious Master teases and taunts his willing captive. Every little squirm and squeal, every mark and bruise, heightens his arousal and readies him for the culminating fuck. Then, with orgasm, the primal urge is satisfied. Personally, I love the game of erotic cat and mouse, but I'm also glad that, unlike the mouse, I don't end up headless and abandoned. Instead, I get cuddled and lots of pillow talk."

The sight of Sharon in supplication before Kirk rouses him. At first, it is her body that stirs him. With her slender arms stretched out before her, they lead to the gentle muscles of her shoulders and back, contours that ripple from decades of modern dance. Like dunes in a desert landscape, the slope of her back leads to the round firmness of her ass, a luscious oasis. If she presents herself with that ass raised high and legs spread wide, Kirk can, if he chooses, examine her readiness—one glance at the slit between her legs reveals much—and he

can admire the hint of breast and nipple, petite things that always present him with much pleasure.

Yes, those things attract Kirk's interest, but it's the other more subtle clues that make his cock swell hard. It's in the quiver of her legs as they tire from the position. It's in the shuddering response of her body when he trails a finger down her back. It's in her moans when he sticks that finger between those lush lips that beckon him from behind.

Those are the things that get him hard. And when he's hard, he's in his element.

However, Kirk never pounces too soon. First, the ritual must be played out. He'll kneel down beside Sharon, take one wrist, and bring it behind her. He'll wrap a leather cuff around that wrist and buckle it fast, then repeat the process with the other wrist. Often, he'll clip them together behind her back. The slim leather collar will follow and with it a slight shiver from Sharon as she feels it touch her skin and draw tight around her throat.

Her reaction to the collar hasn't changed in years. Neither has his. His cock still twitches at the sight of leather on Sharon's skin.

At this point, ritual ends and whim begins.

Kirk took to his overstuffed chair and simply sat there, admiring the woman before him. She was splendid, kneeling before him, her forehead to the ground, arms clipped behind her. He watched the gentle rise and fall of her breathing, patiently waiting for his command. He could not help but remember the countless times his actions propelled her from that peaceful state to one more frantic and frenzied, one where her every breath reflected her anxiety. She would reach that point again, tonight, he knew. But not yet. Not yet.

The thought of what was to come, however, created an urgency of a different sort, and Kirk undid his belt and unzipped his pants.

"Come here," he ordered her.

Sharon rose to her knees and hobbled to him. She had to follow the sound of his voice; a blindfold prevented her from doing otherwise.

As she positioned herself in front of him, he took her by the hair and directed her to his cock. She gasped lightly as she felt his grip, but

he gasped when he felt her wet, full lips around his cock. Her mouth was luscious and willing, just like the rest of her body.

Sharon didn't need to be told to worship his cock. Her eager tongue licked and lapped as she worked up and down his length. Kirk leaned forward and grasped her breasts. He gave them a little squeeze, causing Sharon to moan just enough that it resonated through him. For her part, Sharon sucked a touch more taut, as if to say, "I know how you like this."

If one's dick could swell beyond fullness, Kirk's did, and as he caressed her breasts he marveled. No matter that many years had passed since they first met; every time he touched Sharon, it was as electrical as the first time. Where their friends had either divorced their way out of their disillusioned "later years," or quietly withered into a mutually accepted sexless existence, Kirk and Sharon still lusted after each other.

And why not, Kirk mused? It was the best of two worlds—worlds in which he could take and command as he pleased, hers in which she surrendered to his will. What was not to like? Kirk could cop a feel or a fuck any time he liked and Sharon, by willing acquiescence, received attention and approval, all couched in eroticism and culminating in hot sex.

As Sharon's mouth tugged at Kirk's cock, he thought about their usual Friday night outing at the movies, where once the lights lowered, he would reach for the buttons of her sweater and require her to sit with it unbuttoned. Where he would insist she keep her hand on his lap. Sometimes, he'd even reach inside her sweater and leave a clamp pinching down on a nipple. He loved watching Sharon try to contain herself. She didn't like flinching or squealing in public; she didn't want to draw attention. Attention, after all, meant you could get caught.

Kirk, on the other hand, had no problem with it. Except it made him so hard, it was torture waiting to get home to fuck her.

As he mused, Sharon's mouth had become a slurpy noise, a sure sign of fatigue. Kirk grasped her hair again, this time pulling her off of him.

"Enough," he said. He reached down between her legs and tapped at her thighs. "Spread."

Stiffly, Sharon tottered her legs apart. Like a well-trained dog, she

didn't need detailed instructions. She responded just fine to one word commands. However, she didn't always spread herself well enough. Kirk slapped each thigh quickly with a firm "more!" Sharon gasped, yet complied.

Reaching between her legs, Kirk cupped her and felt flesh, ripe and full. A hint of wetness met his touch. Kirk squeezed her there, groping her cunt as if it was a breast. He nuzzled into her neck and, as he inhaled the scent of Sharon's flesh, he slowly bared his teeth. He squeezed her cunt hard as he bit into her neck. He didn't let go quickly, not even when Sharon squirmed. Squirming was, after all, one of the reasons he did this.

It didn't take long for the pain and pleasure of his bite and his fingers to merge into one shuddering response. It overtook Sharon, transforming her squirming into something more. The clenching throbs Kirk felt in his clutches told him exactly how pain and pleasure played out.

Kirk let go of Sharon's neck and pulled back to admire his work. He could set the mark of his teeth in her flesh, red to the point of purpling. Sharon, suddenly free of his bite, heaved in relief.

"Thank you, thank you!" She spit her gratitude in urgent, breathy little gasps. Kirk knew that no matter how luscious a bite might start out, if he bit fiercely enough, it would escalate to unbearable, and he knew Sharon was genuinely thankful to be free of the burden.

But not free of his whim.

"Did I tell you, you could talk?"

The question was, Sharon knew, rhetorical. Even though he hadn't told her not to speak, she knew that, by merely voicing it, Kirk made it a rule of tonight's engagement. Startled, she squealed.

Kirk smiled wickedly. Squirming *and* squealing. Yes, that's what it was all about—and his to control and invoke. What more could a man ask for? Oh, some men asked for a lot. They wanted to control everything—her dress, her mannerisms, whether she worked and whether she turned in her cash to him, who she fucked, and how. Some men wanted so much control that, to him, it looked like all work, no fun, and so much whoring and pimping.

Neither was dominance all chivalry and romance. It wasn't

starry-eyed, bodice-ripping desire. It didn't rescue or protect. Dominance was something raw and wild for Kirk.

Sex. Dominance was all about sex, unfettered and uninhibited. And Kirk didn't understand why one would want to bother with dominating anything that didn't have an erotic underpinning. If it didn't make his dick twitch, Kirk didn't want anything to do with it.

If her body looked good lying on the floor before him, it looked even better on the bed on all fours. Sharon's hands were now free but she remained blindfolded and unable to anticipate Kirk's actions by sight. She could by sound, though, and Kirk made sure to do everything a little bit louder: grabbing a whip from a drawer, unzipping his pants, even letting them fall to the floor.

Sharon knew what was coming. She didn't know exactly how—whether the whip would be mild or severe, whether he'd fuck her right away or make her wait for it—but she knew. And it made her quake in fear and humiliation.

When Kirk saw Sharon's thighs quiver, he knew what she was thinking. Would she be able to take the whip? What if it was too much? How long could she take it? But he knew that when enough stripes adorned her back, Sharon would feel his cock at the portal of her cunt. He'd push his way in and see to his pleasure. That awareness made her quiver all the more.

Kirk raised the whip he'd selected and let it fly. It struck Sharon's left shoulder. A hiss issued from her and she arched her back, as if to answer the strike. Without waiting, Kirk laid another strike into her skin, this one to her right shoulder. Sharon raised her head and moaned. Kirk knew she now recognized the whip. It was his quirk, a stiff leather thing that was rather unforgiving in its intensity.

Repeatedly, he struck her with it, landing blow after blow to her shoulders until a series of red marks lined her. Sharon yelped and moaned at each stroke, yet no matter how difficult the strike, her cunt grew more and more swollen, revealing how she really felt about it.

It was luscious, that ready hole, and Kirk knew that Sharon liked being his hole. She liked it best when he took her and used her without any concern for her pleasure. So Kirk took his cock in his hand

and aimed it between Sharon's generous labia. He felt them part and welcome him, and he worked the head of his cock into her.

Sharon moaned and raised her ass to Kirk. It was the wordless begging of a woman's cunt. But Kirk only intended to tease; he wasn't yet ready to fuck. He moved slowly and kept his cock right shallow. When Sharon moaned and raised up a second time, he pulled out, swiftly and without warning. Sharon practically collapsed over the sudden void.

"I'm not ready to fuck you yet. You're not marked enough to please me."

But what Kirk really meant was, "It's a setup. I intend to make you utter a word."

He wielded the quirk so hard and fast against her ass that Sharon could barely hold her place, let alone her tongue. When she lurched and struggled, he scolded, "Don't move, cunt. Stay where I put you." When she cried out, he told her, "Your ass is mine and I won't stop until it's red hot." When she choked down a scream, he said nothing. But he whipped her as hard and as fast as his arm would allow.

That did it. That broke Sharon's resolve not to speak. It was more than Sharon could bear.

"Please, please!" she pleaded. Using words like "stop" and "enough" were not within her jurisdiction. They implied she had command and control, and Sharon knew she had willingly ceded both to Kirk. She only had the ability to plead and she begged Kirk to let up.

Kirk stopped and immediately Sharon regretted that he fulfilled her cries. She knew something worse would follow, something that said, "You broke the rule. Now you live with the outcome."

He rummaged again, this time coming up with something Sharon heard as metallic. Metallic chain, to be specific. Kirk imparted more clues to Sharon: His fingers at her nipples said clamps. When the clamps squeezed and burned into her, they hinted at clover clamps. When Kirk pulled the chain tight and an unmistakable pain ripped through her nipples, Sharon knew for sure.

Again, she squirmed, this time in a pain that wouldn't relent. With her back marred and her ass burning red, Sharon looked perfect, ripe for the taking. Once again, he pressed his cock into her. This time, though, he sank deep and wasted no time in fucking her.

As he fucked Sharon, Kirk held the chains as if they were reins, keeping them as taut as possible. Sharon's nipples looked squished, twisted in the mean grip of the clamps, beautifully severe, and although she whimpered at every stroke of his cock, he needed to feel her squirming before him. He needed to feel her body writhing on his cock.

With reins in hand, Kirk stuck his thumb in her ass and reamed it, a sensation so sudden and severe, it shot into her bowels and up the reins to her torture nipples. Squealing, Sharon lurched, practically right off his dick.

"Stay with me, cunt," he uttered. It was exactly what he wanted. A writhing body. It looked primal. Fucking it felt animalistic, timeless, like a caveman's drive to search and seize. Sharon squirming beneath him made her prey—sexual prey. Captured, all it required was conquering.

Kirk had quested after his prey and now he intended to conquer it. He pummeled Sharon, his dick a weapon of conquest and power. Already, a deep, tight heat welled up inside him and it moved toward eruption. He could feel it spread and rise, and, in one last conquering move, he shoved his thumb as deep into Sharon's ass as he could. Sharon shook all over and moaned plaintively, but Kirk could see only one thing: her thighs quivering like gelatin.

Kirk exploded into orgasm. Jets of jism shot from him, flooding Sharon. Defeated, Sharon collapsed onto her elbows, pulling the clamps even tighter. As Kirk felt his orgasm subside, Sharon shook even harder.

Like prey.

Yes, that what dominance was to Kirk—hunter to prey, conqueror to conquered. Primal urges etched erotic. It was rough and wild, and only as tame as one's conscience made it.

For Kirk, tame meant drawing Sharon to him after releasing her from the clamps and the blindfold. Tame meant laying down beside her and curling up around her. Tame meant murmuring what a wicked, wonderful delight she was. It meant urges quelled and exhausted.

• • •

Tame, however, is a relative term and a temporary condition. All too soon, those primal urges will return. The need to feel a body squirm, submit, and surrender will rise again. Desire will fuel preoccupations, and preoccupations will threaten to become obsessions. But Sharon is Kirk's outlet; she keeps him grounded, however wild and raw his cravings might be. When he reaches for her again, she will be ready. She will give herself over to him. He will take and seize and conquer her all over again.

Atonement
by Reese Gabriel

Reese Gabriel is happily married in real life. He and his spouse of fifteen years get to live out lots of his in-print fantasies. He has published numerous novels with Pink Flamingo (pink-flamingo.com) and has a novel coming out with Chimera Books (chimerabooks.co.uk). His love of bondage and of master-slave role play has been lifelong and he is a firm believer in people exploring their sexual desires in safe, sane, and consensual ways.

Of "Atonement," Gabriel says: "Sex for me has always been about masters and slaves. I was the adolescent who inked in collars and chains on my pinups and rooted for the heroines to be caught. My first lover let me tie her down and on my second date with Rose, my wife of fifteen years, we read a Gor book together. Since then, with Rose's wonderful help, I have continued to explore the roots of my dominant desires through role play, fantasy writing, and philosophical speculation.

"This particular story is not autobiographical, although it does reflect an amalgam of fantasies, visions, and ideas that have sprung from relationships forged within the BDSM community. Chief among these, by far, is my association with Lizbeth Dusseau at Pink Flamingo Books, a great lady who I am honored to count not only as my editor and publisher, but a trusted friend and mentor as well."

Crissy is perched on a stranger's lap when I find her, shoes kicked off, the center of attention at a local watering hole known as the Pink Flamingo. Happy and boisterous, a lamb among wolves, the twenty-three-year-old belts an inane Monkees tune off the jukebox, com-

pletely oblivious to the dozen sets of eyes simultaneously tearing away the half-buttoned blouse and skintight miniskirt from the ripe, curvaceous body which is destined, surely, to go home with one of them.

It is barfly heaven; one can almost see the wheels spinning, as each calculates his presumed odds of bedding the busty, barefoot blonde.

The sorry excuse for a bearded yuppie whose crotch Crissy's ass is glued to at the moment would seem to have the edge, though there are other contenders at the table. Chief among them, the balding insurance salesman to her right, furtively rubbing a creamy, stockinged thigh to the beat of "Daydream Believer" (a song I'd found intolerable the first time around) and, to her left, a turtle-necked entrepreneur type who is glaring expectantly down her amply displayed cleavage as he speaks animatedly into her ear.

Whatever he's saying, it must be very funny, because Crissy keeps giggling, shaking her tits and sloshing the contents of a half-finished glass of beer onto the bald man's head.

She's obviously had a couple already, which means she is a sitting duck for whichever of these characters proves strong enough or crafty enough to exploit her special weakness. Crissy, you see, is no mere party girl out for a good time. She's a submissive. A card-carrying member of that special subspecies of women who cannot live without being owned, and while she might have decided for the moment that she is tired of being my slave, she is quite certainly incapable of not being someone's slave.

I decide to announce my presence as calmly as possible. Obviously, I am not particularly thrilled that Crissy has gone to happy hour instead of coming straight home from work like she is supposed to, but this is hardly the time or place to vent my spleen at her disobedience—especially given the fact that the girl and I are living in a relationship based on an institution legally banned a century and a half ago.

"Christine? Excuse me, Christine."

She looks up at me through tawny strands, the vanguard of that kinky, wheat-colored mane in whose tendrils I so thoroughly enjoy burying my fingers during oral intercourse. "M—ma—" she stutters, pale blue eyes wide as saucers, visions of a night in irons dancing through her head.

I interrupt her with a look, warning her not to complete the M word—that time-honored title marking her as my personal property, subject to any form of discipline, confinement, or abuse I may wish to heap.

"I'm her uncle," I explain to the wary, would-be Romeos who have long since sized me up as a gaunt, salt-and-pepper joy-killer of the tallest order. "I've come to fetch her. Christine, I'm glad I caught you. It's your Auntie M. She's gotten worse. Much worse."

Crissy's lower lip slips worriedly between pearl white teeth as she decodes my message. It's abundantly obvious now she's not thought through the consequences of her little rebellion. It is one thing to mouth off to one's master on the phone because he never wants to do anything or go anywhere, not even to a really cool concert that one's been wanting to see for ages and to which one can get really good tickets, but running away—even a few blocks from one's office on a Friday night—that is quite another.

"Pardon me," she hastily tells her skinny, goateed Santa, slipping elf-like from his lap. "I've got to go . . . with my uncle."

Eyes cast down, trembling like a little girl whose father has come out in the middle of the night to collect her from a sleepover for misbehavior, Crissy quickly gathers her shoes, jacket, and purse, and presents herself.

"I'm ready," she whispers. "Sir."

"A little late to close the barn door, don't you think?" I observe curtly, noting the girl's ludicrous attempts to rebutton and tuck her blouse.

I turn in silence on my booted heel, depriving myself deliberately of the pleasure of seeing those pretty eyes lower themselves moistly to the floor, her full cheeks pinkening as she contemplates her sins.

Above all things, Crissy fears my disapproval, and it is this weapon—among others even more subtle and terrible—which I will employ tonight in her chastisement. I know she does not mean to hurt me; in truth she cannot help herself, but I will make her suffer retribution, nonetheless. For her pleasure. And mine.

Crissy is behind me as I burst forth from the smoky den into the clear, crisp air of night. Her jacket and shoes still in tow, she struggles

to keep pace. Although I weigh in at twice the girl's age and change, I am in excellent shape and can eventually wind most people.

"Master," she cries as we reach the sidewalk, "my feet."

I pick up the pace, knowing that the only thing being wounded here is her pride.

"Master, please."

Adding yet another millimeter's width to my lanky stride, I plunge my hands into the field jacket earned honestly, the hard way, sloshing through rice paddies looking for Charlie. If this child thinks she knows suffering . . .

I've parked my car next to hers, two blocks from the Pink Flamingo in the lot of the building where Crissy works as a receptionist. We don't need the money, but I insist on her keeping up with vanilla appearances in case she ever has to go back into that world. For one thing, I won't live forever.

I'm at the door of my nondescript late-model sedan, fiddling with the lock when she catches up.

"Master, will you just talk to me . . . please?" Her voice is high-pitched and desperate over my shoulder. Small hands are clutching my left sleeve. Something tugs at my heart, and I wonder for a split second if I actually love this one.

"I thought you were supposed to be my teacher," she complains now, childish pique coloring her noble play at tragedy, "but it's like you're . . . pouting or something."

I do a 180. The look on her face in response to the look on mine indicates she wishes she'd tried a different strategy to get my attention. "Crissy," I begin, drawing a deep breath. "I have been training slaves since before you were born, and I can assure you, there is nothing you could ever do—not even in your wildest dreams—that would ever cause me to lose my composure. As for teaching you, I hereby absolve myself of that responsibility, once and for all."

I fish in my trouser pocket for the key to the locked collar she wears without exception when we are at home. "Here," I announce, grasping her hand and turning it palm upright to receive the tiny silver object. "You are officially free."

Half woman and half child, Christine looks at me doe-eyed, lips

tremoring, like I have just taken away her pony, stood her up on her first date, and excluded her from a game of jacks all at once.

"But . . . master . . ."

"Goodbye, Crissy." I plant myself behind the wheel. "It's been fun."

Her nose presses to the glass as soon as I close the door. This is the hard part: being a bad ass when all I really want to do is scoop her up in my arms and take her home for a good whipping, a hot fuck, and a couple of cups of cocoa. In that order. But discipline has to come before pleasure. If you can't keep to that basic rule of mastery, then you'll never be anything more than a dilettante, a pathetic dipshit tourist top in need of a good bitch slapping. Believe me, nothing fries my bacon quicker than seeing some selfish little prick taking himself a slave when he doesn't have the balls or brains for the job. A girl like Crissy needs to be dominated, pure and simple. It's what her body craves, and the harder she tests you—tonight being a splendid case in point—the more you need to come down, and come down hard.

"Christine," I depress the electric window a half-inch. "This is becoming tedious. You are not ready. Go home; you still have an apartment, and now you see why I insisted we keep the lease active—not to mention your employment status."

"Just give me another chance," she begs, a latent hiccup punctuating the otherwise flawless plea. "I am ready, I swear! You can do whatever you like. I'll take any punishment."

I feel the familiar tightening in my crotch at the mention of punishment. It is a most delicious word, a verbal aphrodisiac, electric on the lips and a guaranteed entrée for two into the dark world of the flesh.

Oh, yes, I'll punish the girl. But not in the way she thinks.

"All right, then. I'll be back in five minutes." I open the window a little further, handing her a napkin to wipe the rivulets of mascara-colored tears. "If I find you standing in this exact spot, naked, then I'll know you're serious."

Her mouth drops open. Clearly this is a possibility she hadn't entertained. "But . . . master we're . . . outside."

"Yes," I deadpan. "I'd noticed that myself."

She's still staring blankly as I drive off, her perplexed little self neatly framed in the rearview mirror. As far as she knows, I'm really leaving, but as you can probably guess, I have no intention of leaving my lamb unprotected, even for a second. As it works out, one of the security guards for the property is a real stand-up guy named Leon whose acquaintance I've had the pleasure of making through Crissy.

Leon has agreed to keep an eye out tonight, in exchange for a little piece of the action later on. I myself will shortly be enjoying a perfect view of Crissy's impromptu striptease thanks to a pair of binoculars and nearby shrubbery. I'd been planning this little party since five thirty this evening, the exact minute my little pet became officially MIA. My first call was to Larry the bartender at the Flamingo, verifying my hunch as to her hiding place. The second call was to Leon, whose help came with minimal arm-twisting. The high-powered infrared binoculars I'd had in the trunk all along, a gift from another buddy who happens to work in the rather lucrative, if not entirely legal, world of wholesale military sales.

One quick pass around the block and then I slip into position. Needless to say, my little escapee doesn't disappoint. After a brief internal struggle on her part, punctuated by a lot of nervous glances and a rather amusing and totally irrational inspection under a nearby parked car, Crissy returns to the designated spot and begins to work the buttons of her blouse.

Her brazenness pleases me. When I first met her, Crissy had hated her body because she wasn't a size zero or even a three or four. Curse these damned fashion moguls and what they do to kids nowadays; as the great Kurt Vonnegut once said, no man wants to hold a woman who feels like a bunch of coat hangers thrown in a paper bag; he wants Devonshire cream, poured lovingly into a soft, smooth goat's bladder. Or something like that.

My girl is trembling like a leaf. With a little adjustment of the knob I can actually make out goose pimples on her pale skin, patches of them popping up on her upper arms, as she lowers the slinky material, slowly, enticingly. A little south of that are the nipples, hard bumps pushing out through silk cups and with them a pair of silver

rings clearly imprinting themselves from underneath the snow white material.

You gotta love this new technology.

At the last possible second, Crissy yanks the shirt back on. There are no lights in the parking lot, but the moon is more than half full; should anyone look closely, either from the street or out of one of the office windows, they are going to see every detail.

Two more heartbeats pass, then she lets the blouse fall to the ground. Full, perfect tits straining eagerly now at the thin, white bra—the very one Turtleneck had been trying so hard to see down back at the Flamingo. Idly, she touches them with her fingertips. A kind of trance is coming over Crissy, and I doubt she could stop herself from going further even if she tried. Her face has that pouty look, the weak, half-open lips and glazed expression that comes only when she knows she's been completely overpowered—about to be made to do something she really doesn't want but needs all the same.

It's a look I haven't seen in a while. My suspicions are confirmed now that Crissy has become inured to my previous levels of mastery. No wonder she's been challenging me, her body screaming out "clamp down harder, or lose me"—the very opposite of that Hallmark shit about loving something and setting it free.

She works on the skirt next, and in my current crouch I am having to battle a particularly awkward and wicked erection. Unfortunately, my plumbing doesn't understand this waiting and disciplining stuff any better than my heart, but it's got to be done. The unzipping part isn't so hard to take, but she has to do a lot of wriggling to get the material over her graciously endowed hips and it's all I can do to resist running over and taking her on the spot.

One more look around for unseen eyes, and Crissy steps from it at last, reducing herself to underwear and stockings. It is a real act of trust here, and I am proud as hell of her for going this far. She is a gorgeous, kinky little bitch, and she might just make it as a first-class bottom after all.

She opts for the stockings next, giving a little lick of her tongue over her lips for courage. This is the part I've been waiting for. I hap-

pen to love Crissy's legs, among other things. If it weren't for her job, I'd use the crop daily on those meaty thighs, and her rounded belly, too. The ass is mine, though, no holds barred. Read its markings on any given occasion and you'll find an ongoing record of our preceding month's scenes.

One by one, Crissy flexes her luscious calves, peeling the gossamer thin material over her ankles till at last those precious pink feet are bare on the dirty, black asphalt. I can see the shivers in her spine, and not only from the cold; it's nearly payoff time, for both of us. Her breathing is quick and full as she moves her hands behind her back to reach for the bra clasp. It was sheer coincidence I'd let her wear underwear today, but in retrospect the move smacks of sheer genius.

Crissy loves her lingerie, and when she first came to live with me after a brief but torrid Internet affair, she had trunks full of the stuff. Most of it I made her burn, item by item as she related to me the story of each man who'd ever fucked her wearing, or not wearing what. She'd been ashamed of her slutty past, a feeling I'd purged her of both on the rack and in the library. Girls like her move through men not out of moral turpitude, but out of the desperation born of searching for that which exists so infrequently in our hypocritically genteel society: the genuine gentleman barbarian, willing to ravish and ruthlessly possess—through negotiated contract, of course—whomever he desires.

Crissy has to shrug off the cups, so firm are her mammaries. At once, twin globes spring into view, the swollen, rose-red nipples incised horizontally with discrete but entirely functional steel loops. She'd whined and begged about the piercings, but for me it was never an option. They are fun to look at and damn practical, too.

It's amazing how pliant a girl is when she walks with you, her leashed breasts in the palm of your hand. And then there are the attachable nipple weights, an amassed set of them that I treasure and collect the way most men do fishing lures.

I chuckle thinking what Leon, the thrice-divorced security officer, will make of the sexy, unclothed receptionist with her whipped tits and pierced nipples. Supposedly S and M is a fringe thing, a closeted minority movement right up there with foot fetishism and alien spaceship cults, but I've yet to meet a man—at least a heterosexual

one—whose pupils didn't dilate a notch at the sight of a willing slave girl.

The panty-clad Crissy wants very badly to cover herself, or better still, run to her car, but she knows the clock is ticking. Whatever may befall her as a result of public exposure, nothing could be worse than having me return to see her disobeying yet again. The tiny triangular scrap slides down with surprising ease over her freshly shaved sex, though when she goes to kick it off, Rockette-style, the waistband catches on her big toe. Her subsequent removal dance reminds me for a split second just how young she really is. And how inebriated.

The panty battle won, she stands proudly now with that special, paradoxical freedom and ease that only a slave can have. I almost envy her kind at times like this; the peace that must come from totally subsuming one's will, from making your whole world about pleasing and honoring another. There is the atonement aspect, too—that otherwise impossible opportunity to do something real and physical to cleanse one's self of sins.

What else but modern sanitized slavery, safe, sane, and consensual, can offer such a thing? Government? Culture? Religion? Good luck going down one of those roads. For the vast majority, forgiveness is a cold, hard coin, foreign and unspendable, which we wrap up tight and shove deep in some drawer because we're too damned sentimental to throw it away.

I hop back in the car and pull back around front with twenty seconds to spare. Crissy's nude body, precious and pale in the silvery moonlight, illumines into something fiery and wicked under the glare of my high beams. Reaching to the glove box, I pull forth the tools of the trade, implements of the priesthood. A pair of handcuffs, a leather collar with leash, a rubber ball gag, and a blindfold. With these I will lead my lamb to be fucked in the lobby of her own office building by a man whose last name she doesn't even know.

I don't need to say a word. As soon as I toss the bondage gear out the window, Crissy comes running, bounding lightly to retrieve it, like a sprite freshly dropped from some forest, enchanted and untouched by human hands.

She moves to put the gag in first.

"Thank you, Master," she whispers, choosing her last words for the night with admirable care.

I manage a thin smile, pushing down the hard-on that most men my age would give their eyeteeth for. "My pleasure, sweetheart. My pleasure."

In Control
by M. Christian

M. Christian is one of the most widely published writers of erotica. He has written for every subgenre, including gay, straight, bi, trans, kinky, vanilla, and everything in between. M. Christian's work has been, appropriately, published in many "Best of" series, including *Best American Erotica, Best Gay Erotica, Best Lesbian Erotica, Best Bisexual Erotica, Best Fetish Erotica, Best Bondage Erotica,* and *Friction,* as well as more than 150 other anthologies, magazines, and websites. Christian has edited or coedited many anthologies, including *Best S/M Erotica, Love Under Foot, Bad Boys, The Burning Pen, Guilty Pleasures, Eros Ex Machina, The Burning Pen,* and *Midsummer Night's Dreams.* His own short stories have been collected in *Speaking Parts, Filthy, The Bachelor Machine,* and the Lambda-nominated *Dirty Words.* He can be found at www.mchristian.com.

Christian says: "I wrote 'In Control' to play with the idea that behind the roles, the personas, the fantasies, there are some very human needs and desires—often far stronger than the drives that put players into their leather to begin with. I also wanted to show that Masters as well as slaves have something they want out of play—sometimes very innocent but still very important needs."

We met in the dark corner of an Internet chatroom. SLUTSLAVE, a nubile profile full of in-the-know vernacular with damned good typing skills; and MASTER017, my digital persona. We didn't really meet there, of course, but that's where we first started to talk. The dance was slow, at first. I've heard other doms say that they don't like it slow, sedate, careful—they'd rather snap their fingers and have them drop

to their knees. Me? I like the dance, the approach, the "chat" in chat room. Besides, I've had a few of my own snaps, the eager young slaves with sparkles in their eyes, and not a clue between the ears. Give me someone who knows what they're getting into. It's better, after all, to be wanted by someone who wants the best, as opposed to someone who just wants.

So we danced, we chatted, SLUTSLAVE and I—or at least that cyberspace mask I wore. Finally, after many a midnight typing, she complained with a sideways smile—;-)—that she was looking for something where more than just her wrists got a workout.

Like I said: step one, two, three, turn, step one, two, three. Careful moves in this courtship dance. No snap from me. I made her sing for her supper, pushing her along, not making it easy for her. "Do you know what you're asking for, slave?" I asked, clicking and clacking on my keyboard.

She did the same, and the dance changed its tempo: "Yes, Master. I do."

We made a date to get together the next weekend.

A knock on the door. Normally, even when it's expected, it can be jarring. Fist on wood. Bang, bang, bang! But not that night. I opened it. "Welcome."

I had a picture, of course, and the flesh was just like it, though filled out in three-dimensional reality. Unlike the door, seeing her jarred me, but not unpleasantly.

"Thanks," she said with a smile, walking in. I closed the door behind her. Full bodied, curved, somewhere between too young and too old, tight and firm from exercise. Eyes gleaming with sharpness, mouth parted just so with anticipation. Curly dark hair, her skin a Mediterranean patina.

We didn't have to say much, most of our negotiations having been done in e-mails back and forth. I knew she couldn't stay on her feet for too long (plantar fasciitis), didn't like metal restraints or canes—all of it. But her list of yes was longer than her list of no.

"Stand there," I said, pointing to the center of my wool rug. My room looked odd, with all the furniture pushed back, piled up—

spare chairs on my big oak table, ottoman tucked underneath. The room was just the rug, a coarse wool bullseye, and my favorite plush wing-back.

"Yes, sir," she said, the grin never leaving her lips, as she walked to the center.

"Stop." She did, turning slowly to face me. Her breasts were big, wide. Not a girl's, a woman's. Twin peaks on cotton fabric. I reached out to one of the points, circled it slowly with a stiff finger. The smile stayed, but her breathing deepened, sped up. "Did I tell you what to call me?"

"No—" she hissed, trying to swallow a scream, as I pinched her nipple, hard. One of my no's concerned sound. My apartment had thin walls.

"Call me, 'Master,'" I said, low and mean, grumbling and growling, as I pinched even more.

"Yes . . . M-Master," she said, with a delightful stammer against the pain.

I released the pressure. "Pain is your punishment. It will be frequent. Pleasure is your reward. It will be rare. I'm not going to ask you if you understand. If you didn't you wouldn't be here. Undress."

She did, sensually but efficiently. The white cotton dress went first. Under it was an everyday bra, pearl and white, and a pair of everyday panties, just white. No hose, only socks and shoes. As I had requested. Lingerie doesn't interest me. Bodies don't even interest me. She didn't interest me. But what I could do to her—that was what interested me.

She was naked. Her body was good. Not ideal, but with a warmth and reality to her. Big, full tits with just enough sag to mean real and not silicone. A plump little tummy. A plump mons with a gentle tuft of dark hair. It wasn't a body that you'd hang on your wall, but it was a body you'd want to fuck. But that was on her no list, which was fine by me. I definitely wanted to fuck with her, just not with her body.

Her hands kept drifting up, a force of will keeping them from hiding her breasts, covering her nipples. I smiled. SLUTSLAVE had a modest streak. Priceless.

I got out my toolbag, my own kind of wry smile on my face. Other tops went on and on about their toys, pissing on each other

about the quality of the leather, the weight, the evilness of certain objects. I sat back and watched them: wry grin then, wry grin now. If I had a headboard, I'd have it carved: A workman is as good as his tools, it would say. A great one doesn't need them at all.

I added it up once. Fifty dollars was as high as I got. Show me any other hobby that could give as much pleasure as my little bag of toys—or as much wonderful discomfort to SLUTSLAVE.

I laid them out on the rug in front of her. I felt like a surgeon—or a priest. "We're going to play a game," I said. "The rules are very simple. I ask a question. If you tell me the truth you get a reward. If you don't you get punished. Again, I won't ask if you understand."

I picked up a favorite—though to tell my own truth I like them all. This one was just the favorite of the moment. I squeezed, and the clothespin yawned open. I held it out to her nipple, which—I noticed—was nicely wrinkled, erect. "Are you wet?"

"Yes," she said in a breathy whisper. I could tell; her musk was thick in the room. I was hard. Hell, I was hard when I opened the front door, but hearing that, knowing that, my jeans grew that much tighter.

"First lesson. It's an important one. Sometimes even the truth can mean pain," I said, in my best of voices, as I released the spring on the clothespin, letting it bite down sharp and quick on her thickening nipple.

Her sigh was a lovely musical tone, a bass rumble of pain that peaked toward pleasure. Oh, yes, that was it. The first note of a long musical composition. Her knees buckled because of it, and I put a hand on her shoulder to steady her.

I kept it on for a mental beat of ten. Not long, but long enough. I released it, keeping my hand on her shoulder. It always hurts so much worse coming off than it does coming on. Sure enough, her knees buckled even more and she slipped, dropped down to my rug.

Still on her knees, breathing much more regularly, she looked up at me, chin level with my crotch. I knew if I said to, she'd unzip my fly, undo my belt, reach in with eager, strong fingers to fish out my dick, stick it into her hot mouth. She'd do it, I knew, but like the clothespin, it's so much better if you wait. So I did.

I stepped back, grinning at the flicker of disappointment on her

face. You'll have to wait too, I thought. I retrieved my bag, and sat down in my chair, facing her. The clothespin was still in my hand and I found myself absently opening and closing it. A dom's worry bead, I guess. "Stand up. Right now."

She did. Her knees seemed a bit weak. "Come closer." She did, her gait slow and controlled. I reached down to my bag at my feet, picked up something new. "You're mine. You belong to me," I said, looking into her face. Her eyes shone, gleamed. "I won't ask if you understand."

When I was a kid, I used to play with dolls. Well, maybe not "dolls," not exactly. No Raggedy Anns, no Barbies—not like that. I liked that they were mine, they belonged to me. I could make them do anything, at any time, and they didn't say a word. They just did it, forever smiling.

It was a new toy, another deceivingly simple thing. I saw it in some import/export place down in the city. Elegant and simple, black and glossy. Seeing it, I knew I had to have it. Having it, I couldn't wait to use it.

"Lean back," I said. I was tapping it against my palm, a lacquer metronome. Tilted back, her breasts swayed gently apart, just beginning to make that armpit migration—she was younger than I thought.

I ran the tip of the chopstick around her right nipple, feeling it skip and slide over her areola, the contours traveling down the length of it into my finger tips. She sighed, softly.

Way back when, just after I outgrew those plastic dolls, I wondered if I had a dead thing—you know, preferring girls stiff and cold rather than warm and breathing. But that wasn't it. It wasn't them being immobile or plastic—it was me being in control, making them do what I want. Right then, she was my doll, my plaything, and I was completely in control.

I started tapping, steadily, almost softly at first. A smooth double-time. But after a dozen or so beats I moved it up to a harder, more insistent tempo. Her breathing quickened, started to grow close, to almost, maybe match my beats with the lacquered stick. I watched her stomach rise and fall, a background accompaniment, echo to her hisses and sighs.

I moved, circled her breast and nipple with my stick, painting her

with the beats. Tap, tap, tap, sigh, sigh, moan, sigh. Then the other breast, but a little harder this time. She started to glow, shine with gentle sweat. I could smell her, a thick rutting musk. Now she really was wet.

Now just only her nipples. Each impact steady, sure, quick, and hard. She started to unconsciously twist her body, a little this way then the opposite, to get away from the beats. For a moment, I thought about stopping. Make her stand up, make her get dressed, kick her out for such a show of life and independence, but that would mean throwing away, no longer using this lovely new toy. The stick, as well as SLUTSLAVE.

Then I did stop. Time for the next movement. She lifted her head, looking long at me, breathing heavy and hard. Her eyes flicked with a bit of fear, but more than anything, a kind of plea: More.

Back into the bag. Simple. When you have control, you don't need gadgets, gizmos, fine leathers. Fifty dollars in the right hands, with the right toy, and you have all you need. I came up with a pair matching the first clip. Her eyes grew even wider, breathing deeper and quicker. She knew what was coming next. I didn't have to say anything.

The right one first. I leaned down and held it there, open, threatening around her so-hard nipple. She looked at it, then looked at me. Again, fear. But more than anything, a desire for me to let go.

So I did. Her guttural bellow peaked threateningly toward a scream but didn't as she swallowed and swallowed, hissed and hissed it back down into herself. I was impressed.

I kept the clip on. It was wonderful to watch it bob up and down with her steady, deep breaths. I could have watched it all day, thinking: this is mine. This is mine. This is mine. I could have, but I had another tit to play with.

Somewhere during all this, my cock had been confined, trapped in my pants. Turning to the other tit, I felt how very, very hard I'd gotten. But that would wait. I was in control here. Not my dick.

The other one. Again, I held it there, looming over a tight little point of nipple. Again, I let go.

This time a short, quick, honest scream blew past her lips. Sound was a concern, but frankly I didn't care. This was good—damned

good. She was a good toy, a good plaything. She was mine to do with as I wanted.

I watched her, making sure the pain of the clips wasn't too much for her. She whistled her breaths, in and out, belly rising and falling as she tried to accept, flow with, use, and enjoy what was happening to her nipples, breasts, and body. I liked to watch her, knowing that I was the cause of all this. Yes, my cock was hard—steel, stone, rigid—in my pants, but this was almost better. The bliss painting her body in shimmering sweat, making her pant and moan, making her clit twitch wasn't something of mine that could ever go soft, ever come too quick. I could make her come and come and come again and never take off my pants.

Time for the next step. Both pins were in place, both nodded, dipped, and rose from their grips on her nipples as she squirmed against the pain. I picked up the chopstick again. "See this?" I said. She pulled herself up from her blurry rapture. Her eyes took a long time to focus. She looked, she nodded.

I tapped one clothespin, hard, sending serious shocks down through it into her already aching nipple. She squealed in shock, in endorphin delight. I did the same to the other, then back again. Back and forth. She was a wonderful plaything, a fun little toy. I enjoyed playing with her very much. Oh, the things we could do.

I glanced up at the clock. A qualifier of our time together rang in my mind. Just a few hours, she had said, to start. Time had flown.

"Listen to me," I said. Her vision was almost lost against the waves of sensation, but she managed to finally see me. "We're almost finished—for tonight that is. But before we do, I'm going to fuck you."

She frowned past what was happening to her nipples, her tits, her body, her cunt. My words reached through it all and created a worry.

Not good to have my plaything in such a state. Time to demonstrate that I am in control, that for her, I'm the boss, I'm the Master—and she is just a toy, and toys have nothing, not even a worry.

I reached into my bag at my feet, pulled it out, tossed it at her feet. "I said I'm going to fuck you. My dick—right there in front of you—is going in your cunt. Do you have a problem with that?"

She didn't. The smell of her, the grin that flashed on her gleaming

face told me that. Her legs were already gently parted, the kind of reckless, unself-conscious display that only a plaything in the middle of a high-flying pleasure/pain/endorphin rush could have. She may have had a worry, but she was more a hungry cunt. A wet and ready cunt. A wet and very ready cunt with a rubber dick on the floor in front of her.

"Pick it up," I said, though I didn't have to, not really, "and fuck yourself with it."

She bent forward, picked it up. Parting her thighs just a bit more, she showed me her pink wetness. The bare thatch of hair that descended from her mons was matted and gleaming with juice. Her lips were already gently apart, swollen and ready for my store-bought dick.

I knew I could probably have fucked her with my own cock, or simply unzipped my fly and stuck myself into her hot, wet mouth. But that would mean I was flesh and blood, a man, and not the Master I really was. A Master is cold, a Master knows what to do with a plaything, a toy, a doll. I knew what to do. That's what I lived for: that dominance, that authority, that control.

She slipped the dildo into herself, just an inch to start. Then out, then in deeper, with a slow twist. She bit her lip in concentration, she closed her eyes in bliss—lost to the pain in her tits, the cock in her cunt.

Kneeling on my rug, legs very wide, she fucked herself. The gentle part ended quickly. She was now really, strongly fucking herself. A soft foam rimmed her cunt where the plastic slicked in and out. Some of her pubic hairs streaked along the length on the outstroke, curled in on the return. The hiss that had been only from the clips on her nipples was joined by the deeper sounds of a rolling, approaching come.

I didn't know her that well, but a good Master knows the sounds, no matter the toy, and I could tell that she could see it coming, could smell, taste it coming. Her breathing broke, became shorter, panting. Now, right now, I thought as I bent forward and put thumbs and fingers on the pins. I pulled.

Her eyes snapped open, fear lighting her irises. This time she didn't say, without words, more but rather oh my god.

I pulled. Not hard, just enough to drag her orgasm out, draw it

farther out. Her fucking had slowed, eased, but she was too far along to stop. She couldn't if she wanted to.

I didn't want her to. So she didn't. I didn't need to say it, she understood it: the language of Master to SLUTSLAVE. Her fucking increased, pushing herself back up to the precipice. It didn't take long for her to be looking down the fast slope to her come. This time she said, without words, now.

Yes, SLUTSLAVE: Now. The pins came off. Screw noise concerns. Her scream came from her nipples, her tits, but also from her spasming, quivering, quaking cunt. Her come rattled her, making her shake, her head bob back and forth. Her legs, already tensed from holding her forward, collapsed, spilling her backward on my old scratchy rug.

I watched her. Her breathing, after a long while, eased to a regular, resting rhythm. Then I went to my bathroom, got a big fluffy towel and draped it over her. She didn't say anything, not even thanks.

I got her a glass of water from my kitchen, even put a little slice of lemon in it. She took it with gently quivering fingers. Drank all of it, handed it back. Then she said, "Thanks," but for the glass or the evening, I didn't know.

Slowly, she got up, started hunting for her clothes. I helped her, handing them over to her. She seemed to be happy.

Finally, she was dressed, though she looked funny with her hair messed. "Are you okay to go home?" I asked her, my hand on her arm. "Should I call you a cab?"

"I'm—whooo," she breathed, laughing for a second with a shivering after-feeling. "I'm okay. Really. Thank you," she finally said. "That was a blast."

"I'm glad. I'd love to do it again sometime—soon."

"So would I. Really." Her hand was on the doorknob.

"Write me," I said, holding it open for her. "Send me a message and we'll pick a date."

"That'd be fun. Sure." She walked down the hall. When she got to the end she turned, waved to me. I waved back.

· · · ·

I checked my messages an hour or so later. Nothing. I watched some television, something I barely remember. Cops, I think. Or doctors. Something like that. Before I went to bed, I checked again. Nothing. I sent her a message: "Hope you had a good time. Write when you get a chance."

In the morning, nothing. I browsed some of the chat rooms, even though I'd never known her to be there that early. Nothing, of course.

When I got home from work I checked again. Spam. A few messages from some friends. Nothing. She's just busy. Things happen, I told myself, not believing my own thoughts.

Before I went to bed I wrote another message. But I didn't send it. Maybe in a few days, I thought.

In the morning there was nothing. I checked again the instant I walked in after work. Nothing. Nothing at all. I wrote her, against my better judgment. Simple, direct: "Concerned about how you're feeling. Please write."

That will do it, I thought. That'll reach her. Was it too much to ask? I thought she had fun. I thought she did.

But when I went to bed there was nothing but more spam, a few other messages. Nothing from her.

Around midnight, late for me, I went to bed. Nothing at all. I tried to masturbate but it didn't work out.

Eventually I fell asleep.

In the morning I checked again, first thing. Nothing. Nothing at all.

I never used the handle MASTER017 again.

Night at the Trocadero
by Midori

Author of the book *The Seductive Art of Japanese Bondage,* **Midori** is an educator and writer on S and M, fetish, and human sexuality, and she travels the world presenting to university students, S and M clubs, and the general public. Raised in a feminist intellectual Tokyo household, Midori holds a degree in psychology from the University of California at Berkeley. Her work has appeared on HBO and the BBC, and in *Mademoiselle, Playboy, Der Spiegel, Wired, British Esquire, Vogue, Surface,* and many other publications. She is currently working on three new books, including a collection of her essays, a collection of erotic science-fiction stories, and another how-to kink book.

I push the stall door open and sure enough, there you are, with your pierced lips mashed into some black-painted Goth-girl mouth and your right hand buried to the leather-cuffed wrist in her dripping cunt. Goth-girl's eyes pop open and I hear her gurgling some words into your devouring kisses. You won't let her talk. Now, that's Daddy's good grrl. She tries to push you off. You won't let her go. You know you've been caught, so why bother stopping now? Take all you can, grrl, while you can.

The floor throbs to the vicious base from the mosh pit.

I don't try to tear you off of her. I'm not some stoopid bridge-and-tunnel Master with property-rights issues. I got myself a little hunter-bitch and I know how to use her. I lean against the doorframe and kick the door open wide with my knee-high black Docs. Goth-girl relaxes and goes back to sucking face with you. I want to make sure that all the peeps in the stinkin' loo see the action. I want them to know that I've got the nastiest bitch in town and that makes me hard.

Not to mention the sight of your bruised little round ass in torn fishnets bobbing up and down in front of me. That's making Daddy really hard. One foot on the toilet rim, you're fucking her on the cold porcelain tank. Your free hand's pinned both her wrists together over her head.

The lead singer's scream pierces the sticky smoke-filled air.

Reaching into the pocket on my bulletproof vest I pull out a pre-Disney-era Cuban cigar. The real commie stuff; rare goods indeed. The dorks whizzing in the urinals start to turn around. Yeah, that's right. C'mon and see Daddy's grrl put on a show. You ain't seen nothin' yet. I chew off the end and spit it out onto the floor near your spiked heel. I take my time and roll the unlit cig around in my mouth for a while, rolling my tongue around it just like I would your hard clit. With a glance over your shoulder you let go of the bird's wings and reach into your ammo pouch, fumble among the crap in there, and find a light. Without disengaging with the birdie, you reach back and flick the flame in my face, lighting up my red war paint. I suck the cigar deeply from the fire, feeling the dry heat fill my mouth and see the tip glow white-hot. Just a second later on the light and you would have earned another disciplinary action. I don't care what mischief you're up to, it's your job always to light your Daddy's smokes . . . and suck his cock and lick his boots.

Goth-girl moans loudly. My grrl's mohawked head dives down between her legs and licks her clit with the double-pierced tongue. Man, this bird's going to fly to the moon with my sweet baby's piloting! Goth-girl starts to grind harder down onto the hand and my grrl starts to punch fuck the cunt while expertly sucking onto the clit. What can I say, she's good.

The club urchins gather around the door, practically drooling on their precisely shredded leathers and titanium tribal jewelry. The idiots don't know what to do with the show. They don't know how to treat a lady of your ilk. Ripping at the fly of the old Stasi field fatigues, I pull out my rigid tool. The meat's good and thick, but the triple-0 gauge steel PA's the crowning glory: Meet Daddy's little tooth chipper. Puffing slowly on the cigar, I stroke my cock even more slowly, as I watch the wenches fucking.

The urchins follow suit. They pull their dicks out and start to

stroke. There must be a dozen or so gathered around now, all turned on, all watching my grrl like a pack of horny wolves. The dicks grow hard and breathing heavy. They start to shout vicious words at you, telling you what a slut you are and how to fuck harder. You look over your shoulder while keeping a wicked suction lock on the bird's cunt. Your eyes shine a wicked, bitch-in-heat gleam. Your free hand wonders down to your dripping slit and starts to rub that sweet pierced pearl. You look from the hungry boys to me with querying eyes. I nod. Without missing a moment you lunge two fingers deep into your wet pussy. Yeah, baby, you can thank Daddy later. You know exactly how.

The guitars roar a primal scream, barely covering the guttural cum-scream of Goth-girl.

With my dick still hard and hanging out, cigar locked in lips, I pull off my thick leather-studded belt. Unlocking yourself from the chick's cunt, you turn and smack a kiss at me, then go back to biting the girl's ample tits spilling over the black leather corset. Doubled over with the buckle in my hand, I swing back the belt nice and high. You raise your ass and keep it still for just that sweet moment. One hand keeps pumping the bird and with the other hand you're practically fisting yourself. I bring the belt down hard and the leather smack sound flinches a few of the wusses stroking their dicks. I bring the belt down onto your reddening ass over and over again. The welts start to rise. You arch your head back and let out a hell-spun moan. I keep beating you, 'cause I like the demon-bride sounds you make. You're all red welts and old purple bruises now.

I yank your hand out of your cunt and slap the other arm. Abruptly you slide your hand out of your night's-prey's cunt. You smear juices from the pussy-soaked hand across Goth-girl's face and make her suck it off. You're nasty and depraved. I like that in my pets. I grab you by the heavy O ring on the spiked collar and yank you around. Your mouth twists into a sweet sneer. I glance at the filthy floor, all sticky with piss, cum, and beer. Without hesitation you're down on all fours. Your sweet tongue bathes my Docs. I can feel the pressure of your devotion, even through the steel-capped toes.

The ash on the cigar hangs an inch long. I snap my fingers and you're back up on your knees looking up at me. I take the cigar in my

fingers and hover it over your face. Greedily you open your mouth wide and stick your studded tongue out. A single tap and the hot ash drops on the wet pink tongue. With a lascivious curl at the tip of the tongue, you close your mouth and swallow hard. I'm throbbing now.

Someone smashes a guitar on stage and the speakers howl.

Daddy's gonna give you something to wash that ash down with. With one hand wrapping around your jaw, I move your face into my cock. Goth-girl's busy fucking herself at the sight of her predator taken down. Your mouth opens wide to let my piercing in, and maneuvers it past your tongue-piercing. I feel my shaft slide along the tongue and hit the back of your throat. A swallow throbs and tightens around my meat.

Someone's cum hits hot across your face, drips down white and thick. You grin.

You lick and suck Daddy's cock greedily, with your hands smartly crossed behind your back. The guys move in closer and start shooting their loads on you. You suck harder. I know you're wet as hell down there. Good Grrl knows not to touch. Not just yet. You suck and lick like you're going to strip the shine right off my PA. Your nose presses into my body and my cock slides deeper down your throat. I feel that tight ache build up and start humping your face, slow at first, then faster and faster. Yeah, I'm going to fill my bitch-slave's mouth and pump her full of me. I'm going to saturate your every pore from the inside out. I pump my cock faster and deeper, feeling your mouth sucking down, licking, choking, kissing, sucking, gagging, and slurping. I can't stand it any more. I let my wad explode inside of you. You suck at me, cleaning me up nice and dry. My slut-slave loves her Daddy's special cock-tail.

You put my meat back in and button me up. I drag you up by the collar to my chest and give you a deep kiss. You taste of pussy, ash, and my cum. Now, that's Daddy's dirty grrl. Holding on to the collar, I push past the dorks and hit the pit. I gotta dance all that off now. I want to watch you dance and slam. Anyway, you gotta find Daddy another prey to take home later.

Go hunt, grrl, go hunt for Daddy.

Instructor's Fee
by Isaac Walker

Isaac Walker is the pseudonym-shrouded author of several erotic novels and a host of erotic stories. He says of "Instructor's Fee": "I've always wanted to be a teacher—but then, the skills I have to teach aren't exactly community college material. Though, if they were, I would definitely sign up to get a Ph.D. 'Instructor's Fee' is my fantasy of teaching willing men how to give their wives a proper spanking, a skill I would love to help more men acquire."

It amazes me how many people—men and women both—don't know that women can come from a proper spanking.

When I mentioned this fact at the dinner party at Scott and Lisa Carter's house, I must admit I had a bit of an ulterior motive. Knowing Lisa was entirely submissive to Scott, I nonetheless had spent many evenings at their house admiring those firm, toned cheeks of hers, which he always kept in short skirts or exceedingly tight pants. And tonight, Lisa had worn a particularly short, tight skirt, one that showed off the curves of her ass quite admirably and, when she bent over, revealed the top of her thong above the waistband.

"You don't say," Scott mused, puffing on his cigar as the other men and women sitting around the sofa looked only vaguely shocked. "You're saying most women can come that way?"

I quickly scanned the faces trained on me, all listening with rapt attention. There was Carl Winters with his beautiful wife, Justine, two years his senior and raven-haired, her skin the color of unskimmed cream and her eyes as green as unripe oranges. There was Martin Aarund, with his slightly older wife Mary Anne, twenty years his junior and as redheaded as an order of brandies flambé, her eyes hold-

ing the hungry promise of submissions to come. And there were Scott and Lisa, both of whom had been quite plain with me about Lisa's fondness for extreme submission to Scott. Although they were both very much beginners, both had been helped by my suggestions in many nights of pleasure and pain that Scott had told me about during our drinking bouts together.

Now, though, was the first time it had been mentioned with our friends about, or in the presence of both Lisa and Scott. I could see the flush of Lisa's cheeks as she looked down at the floor, obviously quite embarrassed at the effect my revelation was having on her. She wore a very tight top, and the curve of her full breasts was made more evident by the fact that she wasn't wearing a bra.

"Most women, if it's properly done," I said. "It requires a skilled hand."

Scott puffed his cigar, obviously toying with the question of whether or not he should take the next step.

"Perhaps you could demonstrate," said Scott, his voice louder than it should have been. "I'm sure Lisa would be happy to provide an appropriate bottom for you to show us how a woman comes from spanking."

Lisa now flushed deep red, her nipples standing like snow-capped peaks on the mountains of her breasts. She shifted uncomfortably from where she sat on the arm of her husband's chair.

"I would be happy to," I said, setting down my drink. "Lisa, would you care to receive a spanking?"

She looked at Scott for permission as the others sitting around glanced at each other in mixed expressions of horror and excitement. No one got up to leave, however, or to protest my suggestion.

"Yes," said Scott, his eyes locked in his wife's. "She would very much like a spanking."

Lisa turned and looked at me hungrily, knowing that it was not her place to affirm what her husband had said. He had told me his wife wanted a spanking, and now she would receive one.

"Very well," I said, shifting in my armchair. "Lisa, if you would please lay across my lap."

Lisa began walking toward me; I snapped my fingers. "Oh, yes, of

course. It's much more effective without panties, of course. And with her skirt lifted high."

Lisa's face turned still redder, her strawberry-blonde hair bringing out the crimson embarrassment in her cheeks. She brushed a strand of that golden-pink hair out of the way and looked at me nervously.

"Very well," said Scott. "Lisa, take off your panties."

Carl, Justine, Martin, and Mary Anne all watched, rapt, none of them getting up to leave or expressing distaste at this shameless display. Lisa's hands were trembling as she lifted her skirt and took down the tiny white thong she wore. As her skirt fell back into place, I saw that she was shaved and pierced. So did the other guests.

"Skirt up," I said. "It's much more effective that way."

Still blushing fiercely, Lisa lifted her skirt to her waist, exposing her shaved, pierced twat to her guests.

"Good lord," said Martin. "The girl's pierced!"

"Scott . . . Scott likes it," mumbled Lisa nervously. "He said it reminds me that I'm his possession."

Martin and Carl chuckled, and I saw both Mary Anne and Justine staring curiously at Lisa's shaved snatch.

"Across my lap," I told her.

Lisa had clearly received many spankings before. She obediently took her place across my lap. I had chosen one of the chairs without arms in anticipation of this event, though I hadn't dared hope it would come about so easily.

Scott pulled his chair closer to mine and grasped Lisa's hair, placing her face in his lap. I could see his cock was hard in his suit pants, and Lisa's cheek pressed against it as I lifted her skirt higher, exposing her round bum.

"You should come around to the sofa if you'd like to watch," I told the other guests, and they all crowded onto the sofa as I ran my hand over Lisa's perfect bottom. I slipped my fingers between her tightly clamped thighs and could feel the moistness of her slit.

"Legs open or closed?" asked Carl curiously.

"It doesn't matter," I said. "They'll come open soon enough once she's had a few."

Lisa gasped as I brought my hand down firmly on her sweet spot.

She began to wriggle in my lap, her face rubbing against her husband's cock. I spanked her again, and again, slowly building the intensity as I landed each open-palmed blow on her sweet spot.

"Not every woman can come from this," I said as I methodically punished Lisa's bottom. "But I suspect Lisa is one of those who can."

With that, she gave a soft moan and her tightly clamped-together thighs released, spreading slightly to expose her cunt. I slipped one finger into her and withdrew it, rubbing it against my thumb to display the strings of wetness.

"You see? Just a few blows on her ass and she's spreading her legs like a little whore. No offense, Scott."

"None taken," said Scott, caressing his wife's face.

I began spanking her again, well aware of the rapt attention on the faces of the husbands and wives watching. I heard Lisa's moans rising in timber slowly as I increased the force with which I struck her. Her pussy glistened and leaked juice as the sensation increased. Martin lifted his hand and pointed.

"Good God," he said. "Look at what she's doing!"

I looked over at Scott. Lisa had unfastened his pants and had his cock in her mouth, hungrily fellating it as I spanked her. Scott leaned back in his chair, his face a mask of satisfaction.

"By all means, don't stop," said Scott, his voice hoarse. "She's doing quite a wonderful job. Clearly your spanking is having the desired effect."

Lisa continued to suck her husband as I spanked her more rapidly, harder, bringing little whimpers from her throat as she licked Scott's cock all over. Her squirming hips rubbed against my cock and I secretly prayed that Scott might allow me to give it to Lisa as good as he was—perhaps even better, later. I checked her pussy and found it wetter than ever. She gurgled and moaned when I fingered her, and I let my fingertips rub her pierced clit to make sure she was reacting properly.

"She's very close, isn't she?" Justine asked, her eyes focused on the swollen, pink lips of Lisa's sex. I could see Justine's own thighs rubbing together, and I noticed for the first time that she not only had one hand in her husband's lap, but that her other hand was in Martin's. Both men had hard-ons and Justine was stroking them. Mean-

while, Martin had let his hand slide down his wife Mary Anne's shirt, and he was shamelessly caressing her breasts and pinching her nipples as, panting, she watched Lisa's submission.

I reached out and grasped Lisa's hair, pulling her off her husband's cock. She turned her eyes and looked at me, their glossiness only partly due to the tears formed there from when she deepthroated her husband's cock. Her lips were parted, her breath coming short. As she panted, she wriggled her butt in my grasp.

"Yes," I said. "She's very close."

I went back to spanking Lisa as Justine unzipped both Carl's and Martin's pants and took out their hard-ons, slowly jerking them off. Five pairs of eyes were focused on Lisa's ass, thrust up high in the air and eagerly receiving every blow I planted upon it. I could make her come at any moment, but I wanted this moment to last. Justine stroked a cock in each hand as Mary Anne guided her husband's hand down between her thighs and encouraged him to start fingering her. She moaned softly, never letting her eyes stray from Lisa's ass as Justine dropped to her knees and began sucking off Martin, Carl's cock still in her hand.

"She's doing quite a bang-up job," said Scott hoarsely. "She's really quite the little cocksucker when she gets spanked."

"Should I make her come yet?" I asked Lisa's husband, and he shook his head.

"Not until I do," he told me. "I'm damn close."

"You hear that, Lisa? Make your husband come in your mouth. Then I'll bring you off."

With that, Lisa let out a squeal and eagerly began pumping her mouth up and down on Scott's cock. He grumbled softly and lifted his hips to meet the thrusts of her mouth. I kept spanking Lisa, controlling the intensity as I focused on the sweet spot, bringing her closer. Justine was still on her knees, moving back and forth between Martin's cock and that of her husband, while Martin fingered the spread-thighed Mary Anne as she moaned in pleasure.

Scott came first. He grunted "I'm coming!" and Lisa, with a whimper, began sucking him faster, hungry for his spunk. I spanked her harder, focusing exactly on the spot that I had discerned, from her squirmings and whimperings, would drive her over the edge. She

came just as her husband's jizz flooded her mouth, and Justine turned to look, her mouth slick with spittle and pre-come, watching Lisa come before plunging back into sucking Martin's cock and jerking off her husband's. Carl shot his load then, spurting thick jism onto Justine's face as she suckled on Martin's cock, and the grunt Martin gave as he shot in Justine's mouth was drowned out only by the gasping, shrieking orgasm of his wife Mary Anne, who was rubbing her clit furiously as her husband fingerfucked her.

"You see?" I asked. "Clearly it's quite a small matter to make a girl come from being spanked."

"Yes, I see," said Martin, as Justine tucked his cock away and zipped up his pants. "But the spanker is left without reaching satisfaction. Surely that's not acceptable to you?"

I looked at Scott, smiling.

"Your wife can take a spanking," I said. "Can she also give a sucking?"

Scott chuckled. "She certainly gave me one," he said.

I looked over at Carl. "As did yours," I said. "And I suspect Mary Anne, for all her reluctance, would give just as well."

"I've no objection," said Carl with a grin. "Clearly you've earned it."

"Yes," said Martin. "Mary Anne—go to it."

Lisa got off of my lap and sat in Scott's, her skirt still pulled up and her wet pussy running juice down her thighs. The redheaded Mary Anne blushed deep as she slid off the couch and crawled over to kneel before me. Justine joined her, and Scott gave Lisa a little push. The three of them knelt in front of me, looking up at me as I unzipped my pants and took out my hard cock.

I looked down at the three pretty faces so eager to service me. Lisa, the blonde; Justine, the brunette; and Mary Anne, who pretended to be a shy virgin but (I suspected) was in fact every bit as fiery and lusty as any redhead was ever rumored to be—in fact, I guessed that once properly primed, Mary Anne would put the legends about horny, flame-souled redheads to shame.

"You see?" I told them. "A good spanking opens up all sorts of new possibilities."

Justine's mouth descended on my cock, and Mary Anne, vixen that she was, went for my balls. Lisa crawled into my lap again, this

time facing me, and lifted her shirt so she could guide her tits into my mouth. They were small, but delicious, and I suckled them eagerly as Mary Anne and Justine gave me head. Lisa and I kissed, and I heard Scott, Martin, and Carl discussing their wives' various techniques as they focused on my cock.

When I was close to coming, all three couples agreed that Lisa was the one who deserved it. She knelt between my legs and Mary Anne thoughtfully pumped my cock while Lisa's full lips clamped tightly around the head of my cock as I groaned and spurted my come into her.

Which is how Lisa learned to properly take a spanking, and repay the man who gives it to her. My only regret is that I didn't have three orgasms to give, for it was getting late.

But Justine and Mary Anne shan't be disappointed. Carl and Martin have both asked for private lessons, and I always receive my instructor's fee.

Master Spirit
by Cecilia Tan

Cecilia Tan writes about all her passions, including sex, food, and baseball. Her erotic fiction has appeared just about everywhere—*Ms., Penthouse, Best American Erotica,* bathroom-stall walls, etc. . . . She is the author of three books of erotica, *The Velderet, Black Feathers,* and *Telepaths Don't Need Safewords.* She is also the founder and editor of Circlet Press. "Master Spirit" is a prequel to *Telepaths Don't Need Safewords.*

I arrived on the island as summer faded and the days shrank, with scars on my back and my mind still reeling from what I had just been through. But this is not the story of the Emperor and his daughter and all the things that happened to me before. This is the story of what happened to me on the island of Lhysa.

Two of us took the government-sponsored ride from the mainland, me and a woman in her mid-forties, her shoulder-length hair still richly black but shot through with strands of silver. The transport left us at the near-deserted landing point on the island's rocky north side. The white craft lifted off in near silence behind us as we walked from the platform to the intake center. The woman, who had not spoken to me the entire trip from the mainland, asked me as we approached the door, "So, headed for the spas?"

It was a funny question. The reasons for me to go to the island were myriad. I suppose I was there to recuperate, but the healing waters had not been explicit in my plans. I was being kept out of danger, I was curious about my mother's people, and I was very curious about the woman asking me of my destination. I wondered if she had The Sight and raised an eyebrow at her. She raised an eyebrow in return. She was wearing a shirt too large for her, the sleeves rolled up, show-

ing sun-browned arms and empty hands. On her back she had a small pack.

"Well, you don't look like a researcher," she said then. "How long are you going to be staying?"

"Not sure," I told her. I was carrying a small satchel of clothes, some of my father's money, and nothing else. "My plans are kind of open-ended. What do you mean, researcher?"

"Not a scientist?" She pointed to her head and I realized what she meant. There were only three types of people allowed on the island: those who came to study the unique psionic powers of the inhabitants, those who were approved to come for healing treatments at the spas for short periods of time, and those who were descendants of island dwellers. I belonged to this last category, as the pass I showed to the intake clerk read. I was processed in minutes and let through. On the other side of the small building there was nothing but a road leading south and inland.

The woman followed me out. "Welcome back, unduma," she said, using the island word for "homecomer." "I never would have guessed."

"Why?"

"Because you look like one of them." She meant I looked like a Kylar. Tall, rangy, I looked more Kylaran than my own father, who had once been second in command in the empire. "Half blood?"

I wondered if everyone on the island was so direct and nosy. I suppose in a community of mind readers, there is no need for secrecy. "Yes."

"Do you have The Sight?"

"No." We were both walking down the road now, though I did not know where it went. "Not so far as I've noticed."

She nodded. "Not everyone here has it either, you know. Only a few. The gene pool's been watered down over the years."

I murmured in agreement, as if I knew what she was talking about. My mother, at least according to Audan, had various psionic talents. I had been separated from her and sent to foster, as is the Kylaran custom, too young to have known she was different from other humans. "How about you? Can you read my thoughts?" I asked, throwing some of her directness back at her, very curious if her interest in me was genuine or if it was my imagination.

"No," she answered. "Not me."

We walked in silence for a while and I studied her out of the cor-ner of my eye. She was older but still had a kind of beauty, a fine-shaped face and sharp chin—if I had to guess I would have said she was part-Kylar, too. Though the way she had said "them" made me wonder. "What's your name?"

"Vika," she answered. "And yours?"

"Arshan."

She looked at me when I said that. "Like the old emperor?"

"My father has high hopes for me." I tried to make a joke out of it. After all, there must be a Kylaran male born every day who was named for the emperor. But she took it seriously.

"Then what the hell are you doing down here?"

"Staying out of trouble," I replied. Lhysa was perfect for that, in a world that was barely in Kylaran control, plus the island itself was a protected state.

Vika walked in front of me then, stepping backward so she could face me as we went. The land on either side of the road was barren and dry, just a few strange plants twisting up through the reddish soil. "You'll need a place to stay."

I also had a pass to the spas in my satchel, just in case, but her tone of voice intrigued me. "Yes, I suppose I will."

"I have a spare cot you can use for a while," she said, her eyes suddenly shying from mine. "I know it won't be what you're used to, but . . ." She took a deep breath. "But many things here won't be as you're used to."

So much for directness. "What do you mean?"

"I mean, you know. The lifestyle here is different." She had gone from brazen to shy and I could guess why, but something in me wanted to prolong her discomfort.

I suppressed a smile. "How different?"

She stumbled then and fell backward, landing hard on her rump in the middle of the dusty road. I loomed over her as I reached down to help her up. She took hold of my hand with both of hers and ran her cheek along the back of it, speaking fast. "There are few of us here who enjoy . . . I mean, who can satisfy your tastes."

As I suspected. My—or rather the Kylaran—reputation for dom-

inance preceded me. I pulled her to her feet and spoke to her softly. "I am not a lord."

"No, but . . ." she swallowed whatever words she was going to say. Trembling next to me, her hand remained in mine. It was almost a reflex, to reach out and stroke her hair. If it was what she wanted, then she knew the desires of the average Kylaran dominant well. We are groomed for it. She shivered under my touch, and suddenly the fact that she was worldly wise and I was barely an adult did not matter. I kept my voice low and quiet. "Have you served before?"

"Not . . . formally." Her head was bowed, and I almost felt like I could cup her soul in one of my hands. I raised her chin with one finger and her face was scarlet with shame or desire, or both. Then her natural forthrightness came through. "But I thought you might need . . . I mean, if you're going to stay here for a while . . ."

"You thought my knob might need polishing?"

She turned even redder at that. I moved her hand to the loose fabric of my pants where my erection was hardening. I am my father's son, of that there is no doubt, and my body responded to her gesture of submission. She nodded, her breath catching in her throat. "But, but the people here don't understand."

"I know." The Kylar had conquered many places and our customs had come to rule dozens of worlds. But on this island, the old ways remained. Honestly, it was a relief to know that I was not in for months of celibacy. Half-blood or not, I was all Kylar in that sense. We are bred with sharp passions and they need to find release. I looked into her eyes to reassure her. "So let it be our secret."

"Secret," she repeated, her fingers quaking against the stone stillness of my flesh.

She was still on the ground and I pulled her up onto her knees, even as my other hand was freeing my cock. There were questions and protests in her eyes, even as I filled her mouth with me. "There is no one here on the road," I said in answer to her unspoken worries. "We are not even in sight of the town yet. And I need to know if you are worthy of having me sleep on your cot." I tried to make it a joke but the seriousness with which she began tonguing and sucking me proved she did not take it that way.

She may have lacked formal service, but she had years of practice,

or so it seemed, with the Kylaran anatomy. As she licked and drove her head down over me, she kept one hand wrapped around my balls, restricting me somewhat. I could have grown larger, large enough to choke her, if I had wanted. But with her hand there—and my desire was for pleasure, not for punishment—I stayed hard and midsized in her mouth. If I had wanted, I also could have held back my ejaculation. But I let hot liquid jet into her mouth and relished the feeling of her licking me clean. I licked the edges of her mouth then, pulling her up to me and returning her to some semblance of respectability. We shared a laugh, and as we made our way into town she told me some about the island and what I could expect.

It took another hour to cross to the greener side of the island, where the ground was still stony but plants grew and the shore sloped to sandy beaches and calm waves. She led me to a settlement near the ocean, in and around an area of hills and stone outcroppings. Her home was built into the side of a rocky cliff, the front room built of mud-baked bricks, the back disappearing into the island's body. It was five rooms, clean and warm, rustic, and very private in its innermost chambers. I had just put my bag down in the deepest room and was removing my boots when her home system alerted us to someone at the door. She went to answer it while I nosed about, trying to discover where in the rustic architecture the system's speakers were hidden.

Vika came back a few minutes later, worry lining her face.

"What's happened?"

She sat down on the bed pallet next to me. "Our priestess was very sick. She had something even Kylaran medicine wouldn't heal."

"You said was . . ."

"She died yesterday."

"I'm sorry."

"Her funeral will be soon—probably tomorrow or the day after."

"Is that a problem? You look troubled."

She shook her head. "It's a big ritual, supposed to heal her bereft partner. If you're here, they'll expect you to participate. Everyone is expected to be a part of it."

"That's fine with me."

Her mouth relaxed in relief then. "You might find it sort of silly . . ."

I quieted her with a finger to her lips and her eyes widened, as if she suddenly remembered my power over her—such as it was, undeclared, undefined. "My father was a priest once," I told her. "And remember, my mother was from here. I'd be honored to take part in a ritual."

She smiled then, and I could tell she was thinking I wasn't like the other Kylar she had known. I didn't really want her thinking about that too much, though, comparing me to the men who had held her enthralled before me, so I distracted her with a kiss. Her response was polite, schooled, until I dug my fingers into the hair at the back of her scalp and bent her backward. Her lips went soft and the flutter in her chest began again. So soft, so vulnerable. I wanted to make her forget, then, that any other man had ever given her pleasure or pain. My other hand slid under the waistband of her pants, cupped her mound, and then my fingers spread as I pushed deeper between her legs. My longest finger sank into the wetness there—no doubt it had been pooling ever since she had admitted her desire to me on the road. Though her lips were locked in mine she let out a small whimper.

The Kylar have colonized, annexed, or conquered eighty-five other worlds. You can see how hard it is to resist the impulse. How could I hold back from such a treasure as her softest places? I pressed her back into the rumpled blankets on the bed, her legs falling open, eager for me. I withdrew my finger and instead circled her engorged clit with it. When I was sure I had found the right speed and angle, I stiffened my finger against her and she threw her head back. I kept at her, one hand still behind her head but with a loose grip, letting her thrash in the palm of my hand, while the other had but one goal, which was to make her come. As she came close I whispered into her ear, "I want you to come. Be mine. Come for me, come on, let go, give yourself to me." That seemed enough to push her over the edge, as she clamped her legs around my hand and cried out.

When her orgasm subsided, I pushed her pants down her body. She stripped off her shirt and spread herself for me again, but I kept my own clothes on. I gave a small shake of my head as I lay down next to her, hugging her naked body to mine. "I am not finished making you come yet."

She seemed unsure what to say.

"That was only one of my ten fingers. The other nine are waiting to see how you respond." And although I did not have The Sight, I can say with certainty that she responded very well to all of them, though I made her sore and made her beg for a rest before all ten orgasms were done.

We slept the rest of the afternoon like that, atop the blankets, me clothed and her curled naked against me. The island was already being quite restorative to me, it seemed. It was energizing to have a woman give her strength to me that way, a woman who was not part of court politics or maneuvering me for my father's favor. I felt relaxed enough to sleep with her by my side and the empire seemed very far away.

When I awoke she was still in an exhausted sleep and I took the liberty of poking around her kitchen. For all the island's isolation, she still had fruits I recognized, suitable for squeezing into boiling water with sugar. I took a steaming mug out to her front room and into the small courtyard that faced the cobbled street of the village. The sun sank somewhere behind the cliffside and I could smell the sea. In the fading light, I could see only one other person, walking slowly up the street, head down.

A small woman came toward me, her hair hanging in her eyes, and she walked as if she did not see where she was going. She shuffled, and moved her head from side to side, and hugged herself. She put a hand out on the low wall that separated us, steadied herself, and seemed about to move on when she looked up at me.

Her gaze shocked me, like the sudden opening of a too-hot oven, and I wanted to look away but I couldn't. A feeling of grief slapped me, sudden and hard, and I felt my breath catch as my throat closed like a fist. She blinked then, as if seeing me there for the first time. Her hand went over her mouth, and she ran back down the hill. And I could swallow and breathe again.

I was staring into the bottom of the dark and empty mug when Vika came to the doorway. "It's going to get chilly soon," she said to me, beckoning me back inside. "Shall I introduce you to some of the neighbors in the morning?"

I nodded. "I think I just met one of them."

"Oh? Who?"

"Mriah. The priestess's partner." Even as I said it, I knew I had never heard the name before.

Vika pulled me inside and sealed the door behind us. "She told you her name?"

I shook my head. "She didn't say anything. But I think she is . . . sending out signals or something." The ghost of the grief agony still tickled my chest like a cough.

Vika frowned. "Mriah is a seer, too. The two of them had a very deep bond."

I tried not to sound as ignorant as I was. "I've heard that when two telepaths bond, the death of one can drive the other one insane."

Vika shrugged. "It hasn't happened in our lifetime. Not until those two. The bonding, I mean." She pulled the blanket tighter around herself. "As to whether Mriah is insane, or stays that way, may depend on the ritual." And that was all she would say about it that night.

Our thoughts turned to dinner instead, which she wanted to cook for me and which I insisted on helping with, even though I knew less of kitchen craft than I knew of telepaths and their problems.

"But I want to do it," she said, blocking my way into the room.

"And I want to help you do it," I answered. "Whose wishes are we to respect, then?"

She chewed her lip, as the conundrum presented itself to her. She wanted to serve me, to do something for me, but where was servitude and obedience if I wanted something else?

"You're not my servant, Vika, and you're not my slave," I said to her. "If you really want me to stay out of the kitchen, then say so. But don't pretend to . . . don't presume to be other than what you are."

She stepped aside, angry. "And what am I?"

"I haven't the foggiest," I said, as I sat down at the small table in-laid with tile. "All I know about you is you live here on the island, and you offered yourself to me."

Her cheeks were red as she opened a store-box set in the stone wall. She put a pile of vegetables in front of me. "I work for the spas," she said, as she searched for a knife. "I promote the healing treatments on the mainland, and I'm a procurement representative. I'm making sure enough food and goods are making their way here that we're not starving or freezing. It's terribly boring."

"It sounds fascinating," I said. "How many people live on the island?"

"There are about three hundred in this village," she said, handing me the knife. "Another hundred or so live around the spas themselves. And there's a settlement on the north side, with another two hundred or so."

"And do the spas sustain everyone? For the entire year?"

"Yes. Between the government guarantees and the tourist season, we have all we need. That tile is scratch-proof, by the way." She motioned at me to chop the vegetables, and I started on the first one. "Remember, though, that the island was self-sufficient before the integration. It's just considerably more comfortable now."

"How long have the telepathic gifts been on the wane?"

She shrugged. "Hundreds of years. We like to blame that on the Kylar, on integration, but I believe it has been going on much longer than that. Even two to three hundred years ago, our records imply that more than half of the population was fully functioning psionic."

"And now?"

"Now maybe ten percent have a large compliment of gifts. Another ten percent are borderline, or merely sensitive. The rest of us?" She shrugged and began soaking chunks of fish in a bowl of water and spices. I kept asking her questions about her life on the island. In all honesty, I could see why she thought I would be bored with it. It was not a complex or conflict-filled life, which was contrary to everything she had heard about life as a noble-blooded Kylar. I was not bored by her life in the least, but I began to wonder if she was.

We were eating a rich stew of fish and vegetables when I asked her. "How did you develop your taste for Kylaran men?"

She blushed and swished her spoon from side to side in her bowl. "I spend a lot of time on the mainland and in the city."

"I see." The Kylar, on vacation, could be depended upon to be tempted by the local delights, in other words. I certainly was, wasn't I? I pressed my inquiry further, some instinct in me wanting to know her deeper. "Is it just the sex games we play that interest you, Vika, or is something missing in your life?"

She stiffened. "I don't know."

I put my hand onto her wrist and caressed with my fingers. "It's all right to admit if it's just the sex that turns you on."

She twitched a bit as I said that. "Some Kylar are insulted by that prospect."

"Some Kylar have an inconveniently large sense of honor, or are unusually big hypocrites." It was so easy to drop my voice and to see her fall into the aura I projected. "I am not one of those," I said, my fingers traveling up the fuzz of her arm. "I like sex. I like playing with power." I slowed my words. "I like seeing how far I can push things." I was leaning toward her now, my hand slipping under the table to her knee. "Are you sore from this afternoon?"

She nodded, her two knees pressing together.

"Was it worth it?"

She nodded again.

"I am excited by your suffering," I said then, my mouth almost in her hair. These are the kind of games we Kylar learn almost from when we first learn what procreation is. "And my excitement craves release." I kissed her then, a hard, punishing kiss that left her gasping when I stood. "But remember, Vika, what we're playing is a game. We owe each other nothing when it's over."

I was relieved to see she smiled. Smirked, actually, in an inflammatory and insouciant way. I knocked her out of her chair then, and wrestled her to the kitchen floor. She struggled deliciously, letting out small yelps as I bit the backs of her arms and shoulders while tearing the clothes off of her. I penetrated her with my fingers then, sinking two fingers deep into her cleft, my thumb sliding into her asshole. I kept my other hand on the back of her neck and handfucked her that way for a long time, until she was begging me for things, for release, for my cock, for acknowledgement of her plight. I let it go on far too long, probably, but I was young and still finding out how far I could push myself, as well. I resolved not to fuck her for a few days, to give her only my fingers down below, and to use her mouth if I could not stand the mounting pressure myself.

So it was that several days later, after I'd spent the day hiking the stony landscape of the island and she had returned from a meeting with the village elders, that I had still not planted my plow in her fur-

row. No sooner had she sealed the door behind her than she began stripping off her clothing. She crawled to me on hands and knees, and peeled back my trousers, and began tonguing and sucking me. I never ordered her to do so, you understand. I didn't have to. By that time she was so hungry for my flesh, so sure that if I were sufficiently inflamed, I would soon give in, throw her down, and fuck her to both our contentments. Each day she abased herself more for me, wanting it more, waiting for it to come. I had spanked her, by then—spanked her, and bitten her, and struck her across the back with a strap of leather from my bag, and tortured her with tiny flames from her kitchen lighter and fucked her with the vase from her bedside table. It was quite a delightful diversion and I wondered how long we could keep it up. Who would give in first? I was moving cautiously, but it seemed that there was no torture I could devise for her that she would say no to if she thought it would lead to me fucking her in the end. And I was not sure how much longer I wanted to wait for that prize. But a game is a game and I played it well.

That night when we were lying in a sweaty heap she told me the funeral was scheduled for the next day. "At sunset," she said. "It should have happened already, except Mriah was in no shape for it."

"What's going to happen in this ritual?"

Before she would tell me that, she told me the story of Creation, at least as it is told on the island. First Man and First Woman, who were both seers, had lived together in peace and happiness, with all their many children who were grown into a mighty people, until First Man fell ill and died. The Great Spirit Ulun then came and instructed the First Woman that his body must be cast over the edge of the northern cliffs and given back to the sea in payment for all the food her people had taken. And First Woman led all her children to the cliff's edge and cast the body down, but she could not bear to see him disappear beneath the foam, and she cast herself in after him. The suddenness of her death killed half of her children standing there on the shore, and the other half became mortal as a result. "So we're going to cast Narya's body into the waves."

"And what will happen to Mriah?"

"Her pain and grief will be shared among us all, split up among all the souls there, so that her portion may become bearable."

"You do this every time someone dies?"

She laid her head on my chest. "Pretty much."

"But what's to keep her from jumping over the cliff?"

"Usually, it's just ceremonial. No one really expects the bereaved partner to commit suicide. But I was coming to that. Legend has it that the first leader of the people decreed that the family members of the dead be bound to the island. Husbands with leather, wives with rope, and children with cloth."

"I see." I had felt a piece of Mriah's pain and I could see her wanting to leap, to end it. There was a hole in her soul. I shivered, remembering the way it had felt when she looked at me. "Will she be blindfolded?"

"What?"

"Nothing. Never mind." And I asked no more questions that night.

I woke to find Vika on top of me, trying to maneuver my morning erection into her, and we had a fine time wrestling in the bed. (Did I mention I never did sleep on the cot?) To punish her I trapped her facedown against the bed, and teased her between her legs with my cock, rubbing the slick sides of her thighs with it and letting it touch her, lubing it up with her natural ooze while I said things like, "You know Kylaran men can come without ejaculating," and "Once I'm inside you I'm going to make it bigger. I can make you beg me to take it out even though right now you're saying the opposite." When we were both sopping with her juices, I did the only logical thing, and fucked her up the ass. She shrieked and cursed me, but when I quietly reminded her that if she really wanted me to stop all she had to do was say so, she shrieked and cursed me even more, begging me not to stop. Which made me consider stopping, for half a moment, before I continued.

We were considerably more sober when the time for the ritual came. As the afternoon turned to evening, young boys ran through the village ringing small bells, summoning all to the edge of the town. There, a priest wearing nothing but paint and feathers stood. Mriah, clad similarly, stood next to him, swaying slightly as if she were so weak even the breeze could knock her down. As others gathered around, they began to disrobe. "We are all considered naked in the

eyes of the gods," Vika explained. "You don't have to, if you don't want to." I told her not to be silly, that the Kylar customarily wore even less than she did. Vika and I left our clothes folded on the low wall of a nearby cliffhouse and went to join the growing throng.

Massed as we were on the stony, flat plain, it was all the more obvious that I was not completely native. They were mostly of a height, both men and women, ranging from the height of my chest to the height of my chin and not beyond. I could see the shape of my mother's eyes on every face. Perhaps, however, they could see it in mine, too. Few people gave me a second glance as the group began to move on the road to the cliffs. In fact, the only person who did stare was Vika, who saw the scars on my back for the first time.

People began to sing. They sang in a language I had not learned, but I think I am right when I say it was a sad song. People were crying as we walked and now I could see there were four men in the front, bearing a body on a low litter. Mriah and the priest walked beside it, Mriah stumbling from time to time. With my long strides I ended up near the front and lost Vika in the crowd.

Then Mriah stumbled again and would not get up. I saw the priest trying to lift her by one arm. I took the other arm and slung it across my shoulder. The crowd had flowed around us and now we walked in the middle of the pack, toward the setting sun. I squinted and put my head down, and we went on.

She was weeping. The priest was not young and her body was limp. I finally took her in my arms and carried her myself, cradling her small form. She seemed to have shrunk since I had seen her, as if the grief were eating away her substance. I murmured nonsense to her as we walked, in Kylish, as if that might calm her sobbing. Perhaps it did, some part of her listening to my voice by reflex, as I tried to say soothing things, promising her it would all be over soon, it would be all right.

Her head came up then and she looked at me, our eyes meeting for the second time, and I stumbled a little under the weight of the pain that slammed me in the chest. But I stayed upright, and held onto her, and let the crowd push us along as we stared into each other's eyes.

I could see she wanted to die. The void inside her was like a whirlpool, sucking down into its depths all that was good in her. She was trying to wall herself off from the pain, but that only made the void larger, stronger. I don't have any other way of explaining what it was I could see in her eyes. But I understood then the ritual. In the olden days, we would have all been telepaths, seers, we would have all had the power to break down that wall, to take a piece of it into ourselves, to ease the pain and allow her to break free of it, and to fill the void with our own love and caring.

I wasn't sure what was going to happen in the modern day. As far as I knew, from what Vika had said, there were only a few there with the full gifts. What if we failed to heal her and she died that day?

We had reached the shore. The song reached a crescendo. The priest beckoned for me to carry her to the stone where he stood. It was a huge round stone, like it could have once anchored an ancient warship. Ropes and straps wound around it and through the hole in its center, their loose ends pooled at the priest's feet. I put Mriah down in front of him and he began to wrap her in the rope.

And I could see what was going to happen. The old fool had no idea how to tie a person. We were going to lose her, and who knows, maybe lose our minds, too, if she went over the cliff. I took hold of a strap and bound one of her wrists, then the other. The priest did not seem to mind, leaving me to bind her ankles, as well. The rope looked old and weak. I used the leather. For was she not Narya's husband, of a sort?

The priest dropped to his knees, and we all did as he did, and the song ended. He spoke more words, and the bearers of Narya's body dragged the litter to the cliff's edge. Mriah began to scream. They tipped the whole litter then, the entire thing, over the cliff, and others began to scream as well. If they were feeling what I was feeling, I didn't blame them. The pain in my chest flared again, the loss and searing rage pouring out of her into us.

Mriah was standing then, straining against the bonds. I could hardly believe what I was seeing then—she took one step toward the cliffside, dragging the massive stone behind her. Her bare feet fought for purchase in the loose stones and gravel, but a few more inches she

gained as the stone followed her. I did not know if her gifts included the power to move objects or if it was some other power flaring up in her body, making her impervious to the impossible.

But I could see it. See it. She would do it, drag it to the edge, and be crushed on the rocks below—that or even the leather straps would give way . . . Just then, her right arm came free as the leather snapped under the strain. From my knees I reached out and seized her ankle, bringing her down. She turned on me in a fury then, her fist swinging as she twisted beneath me. She connected, to my temple, a glancing blow. Was it reflex that made me slap her across the face? Or was I even then able to see what the effect of it would be?

The pain of the slap echoed through her body, and into mine, and into the others around us, I suppose. The wailing and crying increased and I realized most, if not all, of the people present had been driven into a frenzied trance by her sending. Some were beating their fists on the ground. None were able to come to my aid.

Not that I needed any. Now that I could see. I slapped her again, the pain shocking her and bringing her full attention on me, not on the gulf inside her, not on the walls she was trying to build between the void and herself.

How many times had I held a woman like her in my arms, at that point of no return? I don't mean mad from grief, I mean struggling to fight the pain, rather than letting it shatter her. She clung to her sense of self like a drowning man clutching at a sinking stone, desperately, without realizing it was the very thing dragging her down. I needed to shatter her, to let each of us take a piece of her.

I let my hand sting her face again and then turned her onto her stomach. She snarled and struggled but I had the reach and the advantage and held her down. I was a Kylaran noble's son. I had been taught the seven gateways of the body, the twenty-five points to shock the soul, the hundreds of ways to make a person submit. I struck her on the ass then, where I knew I could strike her as many times as I needed to without damaging her. She cried out and kicked but that did not stop the next blow from coming, or the next. With each new pain on her skin, I felt the stone that was in her heart move inch by inch.

I was speaking to her then, too, more of my usual Kylish, a reflex

I suppose, goading her, coaxing her, promising her I would take care of her if she would only let go, give herself to me, give her soul into my keeping . . . My hand burned on her back, on her thighs. I caught the free ends of the straps flapping at her wrists and bound her hands together behind her neck. I could read every twitch in her body, feel every fiber of her being like I was in some kind of dream. My training and my instincts knew where to go to break her and I went where my vision dictated.

I freed her feet and wrestled with her, inflicting blows and bites as I went. I needed to be stronger than her, faster, I needed to have more stamina. She was starting to tire and yet still she resisted. I bit her nipples and made her cry out, and then almost before I was aware of my goal, I was fucking her. Pinned beneath me, she bucked and cried and yet I could see inside her as clearly as you see into a store box. The pain was wearing thin, transforming into something else, something I would have normally called ecstasy but I am not sure in this case that was the right word. She was trying to resist but at the same time she was losing herself in it, in the sensations that were overloading her body, exactly as I wanted her to. The cries around us were taking on a different tone now, the grief turning to longing, so similar and yet not the same.

Her body and mine were in concert now, the longing we both felt mounting. My hands were on her nipples and my mouth to her ear as I let my organ expand inside her. She was right at the edge and I knew it beyond any doubt. And I was still speaking, saying the things I always said. "I want you to come. Be mine. Come for me, come on, let go, give yourself to me."

She shattered. It felt, to both of us, like the only thing that kept her body from flying apart into pieces was me, was my arms holding onto her, my will closed around her like chains. To say we had an orgasm is to understate the case. Yes, our bodies reached a climax and nerve endings fired, and so much more went on. They say males think visually, and so here is the visual image—she was like an explosion, throwing off sparkling bits of light in all directions, fire and color and blinding sparks. She shattered, just as I'd known she would. Just as I somehow had known she would. Her sense of self was destroyed, torn apart, and into the void within her rushed all of the love and caring of

her people, flowing through me and into her. The pain was transformed into beauty and light as her consciousness expanded and left me blinking. I guess I held on just long enough and was just strong enough that the initial explosion didn't hurt me.

On the second orgasm, however, I passed out.

I came to a few moments later. People were shaking their heads and getting to their feet around us, those that could. I was next to her now, on my back, and she was sitting up, the ritual paint on her barely recognizable among the dirt and marks from my beating her. She looked back at me. Her bonds were loose, flapping from her extremities like some odd costume.

"Arshan," she said in a tone of voice like she knew me. Which of course she now did.

"Yes?"

"Are you all right? Can you sit up?"

I grabbed my own knee and pulled myself upright. "It would appear so."

She stood then, and I marveled at her strength for the second time that day. In the afterglow of the sunset I could not clearly see her face, but I didn't feel I needed to. Then her voice in my head: Let me handle this.

The Priest got to his feet and the two of them began arguing. My ears knew they were speaking the island language that I did not understand, but I did understand. The gist is that he was upset that everyone appeared to have lost their minds and he wanted explanations and reassurances. She gave him none, instead telling him that she had awoken my power and needed his help in training me. I felt his eyes on me in the growing dark. Then his voice in my mind, asking for my mother's name. Then Mriah was at him again, telling him she thought there were others also likely to awaken from latency. He proclaimed it a miracle.

I stood and walked to the cliff's edge, letting the voices recede behind me. I could not see the rocks below in the shadows, but I could hear the rush of the surf against the stone.

Vika appeared at my elbow. "You do realize what you just did, don't you?"

"I'm not sure that I do."

"You probably saved us all from madness and death. Her, too."
She hugged herself against the wind, which was whipping cold now
that the sun had gone. "The two of you are bonded, now. Even I can
see that." I reached for her, feeling her desire for me warring with her
fears. "You're a seer now," she said, as she pulled away. Indeed, I could
see the things in her she wanted to hide, her needless guilt, her fear of
losing herself in another. She stepped back. "I preferred the fantasy
that you could read the depths of my soul to the reality." Then she was
gone in the darkness, and Mriah and the priest were there.

I felt I could see Mriah's face even though it was too dark for that.
She held my hands in hers and said, aloud, "You're going to have an
awful headache tomorrow. But I'll be with you." And in my mind I
heard her say: You have led me through my trials and my life is yours,
now. I know what that means. But I see in your future trials of your
own. It is my turn to help you through them, as soon as you are ready
to face them.

She was right, of course. My father, and the court, and the emperor's daughter awaited. But I said, "My first concern is to get us
back to the village in the dark, naked, in the cold." And she smiled and
took my hand and my life was changed forever.

Cold
by Frank Ramsey

Frank Ramsey's "Cold" is a straightforward tale of sadism, as a dominant enjoys putting his girl through her paces with a new and challenging toy. I love the way it captures the — if you'll forgive the pun — *cold* pleasure of the sadistic act, while simultaneously evoking its sexual heat.

Amber's wrists and ankles were circled by padded leather restraints. Her wrists were padlocked to straps around her thighs, her ankles tied to the bottom of the four-poster bed. Underneath her stomach were a large number of pillows, lifting her pretty ass high in the air and exposing her luscious pussy. She was gagged with a ball gag, and blindfolded, but she could still hear.

I knew what she'd be thinking. I knew what she'd expect when she heard me walking across our small studio apartment to the kitchenette. Perhaps she'd think, for a moment, that there would be some food involved—chocolates, or hot peppers, or fruit slices. When she heard the refrigerator opening, it would hit her: Ice.

Amber loves sensation play; I tie her up and torture her for hours. It becomes a game between us for me to push her as far as she's always wanted to go. She's not so much a pain fetishist—what turns her on is discomfort and being challenged, pushed, edged toward her personal boundaries. Tight bondage. Awkward positions. Fear. Spanking.

And ice. Amber loves ice.

When I returned to the bed, I could sense the ecstatic anticipation in Amber's body. Her ass wriggled back and forth, expecting a smooth, seductive slide of ice up and down it, perhaps around the swollen, wet lips of her pussy. I chuckled.

I took the first dildo out of the plastic mold.

When she felt the first touch of the head between her pussy lips, she moaned, perhaps thinking it was a conventional ice cube. I heard her gasp as I pushed the head in—it was quite a sizable dildo, and its freezing-cold head spreading her pussy lips and entering her had an immediately obvious effect.

I could hear Amber moaning behind the ball gag, her sounds muffled and distant. She still clutched the handkerchief in her right hand—if she dropped it, I'd stop.

But she wasn't dropping it.

I pushed the ice dildo as deep as it would go into Amber's pussy, watching her ass buck and pump as the intense sensations of the cold filled her pussy and then her entire body. I could tell that Amber was right at the edge, and I took a moment to tease her clit, savoring the confusion in sensations between the torturously cold dildo inside her and the pulsing heat of her clit, which wanted so badly to come.

Then I squeezed some lube onto my hand and slid my finger inside her ass.

If there's one thing that'll make Amber come quickly, it's anal stimulation. She loves it. I could feel her asshole tightening around my finger, and I knew she was close. Very, very close.

But I also knew I had only a few minutes to fuck her with the ice dildo—after that, I might cause damage. Too much cold is not a good thing.

Amber's ass pumped up and down, begging for more. She wanted more fingers in her ass; she wanted my cock.

I cracked open the second mold and eased the tip of the butt plug up to her lubricated asshole. She gasped behind her gag, and gripped the handkerchief tighter than ever, desperate not to drop it.

Her muffled moan, this time, was louder than ever—almost a scream. Her ass pumped wildly as I held both pieces of ice deep inside her with my spread palm and began to rub her clit. I could tell her body was awash in confusion—the cold of the dildos mixed with the heat of her hunger. She'd been so close, and anal penetration always made Amber come.

And this time would be no different, despite the conflicting sensations exploding through Amber's body.

I rubbed her clit in quick circles, forcing her closer. She struggled against it, as if her body wasn't sure what was happening. Then she came, moaning so loud behind the gag that if she hadn't been wearing it, the neighbors would have called the cops.

I kept rubbing her clit and nestled the ice dildos deeper inside her, pumping her as she came, her orgasm clearly intense from the way her naked body twisted and the way her ass lifted up, begging me for more.

I pulled the butt plug out of her and left the ice dildo in place as I added more lube and mounted her. Driving my cock into her tight asshole, I could feel the embrace of the ice-cold channel, feeling so different than ever before. But the friction of my cock plunging into her heated it up. When I moaned and came, I knew the cold would still be there, salved by the heat of my come filling her ass.

The dildo slid out of her pussy, leaving a big wet stain on the bed. I picked it up and ran the tip of it, now melted and misshapen in the form of her vagina, down Amber's back.

As I did, she shivered, and lifted her ass in the air for more.

Taking Dictation
by N. T. Morley

My own contribution to *MASTER* is an exploration of one of my
favorite power relationships — that of employer and employee —
in one of my favorite settings: the office.

"I'll be dictating a personal letter today, Miss White. I assume you
have no objection?"

Miss White crosses and uncrosses her legs, tugging at her short
skirt to hide the lace tops of her nude-colored seamed stockings,
which clip to her off-white garters. She clears her throat and adjusts
her pad of paper.

"Certainly not, Mr. Williams."

"All right then. 'Dear Kymberlee.' That's with a y and two e's."

"Yes, sir."

" 'Dear Kymberlee. It was great to meet you recently at the Plaza
Hotel to discuss our mutual business concerns. In particular, I enjoyed discussing the possibility of an exchange of ideas for office
reorganization, which promises to be quite fruitful.' That's 'reorganization,' one word, Miss White."

"Yes, sir, I know."

Mr. Williams gets out of his plush leather chair and comes around
the side of the desk, sitting on the edge of it, very close to Miss White.
The secretary looks up at him. She always feels a little fluttery when
his eyes rove over her, and today she's wearing a particularly low-cut
blouse, one with a V-neck that shows a hint of cleavage. She wonders
if she should have worn a more substantial brassiere.

" 'Pursuant to our conversation, I should like to offer you a position as office manager at our firm with the very terms we discussed,

which I've attached in this memo.' Attach office memo 473, Miss White, offering a salary of $56,000."

The secretary's eyes widen slightly. "Yes, sir."

Mr. Williams leans closer and clears his throat. " 'More importantly, however, I wish to compliment you on your interview techniques. Suggesting we meet for such a late lunch in the bar at the hotel was an inspired choice. This, I think, underlines your suitability for the position. I would have suggested an earlier meeting, perhaps at a more public restaurant, which wouldn't have allowed for the quality of discourse we enjoyed.' That's discourse, o-u-r-s-e, Miss White."

"Yes, sir. I know."

" 'Furthermore, attending the meeting without wearing panties was a commendable if slightly daring career move. Clearly you'd planned well, as the tables at the Plaza are just small enough that you could reach out and guide my hand up that impossibly short skirt you wore to touch your pussy. When I found out you were wet, I'll admit, I was inclined to make an offer right then and there. The fact that you were shaved smooth like a kinky little tart sweetened things immeasurably. But I then refrained from showing my hand, Kymberlee, because I wanted to see if you'd really put out for a job like the tawdry ho I suspected you were.' That's 'ho,' h-o, Miss White."

Miss White shifts uncomfortably in her chair. Mr. Williams' eyes are locked quite firmly on her cleavage, and though she doesn't turn to meet his eyes, she can't help but notice from the corner of her vision that his eyes are sweeping lower, savoring the curve of her thighs. She notices with some excitement that the skirt is riding up and the lace tops of her stockings are again showing. She feels her nipples hardening and knows they'll show quite plainly through her top. When she glances up at Mr. Williams, she immediately notices the unexpected distension in his pants.

"Do you wear panties to business meetings?"

Miss White clears her throat and locks eyes with Mr. Williams. The intensity of his gaze sends a pulse through her body, and she squirms a little, her butt wriggling in the secretarial chair.

"Is . . . is that part of the letter, sir?"

"No, Miss White. It's a question. Do you wear panties to business meetings, Miss White?"

"Um," says the secretary. "Ordinarily I do, Mr. Williams."

"But on special occasions?"

Miss White reddens slightly. "On special occasions I might not."

Mr. Williams chuckles. "We'll have to evaluate your job duties, Miss White. See if we can provide some of those special occasions. Are you wearing panties today?"

"Yes, sir, I am."

"What kind?"

"A pearl-colored thong," says the secretary. "With pink lace."

"Very nice," hums Mr. Williams. "Rather skimpy?"

"I . . . I prefer them skimpy," says Miss White. "They're . . . they're more comfortable that way, sir."

"Are you aware that when you bend over in that skirt I can see not only your stockings but the line of your thong running up the crack of your ass?"

"I . . . I didn't know, sir."

"Come now," says Mr. Williams. "I think you did."

"I . . . perhaps I suspected, sir."

"But you don't mind if I look, do you, Miss White? You like men to look at you? To know what you're wearing under that tight skirt?"

"Y . . . yes, sir," says the secretary. "I think . . . I do like it, yes."

He clears his throat, and says more loudly: " 'Kymberlee, when you reached out and grabbed my cock, I must say I expected you to just jerk me off there under the table. Which would have been quite a delicious treat, but I was even more pleasantly surprised when you leaned close to me and told me you'd already rented a room. When I asked you if you swallow, you told me to come upstairs and find out.' Do your panties have a cotton crotch, Miss White?"

Her face pink, her nipples showing clearly through the tight top, Miss White says falteringly: "I'm afraid they don't, sir."

"But you're beginning to wish they did, aren't you?"

"Uh-huh," mutters Miss White.

"Perhaps you could show me."

"Show you . . ."

"Show me your panties. Come now, you've told me all about them. You've even admitted the tiny things are soaked through. The least you can do is prove it."

Miss White sets her pad on the arm of the chair and stands up, reaching for the hem of her skirt.

"Bring your pad," says Mr. Williams.

Obediently, Miss White picks up the pad and pencil with faltering hands. She sets it on the edge of the desk close to her and pulls up her skirt slowly, revealing first the lacy bands of her stockings, then the pearl-colored garters, then finally the tiny iridescent thong with its low-plunging front ringed by a splash of pink lace.

Mr. Williams looks over Miss White's crotch quite appreciatively.

"You look like you're shaved under there, Miss White. Freshly shaved."

"Yes, sir," says Miss White.

"Just this morning?"

"Yes," says Miss White. "It's still a little tingly."

"Show me."

Her legs quivering, Miss White tucks her fingers under the straps of her thong and pulls it down her thighs, hesitating when the slip of silky lace is just below her moist, pink-swollen pussy.

"Take them off," says Mr. Williams.

Miss White obediently steps out of the thong, awkwardly lifting her feet through in their high-heeled shoes. Mr. Williams snatches the thong from Miss White's hand, brings it to his face, and inhales.

"You do wish you had a cotton crotch, Miss White. It's only ten o'clock in the morning."

"Yes, sir, I know," says Miss White, quivering as she stands there with her skirt pulled up.

"You've been gushing wet ever since you walked in here, haven't you?"

"Yes, sir," says Miss White, meekly.

"You certainly seem like you need a good raw fucking," says Mr. Williams. "As good as I gave it to Kymberlee, and then some."

"Y . . . yes, sir," says Miss White. "I suppose I do."

"Bend over the desk, then, and let's finish the letter."

Tucking the hem of her skirt into her waistband, Miss White

bends over the big oak desk, which is just high enough to lift her heels off the ground when she rests her hips on it. She spreads her legs, having to stand on tiptoes to do so. She takes the steno pad and her rapidly dulling pencil and stands ready, her breasts pushed uncomfortably against the desk and her ass lifted high for Mr. Williams. Mr. Williams undoes his pants and pulls out his cock, hard with desire. He presses up behind Miss White and begins to dictate.

" 'When you lifted your skirt and bent over and put your pretty ass in the air,' " Mr. Williams says, guiding his cockhead to Miss White's entrance as she scrawls furiously with shaking hands. " 'I knew I wanted to fuck you in the ass as well as the pussy. But I had no idea how good that tight cunt of yours would feel wrapped around my cock. When I rammed it home, you squealed like a pig, Kymberlee, and I thought I'd hurt you—except that I really didn't care.' "

With a shudder, Mr. Williams drives his cock into Miss White's pussy, eliciting from her full, lipsticked lips a squeal remarkably like the one Mr. Williams just finished describing. Miss White wriggles her ass back and forth, snugging her cunt down onto Mr. Williams' shaft as he begins to pound her. Her shorthand is becoming quite illegible, but she continues to scrawl as Mr. Williams dictates.

" 'From the way you pumped back onto my cock, though,' " grunted Mr. Williams, in time with his thrusts into Miss White, " 'I knew right away that you wanted it as bad as I did. I fucked you good, Kymberlee, and you gave as good as you got. I fully intended to take that snug little back door of yours, Kymberlee, but you were even more eager than I was. You looked over your shoulder and begged me to fuck you in the ass. "Ram it in my butthole," I think, were your exact words, "make me your little fucking ass-bitch." Excellent choice of words, Kymberlee, reinforcing my confidence that your oral skills were more than adequate for the tasks of this job.' Do you like to get fucked in the ass, Miss White? Miss White, you're not transcribing."

Miss White is sprawled across the desk, moaning uncontrollably, a puddle of drool having formed under her red-painted lips on the glistening surface of the polished oak desk. Her ass is lifted high to receive the thrusts of Mr. Williams' cock, and her eyes are shut tight as she shudders in bliss.

"Miss White!"

"S . . . sorry," mumbles Miss White, and grasps the steno pad and pencil. "Wh . . . where were we?"

Mr. Williams pounds harder into Miss White's cunt, making her utter a great moan of release as she finally reaches the orgasm she'd been striving for when she lost track of the steno pad. "What was the last thing you got, Miss White?"

Miss White's voice is hoarse from moaning so loud. " 'Make me your little fucking ass-bitch,' " she whimpers. " 'Make me your little fucking ass-bitch, Excellent choice . . .' "

"Do you like to get fucked in the ass, Miss White?"

"Right now," moans Miss White. "God yes," she wails. "Fuck me in the ass!"

"Keep transcribing. I've got a ten-thirty."

"Yes, sir," whimpers Miss White, grasping the steno pad with some difficulty as Mr. Williams pulls out of her cunt. His cock, glistening with her copious juices, travels up a miniscule distance until the head rests between the curve of Miss White's pretty ass cheeks, at the very entrance to her rosebud. "Please," she moans desperately. "Please, please, in the ass, make me your little fucking ass-bitch . . ."

"The willingness of an office manager to beg for it in the ass is critically important," says Mr. Williams, his breath coming out in a rush as his hips pivot, driving his mammoth organ into Miss White's uncooperative back door. With a yelp, Miss White straightens, then moans low and long as she settles back down onto the desk, scrawling furiously "Make me your ass-bitch" over and over again in shorthand as her ass surrenders its sanctity and Mr. Williams' cock slides all the way into it, until his balls gently tickle her vulvar lips. " 'Kymberlee, office politics demands frequent ass-fuckings, and you showed your willingness to put out in whatever way required when I rammed my gargantuan thing into that filthy crack of yours.' "

"Garg . . ." moans Miss White. "Gargan . . . tu . . ."

"G-a-r-g-a-n-t-u-a-n," grunts Mr. Williams, his voice coming out in time with each pounding thrust deep into Miss White's rear passage.

"Th . . . thank you," groans Miss White.

" 'But Kymberlee, the final decision was made when you begged me to whip my cock out of your ass and shoot all over that pretty face

of yours. Nothing pleases me more rather than an applicant willing to undergo any degree of filthy degradation for the sake of employment.'"

"Yes, yes," gasped Miss White. "Come on my face! Come, please, come on my face!"

Pulling his cock out of Miss White's ass, Mr. Williams steps back as Miss White slides off the desk and kneels before him, clutching the steno pad. Mr. Williams' hand pumps up and down on his cock and within moments great streams of white jizz shoot out and onto Miss White's upturned face, coating her cheeks and soaking her hair with Mr. Williams' thick, pungent issue.

Come dribbles down Miss White's face and onto the steno pad, soaking the sheet that held all her shorthand scribblings.

Mr. Williams clears his throat.

" 'Therefore, if you accept this offer, please report to my office at 9:00 A.M. Monday morning for intake processing; I'll have your employment contract ready. Yours very truly, Mr. Anthony Williams, Chairman and CEO, etc. etc.'"

Miss White is having some trouble getting her pencil to work because her hand is so slippery with Mr. Williams' come. She rips a hole in the jizz-soaked steno page and has to take a fresh sheet to get the salutation down.

Mr. Williams hands her a wad of tissues from the box on his desk.

"Thank you," says Miss White, dabbing the come off her cheeks and licking her lips. Mr. Williams tucks his cock away and zips up. Miss White pulls down her skirt, not bothering with the soaked panties, discarded casually across Mr. Williams' oak desk.

"Now, I've got my 10:30," says Mr. Williams, leaning close to Miss White. "And you've got to prepare for the transition." He clutches her to his chest and growls into her ear.

"But I'll see you tonight at my place, Kym?"

"I'm counting on it, Tony," Miss White whispers back, and turns to leave. "Thanks for the raise."

"Don't mention it," says Mr. Williams, and slaps her ass as she scurries away.

The Wealth of Pearls
by Dominic Santi

Dozens of **Dominic Santi** stories have been published in various anthologies and magazines. Santi's anthology *Strange Bedfellows*, coedited with *MASTER* contributor Debra Hyde, is available through Venus Book Club.

Santi's "The Wealth of Pearls" is a refreshing exploration of the eroticism of Renaissance Faires—and as anyone who's ever worked at one knows, there can be powerful BDSM undercurrents flowing through the complex and antiquated social codes of such events. This story takes us in to that world. Santi says that "The Wealth of Pearls" was written because "I like being on the dominant side of sexual power plays, I like historical reenactment, I like pearls, and I'm an incorrigible voyeur—especially when people are wearing or disrobing from period garb."

I have a fondness for seeing Genevra's breasts exposed. She is, as the current norm describes her, full-figured. The historical period we reenact at Renaissance faires and the like is well known for bodices so low-cut they pressed the edges of decency, in either current times or the past. In public, even when Genevra is wearing period garb, I usually allow her to cover her nipples—so long as her cleavage is well displayed. I am especially fond of seeing her long, waving tresses resting on her creamy bosom. At forty-two, her hair is still a pure chestnut brown. She does not think I notice the occasional gray hair she so diligently plucks. After all, since she is a woman of a certain age, the decorum expected of her is directly proportional to my position as marshal of the barony.

Genevra is an excellent seamstress, so her garb is always exquisite. I insist she use only the finest linens and brocades. Modern boning is

acceptable, as I want her able to breathe while her bodice cinches her waist and lifts her voluptuous breasts. But I allow no brassiere, of course. They did not exist in the period we reenact. Her creamy linen blouse holds her straining breasts as she raises her skirts and weaves her way through the campsite. She has perfected a slow, sensuous gait, one that causes her hips to sway sensuously yet allows no sudden movements. Her blouse just barely covers her nipples. Men, and often women, stare at the large, shadowed areolas beneath the creamy white fabric, at the occasional glimpse of a rosy pink edge when she turns too quickly. With one reckless move, one unexpected tug on the satin string holding her blouse closed, the linen pulls away to reveal the dark red satin of her large, sensitive, and oh, so obviously well-suckled nipples.

Such exposures embarrass my Genevra terribly. In private, she gives herself easily and completely to me. Her body is mine to use and her orgasms ferocious when I use her hard and well. In public, however, she is much too shy to act on the exhibitionist streak that gets her pussy dripping—unless she is ordered to. So I insist only judiciously. Occasional "accidental" exposures, when I pull her blouse down just a fraction more, so that her nipple then pops free while she is cooking or lifting her sewing basket. Those are just training reminders—"down" commands, if you will—to remind her who put the delicate gold chain with the permanently locked clasp around her neck. The gold chain with the heavy pearl pendant that hangs just above her cleavage. The chain that says she is mine.

There are also the simple reminders when my fingertips slide into the edge of her blouse, exposing her nipples, if only under my hands, while I spread sunblock over her in the early morning light. Or when, unseen to others, I quite deliberately tug her dress while she is cooking. Her face flushes beautifully as she fumbles with the front of her dress, pretending her hands are full with dinner, dishes, or the like, while in reality, she obediently awaits my permission to raise her blouse again. If we are alone in camp, I sometimes ignore the sounds of people walking by and wait to give my command, watching the sweat run down her breasts and drip off her nipples onto her apron. I relish the feel of blood rushing to my cock at her embarrassment and her obedience.

At one time, however, Genevra's reticence was more than simple shyness. She had told me that while she desired to flaunt her body for me, she was afraid to be completely vulnerable if other men were close by while I was distracted and aroused. It had become a trust issue for us, and one I wished to put to rest.

We had known both Thor and Lorenzo for well over a year. We'd met several times at modern-day BDSM parties. They were fairly new to that community, but veterans of reenactment groups. Neither of them currently had a submissive, and they were most anxious to learn. They had both watched us, appreciatively and at a respectful distance, enough times at modern play parties that I believed opening our tent to them would allow Genevra to feel safe while I led her into more intense vulnerability. Genevra agreed, and while she was nervous about the upcoming night, she was comfortable with the idea of them as our guests.

"I will not require you to speak this evening," I said, sliding my hand under the edge of her blouse. It was morning and though the sun had barely risen, I did not want her sunburned while she prepared our breakfast. Her nipple stiffened quickly to my slippery, sunblock-covered fingers. "Wear the blue and gold brocade dress, the one with the bodice that laces up the front. I will display you for my pleasure while I speak with our guests." I pinched her nipple. She shivered, and I smiled. The beautiful flush lighting her face let me know that by nightfall, she would be wet with anticipation.

Our pavilion is round and a good twenty feet in diameter. I had toyed with the idea of darker canvas for the walls, but in the end, I stayed with the traditional heavy cream fabric. With bright lights, movement inside the tent would have been visible from outside. Our lighting was candle lanterns, though, well-encased in glass and hanging from sturdy hooks on the tent poles. From outside, one might see vague movement inside. But the only real clarity would be inside the tent, where candle lanterns glowed golden on bare skin.

For the evening, I had pushed our personal belongings to the sides of the tent. In the center, on top of the thick red and gold rug, I had positioned two large piles of velvet-covered pillows across from each other. On one side, Thor and Lorenzo reclined, nibbling on grapes and cheese and drinking lemon tea from their mugs.

Thor's persona was that of a Viking. He wore full woolen pants, a linen shirt, and a heavy brown wool tunic. His long, dark blond hair was pulled back in a ponytail. Tall and muscular, he looked like a modern-day Norseman with a clear, easy laugh and intelligent blue eyes. Lorenzo was a short, slender Renaissance Italian with thick dark curls and flashing brown eyes. He wore the short doublet, loose shirt, and skintight hose so common to the young men of his time. Tonight his hose were bright red, with a black-and-white striped codpiece that immediately drew the eye to the sizable mound of flesh cupped therein.

I reclined on the other side of the tent, eating a small bunch of sweet purple grapes and nonchalantly fondling my swollen crotch as Genevra again filled my cup. I had not invited the others to touch themselves, so they carefully kept their hands on their mugs or to their sides. With their eyes, however, they flagrantly admired Genevra's breasts straining against the linen of her blouse as she leaned over me. I tossed the grape stems aside and tugged the front of her blouse down just enough to make a nipple pop free. She inhaled sharply as I ran my fingertips over the satin of her large, dark pink areola. It was still dark and tender from my ministrations the night before.

"I will be the only one touching you tonight, beloved. The others may admire your beauty and your sexuality from a distance, but they may not touch you. They may not even touch themselves, except by my command. Do you understand?" I rubbed the stiffening tip as she nodded, waiting until she also whispered, "Yes, m'lord" before I took the now-hard point between the pads of my fingers and stroked it with my thumb. With my other hand, I lifted her chin so her eyes met mine.

"If at any point you become afraid or truly do wish not to continue, you will tell me in so many words. 'I am afraid, my lord' or 'I do not wish to continue, my lord.' Do you agree, Genevra?"

Her eyes flicked to Thor and Lorenzo, then down to where my hand stroked her. Even in the glow of the candlelight, her blush was beautiful as she again met my gaze and nodded.

"I agree, my lord."

I leaned up and kissed her nipple. She shivered, her blush deep-

ening at the wetness I left glistening on her skin. I laid back and motioned her to fill the others' cups. She reached to tug up her blouse.

"Leave it."

Her eyes widened as she stared down at me, but I held her gaze until she took a deep breath and turned to face the others. Thor and Lorenzo were both avowed breast men and had told me, respectfully and at a proper distance, though still within my submissive's presence, how much they admired her voluptuousness and her beauty. She knew them well enough to know they were respectful. And she knew they were drinking lemon tea and not alcohol.

To their credit, neither Thor nor Lorenzo so much as looked at her as she filled their cups. They kept their eyes on me, talking about the silversmithing they were doing, modeling after paintings and pieces in museums. As she turned back to me, however, both sets of eyes shifted appreciatively to her exposed nipple, then immediately back to me, again giving me their full attention. Genevra set the pitcher on a chest, her relief clearly visible in the now-relaxed set of her shoulders. It was only then that I released my grip on my mug. She had passed a milestone in trusting them not to grab her without permission. Now we would see to expanding that trust to letting them remain even when I lost myself to an orgasm. I patted the pillows next to me and she sank down to my side.

"I'm proud of you," I said quietly. With my eyes on Thor, I took a deep drink of my tea. Then, without looking at her, I tugged down the other side of her blouse and set my fingers to her other nipple. Her shiver made my cock swell hard, but I didn't touch myself. I kept my eyes and attention on Thor while I rewarded Genevra with the nipple stimulation that I knew would drench her pussy with desire.

In truth, I greatly admired the way both Thor and Lorenzo kept the conversation flowing with minimal input from me. They spoke in detail and at length, always addressing their comments respectfully to me. I gave them mostly noncommittal responses, acknowledging them, yet not truly giving them my full attention as I pulled Genevra into my arms and gradually unlaced the front of her bodice completely. When her breasts hung full and heavy in my hands, my fingers traced the outline of each curve, milking her nipples until she was trembling.

Lorenzo finished one truly humorous anecdote, and when we finished laughing, I said, "Please, continue." Then I leaned down onto my elbow, cupped her breast, and lifted it to my lips. I swiped my tongue over her areola. Genevra gasped and Lorenzo stammered. Genevra tensed, her eyes flickering to him. But when he immediately picked up his story, I sucked her nipple between my lips, holding her firmly until she relaxed into my arms. Lorenzo's voice, then Thor's, droned on in the background, drowning out the distant sound of drums and singing in other encampments. I suckled her long and deeply, until her nipple was stretched out onto my tongue and she was moaning in my arms. Lorenzo's and Thor's breaks in speaking, followed by the sound of drinking, were becoming more and more frequent. I drew back, blowing softly on Genevra's wetted skin. She shivered hard.

"She is most beautiful, is she not?" I said quietly. I swiped my tongue over her other nipple. Her moan was loud and heartfelt. Thor's and Lorenzo's voices were clear and touched with humor as they answered, "Yes, my lord." Genevra trembled again, but this time, she did not stiffen. I smiled and kissed her soundly.

"Our guests appreciate you as well, my love. And from their swollen crotches, I see their need is also great." Genevra stilled in my arms. I reached up and stroked her hair. "I am going to tell them they may show their appreciation by fondling themselves through their clothes. Do you cry nay to that, my love?"

For a moment, Genevra hesitated. I did not kiss her, did not touch her with my mouth. I just held her in the safety of my arms and waited. Eventually, she shook her head and smiled at me. "Men touching themselves through their clothing does not frighten me, my lord, when you are here and they are across the room."

"Indeed." My voice was gruffer than I'd expected. I turned my head toward our guests. The front of Thor's pants poked out like a tent pole. Lorenzo's shaft strained against his codpiece, spreading the black-and-white stripes wide, his cock so hard pink flesh extended out to stain a dark, wet circle on the front of his doublet. But both had one hand on a mug, the other resting steadily to the side, nowhere near their straining erections. I nodded once toward both of them. "You honor my lady's beauty, my guests. Should it please you, you may pleasure yourselves through the fabric of your clothing."

To Lorenzo's great credit, when he moved his hand between his legs, he pulled his shirt out to cover the head of his cock before he cupped his impressive erection. While they paused more often in their discussions now, they both continued to speak as if there had been no interruption. I turned my head back to Genevra's breast and suckled that nipple as well to a dark and tender arousal. She was completely vulnerable now, her total trust apparent in the uninhibited relaxation she maintained as I turned her further into my arms and raised her skirt. Though I pressed my erection against her, letting her know my own arousal, and thus my own vulnerability, she still did not stiffen in fear. Instead she moaned, whispering an urgent, "Oh, yes!" as my fingers slid between her thighs.

Genevra's pussy was sopping. I rose up onto my knees and laid her down with the pillows running from her head down the length of her spine. Her arms and legs fell naturally over the sides, her breasts lying in comfortably flattened mounds above her open bodice. I shoved her skirts up to her waist. The rich dark curls between her legs glistened in the candlelight. I pressed her legs farther apart, exposing the dark pink slit hidden between her labia. I slid my hands up her thighs, touching one finger to her core and slowly stroking upwards. When I reached her upthrust nubbin, Genevra arched up, crying out. Lorenzo stopped in mid-sentence, his discourse on silver-casting abandoned as his breath came harsh and fast. This time, Thor, his breathing as hard as Lorenzo's, did not speak to fill the silence. I rubbed Genevra's slippery clit, locking my gaze on hers as she moaned and arched against my hand. Her eyes were glazed with desire, and this time, though my cock was rock hard and we had an audience of fully aroused men, my Genevra's eyes did not cloud with fear. Instead she smiled and closed her eyes, entrusting all her defenses to me.

I turned my hand, sliding three fingers deep into her cunt and sliding my thumb over her clit. Genevra groaned, bucking hard against me. I set my other hand to her breast, milking her nipple as I growled to Thor and Lorenzo, "Open your pants if you will, and jerk your cocks to spewing. There are linen napkins beside you to catch your come." I leaned down and bit Genevra's nipple. She yelped. "My

lady wife will enjoy displaying her climax for your pleasure—and especially for mine."

I had not even finished speaking when the sound of fabric moving was replaced by the soft slap of skin on skin. I looked up to see that Thor and Lorenzo were both leaning back onto the pillows, Thor's pants shoved down to his thighs and the front of Lorenzo's codpiece thrown open. Thor was uncircumcised, working his foreskin feverishly over his cockhead. Lorenzo spit copiously into his hand, encircled his huge shaft, and began stroking rapidly. I doubt either of them noticed my observation. Their eyes were glued to where my hand slid in and out of Genevra's pussy, to where the sight of my hand fucking my lady wife's cunt made their cocks drool with envious desperation. I pressed up hard into the knot of flesh on the top of Genevra's cunt. She screamed, digging her heels into the carpet and arcing up. Her pussy clamped down hard around my fingers and a thin, clear stream of juice spurted onto my arm. Thor grunted and Genevra reached out, tugging at the front of my pants as she pleaded. "More, my lord. Please!"

I pressed into her again. Her cunt tightened around my fingers as she squealed again, shaking beneath me as her pussy walls spasmed and another climax rolled through her. Still pressing, I tore the front of my pants open and leaned forward, shoving my cock in her mouth.

"Suck me, wench. Suck me while you come again, loud and slutty." Her mouth was hot and wet. She sucked me so deeply and so sweetly I could barely choke out my commands. "Your body is mine to take. Mine to use. Mine, no matter who watches . . ."

She swallowed and my cock exploded into her throat. I pulled back, spewing my juices onto her face and neck and her glorious breasts as my shout matched that of Lorenzo's in back of me. Again Genevra's pussy clamped around my hand, and this time, when her shaking stopped, she leaned up, swiping the last lingering drop from my cock slit and onto the tip of her tongue. I shook as she licked my cockhead clean with long, thorough, tender strokes over my now hypersensitive shaft. When she laid back down, I withdrew my hand and leaned back onto the pillows, holding my sticky fingers to her lips where she licked them clean as well. I did not lower her skirts, leaving

them instead at her waist so our guests could admire her well-satisfied pussy while they composed themselves.

When I looked back at them again, Thor and Lorenzo were once more dressed and leaning back against the pillows, casually sipping their drinks. A pile of discarded linen napkins lay between them, and the air was thick with the scent of sex and semen.

Genevra kissed my cleaned fingertips and set my hand on her chest as she smiled up at me. I gently traced my fingers through the sticky puddles on her breasts.

"Did you know that pearls were the most expensive jewels of our time?"

Lorenzo's roar of laughter drowned out Genevra's quiet giggle as she hid her face against my arm.

"I think, m'lord, that your lady wife is wealthy indeed," Thor laughed, retying his belt as he and Lorenzo gathered their things to go. The drums in the distance still throbbed as I closed my pants. The public revelry would still go on for hours. But I was quietly contented to end our socializing for the evening. I left Genevra lying sleepy and exposed on the pillows as I refilled our guests' cups and showed them to the door. When my lady and I were alone again, I stripped us both naked, blew out the candles, and carried her to bed.

"You did well tonight, wench," I growled, pulling her close under the covers. "I'll reward you with a good, hard fuck in the morning."

It was too dark for me to see her eyes, but I felt her smile against my chest. "Perhaps you could even fuck me in front of guests, m'lord. If it pleases you."

"I have created a monster," I growled, hugging her tightly to me. I was exhausted, but my cock still twitched at the idea. My mind was already racing at the possibilities. I was indeed a wealthy man.

Controlling the Accident
by Tom Piccirilli

In addition to being the author of ten novels, including *The Night Class, A Choir of Ill Children, A Lower Deep, Hexes, The Deceased,* and *Grave Men,* **Tom Piccirilli** has published more than 150 stories in the mystery, horror, erotica, and science fiction fields. Tom has also been a final nominee for the World Fantasy Award and is the winner of a Bram Stoker Award (the award given annually by the Horror Writers Association for achievement in the horror genre) — the very first Stoker given in the category of Outstanding Achievement in Poetry.

Piccirilli is also known as a writer of erotica, and his "Controlling the Accident" is a perfect example of the intense, no-holds-barred prose that has made him both a master of the horror genre and a writer to watch in the field of erotica.

You always need to be careful in a situation like this.

What works on the phone, what's fun in e-mail, isn't the same when you crawl out of the electrical line and into the rest of reality. It's exciting but there are ramifications. Everything has its price. You know the truth but can't help yourself anyway, and now you're on the East Side heading for Le Belle Bleu and you really don't know what the hell is going to happen.

The pulse throbs in your neck and the base of your spine, and you keep clicking your canines together, consciously having to keep the growl down in your chest. You are low-slung pale in black, wearing your grandfather's gold cufflinks, the weight of your years in perfect control and under wraps for the moment.

The East Side might as well be the outskirts of Paris, Mazatlan,

Machu Picchu, or Long Island. You feel yourself out of tune with the streets, at a loss wherever you look. You're tripping over curbs a lot, and you give the killing glare to anybody who risks giving a look. The voices seem foreign and take a second to decipher. How the hell does anybody live over here? The East Side is purgatory, you only come this way when you're punishing yourself, or when you're going to try something new.

You've known her for years, via the web, and through a few phone calls. There's a flirtation that's built up, a common well of fire and creativity that burns in the wrong kind of way too often. She fiddles with your guts, and you can feel her hands too deep inside you, grabbing at whatever she can get hold of.

One of you—or perhaps both of you—decided to bring it into the world, if only for a few hours. She probably couldn't deal with you for more than that, which is fine. She suggested . . . or was it you . . . was it? . . . to meet at the restaurant for dinner tonight. You're to talk of writing, of publishing, the theater, the Whitney Museum of American Art. Perhaps it's not beyond your means.

You walk into Le Belle Bleu full of cool in the tip of your tool. Your heart rate has downshifted. The muscles in your belly and back are tense, hard as shale, able to deflect switchblades. The role slides on like an oil that warms up with your body temperature. You're at about a hundred and one and rising.

The suit cost eight hundred and you've only worn it once: to your father's funeral, a year and a half ago. Seeing him there in the coffin opened up a whole new landscape of possibilities. The old man is smiling up at you from hell, holding a whiskey and water and making one of those Irish toasts that tell the story of some goddamn battle from twelve centuries ago. It'll end in laughter and cheers from fifty other dead guys, and you wander into the dining area with his brogue in your ears.

Words are more or less meaningless now because you're so far into your own appetite. Everything else—the friendship, the exchange of ideas and memories, maybe even some kind of fuckin' spirituality, who knows—is faded into the background, a mist writhing around the room.

There she is.

Whatever you might say to one another is too circumspect now. There's a bridge to cross first, and you might as well take a running jump and get over to the other side. Once there, you can feed the fever, put your thoughts in order, and follow the proper course, but for now you're nothing but coiling, sharpened need.

She's so tiny, smaller than you remember from the downloaded jpg's, and she's acting a touch too shy. It throws you off even more, but you've learned patience over the years. You don't press. Don't let the animal out yet. You've got cages within cages going all the way into the center of yourself. It was tough in the beginning, but you've found ways to lock doors that once threatened to let loose every heartache, desire, and twisted passion, streaming in and out. Timing is important. Dominion, mastery. You're finally better at filtering yourself.

Not as much comes through, and when it does, there's a purity to it.

She's elfin, with intensely black short hair, dark eyes, and a face made up of soft angles and planes, that hyper-cuteness in effect, the way you like it. The animal does a happy prance in place. She's nearly thirty, but could pass for fourteen, and you imagine all the kiddie games you might play. Cheerleader and dirty old man, baby darling and sicko daddy, niece in a tight teddy and perverted uncle with a lollipop. It might work out.

You sit, and she's about to make some nominal greeting when you rest your lips against hers, holding the pose, pressing your tongue slightly against hers, letting it go on for maybe three seconds too long. She looks a little spooked and swallows heavily, a slight flush to the lovely cusp of her jawline. She has only an instant to decide what to do.

Blinking twice with those huge eyes, her thoughts wheeling one way and another, her gaze settles on you again. The gently yielding surrender of her self is as clear as if she'd just stuck her wrists out and thrown them down against a rope. Waiting for the binding, some nice complex knots ending in a pretty looping bow.

Your right hand, with fingers splayed, is damn near as big as her entire chest. You could put your palm over her heart and feel her placid, slow intake of air from her throat to her diaphragm. The shadow of her throat pleads for attention. You want a taste.

She is talking and you are responding, but it's all autopilot. It's

necessary to comfort the conscience, to soothe all the grandmothers and priests in your blood. They've been screaming the word *sin* at you for so long that you're beginning to like the sound of it.

She's asking you about yourself and you tell the truth. Only the sovereign don't lie. You're sincere, honest, witty, and even deep, yet it's still as if somebody else is doing the talking. You talk about your father in the gutter, your sister the novitiate going for her final vows next month. There's more emotion in your words than you ever intended. Odd, that. You hear it and listen to her chatting, but it's damn near to eavesdropping on somebody else's conversation.

So you go through the entire dinner without tasting a single bite, watching her eat with great prudence, unsure if she's allowed to do what's being done. The young girl vibe electrifies the room. The plates continue arriving, but you've no concept of what the food is like. She looks up between bites, waiting, and you nod, urging her to proceed. To take a sip of the wine.

It's a good thing you hate French cuisine. Your tongue can't taste anything except what you've been dreaming, what's inside demanding release. Your tongue is for her. Your tongue will never taste anything again until it savors her.

The sword cuts both ways, ain't that some shit.

Suddenly, she is close to you, at your side. It takes a second to realize you've shifted seats and moved to put your arm around her. There's a fog of fear in her eyes, a touch of guilt, amazement, and even anger. It's to be expected.

She trembles, but not enough.

Your features frame a fiery scowl. Three shivers quake down her back and visibly rock her. You place your hand on her knee firmly enough for her to feel how strong you can be when it's necessary.

The cages within are rattling and thumping, the animal beginning to snarl and snap. You try to calm your own respiration but it's difficult, and your breath comes in bites.

Energy whirls around the restaurant. You can almost see a corona around the other people dining, the waiters rushing in and out. Colors bleed from the edge of your vision. The world wavers, first in black and white, then thickening into blue and red. You stare at the side of her face and you can sense the blood coursing beneath the soft

palette of her flesh. Her chin attracts you especially—you don't question, there's no point. These small temptations contain great power, and they are at your disposal.

You lean over and begin the walk down the darkening road. You may never find your way back but you can't think of everything.

Now, you lick her throat, behind the left ear. It's a very specific place you have in mind for some reason. Instinct leads. Right here, this vein, this inch of skin, it means everything to you for the next ten seconds.

You gnaw as you have never done before, with every ounce of your soul. It's an unfamiliar feeling, and she responds with a moan.

The waiter brings coffee and you run your hand along her inner thigh, petting the boundaries of her pubis. She begins to clamp her legs shut but your fist is stone. You flex your hand and her knees snap apart.

Leave them open.

She starts to protest but her complaint dies before she can form a complete sentence. Only now do you allow yourself to recall that she's married.

You pour more milk than you actually like into the coffee, but everything now has a purpose. These are instruments for your use, exactly the same as she is. The coffee's now cool enough for you to finish in three gulps. You gesture to the waiter and he returns with another pot. Even he has a design.

You reach between her legs, draw her panties aside, and place two fingers into her cunt. She sits up fast and straight as if you've just stuck her with a cattle prod.

The waiter can't help but see. His flat face freezes in an expression of shock. It doesn't matter—he's no more capable of judgment than a dildo or an X-rated DVD. He's an apparatus, a gadget you use because it's nearby.

You probe harder and slide in past the second knuckle. Her rapt grunts are peppered with "eep" sounds of panic. You fingerfuck her with one hand and hold your cup up with the other one, catching the trembling pot under the steel lip and steadying it as the waiter quivers, bottom jaw touching his chest. Games can get dangerous; you could scorch your lap.

The guy is about to skip off. You pluck your fingers free and use them to wave him closer. He stares at the glimmering wetness on your nails and isn't sure if he's horny or nauseous. You don't give a damn and tell him you need more milk.

You ignore her as she reaches up and begins to rub her cheek against your upper arm. The waiter returns with more milk, still gun-shy but grinning now.

Stupid move—never let on you've been watching other people's games. He'll get a five percent tip now, the prick.

His smile is shit-smear fish-gape and you tell him to get the fuck away from you.

She's dry humping your thigh, slowly, with a puzzled frown, like she's surprised to find herself acting like this. She hisses in your ear.

Rub me, you tell her. Your voice is forceful, a full octave lower than when you first walked in. You sip your coffee black, the bitter taste a nice contrapuntal to the syrup of her loving whispers.

She starts at your chest and you give her the death gaze. Back teeth grind together and your upper lip curls into a snarl. You won't repeat yourself—if you did you'd be the wrong man for the job anyway.

So, it's like this, she catches the fervid heat of the beast. Body temp at a hundred and three now, and she's close enough to feel the feverish warmth wafting off you. The veins in your wrists stand out, thick as tubers. You say things once, and she either does them or the threat of the animal crawls forward close enough to lunge and tear out a throat.

Yes, she murmurs, and places her palm solidly over your cock. With all these goddamn raging hormones you'd think you might be hard, but you're not. It's not exactly sex yet, and maybe it never quite will be. This is a different, much more genuine dance that goes back the unfathomable ages to when you were a critter scratching at the dirt and keening in torrential storms.

Unzip me first.

She does, slowly, finding your rhythm, at last understanding when to be quick and when to make it last. She reaches into your box-ers and begins to squeeze your cock, flicking her nails over the head, jacking casually but with great intent. You fuck her hand and when she smirks, as if she's in charge, you stop and stare and wait for the

abashed shame to crawl into her face again. Until her eyes begin to tear up and she implores to be forgiven.

You say something unintelligible, but she understands.

Again.

Good, you're getting somewhere.

You can relax a little, but not much. Someone's got a price to pay, and it's probably you. She jerks roughly and comments on your size, now that you're growing firm, inflexible. It doesn't take long. Her hand is already filled with pre-cum. She's about to wipe off on the silk napkin but stops, picking up the finer subtleties. She gives a sidelong glance and purses her lips, going green around the gills.

Lick it.

She closes her eyes and makes a face of loathing. For a second you wonder about the husband, if she's the kind who only swallows in the heat of passion, only when the cock is already halfway down her throat. But to think about it—to catch cum in a cup and leave it in the fridge overnight—now there's a woman.

You take another sip of the lukewarm coffee. It's all you're getting for the rest of the night—that dimwit waiter isn't going to show his face again.

Her eyes open and she stares at the transparent drops beginning to pool together in the center of her hand. Goose bumps rise on the backs of her arms. Another line in the hot sand to cross, and it's just the way it's got to be. She smiles, blushing, and leans closer, closer, inching her mouth to the cream. Your cum slips into the ridge of her lifeline and glides off in another direction, just as her tongue dips in. She hums.

Let's go.

Where? You haven't paid the check.

She begins to scurry from her chair but you hold her close, angling her ass to cover your exposed cock. You don't zip up. The two of you get up together and you're poking her in the soft fold of her anus, guiding her from behind toward the men's room.

In.

Aren't you going to check first?

But no, you aren't. The universe is finally in sync with your beat, all of nature working at your behest. You could hold out your hand and a fifty-dollar bill would fall from the ceiling if you needed it.

You slap the door open with your shoulder and whirl inside with her, keeping your crooning lament to yourself as you press your teeth against her throat again.

She heads for a stall but you steer her to the sink counter instead. She walks straight into it and you put your hand against the middle of her back, barely doing anything at all to turn her around to face you. She's listening to your merest caress now.

Okay, so she's wondering whether she should kneel in front of you, jack you up some more, suck it, or what. You reach out for her hips and she does a little leap. It's like you've been training in the circus together for years, the Flying Humpendas. She weighs nothing and floats into the air, up onto the counter. She parts her legs but her panties have fallen back into place, covering her cunt.

It might as well be a stainless steel chastity belt.

Let me in, you say.

Getting to the risky part now. A handjob is one thing—her conscience could be eased with all kinds of pretext and excuses and self-evasion. But the deed is another matter.

She snorts and looks toward the ceiling, a hint of regret passing across her face. The husband is here with you in the shitter for a moment, his presence a bitter force in the night. So let's see.

The dare's in the air. You brush your fingers against the panties, back and forth, and your cock is rigid and laid against her thigh.

Of course you could shred them, take her, and you will, but first she's got a hell of a lot to give back. This is no simple diversion. You put your life on the line, your complete resolve. You could get hit by a celebrity limousine out there, trying to get home from the fuckin' East Side. You are never completely safe. She could always rise up and champ her teeth on your carotid and leave you spurting red against the Tunisian glazed tiles.

The gamble is the action.

What are you doing to me? she cries, staring at you curiously and panting heavily. A trace of rage—even hate—flashes in her eyes. Her face is dappled with sweat and the short hair is pasted against her forehead. The sheen reflects the retro-hip, recessed gallery lighting.

You don't answer. To respond is to initiate dialogue, and that's not the way to accomplish anything. You don't shove forward even

though the animal is screaming, your compulsion backing up into your heart.

She plucks at the panties. Your cock represents your ties to the generations of your forefathers, your lineage, your children, but as brutal as this is for you, maybe it's more so for her.

She flinches as if you're pinching her ass, smacking her in the face, yanking at her ropes and shackles, and she's still toying with the idea of halting everything in its tracks. You wait. You have a greater patience than anyone you've ever fucked.

This is pain.

You remain stone. Not bad for thirty-seven. You tilt forward and take her earlobe in your teeth and bite until you swallow blood, but she hasn't made a sound.

She draws the lace aside an inch, but that's still not enough. She's the kind of woman you want to either screw or kill. How she loves kneeling beside the wolf, taking a chance it won't murder her where she sits.

Someone invades the domain, tries to get in. You're close enough to slide a foot backward and brace it against the bottom of the door, keeping it shut.

Fancy-ass French restaurant and there's no lock.

Hey, the dumb shit says. Someone in there? Hello?

Piss in the Deviled Eggs à la Dijonnaise, frog lover!

Your snarl is soft but lethal in its implication. You hear the bastard drifting back down the corridor, muttering to himself.

She responds, yanks the panties aside and says, Now.

Frig that shit.

You hold off. She doesn't demand a damn thing. The hell is this upstart crap? The beast throws itself against the bars but you can hold off, hold the shrieking in your veins back for another minute. You press your lips against hers and let her taste her own blood.

Now, please.

Beg, you tell her.

Oh God.

Better than that.

Fuck me, give me your cock, I love you . . . I love you, do me, do your girl . . . I'm your girl, I'll always be yours.

You slide in and bellow and oink. She makes loud guttural noises of pleasure that drive you to pump harder, giving it your all.

Body and whatever soul you've got left.

You pull out and position her so she's leaning at such an angle you actually pop free. The horror and dismay on her features makes you chuckle. You jab forward brutally against her clitoris, pounding at the red bud beautiful as a ruby. You reach up and pull her dress down to her waist, freeing her tits. Her nipples are erect and you eagerly suck at them as she twists and squirms. She begs that you don't bite so hard, so you really kick it up and start chewing. Leave something for the husband to see.

Somehow you've set off the water taps in the sinks on either side and the blasting hot water begins to steam the mirrors.

She lays there, helpless, the way you need it to be, and finally you slip back into her. That's it. Her cunt's warmer and you can feel the splashing cream wetting your nuts. You begin to urgently, mercilessly, fuck her as she whimpers and whines. The sound of her supplication makes you roar.

Excitement wedges molten spikes into the back of your head as you bring each other to the brim. She senses this and places her hands on your ass as if to draw you closer but she doesn't dare pull. Her tits are covered with your spit and teeth marks, thin rivulets of blood coiling down across her chest, her belly. You can't hold off anymore and she cries out in your ear as you spurt deeply inside her, every muscle in both your bodies locked in place.

She continues to hump against your softening cock, milking each drop. You gather a handful of cum, grab the back of her head and haul her sideways so she's laid out like a sacrifice. You rub your cream in with her blood, working every inch from her clit to her forehead.

You're my girl.

It lasts as long as it lasts.

Then it's over, the cage door slamming shut, the animal in the corner nuzzling mud and hay.

She nearly flops off the counter, weak-kneed, wincing, and falls heavily into your arms. The silence is all-encompassing as the fever breaks. Your vision is red around the borders and filled with black spots, but your head is clearing. Feels like the first time in months.

You carefully wash the pink froth from her, dappling her face with faint kisses. You dress her slowly and she says nothing, staring at you lovingly, as if this has a chance to go beyond where it is.

When she begins to speak again, you feel it with a sinking of the heart. She starts playing with words like fate, chance, and other concepts you don't believe in.

This is nothing more than an accident still in the process of occurring. You ease off the gas, you don't hit the brake. You calmly continue steering through the wildly outrageous skid, ride the centerline, doing what you can to avoid obstacles and outcroppings of terror. It's no easy task taking control of the accident.

You walk with her from the bathroom, chin high and eyes like shards of flint. As you pass your table you toss a few bills down, unsure if it covers the check or not. Nobody's going to stop you anyway.

You shove her into the back of a cab listening to promises with a rictus grin. She looks back through the rear window and waves. Kisses her fingers, presses them to the glass.

There's the smell of rain in the wind.

You stumble over the goddamn curb and try to get your bearings. You start off in some direction, not knowing where it'll take you.

Frickin' East Side.

Misty's Clothes
by Daniel Harris

The BDSM player writing as **Daniel Harris** says of "Misty's Clothes": "I love dressing women up, 'forcing' them to wear the kind of slutty clothes that many of them feel too guilty or disempowered to wear. For many women, dressing like a whore can be so risky, knowing that people will judge her cruelly because of too tight a skirt, too low-cut a top, or the sight of her nipples, erect and braless, through a thin top. With all the myths about sexy, promiscuous, or provocatively dressed women deserving to be treated as less capable than more conservatively garbed women, it's no surprise to find women afraid of being accused of dressing like a slut.

"That's where I come in: If I 'make' her wear those clothes, how can she be blamed? I may still judge her—after all, when I'm finished dressing her up, she'll *definitely* be a slut. And I'll give her everything a slut deserves. Misty is a composite of all the women I've taken shopping."

Misty wears sexy lingerie. She dresses like a slut. Always. Whether I'm around or not.

It didn't used to be that way: Though an erotic and supremely feminine woman, Misty never showed herself off like a shameless tart until I told her she was going to. Now, her lithe, lush body is visible to everyone who sees her, every day.

Misty has that trait most cherished in a submissive: She's eager to please. Desperate, even. When I lift her tiny skirt or bend her over and pull down her low-slung pants, I know that ninety-nine times out of a hundred, I'll find the sexy, skimpy see-through lace or mesh or fish-

net I demand of her. And the one time, Misty knows she'll be spanked—or worse.

That didn't used to be true. The first time we slept together, when she confessed to me her need to be dominated, controlled, instructed, it was at her apartment on a Saturday night. That night I undressed her slowly, savoring the exploration of her body, and it took quite some time. She'd dressed up for our date, which means she wore baggy slacks, a silk blouse, a blazer, lacy panties and bra—I would find out later, the only items of lace she owned.

Sunday morning, I got out of bed while she was making breakfast. I went through her top two drawers and made a mental inventory. They were filled with cotton briefs, sports bras, T-shirts. Her other drawers were filled with sweaters, jeans, extra-large T-shirts. I had noticed as we'd courted that Misty harbored a deep need to be a slut, but camouflaged it in heavy clothing. I resolved to change that, without preliminaries.

When she returned to the bedroom wearing a terrycloth robe, holding her breakfast tray, she saw me looking through her drawers and blushed.

"Unacceptable," I told her. "If you're going to be mine, you'll be dressing like a slut. We're going shopping today."

"Yes, Sir," she told me.

I enjoyed the breakfast my new slave had cooked, then enjoyed her again, stretching her nude over my bed and spanking her before fucking her again until she came. Then I told her to get dressed, and asked her if she had any sexy lingerie.

I could see her, despite her recent orgasm, flushing with heat as I queried her.

"Not really, Sir," she told me. "I mostly wear cotton."

"That's going to change. Wear your tightest pair of jeans with nothing underneath."

"Yes, Sir."

The pair of jeans she selected was just barely adequate, and I could see her squirming as I ran my hands over her tightly encased behind. She wasn't accustomed to going without underwear.

We went to the shopping mall and spent the next four hours pick-

ing out a whole new wardrobe for her. The sales clerks in the lingerie store looked at us with warmth, like they were charmed by my considerate nature in helping my girlfriend pick out her under-things. Misty blushed, looking nervous as I selected infinitesimal mesh thongs, lace garter belts, push-up bras. She tried each one on, tempting me into the dressing room to approve or disapprove each item. I paid with my credit card and we moved on to a series of stores aimed at juniors, selecting tiny skirts, skimpy minidresses, snug hot-pants, and skintight hip-hugger slacks. We got a pair of ultra-low-slung jeans so tight she had to wriggle her pretty butt to get into them. Her underwear showed plainly above the hem, especially since I didn't allow her to buy a belt.

I could see Misty squirming uncomfortably as she tried everything on for me. When I sneaked into the dressing room with her and slid my hand down a pair of silky stretch trousers, I found her so wet I had to make her lick my hand clean. That inspired me to take her to the "novelty" store, where once I'd spied a line of jaunty cotton thongs that said naughty things on the front. Misty blushed as I selected them for her. SLUT. WHORE. HOOCHIE. PARKING IN REAR. IF FOUND, RETURN TO _____. I told her she was going to write her name on that last one in indelible marker, because a slut like her might lose her underwear.

Misty said, "Yes, Sir."

I also knew Misty liked to keep in shape by going to the gym. That was, in fact, where I had met her. I'd seen her working out in sweats, baggy shorts, heavy T-shirts. We went to the sporting goods store and walked out with bags crammed full of the tightest possible running shorts, tiny leotards, and skintight sports bras I knew would reveal those perfect, hard nipples of hers. Since it was late winter and I know Misty likes to swim—it's one of the reasons her body was so perfect—we also bought her two swimsuits. The first was a white one-piece, though it was hardly what you would call "practical." A mere string in back, it plunged so low in front that Misty's slight breasts bulged through the fabric invitingly, creating cleavage where there had been none. The second suit was a string bikini, Brazilian in style, so incredibly tiny that it showed the rich dusting of Misty's blonde pubic hair as she broke the state health code and tried it on

with nothing underneath. "You'll have to shave this," I told her, stroking her hair, crowded illicitly into the dressing room with her. "Shave it bare."

"Yes, Sir," she murmured.

Our last purchase at the sporting goods store was a pair of athletic shoes. It was no small matter to find a pair of slutty running shoes, but I managed—they were pink, with a picture of a famous 1920s cartoon slut on the side. As I'd noticed Misty wore tube socks exclusively when she worked out, I selected several packages of ankle socks. There would be no excuse for covering up flesh unnecessarily.

Between each shop, we filled the trunk of my car with Misty's new wardrobe. Each time, she thought the restructuring of her fashion sense was completed. Each time, I brought her back into the mall to endow her further with the slutty clothes she would be wearing for me.

Lastly, we purchased several new pairs of shoes—high-heeled strap pumps, flashy red heels, a pair of black shiny patent-leather lace-ups, and a pair of athletic shoes—pink. I could see Misty's reaction to all these purchases, which I paid for with my credit card. She was an independent girl, not used to being told what to do, and certainly not used to having her new lovers buy things for her. But I could see that some part of her had forever longed for this.

We returned home in the late afternoon and I told her to gather up all her old clothes and put them in a black garbage bag.

"Yes, Sir," said Misty.

I allowed her to keep the tight pair of jeans, which were now soaked with her juices after spending a long day cradling her pussy without underwear. Everything else went in the bag.

Only when her drawers and closet were empty and the garbage bags were stuffed full did I allow her to unpack the bags from the mall and fill her drawers with her new garments.

"Try something on," I said. "Show me."

Misty's hands shook a little; I could tell that, not being a lingerie girl, she wasn't sure what to wear. She finally selected a tiny white mesh thong, a matching see-through bra, and a white lace garter belt.

"Wrong," I told her as she climbed into her new outfit. "Panties go on the outside of garters."

"Yes, Sir," she said.

When she was dressed up for me, I inspected every inch of her with my fingertips, appreciating the way the tiny garments revealed her slim, pale body, adoring the way she shivered as I explored her. I plucked her thong out of the way and entered her from behind, finding her even wetter than she'd been the previous night after her spanking. I fucked her until she clawed the bedsheets, coming twice before I emptied myself into her.

"From now on," I told her, "You'll dress like this every day. Wherever you go, whether or not you and I are going to see each other. I'll drop your old clothes in the garbage on my way out."

Still shimmering with sweat from the hard fucking I'd just given her, Misty said the words I so loved to hear from her.

"Yes, Sir."

Now, Misty dresses like a slut. Whether she's going to work, out to dinner with girlfriends, or out on a date with me, she wears short skirts, tight, low-slung pants, revealing minidresses, high heels. When she goes to the gym, she wears a tiny sports bra and bicycling shorts so tight every curve of her ass and the full swell of her sex lips show through to anyone watching. When she swims for fitness or recreation, she calls me on my cell phone before changing. She asks permission to wear her white one-piece instead of her string bikini. I usually grant it, but she never knows for sure. Sometimes Misty finds herself doing laps in a string bikini so small she has to tug it back over her nipples and pluck the thong out of her sex lips each time she reaches the deep end.

I didn't throw her old clothing away, of course—I stashed them in a locked trunk in my closet. I couldn't be responsible for the erasure of the old Misty—not until I knew it would last. You never know if your slave will prove to be the kind that remains, or for whom submission is merely a walk on the wild side of which she soon tires. But now, after the two years Misty and I have spent together, I'm certain. I doubt my slutty tart is ever going to change back to her dowdy self.

She surrendered to it long ago, you see. Several weekends a month we go shopping and I no longer have to select clothes for her. In fact, when I'm buying, which is always, Misty is even more adventurous than I demand of her. The clothes she selects are exactly what

I would have picked—or, at times, even more revealing, more daring, sluttier.

Misty's confessed how much she loves being cherished like this. She's confessed she never wants to dress the way she used to. She wants to be my tawdry little slut forever.

I think it's finally time to consign Misty's old persona to the trash heap.

But not before she accepts. I plan to go down on one knee when I propose, which will be the first time she's ever seen me there. Many times I've imagined the look of rapture on her face, the tears of joy on her eyes as she accepts my ring.

It should look nice tucked into one of those see-through thongs, nestled between her shaved lips.

Becoming Veronika Vale
by Simon Sheppard

Simon Sheppard is the author of *Kinkorama: Dispatches from the Front Lines of Perversion; Hotter Than Hell and Other Stories;* and the syndicated column "Sex Talk." His work also appears in more than one hundred anthologies, including many editions of *Best American Erotica* and *Best Gay Erotica.* His next collection, *In Deep,* will be published in the fall of 2004 by Alyson Books. He hangs out at www.simonsheppard.com.

When I first met her, I had no idea.

It was at one of those classical music get-togethers for no-longer-so-young singles, wine and cheese followed by Debussy and Dvorak. I had more interest in pussy than in music, but my pal Tony had convinced me to give the high-culture route a try.

At intermission, she approached me in the lobby of Symphony Hall. "Hey, you're Rob, right?"

"Yeah, Rob Wayne. But I'm sorry, I've forgotten your name." She was no longer wearing one of those awful name tags that went with the brie en croute. I remembered her, though; she was someone I'd immediately checked off my list as both "too demure" and "too good for me."

"Laurie." She smiled. "Laurie Courtauld. Listen, can we go somewhere after all this for a drink?"

"How about now?"

Fuck Dvorak.

Now, I wasn't desperate, not really. But Laurie was beautiful, insistent, and she seemed to see something in me that few other women had. So

I ended up in her bed that night. Naked, she was even more attractive than she'd been in what I guess some fashion writer would have called her chicly understated clothes. Smallish, perfect breasts, a gorgeous ass, and a cunt that was wet, welcoming, and anxious for my dick. She straddled me as I lay on my back, riding my hard-on till I shot, me rubbing her clit till she came, too.

"I should get going," I said, after we'd barely caught our breath. "I have to work tomorrow."

"Oh, stay," she purred. "I'll make sure you get up in time." She reached down for my hand, pulled it to her lips, and sucked my forefinger, the one that had gotten her off, with her lovely mouth. Amazingly, I felt my cock stirring again. I had no idea what I'd done to deserve her, but sometimes it's better not to ask too many questions. Or to argue. I stayed the night. And several nights thereafter.

It wasn't till date number five, on the way back to her apartment, that she gave some hint of what was to come. "I want you to see something," she said.

"Something" turned out to be, when we got back to her apartment, a videotape. She popped it into the VCR, and the title, in Gothic script, appeared on the screen. HOUSE OF CHAINS.

"I'll be right back," she said, and left me sitting there watching the video. Now, I was no babe in the woods; I knew something about kink, read *Penthouse Variations*, had even plowed through one of those books Anne Rice had written under some pen name. Still, there was something a bit weird about watching bondage porn while my new I-guess-girlfriend was in the next room. Weird.

Up on screen, a lithe woman with hennaed hair, wearing nothing but a corset, net stockings, and high-heeled knee-high boots, was being tied to a chair by two strapping men in hoods. Her knees were spread wide, her shaved cunt open to view. Her position, hands tied behind her back, made her ample breasts jut out from the top of her black leather corset. One of the men grabbed her long, red-tinged hair and pulled her head back, while the other one pulled his big, swollen dick from his leather codpiece and jammed it between her scarlet lips. That kind of brutality really wasn't my thing, but I realized , guiltily, that my own dick was hard too. If I hadn't been such a gentleman, I would have reached down and played with myself.

"You enjoying it?" said Laurie, sneaking up behind me. I jumped, then turned and started to say something. Only started to, because when I saw her, the words caught in my throat. She was dressed like the woman in the video, corset tightly laced, spike-heeled boots gleaming, pussy newly shaved.

"I want you to use me," she said. "Sir, I want to be your slave."

I write advertising copy for a living, so I'm rarely at a loss for words. But I was at a loss for words. She walked over to the chair and stood before me, her crotch at eye level. She pushed her hips toward me; I could smell her cunt.

"Don't you want me, Sir?"

I still find it hard to say what came over me. I rose to my feet, grabbed her by the hair, and forced her to her knees. Tearing open my fly, I pulled out my hard-on and slapped it against her face. She whimpered, then opened her mouth. I fucked her face as brutally as I could. It didn't take long for me to shoot down her throat.

"Thank you, Sir," she said, cum trickling from her scarlet lips.

Without a word I stuffed my cock in my pants, turned, and walked out of her apartment. Somewhat woozily, I headed home.

I spent the next day in a state of confusion, wondering what I could possibly say to a woman I'd treated so badly. Even if the bitch had been asking for it. And she had. No, no, that wasn't the way to look at it at all . . . Or maybe it was.

When I got home from work, there was a message waiting on my machine.

"Thank you so very much for last night, Sir. I'm so glad you found me worthy of your use."

Well, it was hell on my self-image, but those few words got my dick rock hard. Within a couple of hours, I was back at Laurie's apartment. This time she met me at the door naked, wearing only a studded leather collar, a leash in her hand.

"Permission to speak, Sir?"

"Um, permission granted."

"Sir, from the first moment I saw you, I knew you were meant to be my Master."

I'd heard a lot of strange things in my life, but that was a new one. Still, when I looked down at Laurie's beautiful face, her eyes glistening with what looked a lot like devotion, I was in no mood to contradict her.

"Would you care to come in, Master? Your unworthy slave is at your disposal."

I took the leash from her hand and snapped it onto her collar. "On all fours, bitch." I wasn't sure whether that was just the right thing to say, but it sounded okay. In any case, she dropped to her hands and knees, her perfect back tapering into her gorgeously rounded ass. I slapped one of her cheeks, because that was what I thought I was supposed to do. And then I slapped the other one because that's what I wanted to do. She shuddered and moaned softly. So fuckable.

As I led her to the living room, I noticed the TV was on again. The same woman I'd seen before was onscreen, her hair still hennaed, but cropped short; evidently this was a different video. And this time, the woman onscreen was, like Laurie, wearing nothing but a collar and leash, being led around by a guy who looked like a football player gone to seed. As the camera zoomed in, he hooked a couple of fingers into the woman's cunt and pulled her toward him.

"Who's that woman?" I asked my new slave.

"That's Veronika Vale, Master. She's my favorite actress. I hope that someday I can be just like her."

Well, Laurie was already more beautiful than her—she lacked the been-through-the-mill look so many porn stars have. And I didn't have the heart to point out that Veronika Vale was, presumably, playing a part, one she'd been paid to play. I looked down at lovely Laurie Courtauld and, obligingly, reached between her thighs and hooked a couple of fingers between her hungry wet cunt lips.

"You're going to be my slave, full-time. From now till forever."

"Oh, Master, thank you. It thanks you so much, Sir."

The dialogue was coming from the TV, but it gave me ideas.

Over the next few weeks, our relationship became more intense, more structured. I, basically, took possession of Laurie Courtauld. I de-

manded, and got, the key to her apartment. I ordered that she be naked and collared whenever she was at home, and she gratefully agreed. I suppose that if I'd been a good slave owner, I'd have demanded she move in with me, but there was something reassuring about the current arrangement. She was there whenever I wanted her, ready to give me her mouth, her pussy, and, later, her ass when I wanted it. She was mine, all right, but I bore no responsibility, could walk away from the scene whenever I liked, back to my everyday, normal life. If she was unhappy with what was happening, the slut kept it to herself. I was, I had to admit, living every man's dream.

Often when I left her apartment, I found a gift waiting for me on the table in the hall, always neatly wrapped, always tagged "For my MASTER." Each and every one was a video, a porno starring Veronika Vale. I'd take them home and watch them. Veronika chained up in the dungeon of what was supposed to be a French chateau, but was more likely the basement of a house in Orange County. Veronika in Victorian times, a serving wench at the beck and call of a roomful of hungry sadists named Lord This and Baron That. Veronika dressed up as a pony. (That one made me guiltily guffaw.) And all that was what my girlfriend aspired to. I found the whole situation a bit sad, more than a little odd, and very, very hot.

Not every video was followed by an acting-out by Laurie and me, but a goodly number of them were. In one of the videos, *Pussies Whipped*, an evil top with a dick the size of Maryland jacked off while he ordered a supposedly reluctant Veronika to eat out another woman's cunt. Sure enough, the next time I visited my slave's house, a second woman was there, too, a petite Asian wearing a red lace bra and panties.

"Master, permission to speak?"

"Granted."

"I've gone to the liberty of providing Mitsouko as a gift for you. I hope she does not displease you." It sounded a lot like a line from *Pussies Whipped*.

I spent that night playing director, sitting in an armchair and jacking off while I ordered Veronika, er, Laurie to suck Mitsouko's hard, dark nipples, to lick her Japanese cunt, to suck on her swollen clit as my gift writhed and moaned, a bit theatrically but convincingly

nonetheless. As I sat sipping Laurie's Chardonnay while Mitsouko used her long, dark hair to flog my slave's beautiful ass, I got an evil idea. Early on, before the Master/slave thing, Laurie had refused to rim me. It was, she confessed later, a sexual taboo she couldn't get past, something that deeply disgusted her. So I never forced the issue, not even when things had gotten to the point of my pissing on her naked body, hot liquid shining on naked flesh. But now . . .

"Slave," I said to her, "rim Mitsouko's ass."

I saw her look up at me with a glance that was, for a moment, something besides the adoring look of total submission. But that vanished quickly. Mitsouko got on all fours and pushed her ass out as my slave kneeled behind her. Laurie put her hands on the woman's butt cheeks and spread them, then stared at the waiting hole.

"Do it, you cunt," I growled, pretty much beside myself with lust. "Do it now." Laurie closed her eyes, stuck out her tongue, and leaned into Mitsouko's butt. She licked at the small, puckered hole, tentatively at first, then hungrily, spreading the hole wider, shoving her tongue further in. Mitsouko moaned like she meant it.

Laurie took her tongue from the hole and looked up at me, with what seemed like tears in her eyes. "Is slave doing it right for you, Master?" she asked. I could no longer restrain myself. Grunting blindly, I shot my load across the hardwood floor. Immediately Mitsouko and Laurie were at my feet, licking the sperm off the polished oak, then snuggling up against my legs like the two pussies they quite apparently were.

"Slave trusts its gift pleased you, Master," Laurie said.

Um, yeah. You bet.

The next time I saw Laurie, she asked for permission to speak frankly. I granted it.

"Sir, slave hopes this doesn't sound impertinent. But slave yearns to give even more, to quit its job and move in with Sir, to become all his, full-time and fully."

I was taken aback. I realized then that Laurie hadn't ever been to my apartment. And that I'd kind of liked it that way. I bent the truth.

"I'm not sure that's possible at the present time."

"Why not?" That was the kind of thing a slave wasn't supposed to say, spoken in a tone a slave wasn't supposed to use.

I found myself more upset with her than I'd ever been. "I think tonight's session is at an end." I pulled my clothes on and left her huddled semipathetically on the floor.

The next day at work I found myself obsessed by the look she'd given me when I refused her offer of full-time servitude. Maybe moving her in with me wouldn't be such a bad idea after all. On the other hand, without a job—and I was brought up short when I realized I didn't have the slightest idea of what she did for a living—she'd be totally dependent on me. And she'd always be there. Waiting on me hand and foot, of course, but there.

Hell, had I gotten myself in over my head?

I decided not to go to Laurie's that night. Since I'd met her, the rest of my social life had dwindled down to nothing. I hadn't seen Tony since that night at Symphony Hall, so I phoned him up and arranged to meet for an after-work beer.

"Long time no see, Rob. What you been up to?"

I hadn't planned to tell him the truth, not at all. But I guess I had to talk to someone, and he was handy. So I told him about Laurie—not all of it, not by a long shot—but enough of it so he could get the drift.

"Rob, I'd be careful if I were you."

Which is not exactly what I wanted to hear.

"Jesus, Tony, I didn't figure you for a prude." Or maybe he was just envious?

"It's not that. I don't give a fuck what consenting adults do, as long as they don't leave a mess on my lawn. But . . ." He looked long and hard at me. "Correct me if I'm wrong, but seems to me you've fallen in love with her."

Oh fuck, maybe he was right.

"You sure that she's what you want, Rob? I mean, if she is . . ."

By the time I left the bar, I realized that my feelings were a fucked-up mess. Here was this immensely desirable woman, a

woman who'd given herself to me body and soul, who was ready to do anything for me, and she'd offered me the gift of her self, all of it. And what had I said? "Er, I'm not so sure." What a complete shit I was.

I stopped by an adult bookstore for a peace offering. I'd seen almost all of the Veronika Vale videos. But there was one, *Bitches in Revolt*, that didn't sound familiar at all. When I joked with the skinny blond clerk to giftwrap it, he didn't get the jest. Instead, he reached under the counter and pulled out a roll of vagina-pink paper and expertly wrapped up the video. I shoved it in my overcoat pocket and headed for Laurie's.

When I let myself in, Laurie was fully dressed, sitting on the sofa watching *Friends*, eating Lean Cuisine.

"Oh God," she said when she saw me. "I wasn't expecting you Rob . . . Master." She put the plastic tray aside, and stood up, starting to peel off her sweater.

"No, wait, Laurie. We should talk. We really have to talk."

"About what?"

"Listen, Laurie, I like you a lot. A lot."

"I hear a 'but' there. What's the 'but'?"

This wasn't going the way I'd planned. I plunged ahead. "I just don't know if I'm ready for a full-time commitment."

"Listen, mister, I've offered my whole self to you." Her tone was more querulous than I'd ever heard.

"And I appreciate it, but . . ."

"There it is. The 'but.' How could you treat me this way, Rob?"

" 'Master'; call me 'Master.' "

She snarled. "You son of a bitch."

I slapped her across the face. Hard. I'd never hit a woman before, not in anger. Before I met Laurie, I'd never slapped a woman at all.

"You think you're such a big deal, Rob? You're not worthy of me, not fit to be my Master. Not even to be my boyfriend. You want to know why I chose you?"

I didn't want to know, but she told me anyway.

"Because I could sense you were weak, that I could mold you into whatever I wanted. And I was right, up to a point. But you were too much of a fucking pussy . . ."

I hit her again. Blood trickled from her lip. I felt like I was either going to cry or kill her. Maybe both.

"Get the fuck out of here, you fucking loser," Laurie screamed.

So I did.

As bad luck would have it, I'd chosen that fucked-up night to lose my house keys. I had to go down the block and dig up my spare set from where they were still, fortunately, buried beneath a tree. Fucking idiot. I was a fucking careless, ungrateful, confused, self-deluded idiot.

When I finally got home, I poured myself a scotch, then a second. It took me a few hours to calm down, to sort things out. Would I miss Laurie? Well, I'd miss the sense of omnipotence she'd given me, the mantle of Master I'd reluctantly donned. And yet, if I were honest with myself, I'd have to admit to a feeling of immense relief, as though I'd been fired from a high-paying job that I hated.

Veronika Vale. Who in her right mind would want to be Veronika Vale? Or her boyfriend?

It was then that I remembered the gift-wrapped video that still sat in my overcoat pocket. I decided on an exorcism. I tore open the wrapping, peeled the plastic from the box, and popped the cassette into my VCR.

"Bitches in Revolt," the badly drawn title read. "Starring Veronika Vale. With Alan Troy as Lance. And featuring Mitsouko." I got a funny feeling in my stomach.

Sure enough, it was the same Mitsouko that Laurie had apparently hired for my entertainment. Vale played a woman named Laura. Mitsouko played Laura's best friend. Laura was Lance's contractual slave, her utter submission dramatized by extended close-ups of clothespins being put on her nipples and labia. Laura was the perfect slave, all selfless devotion, and Lance masterfully used her every hole. But then she discovered that Master Lance had been carrying on with Mitsouko behind her back.

"I know that being a slave means that slave deserves no influence

over a Master's behavior, nor should slave ever judge him," Veronika/Laura said in a voice-over. "But I wasn't a good slave, after all. I was just a rejected woman, a weak woman with a broken heart, and so I did the unthinkable."

Next came a badly acted scene in which Laura walked out on Lance, then an extended fuckfest between Lance and Mitsouko, and, finally, a scene where Laura returned to Lance's house. She let herself in, using a key she'd stolen from him. It was the middle of the night and Lance lay naked in bed, Mitsouko having conveniently vanished somewhere. Laura crept into Lance's bedroom, clumsily fished a knife out of her pocket, reached down for his cock, and . . .

I hurriedly pushed stop on the remote.

I had to relax. I'd lost my keys, that was all. Laurie didn't even know where I lived. But why not? She could easily have found out. Easily. I went to the front door, ready to throw the bolt. But I didn't. I didn't because I knew I was being silly. Because maybe Laurie hadn't even seen *Bitches in Revolt*. And because, hell, some things just have to play themselves out, that's all.

And that was over two hours ago. Since then, I've been lying in bed, naked, on my back, no blanket, dick exposed. Waiting. With every noise, my cock gets hard, waiting, then finally sinks back down. Until the next sound in the night. And maybe until, until . . .

Something She's Not Telling You
by Jim Barker

In the Daddy/girl story "Something She's Not Telling You," newcomer **Jim Barker** spins the clever tale of a submissive traveling to make contact with her first master, whom she's met online. What I like so much about it is the idea of a submissive being marked, one of my favorite fantasies—but one that always makes me wonder what happens with the submissive's *next* master. In my own erotic novels, consensual enslavement lasts a lifetime, but here Barker plays with the idea of a slave's existing tattoos and the way they hint at previous fantasy scenes.

I was waiting for her at the airline gate, prepared for the worst. When you meet a girl online, especially if there's an immediate connection, there's always something she's not telling you. I had long ago resolved to be completely honest online, but Erica, in particular, promised to be much too good to be true.

When I saw her coming off the plane, I couldn't believe it. She looked exactly like her picture—if anything, she looked better. Twenty-eight, slim, pretty, with long, dirty blonde hair and firm, small tits. I could see from across the terminal that she had followed my instructions: She definitely wasn't wearing a bra under that tight top. Her nipples were hard and I could see them already. Perhaps they were hard with anticipation at meeting me.

I wondered if she'd also followed my instructions not to wear panties under her plaid skirt. From her photograph, I knew that pretty cunt would be tattooed: A single, stylized CUNT right where her pubic hair would be if she didn't shave it.

She recognized me from my picture and ran to me, smiling.

She hugged me, whispered in my ear. "Hello, Daddy," she said.

"Hello, Erica. You're as beautiful as your picture."

She blushed deep red—and my caution was evoked. It didn't look like a blush from modesty. Rather, I had the sense that there was something she wasn't telling me.

"My car's waiting," I told her. "Let's go."

She didn't have any bags; I had instructed her not to bring any. She wouldn't be wearing much this weekend. All she carried was a tiny purse, and I knew that the only garment inside would be a black leather collar. We went to my car and I opened the door for her.

Once inside the car, I lunged at her. I kissed her hard, and put my hand up her skirt and felt her pussy, wet and bare and shaved, as I'd instructed.

"I see you really can follow instructions," I said. "Girl."

She moaned softly as I fingered her wet pussy, and she whispered back: "Yes, Daddy."

I turned, put the car in gear and drove out onto the highway.

"Are you disappointed in me?" she asked.

"Not at all," I told her. "You're even more beautiful than your picture. You followed all my instructions. Usually people you meet online lie about something. You haven't lied about a thing."

She blushed again, bit her finger.

"Daddy, I'm sorry," she said. "I did lie about something."

My eyes narrowed. "You're married," I said.

"No," she said.

"You were once a man? I've already felt your pussy, so I know you're not one now. What's the problem?"

She giggled. "No," she said. "I was born this way."

"Slutty?"

She blushed and smiled.

"Yes, Daddy."

"Let's see if I can figure out what you lied about," I told her. "While I fuck you."

We pulled into my driveway and went into my house. Immediately I pushed Erica against the wall with her wrists flat to it, and I

started to kiss her. I was hard instantly, and when I pushed her to her knees she didn't hesitate. She opened my pants, took my cock out, and began to suck me.

"Say it," I said.

"Thank you, Daddy," she whispered, her breath hot on my cock. "Thank you for letting me suck Daddy's cock."

I pulled her to her feet and carried her into the bedroom. I dumped her on the bed and said, "Strip."

Erica looked so pretty with her red lipstick smeared across her face from the enthusiastic way she'd just sucked my cock. I knew fucking her was going to be a dream. "Daddy," she said. "I . . . you're going to find out what I lied about."

"I said strip, Girl."

Erica knelt on the bed and lifted her tight T-shirt over her head, revealing her perfect tits. Then she kicked off her shoes and squirmed back onto the bed, wriggling out of her plaid skirt. She leaned against the headboard and spread her legs very wide. She blushed deep red and looked down, ashamed.

"I'm sorry, Master."

"Good Lord," I said. "You're going to get a very stern punishment, young lady. Where did you get the photo?"

"That was someone else's," she said. "I found it on the web."

I climbed onto the bed and ran my fingers over the tattoo, smiling.

There it was, and she had lied. She'd shown me a photo of a pussy that was tattooed CUNT.

This one said DADDY'S CUNT.

I smiled.

"Lying is punished most severely," I told her.

She nodded.

"Yes, Master."

"Why did you lie?"

She looked ashamed. "I didn't want you to think I was too slutty."

I laughed. "The cat's out of the bag now," I said, and leapt on top of her. She moaned as I pushed her into the bed, forcing her legs wide open. My cock was rock hard already, and I had been anticipating this moment since the first time I'd seen her photo online. I pushed my

cockhead between her pussy lips and entered her, deep, making a moan burst forth from her mouth. She wrapped her arms and legs around me as I pounded her.

"Yes, Daddy, oh God yes, Daddy, thank you for fucking me . . . thank you for fucking my cunt . . . it's Daddy's cunt . . ."

She came just before I did, moaning and thrashing on the bed as I fucked Daddy's cunt good. When I came deep inside her, she moaned softly into my ear: "Thank you, Daddy. Thank you for coming inside my cunt."

I pulled my cock out of her and guided it to her mouth. Eagerly, she licked it clean, tasting Daddy's cunt and Daddy's come. I ran my fingers through her hair as she looked up at me with her pretty eyes, her mouth wrapped around my softening cock.

I pulled her face off my cock and sat up against the headboard. "You lied to Daddy," I said.

"I know, Daddy. I'm sorry."

"Get over my knee."

She blushed again.

"There's something else I lied about, Master."

"Good Lord," I said. "I'm going to be busy punishing you all night. Get over my knee."

"Yes, Master."

Erica crawled over my knee, her naked ass pushed high up in the air. I ran my fingers over her ass. A drizzle of my come ran down the inside of her thigh. I dipped my finger in it and pressed my middle finger between her cheeks. She moaned and writhed in my lap. I chuckled.

"Is this true, too?" I asked her.

"Yes, Daddy. It's true. It belongs to you."

There, at the top of her rear furrow, was tattooed DADDY'S ASS.

"But you were afraid I'd think you were too slutty," I said.

"Don't you, Daddy? I knew you'd be angry and punish me if I was too slutty. Don't you think I'm too slutty?"

"I do," I said. "You're much too fucking slutty. And if it's Daddy's ass, then Daddy can do whatever he wants with it, can't he?"

I pushed my middle finger, slick with my come, deep into her ass-

hole, and she gasped, loudly, her back straightening as she clutched at the bedsheets. She settled down into my grasp and sighed as her asshole loosened around my finger.

"Yes, Daddy," she said, and pushed her ass back, forcing herself more fully onto my finger.

Office Copier
by Keith Walsh

"Office Copier" is the kind of short, sexy, tongue-in-cheek story I've come to love. I like to call this sort of thing "flash erotica," which is uniquely appropriate for this particular scenario.

I catch her by the copy machine. She's making photocopies of something very naughty. A story she found in some two-bit magazine with spreads of naked women opening their legs for all to see. She's so engrossed in her task that she doesn't hear me come into the copy room. I lock the door behind me.

I reach around her from behind, seize the magazine from her hands. I can see the back of her neck turning red as I look at the cover. It's a tabloid-sized magazine with a lingerie-clad whore on the cover. *Shameless Slut Weekly*.

"I—I was just making some copies," she begins, and I cut her off by grabbing her neatly bound bun of hair and forcing her down against the copier.

"Let's make our own porn," I growl into her ear as I grind my crotch against her ass. She's wearing a very tight skirt, and I can feel her push back against me, moaning as I reach under her and pull at her blouse. It tears open with a scattering of buttons, and I push her against the smooth glass of the copy machine and hit the button. She's bathed in light, moaning as the warmth washes over her. A perfect picture of her lace-clad tits comes out. I grab it and hold it up for her to see.

"There," I say. "Much prettier than anything in that magazine, wouldn't you say? But I think we can get more hardcore than that, can't we?"

She moans as I pull up her skirt and force her legs apart. She's

pressing back against me, lifting her ass high into the air. She's wearing garters and no panties under the tight, short skirt. My cock's already quite hard, and I enter her in one quick thrust. She gasps and grips the edges of the copy machine.

I undo the front clasp of her bra and peel the sweaty lace off of her. Grasping her hair as I fuck her from behind, I push her naked tits to the copier, punch in 100, and hit START.

She moans as the hot glass sears her hard nipples, and as pictures of her full, round tits start coming out. I continue fucking her, hard, holding her tight against the copier as her hips grind back against my body, forcing her cunt more firmly onto my cock. She looks down at the pictures of her breasts as they scatter everywhere, sailing out of the slot with increasing speed.

"Very nice, wouldn't you say? They look a little smashed, but still very pretty."

She moans and comes, her pussy spasming around my thrusting shaft. A moment later I come inside her, filling her cunt with a thick load of my juice. When I pull out of her, a thin stream of semen drizzles down the inside of her thigh.

I hold up one of the copies of her naked breasts.

"Very pretty," I say. "I think the rest of the company would appreciate it, don't you?"

She murmurs meekly, her face flushed from the heat of the copier and the exertion of fucking herself onto my cock.

I pull away from her, zip up my pants, and turn to leave the copy room. She's still slumped over the copier, panting and moaning.

"Distribute this as an all-staff memo along with whatever story it was you were photocopying," I say. "Have it out by the end of the day."

Breathlessly, she says: "Yes, Sir."

Kyree
by Marcus Lord

Marcus Lord is the pseudonym for a popular author of erotica with Pink Flamingo Books and Chimera Books. Lord says he has had a lifelong fascination with bondage fantasy as well as with the seamy underworld so familiar to readers of detective thrillers. At the same time, he has a soft spot for true love, the tension of which runs throughout this unusual and unique story. The edge is as fine as a knife, but in the end, it cuts toward pleasure . . . for Master and slave alike.

Of this story, Marcus Lord says: "The Crime Fighter lives on the edge: between pleasure and pain, between right and wrong. This is his story, played out on the dark streets of an unnamed but all too familiar urban landscape. More than anything, the crusty detective longs to escape his past and his violent present, but inside rages the spirit of the wolf. Is there a woman to bring him peace—the perfect slave for this most formidable and jaded of Masters?"

The Crime Fighter doesn't cane her straightaway.

It's a ritual he has. First, the door must be locked and double locked—as if anyone would dare to enter! Then he takes his trench coat off, hanging it on the middle hook of the bottom row on the old brass coatrack, the kind you'd find at a garage sale. After this, he rolls the sleeves of his white or blue or salmon-colored dress shirt and goes to the sink.

She will start a little as he turns the faucet on, her slender, vertically shackled body responding like a filament about to be lit. The water is cold already, but he likes it colder. For a while, he'll just stare down, his hands on the edge of the sink, letting the water splash onto

the rust-stained porcelain, till the temperature's right so he can douse his hands and anoint his face.

It will be night by now, and he'll have stubble. Sometimes, afterward, he'll let her run her fingers over the sandpaper roughness and look into his eyes while they lay in bed, listening to the jagged chants of Chinatown, its essence carried from the street below on wings of myriad colors and strange, exotic scents.

The Crime Fighter tolerates these times, but they are not his favorite.

He snatches up the towel next, threadbare, a complete mismatch to the faded yellow wallpaper. When his hands are dry, he'll toss it onto the four-poster bed, which has been fixed with permanent restraints of gleaming steel. Like all the furniture in the room, it is designed for the use of the guests and not for the girl herself.

The Crime Fighter, whose name is Sergeant Ryan, could give a damn about furniture, here or in the room he rents downtown. For an address he might as well list the battered metal desk he occupies at the precinct, or else the litter-laden front seat of the unmarked cruiser in which no one else will willingly ride, not even the dogs from the K-9 unit.

Sometimes he takes the gun off at this point, and sometimes not. Tonight he leaves it on, because there are three separate murders he cannot solve and they are eating at his brain and he knows there's got to be some connection no one's seen as yet.

The girl, meanwhile, is taut as a cable, a violin string to be plucked. She is on tiptoes, the shackles digging into her wrists. One of the house staff, or else one of Johnny Shin Tao's boys will have placed her like this an hour ago. The Crime Fighter likes to know she's been waiting for him, and sometimes he thinks of her, even during the day.

Living in this one small room, eating, sleeping, fucking.

Officially, places like this don't exist. Houses crammed with immigrant girls, working off transport from shithole countries with their bodies. Not ladies of the evening or even whores, but slaves. Street vermin like Johnny Shin Tao had ways of making it permanent, too, by charging the girls for room and board, not to mention the laughable "protection fees" to insure no one compromised their honor.

The Crime Fighter isn't sure what it is about this particular girl,

this improbable slip of a woman that so holds his interest. Certainly she's exotic. All of nineteen, and an ethnic meatloaf: Javan and Sumatran, a sprinkling of jade and ebony, a dash of vanilla. Eurasian, Polynesian, "the hope of humanity," as some bullshit sociologist might say. More likely, it's her capacity for pain that attracts him. Sergeant Frank Ryan likes pain—likes dispensing it on the helpless bodies of attractive young females. And not just the act of whipping or caning, either, but everything that leads up to it and all that follows as well.

The way a girl anticipates what is going to be done; the way her body begins to smell, how it feels to the touch, and the way her nipples rise in fear, wonder, and need all mixed together. The way she says "yes," though she hates what is going to be done, her whole body screaming out to fight when her cunt—and her brain—are needing to go on.

And afterward, when she hangs so limp, like she's been fucked, her body aglow, hot to the touch and covered in fresh wounds. Endless varieties of them . . . no two the same. Welts and sears, fine cuts and bruises in green and blue and black, like Rorschach blots, filling your mind with wicked dreams and making your cock swell so hard you think it will burst your pants, like you're seventeen all over again.

And then, when you finally free her from her bonds, when you let her down, there is this moment, her eyes reflecting yours in which you feel all-powerful. Like some kind of god. It is all the Crime Fighter can do at times like these to get a girl in place for fucking before he explodes in his pants.

Did all this make him some sort of pervert or psychopath? No. Psychopaths are those who don't ask, who don't care, and who wound only to kill.

Kowalski, Frank's sometime partner, calls him a hypocrite for claiming a difference between his own activities and those of the men they hunt down and put away under the auspices of SCU, the city's Special Crimes Unit.

"You think them girls got a choice?" the combed-over walking coronary would say, his mouth invariably stuffed with some piece of sausage or burrito. "Bullshit. You're a predator, my friend. Which is why you're so fucking good at catching the bad guys."

This particular girl has a name in her native language, but when

she tries to say it, all the sergeant hears is a little song with no discernible words. The closest he can come to pronouncing it is "Kyree," so that is what he calls her. They do not often use each other's names. For that matter, they seldom speak at all now, since she has learned his rhythms, and he hers.

Which is what makes it so unusual on this particular occasion when she addresses him face to face, just as he is about to present the cane for her to kiss. "Master," says Kyree, using a term the Crime Fighter thinks vastly inappropriate but which he has tired of constantly correcting her over, "something bad happen to Kyree."

The sergeant frowns, weighing the bamboo in his hands. He keeps it balanced, resting it against his muscled thighs that once belonged to a Special Forces soldier and before that a running back.

"Bad, Kyree? What do you mean, bad?"

The truth is, he would kill for her, though neither has yet been ready to face the implications of this.

Kyree chews her lip. Amber gold eyes blink on a perfectly ovaled face. "Johnny sell Kyree," come the words from lightly painted lips— the only covering besides mascara that she is ever allowed in the house.

Something clutches at the Crime Fighter's chest. "Sell?" he repeats. "Look at me, Kyree. What do you mean 'sell'? You're working off your debt to him, aren't you?"

She shakes her head. "Rich man pay debt," she tries to explain, straining her limited English. "Take me away . . . soon."

The Crime Fighter chides himself for his momentary naivete. Of course such things were not only possible, but probable. Johnny Shin Tao was a scumbag of the highest order, and while he was obviously enjoying keeping the pretty young woman in squalor and torturing her with an endless stream of cruel abusers, he was also a businessman. A girl like Kyree was worth big money. Her value on the slave markets would far exceed anything he could ever squeeze out of her here. Yes, it was all very clear. The only thing that should have surprised him at all was that the smooth-talking hustler and pimp hadn't made the move sooner.

"You're talking nonsense," he silences her, determined to enjoy what is likely to be their last session. "I don't want to hear another word about it. Is that clear?"

Kyree nods her agreement, though Ryan has already moved on to the foreplay, running the tip of the cane over her small, high-peaked breasts. She is so very beautiful—and so powerless to stop him as he toys with her, flicking and jiggling the soft, firm flesh at will, making painfully obvious her submissive needs.

She wants more and he gives it, pressing the tip cruelly against her nipples, one by one, then sliding it down over her concave belly to that magic place between her thighs. He is caught up himself now, in the drama that is Kyree's flesh—in what he can do to it, to her. He wants to make her sing and cry and laugh. He needs her to worship him and need him and . . .

The Crime Fighter stops himself before he finishes the thought. Had he been about to say he needed her to love him as well?

The hanging girl eventually yields, her eyes beholding him in wonder, her cheeks freshly pinkening as he finishes masturbating her. The last of the old-school dressers, the sergeant opens the neck of his polyester shirt and yanks loose the tie. He is feeling his pulse in his throat, the throbbing of blood in his crotch.

This is the part that always gets to him most about Kyree. The fact that no matter how many times he does this, it is like the first. Like her virginity has some kind of phoenix power to be reborn after each and every violation.

It boggled the mind. Three times a week she'd been taking it from him for, what was it now, four months? And that didn't even begin to touch what the others did to her. Granted, he'd paid extra and pulled some favors off of the fast-talking, Hong Kong suit-wearing Shin Tao to keep her free from the worst of it, but still . . .

"Master," he hears her say, the word a statement, question, and declaration all at once.

"I'm not your master," he grumbles, delivering an administrator's smack to her left hip. "When are you going to get that straight?"

Kyree mumbles an apology. Her hair, jet black with bangs that need trimming, is already wet, as wet as the oil slick between her legs. She will come two or three more times before he has finished caning her.

Truly, she is a marvel, and the Crime Fighter—who is pushing fifty and has to work a little harder every goddamn day just to stay be-

hind the eight ball and ahead of the smart ass detective recruits, perps, and walking whack jobs—has never seen anything like her, even in his heyday. Not in the whorehouses on the south side, not in his wildest fantasies, not even in the military, where he's visited the fleshpots of Bangkok and a half-dozen other places whose names he can't ever reveal because, according to the government, he's never been.

"Cheer up, kid," he lifts her chin, not liking the deep sadness he sees.

She tries to conjure a smile; he doesn't force the matter any further. Unlike the others who use her, the Crime Fighter spares her dignity, giving her privacy, at least in her feelings if not her body. Supposedly she is some kind of princess back home, the daughter of a native king or chieftain. She's never said so to him and he hasn't asked. The only one whose word he has on this is that of Johnny himself, the two-bit hood who is always trying to sound like a mix between Edward G. Robinson and Brando's *Godfather*.

"Hey, Ryan, you dirty rat," he was forever drawling in his thick Chinese accent. "I make-a you offer you no refuse, okay?"

"Just keep your nose clean around me, Johnny," was the Crime Fighter's stock answer. "And we'll get along just fine."

Hell, the Crime Fighter wasn't a vice cop, anyway. As far as he was concerned, the Johnny Shin Taos of the world were performing a necessary service. Relieving the pressure, keeping the steam from building too high.

"We have a lead on the Quinto killing," said the Crime Fighter, letting loose the cane, giving it a smooth test pass through the air. "A low-level dealer gave us a plate."

Kyree made no response; she never did, and he wasn't sure how much of it she even understood. The information was confidential, of course, but where would she go with it? Who would she tell? Her slobbering, degenerate, so-called customers? The buffoonish Johnny or one of his half-brain associates?

The cane landed now with a satisfying thwack, the jiggling buttocks recoiling, but unable to avoid the damage as he gave her details as to the owner of the car whose license plate they'd traced. It was always this way, and depending on the backlog, she would endure anywhere from ten to twenty blows before he was done.

The choice was his. Kyree's ass was on permanent loan to the Crime Fighter; that much had been secured from Johnny. The marks she bore on those perfect globes were his alone, a living record of his trials and tribulations. Sometimes he would put her on all fours just so he could run his fingers over them, feeling the reality of his life in ways he never could on the street.

Today he gives her twelve—a moderate amount, though he does intend to take her hard right after, maybe even twice. Like a marionette, fallen from favor, Kyree collapses at his feet as soon as the shackles are opened.

"Hands and knees," he tells her, indicating the position she is to assume on the bed.

The command is standard between them; her response is not. He has to restrain himself from drawing back his foot as she lowers her head, placing delicate kisses on the worn leather of his standard-issue cop shoe. It isn't the act of obeisance that makes him uncomfortable, but the implied sentimentality.

"Hands and knees," he repeats more forcefully, striking savagely with the instrument of torture he is still holding.

Kyree shudders at his feet, the waves of another orgasm passing through her captive flesh. "Buy Kyree," she whispers. "Please, Master?"

He speaks her name harshly, the effect far greater than any corporal punishment. Head down, she crawls, her well-abused ass on fine display. The Crime Fighter wants to undress, but pauses first to watch her climb up onto the feather mattress. She is like a cat, sleek and ready to be collared. Her whole body is vibrating like a tuning fork as she takes up her position, sex holes open and facing him as she waits on all fours.

The bed is a turn-on for them both because of what it symbolizes; Kyree may not go upon it except when she is being used. Sleeping is something the indentured girl does only on the floor, her body curled on a mat, her ankle chained to one of the bedposts. The Crime Fighter knows for a fact that Johnny Shin Tao sees to this himself every night, right after he makes her choke down a load of his fresh come.

The very thought makes the Crime Fighter sick, not to mention pissed as hell. "You suck my dick," he can imagine Johnny saying, "you dirty rat."

Kyree says the words again just as he's ready to enter her, his manhood poised, the helmet grazing her opening. They hit him like the cane, like a slice from the bullwhip.

Buy Kyree. Please, Master?

"What the fuck for?" he pulls back her head by the hair, the swiftness of his own anger surprising even him. "So I can set you free?"

Kyree arches her back, making the position look natural. "No, master," she says simply. "Buy Kyree to keep . . . how you want."

"The hell you know what I want," he growls, shoving himself in hard and to the quick.

The girl clenches round his penis, holding him for the moment within her conquered chasm. "Kyree," she hisses in short, spasmodic blasts. "Belong to master; master own her, make her feel . . . alive."

He tries to hold back, denying the overwhelming rush—the exhilarating thought of having the lovely creature for his very own, night and day, waiting for him when he comes home, naked and kneeling, head to the floor, ready to serve, to suck, to be or do whatever he wants, the whole of her body for his pleasure, to be marked and abused . . . and above all, that look he would find in her eyes, the one that says he is her god.

"Kyree," she moans boldly as his emission floods her, "want . . . be master's pet."

He withdraws as soon as he's done lest the words, charged as they are, prime him all over again. "Sorry," he slaps her welted, vein marked cheeks, the dribbling line of come already reemerging from her sex, "but I have a no-pet clause in my lease."

He leaves her that way, not bothering to kiss or touch or even tether her. It is only when he hears her sobbing, just as he is about to open the door, that he feels the tugging in his heart. He heads straight for Muldoon's, but the pair of double shots and chasers only serve to focus the pain.

Harry the bartender, who hasn't seen him in here since the bad old days, asks if he wants to talk. The Crime Fighter tells him no.

The way he sees it, the thing is crazy, no matter how he slices it. Joan was the last decent woman he'd touched and the night he'd come home loaded, wanting to put her in handcuffs and a teddy, she'd gone through the roof, and straight back to her mother's, in that order. He

hadn't raised a squawk over the divorce settlement. There were no kids and nothing to fight over except for his pension, and it'd be another five years before she could get her claws into that.

No, that wasn't fair; Joan was a decent woman, like he'd said. It was all on him, his playing into all the stereotypes: the perverted, drunk, over-the-edge psycho cop. The shrinks had wanted to put him on the Bow and Arrow Squad—no gun, no dignity—but his captain had fought hard for him. The road was long, and Kowalski, pain in the ass that he was, had seen him through most of it.

And then he'd found Kyree. The most improbable antidote to his gaping wounds. It hadn't even dawned on him till just this moment how much better he'd felt, how much easier it was not to drink since he'd known her. It didn't make sense, but it was true. The girl could barely speak English, but he felt connected with her, accepted. It wasn't just that she took a beating; she made him feel wanted, made him feel like a man again.

"Heading out, Frank?"

Ryan nods, leaving a pair of twenties on the bar. "Got somewhere to be."

Harry towel-dries a beer mug. "Will we see you again?"

"No, Harry, I don't think so."

The Crime Fighter gets back into his four-door and clunks the magnetic light on the roof so he can cut through the crosstown traffic a little quicker. He doesn't bother parking round the back of Johnny's place the way he always does, but leaves the sedan right out front. Johnny is in the backroom, counting the daily proceeds from the numbers racket he runs out of Chinatown.

Two of Johnny's associates leap from their chairs at his unannounced entry. Their hands are inside their suit jacket pockets for nine-millimeter pistols, but Johnny makes a joke out of the thing.

"Hey, Sergeant Frank," he quips, rising to his feet behind the oak desk. "You are just the man I want to see. I been working on new impression. You want to hear?"

Ryan watches as the gangster's face contorts and compresses in some bizarre version of method acting. A moment later Johnny clears his throat and lets loose.

"Hey, are you lookin' at me? Huh? Are *you* lookin' at me?"

The Crime Fighter has to laugh at the piss-poor De Niro.

"So, what you think?" Johnny wants to know.

"Well, Johnny," he runs his hand through his thinning hair. "I would have to say, without a doubt, that was the worst single fucking piece of acting I have ever had the misfortune to witness."

Johnny's henchmen are laughing now, and the tension is down to zero.

"You guys are dirty rats," he complains.

"Listen up, Johnny," says the Crime Fighter. "You and I need to talk."

Johnny, a vision of sky blue in his knockoff Versace, throws up his hands like an old woman. "An offer I can't refuse . . . I know, I know. It's the girl you come for."

He cocks his head. "How did you know?"

Johnny snorts. "She do nothing but cry since you leave. Hell, Mr. John Wayne Junior, that girl, she cry after every time you leave. And don't think you fool me; I know how you watch over her all the time." He reaches down to the desk for a piece of paper. "Here, this what you lookin' for."

Ryan regards the invoice. The writing is Chinese, but the amount at the bottom is clear enough. "Eight dollars," he reads. "What the fuck is this?"

"That's how much left on girl's account—I subtract a lot, because you and me, we do business, right?"

"Not business," Ryan corrects him. "We have an understanding, that's all. You help me with tips and stay out of the serious shit and in exchange I overlook what a total sleaze ball you are."

"Hey, you really know how to hurt a guy," Johnny whines. "And here I give you big gift, too."

"Kyree said you were selling her to a rich man."

"Right, just as soon as you give me my eight dollars."

"But I'm not rich."

"You are to her," he sticks out his hand impatiently. "Now give me my money."

Ryan takes out a ten. "Keep the change," he tosses it on the desk and turns to go.

"Hey, you forget something!"

The Crime Fighter looks over his shoulder. "What's that?"

Johnny Shin Tao is beaming ear to ear. "You forget to say 'thank you.'"

Ryan inclines his head to the pile of illegally collected cash on the card table between the two silk-suited hoods. "I didn't bust you for running numbers; that's thanks enough in my book."

The Crime Fighter finds the girl still on the bed, curled up and shivering under a blanket. Someone has shown her a little mercy, apparently. "Kyree," he whispers in her ear.

She opens her eyes immediately. "Master?"

"Yeah," he nods. "Come on, let's go."

She sits up, like she's still dreaming. "Kyree no understand."

He takes off his trench coat. "I don't feel like explaining now. Put this on and we'll talk in the car."

"We talk . . . *in car*?" She pronounces the words with disbelief.

"How else are we going to get home?" he chides, helping her to her feet. "And since when did you stop calling me 'master'?"

She leans into him as he wraps the coat over her shoulders. She is so small that it hangs to the floor. "Master," she sighs, "forgive me."

The Crime Fighter, Sergeant Frank Ryan, lately become Master Frank the slave owner, pushes down the newly sprung hard-on. "I'll consider it," he says, grabbing her well-pummeled ass through the material, "after your next punishment."

"Yes, master," she trembles, deliciously anticipating his wrath. "Whatever master say."

Fisting
by Andre Farmer

Fisting is one of the deepest acts of dominance and submission that two people can share. While it's not always a BDSM activity, the sheer intensity of the act guarantees that powerful forces are involved. Here, **Andre Farmer**, who refers to himself as a "weekend outlaw biker" who has posted short stories to the Internet on several small websites, plays with the idea of "forced" or "semi-forced" fisting, which I can testify from personal experience is a physical impossibility. But every woman I've known who has engaged in vaginal fisting knows that the sense of accomplishment and the connection required between the two partners makes fisting a ready-made form of powerful submission, an offering to a slave's Master. "Fisting" describes a relationship wherein a Master and slave investigate that bond, with pyrotechnic results.

Naomi didn't believe me, at first, when I told her she was going to take my fist. "It's impossible," she said. "Women can't do that, can they?"

She is younger than me and less experienced in the art of extreme sex. I found her naivete charming, and resolved to maintain it until the last possible moment. Her fear of being taken that way only excited me more though, and I never wavered for an instant. I wouldn't have dreamed of actually hurting her. In a way that caused damage, that is.

This, however, presented something of a problem. You see, the critical elements in fisting a woman are time, patience, lubricant, and an unwavering belief on her part that she can accept your whole hand

into her cunt. Without that last part, I knew, it would be a much greater matter for me to take Naomi with my fist.

I, therefore, took my time. Naomi and I had long ago established a power arrangement where she does everything—everything—I demand of her. It was as arousing to her as it is to me, and it grows from her knowledge that I would never do anything to hurt her. Cause pain, yes, but that's not the same as hurting her.

With the matter of fisting, however, her mind refused to comprehend it.

And so I set about to remind her, during our sex, that she was going to accept my fist. Not now, not tomorrow, but eventually.

When spanking her, I would bring her to the edge of orgasm, rub her pussy, and run my knuckles over her behind. Then I would ask her: "Where is this fist going to go, Naomi?"

When she balked, I would withhold the blows that would drive her over the edge until she had whispered, her voice quavering with fear: "In my cunt, Master."

Only then would I let her come.

When we were fucking, I would wait until she was close, and ask her: "What's going in this cunt, Naomi?"

Eventually, she learned the answer I wanted, and she gave it: "Your fist, Master."

Some months went on this way. Naomi got used to the idea of telling me her cunt would taste my fist. I got quite used to the idea of waiting. It became a conditioned response: She knew that before she could come—ever—she had to admit that her pussy would open up for my whole hand.

Soon it was time to get started.

I installed a sling in the bedroom, asking Naomi what she thought it was for.

"So you can fist my cunt, Master," she said.

"And I'm going to fist your cunt, aren't I, Naomi?"

"Yes, Master."

"When am I going to fist your cunt, Naomi?"

"When . . . whenever you want to, Master."

"And if I wanted to do it right now?"

"Then you'd fist my cunt right now, Master."

I still don't think she believed it, but I could tell the idea was sinking in. I left the sling there untouched for another month, building up Naomi's comfort with it. I instructed her to polish the sling's leather every day, however. Then, one Saturday night, I fucked her in it.

The advantage of this particular sling is that it raised the ass quite high in the air. I could take Naomi's pussy and ass one after the other. I enjoyed her this way several times, each time asking her before she came what was going to happen in this sling.

"You're going to fist my cunt, Master," Naomi would say, and I would allow her to climax.

The day finally came, and I rejoiced.

Kneeling on the floor as we watched television, Naomi looked up at me and said: "May I speak, Master?"

"Yes, slave," I told her.

Her face was red with embarrassment.

"When are you going to fist my cunt, Master?" she asked.

"Whenever I want to, slave."

"Master, when . . . when will that—why haven't you fisted it yet?"

"Because you once told me it couldn't be done," I told her. "Do you still think that?"

"I . . . I don't know."

"Do you want your cunt fisted?"

Naomi turned still redder, looked down at the ground.

"I . . . I think so, Master."

"When am I going to fist your cunt, Naomi?"

"Whenever you want to, Master."

"And when are you going to beg me to fist your cunt, Naomi?"

Naomi's breathing came quick.

"Now, Master."

"All right."

"Will you fist my cunt, Master?"

"That's hardly begging, Naomi."

"Please, Master," she whimpered. "I . . . I think I'd like it. I think I'd like it very much."

"Not good enough," I said.

"Please, Master," she said. "Please fist me."

I took her into the bedroom and put her in the sling. I stripped down and fucked first her cunt and then her ass. When I came inside her, she begged, "Please, Master, please fist my cunt."

"Time for bed," I told her.

After that, she begged me each time we fucked, and other times, too. It had been a mantra for her, and she never forgot it. I knew, now, that the choice was mine—she believed it could be done, and I would do it when it amused me.

But Naomi had no idea when it would amuse me. So she begged, constantly.

Finally, the night came. She was in the sling. I had lovingly buckled her wrists into restraints and spread them wide above her. Her ankles, too, were cuffed to the chains that held the sling. I was ready to fuck her with my hand, and something told me tonight would be the night her cunt would accept me.

"What am I going to do tonight, Naomi?" I asked her as I put on the gloves.

Her eyes went wide, sparkled. "Are . . . are you going to fist me, Master?"

"Of course," I said. "You're going to take my whole fist in your cunt.

"I . . . I don't know if I can," she said, her voice quavering.

"You've been begging for it for weeks," I said. "No use trying to back out now."

I saw Naomi's body give a little shiver of excitement at those words. Of course, at the first hint that my fist was beyond my capacity, the goal-oriented scene would end. But she didn't need to know that; for Naomi, the fear and excitement of being fucked by my whole hand was much more important than actually taking it.

I started out with my well-lubed fingers fucking her two at a time. Naomi moaned and came within a minute. Then three fingers, and she eventually came again. She squirmed in her bonds and the chains rattled against her. By the time I had given her four orgasms, two hours had passed.

"I can't . . ." she moaned. "I can't take any more . . ."

"All right," I said, fucking her with four fingers. "We'll just keep going like this, then."

By the time she came a fourth time, her naked body was moist with sweat and her face was slack. She looked at me wide-eyed, and moaned.

"Please, Master. Please put your fist inside me."

"Beg," I told her.

"Please," she whimpered. "Please, Master, I want your fist. Please give me your fist in my cunt."

I tucked my thumb under and added still more lube. The towel under the sling was soaked already, and more drops poured out onto it. I worked my fingers around in a slow clockwise, then counter-clockwise circle. Naomi came again and her pussy tightened up.

"Open wide," I told her, caressing her, forcing her open.

After her pussy relaxed from its most recent orgasm, I could feel it loose against my hand. I knew she was ready.

"Tell me when," I told her.

"Master . . . Master I don't know if I can . . ."

"Sure you can," I told her. "I'll just stay here until you want it bad enough."

I kept twisting my hand in and out of her pussy, each time the knuckles forcing her almost open wide enough to take my whole fist—almost, but not quite. I added more lube each time, knowing there would be a stain on the carpet—and not caring. Finally, I felt her opening for it, the critical point having been reached.

"Oh God," she moaned. "Please, Master, please fist me!"

You don't force your fist into a cunt—it opens up for you. And Naomi opened up like a blooming flower, her cunt finally giving way and letting me in. Her eyes went very wide and she let out a moan bordering on a scream as I entered her fully, her cunt closing tight around my wrist.

"Oh God, Master, oh God . . ." she moaned.

"It's inside," I said. "How does it feel?"

She answered by shuddering all over, and I felt the powerful con-tractions of her cunt, almost strong enough to break my bones. I smiled as Naomi gripped the straps of the sling, her eyes shut tight as she came. Then she opened wide and she looked at me.

"You took my whole fist," I told her. "Congratulations."

"I . . . I love you, Master," she moaned. "Thank you."

"Now I own all of you," I said, and she looked down at the place where we joined. She nodded.

"You own all of me," she said.

"And what am I going to do from now on?" I asked her.

"You're going to fist my cunt," she said. "Master."

"And when am I going to do it, Naomi?"

"Whenever you feel like it, Master."

I smiled at her and began moving my fist in tiny, gentle circles inside her. Moaning, Naomi begged me for more.

Oral Arguments
by Christopher Becker

Christopher Becker is the pseudonym of an erotic writer who describes himself as "mostly vanilla." Of "Oral Arguments," he says, "I've always been fascinated by the idea that going down on someone is seen as a submissive act. I can identify with the sense of intense power I feel when I'm holding my lover down and orally pleasing her, and she makes it very clear with her body language that at that moment before orgasm she is utterly submissive—in the sense that I have total control over her. Also, since my wife is a lawyer, I also couldn't resist the pun in the title."

"I hate this," said Annie, throwing down the manuscript in disgust.

I looked up from the book I was reading. Annie was curled up on the far end of the sofa, her legs tucked deliciously under her. It was a hot evening in the summer and she wore a pair of tight shorts and a top that left her belly bare, revealing her pretty navel with its glittering jeweled ring. She wasn't wearing a bra.

"What do you hate?" I asked her, looking back down, with some effort, at my book.

"Men," she said. "I hate men."

"Bummer for me," I said.

"They all think it's incredibly dominant to tie up a woman and go down on her."

I looked up at her, my eyes narrowed in puzzlement.

"Excuse me?"

A law student in real life, Annie was getting her thrills by copyediting a website for her friend Sarah—a website that published large quantities of erotica. It was all user-generated, the carefully selected fantasies of the readers who wanked to the site's naughty tales. Sarah

selected the pieces, and Annie had expressed her frustration with Sarah's taste—it seems her friend wasn't nearly kinky enough to satisfy Annie.

Annie always edited in hard copy on a jet-black clipboard with the image of an anthropomorphic Japanese cartoon femme on it.

"Men," she said. "These guys write stories about being dominant. They tie up women and go down on them. I don't understand why they think it's dominating a woman to go down on her."

Annie, like most women, was partial to cunnilingus. But her submissive fantasies revolved, primarily, around giving lots and lots of head. I'd felt the benefits of those submissive fantasies more times than I could count, and Annie was one of the most accomplished oral submissives I'd ever been with. But when it came to receiving oral sex, it was all about being loved, not being dominated.

"You like head," I told her, not looking up from my book. "In fact, as I recall, you seem to love getting head."

"I know," she said. "But it doesn't make me feel submissive. I mean, I guess guys can get off on whatever they want, but these stories are really annoying. I can't tell you how many guys write stories about topping a woman by eating her out."

"It's possible," I said. I still didn't look up from my book, but that was mostly for effect. The machinations of a supermassive star in the last moments before supernova had lost my interest the moment I'd noticed how hot Annie's tits looked in that tight crop-top.

"What's possible?"

"To top a woman by giving her head."

"Sure, I guess," she said skeptically.

I don't know if Annie was playing dumb, or if she really never saw it coming. I was on her in an instant, dragging her by the shoulders, stretching her out on the couch, pressing her roughly into it. My kiss was savage, my tongue plunging into her mouth as she moaned softly and arched her back, pressing her tits up against me. I could feel her hard nipples through the thin cotton.

Annie's hips lifted slightly as she spread her legs, grinding her crotch into mine. She could feel I was already hard, and her shorts were tight enough that I could feel the slight indentation where her pussy lips parted around the thin cotton.

I leaned back off of her, got my hand around her wrist, my other hand under her waist. I wrenched her off the sofa and she squealed as I forced her to her feet, standing up like a rag doll. I came off the couch as I stood her up, and I pushed her toward the full-length mirror. I now had her arm twisted behind her with one of my hands, which was big enough to go effortlessly around Annie's petite wrist. My other hand grabbed her long hair and her butterfly clips went springing out of it as I tangled my fingers in her auburn locks and held on, pushing my gasping girlfriend toward the full-length mirror.

"Take off your clothes," I growled, looking over her shoulder.

"Give me my arm," she said.

"One hand," I told her. "Take them off with one hand, counselor."

It was harder than it sounded, but that was partially because I had Annie's other arm pushed hard into the small of her back, forcing her to keep her hips pivoted forward. She awkwardly slipped her hand under the waistband of her tight gym shorts and pulled them down over her hips, letting them slide past her pussy and bunch around her ankles. She stepped out of them obediently. Her shaved pussy glittered from between her legs, displaying the jeweled clit ring I'd put there.

"Now the shirt," I said.

That was even more difficult. She wriggled her arm out of the T-shirt and pulled it over her head, revealing her perfect B-cup tits with their silver rings through the nipples. I'd put those there, too, a present for her twenty-fifth birthday. I never let her go, instead switching arms so that by the time she slipped the top over her wrist, I had her other wrist—pulled up hard behind her back. I still had her head, and was holding her face up so as to make her watch herself in the mirror—naked, shaved, pierced, and in serious distress.

"Is this a dominant woman?" I growled.

"No," she whimpered, looking at herself in the mirror.

"You feel good and submissive right now, don't you?"

"Uh-huh," she said, her full lips parted, her pierced tongue lolling out.

"Stay that way, counselor," I instructed her, and frog-marched her toward the bedroom. I spun her around and forced her onto the bed,

feeling her topple and go down underneath me as I jammed my knee into her crotch to hold her down. The restraints were already in place—padded metal circlets that I clamped easily around first one wrist, then the other. Annie squirmed with her arms spread wide; I gave her legs the same treatment, stretching her spread-eagled against the unmade bed. Then I stood and looked at her as I took off my clothes.

"I'm going to give you head, you little slut," I said. "Whether you like it or not."

There's something that happens to Annie when she gets real, real submissive. It's a look in her eye, a tension to her face, a hungry, desperate need to please. I knew her cunt was pulsing hard, going so wet it'd be dripping in a moment.

"Yes, Master," she said.

When I was naked, I dove on top of her and pressed my mouth hard to hers. I heard the tiny moan deep in her throat as I plundered her mouth with my tongue, my hands roving over her tits and pinching her pierced nipples.

"I'm not going to find out you want this, am I?" I growled.

She didn't answer. She just blushed deep red, something she still manages to do despite her shameless pursuit of kinky sex. My cock was immediately harder than it had ever been.

I licked my way down her belly and plunged my mouth between her thighs. The second my tongue touched her clit, Annie's ass lifted off the bed, her back arching and straightening, her hips unable to control their desperate grinding. I pressed hard, licking her clit so firmly that I heard her gasp in surprise. Then I licked down to her pussy and wriggled my tongue inside, feeling the drizzle of pussy juice that came with Annie's intense arousal.

"You do want this," I said. "You've been wanting to get head all day."

Annie's only response was a long, low moan of ecstasy as my tongue returned to her clit. I slid two fingers into her pussy and fucked her as I ate her out. I've gotten very good at gauging how turned on Annie is, and I'd never seen her as hot as she was right now. I pursed my lips and suckled lightly and rhythmically on her clit,

something that always drives her right to orgasm. But this time, after several minutes of that, as I heard her moans changing, indicating the approach of orgasm, I stopped.

"Beg for it."

"Please," she gasped.

"Not good enough," I said.

"Please," she moaned desperately, her voice shaking as if she was on the verge of tears. It wasn't acting. "Please, Master, please, please make me come Master . . ."

My tongue pressed hard against her clit and pushed her over. I felt Annie crumbling under me as her long torture exploded in an orgasm that seized her naked, bound body and made her groan wildly. As she came, she pulled on the manacles, understanding in the instant of her orgasmic surrender that she was captive—that she belonged to me, as did her orgasm.

When she was finished coming, I climbed on top of Annie and slid into her. After she comes, Annie's pussy is incredibly sensitive, and it's torture for her to be fucked. But such succulent torture. She moaned softly into my ear as I fucked her. I would have tortured her longer, but she felt so good, wet and tight around my cock, that I came within moments, moaning as I fucked my cock into her pussy, taking her, releasing myself inside her body.

I grasped her head and turned her face to the side, pressing my lips up against her ear.

"Do you feel dominant?" I asked.

"No, Master," she whispered.

"What do you feel?"

"Submissive, Master," she said.

"I rest my case, counselor. The jury finds in favor of cunnilingus being a brutal act of violation and domination."

Annie shivered underneath me, arching her back and pushing her perfect, pierced tits up against my chest.

"Yes, Master," she said.

Grifter
by Carol Queen

Carol Queen got a doctorate in sexology so she could impart more realistic detail to her smut. She is an award-winning erotic author and also writes personal essays about sexual diversity. For a complete listing of her work, see www.carolqueen.com. Her classic erotic novel *The Leather Daddy and the Femme* was reissued in 2003 by Down There Press. She works at San Francisco's Good Vibrations (www.goodvibes.com).

Queen says: "I wrote 'Grifter' to challenge myself; I wanted to write something about nonconsensual play. I don't really *believe* in nonconsensual play, so to do it, I needed to set up strongly worked characters and motives and a moral situation that, while not *too* black and white, makes one person the 'bad guy'—all the while letting the other characters explore their own sorts of badness. Also, I'm not a top (at least, not this kind), so the punishment scenario gave me something to work from in trying to craft a credible scene."

I wouldn't have gotten involved, except that Joe was such an old friend. I've known him since college, long enough for either of us to have raised kids if we were the marrying kind. He certainly never was—I've watched him go through a succession of blondes, the hairstyles changing with the decades, from long and straight to big and fluffy and back again. If any of them loved him, I'd be surprised. He was a success right away—in fact, he came to school with enough money to impress any girl he wanted, and they just lined right up. It was never that easy for me back in those days, and it didn't help my opinion of women, watching them cuddle up to his bank balance and not to him.

Then I started meeting women who didn't care about that. The entire sex was redeemed by one barefoot girl who liked to smoke pot and recite poetry to me before I tied her to the bed.

Joe and I could never double date because our girls couldn't get along. Blonde bubbleheads or connivers setting themselves up to be Mrs. Money struggled to make small talk with kinky grad students. It was partly my influence that none of them ever grabbed the ring, though a few of them earned themselves a few years at his side, shacked up, playing house, and then leaving him—if the leave-taking was civilized—with a car or a condo or a no-strings loan to start a business. They were all gold diggers, as near as I could figure, but mostly honest about it. As one of my ethereal bondage-queen girl-friends explained, it was just what their mothers had taught them to do. It was how the whole straight world worked. He had fun with them, they looked good on his arm—and it wasn't really my business.

Until Alice came along, and we're not talking Wonderland. My old pal Joe, now something like the seventeenth-richest man in the country, came face to face with the kind of succubus that wants nothing more than to eat a man like him, spit out the husk, and pick her teeth with his bones. He'd finally stumbled into the sights of a grifter.

None of Joe's friends noticed anything different at first: She was blonde and gorgeous, and could keep up her end of any conversation. She said she was an attorney, but had a surprising amount of free time, always ready to take Joe's arm for an outing, and the more caviar or ski chalets involved, the quicker she could go. Like I said, there was nothing so different about that. But where Blondes One through One Hundred were eager to put out, understanding the con-nection between their visits to the money tree and their ability to keep Joe well-fucked—and God knows there was someone nearby to take the place of any doll with too-frequent headaches—Alice se-duced and then dangled the prize just out of Joe's reach. He strove for that sweet carrot like the dumbest mule who ever plodded through Tennessee dirt. It might just have been a new technique—the latest Blonde Strategy, passed along in tony ladies' rooms as guys smoked their fat cigars—and it's true he fell for it hook, line, and sinker. He was used to dropping his pants when and where he wanted, but Alice wasn't having any of that. My babe du jour—an aspiring-if-decades-

late Beat poet when she wasn't singing the older laments and praises to the tune of my cat—speculated that maybe she had read *The Rules*. Joe wasn't the marrying kind, true, but he wasn't getting any younger. Maybe his mother'd been pressuring him about an heir.

You could see it unbalanced Joe. Alice was there at his beck and call, always dressed to eat caviar. But she never put out, teasing him with very un-Joe-like notions: "You have no idea how much better it can be," she purred, "when you wait."

My little beatnik and I got a good laugh out of that. We had waited a good fifteen minutes our first time, though it's true I hadn't gotten out the bondage gear till our third date. Joe was entering his own kind of bondage, beginning to get a little sloppy. He was already offering her things. We worried he'd buy the cow without tasting the milk. Sure, I know that's crass. But love or no love (and I've been around the block enough to know this wasn't any kind of love I'd ever seen), before you go buying diamonds don't you want to know whether tab A and slot B are a righteous fit? Joe used to think that way, but his brain was not working the way it ever had before.

Anyway, what's a nice fur coat between friends? It wasn't like it hurt him to spend the money. She hinted at more esoteric pleasures if he'd only equip her for them. In his circle, I'm the acknowledged expert on esoteric pleasures, so he came to me.

"I've never felt so . . . enthralled! So ready for something new, something I've never experienced!" Joe wasn't the pay-his-way-up-Everest kind of rich guy, exactly, but it came out that he was planning to set her up in a condo, complete with everything money could buy. He simply had to experience it all for himself, and she was his key, his Beatrice.

I didn't think so. Hey, if Joe had ever wanted to play slap and tickle, he'd have been welcome at my place: a pretty-nicely tricked-out dungeon if I do say so myself, even if I did have to build most of it from scratch. Joe knew he was always welcome—he could bring any blonde he liked. In a pinch, I knew a blonde or two who were at the top of their game. If ecstatic torture was this year's new flavor, it could be had, with girls dressed in any color of black. Most of them even

had their own outfits, unlike Alice, whose trendy dominatrix look was courtesy of Joe's credit cards.

But by now Joe had swallowed the bait. He wouldn't place his lily-white ass in anyone's hands but Alice's, much as I tried to convince him he ought to have at least one good experience to compare to her chatroom-tutored ministrations. I was pretty sure this girl was a gold-plated phony, but he wouldn't even let her out of his sight to play with me. I tried to explain how important it was that she be road tested, but no such luck. By now he'd convinced himself that her piss tasted like high-class chardonnay.

Not that she'd let him near her piss, even.

So I invited him to bring her over to my playroom. Then I called Micki, an ex who worked for a private eye.

She ran Alice every which way, and guess what? She wasn't a lawyer, though let's just say she'd been close to lawyers in the past . . . and I mean that in both the biblical and the jurisprudential senses. She was nearby a couple of rich old men when they bit the dust, and close enough to see some of the profit. My hunch about her S and M credentials seemed to play out—no one had ever heard of or played with her. Although, of course, she could have an Internet alias that regularly committed unspeakable acts upon the absent, insensate bodies of her submissives. Speaking of aliases, Micki found a couple, one that claimed Alice to be just once-removed from deposed European royalty. Well, whatever—she *did* have the cheekbones. But way past that, she had the cheek—it turned out she wasn't even an American citizen, although she would be, of course, if any rich schmucks like my old friend Joe saw fit to waltz her down the aisle.

"Right," said Micki, "if he lives that long."

"Oh, he'll live that long, all right, though odds are pretty good they won't grow old together." I pondered this setup. Did I give a shit? Was this, on some level, what Joe deserved? He'd had decent luck with blondes so far; maybe the inevitable bad apple had just turned up, and it was meant to be.

Naaah, I finally decided. Joe wasn't a bad guy. No, in this picture, the bad guy had 38DD's.

•   •   •

Our double date was set up, and we still had a week to go. This gave Micki time to do a little more digging. She had a real prejudice against blondes, Micki did, and I saw a predatory side of her emerge that had never come out while she was tied to my rack. On Wednesday she hit pay dirt—she turned up a real boyfriend in Alice's closet. Not in her past—Alice was giving away plenty of milk, just not to Joe. He subconsciously honed in on her well-fucked radiance, wanting whatever it signified. But Joe had no idea it signified a small-time thief with big brown eyes and a really big cock named Johnny. Johnny had one strike to go—no wonder Alice was head-of-household.

It turned out that I was the lightest-weight guy Micki ever played with. She'd been on both sides of the fence and had a friend or two, who still owed her favors. On Friday afternoon, a couple of them popped up on either side of Johnny's bar stool. He got an early start at the Dew Drop Inn, or whatever his joint-of-choice was called— obviously no one had taught him the finer things, like no cheap whisky before noon. Only one trip to the alley, a view of a different kind of 38, and a couple of well-placed suggestions later, and Johnny decided to go home to Chicago. Micki paid for the bus trip. Damn, she really got involved with her work.

So Alice came back to the abode to find it cleared out—no Johnny, no note. Also absent was a fair amount of the jewelry she'd already gotten from Joe—good-quality trinkets, really, but Johnny'd need some walking-around money when he got back home.

You'd have had to be looking closely to see that Alice wasn't quite herself when our big date rolled around on Saturday night. Joe obviously didn't notice—she had him so snowed, nothing would have sunk in. Maybe a shaved head, but she was done up as flawlessly as ever. If mascara had raccooned around her eyes last night as she sobbed over the loss of her bunny-boy, she'd had time to put the toner on. And in fact, Joe was even more obsequious than ever, trying to get into what he thought was the proper mood for his kinky date. His slavish attention stabilized her somewhat. That, after all, was the name of the game.

This was a double date only because we were using my space and my gear, and I insisted that Micki and I chaperone. Alice had no time for us, intent only on trussing up Joe. Micki muttered under her

breath that this was Alice's way of keeping Joe's hands off her, and indeed, she had him in cuffs in record time. In a perfect X on my St. Andrew's cross a naked Joe was soon immobile, Alice purring around him as she tied half-assed knots and tweaked his tits. Micki and I occupied the other side of the room, managing to look busy while we kept an eye on things. Joe was hard as a rock—this was probably true nearly all the time when Alice was around, she got him so worked up—and she even deigned to put a cock ring on him and run her nails along the engorged flesh. This was almost certainly the closest he'd gotten to scoring with her after all this time, so he paid complete attention.

Micki and I were of two minds about strategy. One option was to wait until Alice fucked something up, as we were pretty certain she would. But our plan as it unfolded would seem like a pretty extreme overreaction to a bondage faux pas. It didn't really have any logic connecting Alice's eventual mistake to what we planned to do, and besides, when you got right down to it, Alice's very presence in Joe's life was mistake enough. So Plan B, we decided, was simpler: Just do it.

Micki was integral to this. I'm a pretty nice guy. Sure, I like hurting women, but only the ones who want to be hurt. I'd just as happily lick a girl's clit until tomorrow morning as whip her—as long as she's tied up, anyway. The bondage is really my lech. Pain is an extra, and like most nice guys, I take the concept of consent very seriously. I don't even know if I could inflict nonconsensual pain or distress—even on Alice, despite my dreams of tying her wrists and dangling her over the balcony.

Micki was another story. Micki liked pain, and she liked both sides—she was an equal opportunity woman in that respect, as switchable as it gets. Some of the things she'd gotten me to do to her would qualify as horrific, if it hadn't been for the look on her face—pure nirvana, a sensation slut in her true element. And Micki usually played fair when she topped, but the plain fact was, she didn't care whether or not her willing victim liked the games she played. The fact that her bottom had agreed to play was what mattered. And there was one final, secret side to Micki—when she got irritated, it didn't really matter whether you were a willing victim at all.

"I could be on the other side of the law pretty easily myself," she

told me once. "It's all a rush. A little vicious part of me doesn't give a shit about consent. I just have too much superego to go all the way—most of the time. I keep that side of me in a pen, but that doesn't mean it's not there."

I pictured that part of Micki, which I had heard about but never met, as a snarling weasel—a cute but feral powerhouse with sharp, sharp teeth. Micki had a special way of thinking about wrongdoing, and for her, taking Alice down was logical in two ways: Alice was asking for it by fucking around and grifting, and Micki deserved to do it, because there were so many times she'd wanted to do something like it and never had. It was like cleaning your room on a sunny day when you'd rather be outside: You cleaned it, and then you got to eat cake. Except this time, she was going to eat Alice.

Joe was trussed and hard, and Alice buzzed around him like a bee on a flower. They were paying no attention to Micki and me at all. We could have gotten into a nice loud scene and the lovebirds wouldn't have noticed. So it was ridiculously easy for me to slip up behind Alice and grab her wrists. Micki, right there with the cuffs, slapped them on and shoved. Between us we quickly had a spitting-mad Alice bent over a horse, blonde as Gwendoline and just as immobile. I held her there while Micki grabbed a portable set of stocks that chained to the legs of the horse. Over her neck and locked into place, Alice could rage and wiggle, but she couldn't go anywhere. Red-faced and furious, she spewed some pretty impressive invective—hadn't learned talk like *that* in any of the courts of Europe—but Micki shut her up momentarily with several hard thwacks to the ass.

Joe hadn't said a word. Still tied up the way Alice had left him, he stared at the new tableau, dumbfounded.

Micki bent down so she could look Alice in the eye. "Wondering why we've convened this little meeting?"

"You shit-sucking bitch, what the fuck are you doing?" Damn, Alice seemed so much less elegant when she was pissed. It became easier to see what Johnny saw in her.

"Show a little respect, babe," said Micki, punctuating it with a resounding slap. Alice's eyes went involuntarily wide. "We're holding a

little tribunal, that's what, babe. A truth-telling commission, how does that sound?"

I stepped over to Joe and uncuffed his hands, though he was still wound to the posts of the cross like a kid who got on the wrong side of a rough game of cowboys and Indians. He wasn't going anywhere. I patted him on the shoulder and interrupted the resumed flow of Alice's swearing. "See, Alice, we've been really concerned that you don't fit in very well with our crowd. Joe deserves the best, and he doesn't seem to be getting it from you. He doesn't seem to be getting anything but a snow job, to tell you the truth."

Micki cut in. "As a matter of fact, you really remind me of somebody who'll only put out after the wedding day, and only if well-stocked with Viagra and poppers." Joe was oblivious to this, but Alice's expression changed just enough to make me think that this possibly lethal combo might in fact be in the medicine chest, just waiting for Joe to sign the right papers. Micki ran a spiky nail across Alice's throat while she stalked back and forth in front of her, leaving the fine pale length marked with a glowing red slash. "Foxglove takes too long, huh, baby? We wouldn't want to whore ourselves out *too* long, just to get our hands on some money. That's just so bad for a girl's self-esteem, isn't it?"

Alice hissed.

"Hey, speaking of whoring, where's that little fuck-boy you lived with up until day before yesterday? Where'd he go?"

Alice started up with the verbal vitriol. Joe's eyes went a little wider in their already-evident confusion, kind of like a dog who twists its head sideways and you could swear it just said "Huh?" Instead, what came out of his mouth was, "What the . . . ?" I figured we should let him stay trussed to the St. Andrew's cross for at least a little while. It was a ringside seat, after all, but also, I wasn't sure this was going to feel any more consensual to Joe than it did to Alice. At least, not at first.

Micki saw Joe's doglike confusion and lifted Alice's chin with the point of one nail so Joe could look her in the face. Alice's eyes darted around, like she was looking for the magic key that would let her out of this predicament. She sure didn't seem to want to meet his look, into which a certain mix of hurt and almost-but-not-quite-anger had

begun to seep. But Micki's sharp direction wouldn't let her look away. Alice's expression began to resemble a teenager whose overindulgent mom has finally found her little darling's stash of coke, hash oil, and stolen pharmaceuticals.

Micki wasn't overindulgent at all, except occasionally to her own dark side. "Why don't you tell Joe about Johnny, Alice? Don't you think he deserves to know that he's helping support a no-good, big-cocked fucklush who isn't even his own goddamned illegitimate kid? That he's paying some guy's rent so you can take it in the ass all night after sending him home with blue balls? It seems to me, any guy who's taking you on ski vacations and buying expensive champagne would want to know that kind of detail, you little cunt."

This last statement finished with a stinging slap, as punctuation. Joe was starting to look maybe a little less confused and maybe a little more irritated—after all, Alice hadn't opened her mouth to deny any of it. Her considerable conversational skills seemed reduced to calling Micki a fucking bitch.

Micki had a lot more verbal acuity than this. "So is this little scam all your plan, missy? If Johnny was pimping you out, I can't imagine he'd have cut out on you quite so fast. Hasn't called yet, huh?" Nothing but a glare from the trussed-up blonde—plus an attempt to struggle her way out of the bondage.

"Hey, Alice," I cut in, "When you try to get away, it makes your ass look really hot. I'm beginning to see what Joe likes about you." Alice roared, with just the hint of unintelligible invective at the center of the noise.

Micki took over again. "You know, what you're doing with old Joe here *reeeallly* irritates me, Alice. Would you like to know why?"

Alice was beginning to get back up to speed, expletive-wise. Micki rummaged around in a toy bag and came up with a ball gag. The verbiage continued to spew as Micki dangled it a few inches from Alice's eyes.

"Sweetie, when you took your little Internet correspondence course on pro domination, did they mention this? It's a really handy toy to have when someone just won't shut up." Micki's considerable professional skills included takedowns, and the gag went into Alice's mouth with almost no fuss. Micki just waited till the yowling blonde

reached a particularly open-mouthed yell, and in the gag went. It had a buckle, so she didn't need to call upon her knot-tying abilities as Alice tried to Linda Blair her head out of Micki's reach. In a few short seconds, the gag was in and the tirade had turned to muffled bellows of impotent rage.

"Alice, shut the fuck up. I want to explain something to you." The next slap *did* shut Alice up, at least briefly. "You know, cunt, in a perfect world, it would be no big deal if you wanted to suck rich guys' souls. We wouldn't even have cared this time, except Joe's not an asshole. When you do your little game on assholes, the world stays balanced. When you do it to decent guys, you fuck things up. It makes bad feng shui everywhere. It makes your karma suck and it makes it harder for decent women to get what they want."

Did I mention Micki was a very spiritual person?

"I don't know if you learned this shit from your mother or made it up as you went along, and I bet *you* think it's the law of the jungle. But I want something really different from the men in my life, and if you've been through the room before I get there, it makes the men turn into jerks. A rich jerk can cause a lot of trouble. A rich jerk who wants revenge on women can *really* cause a lot of trouble. So while you move on to the next mark, other women get the backwash. You're fucking it up for everybody. And what makes it worse is you're smart. You could be doing something useful." The word "smart" was punctuated by a sharp movement—Micki plunging her fist into Alice's hair and jerking up, as close to her brain as Micki could get—for now, anyway. I wasn't sure how much Hannibal Lecter she had in her when she got this way.

"You have completely fucked-up your abilities. You have let me and all other women down. You're not even doing anything useful with the fucking money you do get. You're a blonde fucking bleached fucking leech."

Joe finally sputtered into action—sort of. "Alice, er, is this true?" Alice only glared at him, which was its own sort of simple communication. I would almost—almost!—have given up the pleasure of doing this to Alice, if it meant I'd never had to see my friend look so dispirited. But I'd gotten him into this, and I figured he deserved an answer.

"It's true, Joe. Micki ran her, and she's a class-A grifter. While you fed her filet, she was getting porked by a punk she kept in style, courtesy of you. After you married her she was probably gonna set up the kid as your driver. If you lived long enough to drive anywhere."

Micki looked up from her ministrations. She'd been doing quietly fucked-up things to Alice, who was finally looking a little scared—still pissed, but scared. "Joe, I'm sorry we couldn't just tell you. But I've been around a lot of guys, and I don't think you would've bought it if we'd just told you over lunch." Joe shook his head a little. "We're not going to do anything drastic to Miss Gold Digger here, don't worry—but when I'm done with her she might be less willing to fuck up the life of the next five rich guys she meets."

"Joe," I said carefully, "do you want to help us out here?"

"Yeah, we thought you might like to throw one good fuck into her before you never see her again." Micki was remarkably cheerful-sounding; she just wasn't willing to grasp that Joe was in love with Alice, or had been until three minutes ago. Besides, Micki would have loved to provide the soundtrack while Joe finally tasted the milk. You couldn't have wanted a better trash-talker in your bed than Micki, and just opening her mouth she could have doubled the indignity for Alice—Joe's cock hammering somewhere down south, Micki reading her beads like only a truly vicious girl can do.

But Joe was, as I told you, a decent guy. What were the odds, I wondered silently, of two such decent guys as me and him getting caught up with two evil women like Alice and Micki? Though Micki *did* keep a lid on it most of the time, I had a feeling the lid would come off pretty soon.

"No, let me leave," said Joe. Though it took the next five minutes for me to get him out—Alice had clearly never heard of panic snaps, and he was tied to the cross in an absolute gnarl of ropes—I was finally able to support him as he lowered his arms, get him some water, and help him find his coat. "I don't want to know what happens after I go," he said, and closed the door quietly on his way out. He never once looked back at Alice.

Although it would have been sweet porn indeed to see Joe throw a savage fuck, Micki was actually, I suspected, a tougher fuck than Joe would ever be—and she was still in the room. Part A of the mission

had been simple—get Joe out of this bitch's thrall. Part B was really Micki's primary agenda: Teach her a bitter and thorough lesson. Micki cared very passionately about right and wrong, probably because her own self-control was fairly hard-won. This is the kind of superego that, when blended in a perfect yin-yang with one's id, makes for a diamond-hard and implacable top. In fact, I was pretty sure that while she punished Alice, she'd be sending an internal message to herself: Crime doesn't pay, babe. Is that the secret motivation of sadistic cops and prison guards everywhere? I'd have to remember to ask her this later, when we were doing one of three logical post-scene activities: enjoying a drink and going back over every little element of the evening; fucking like crazed, power-drunk weasels; or running for the border after we dumped the body.

But I'd made Micki promise she wouldn't kill her.

"Don't worry, sweetie," Micki was in fact saying, "we're not going to kill you. I don't even think we plan to disfigure you, but you might want to try to hold still, just in case."

Alice gave her a look that was reminiscent of an alley cat wrapped in duct tape.

"We might talk a little about whether you *deserve* to be killed," Micki continued, "but we won't actually do it. However, I fervently hope that when I get done with you, you will never—*never!*—ever pull another scam. I want you to walk out of here tonight, if you can walk at all, thinking you can't wait to take a Greyhound to Chicago, move back in with Johnny, and get a nice job at a Krispy Kreme."

The cat started to hiss.

"Because you are never going to use your skills to fuck with people," Micki said, "*ever*"—she punctuated this with a ringing slap—"*again!*"

Alice's eyes filled with tears, though none of the rage left them.

"You're also not going to turn us in, and do you know why?" Micki pulled a computer printout from her pocket, folded multiple times and scored down the sides with the regular pattern of holes that said "old funky printer in a PI's office." She unscrolled it and began to read all the dirt she had on Alice, including birth name and the year she first got sent to juvenile court. "Alice, if there's anything that's not on here, it would just make me want to fuck you up worse. So take

your medicine and crawl home, and no later than tomorrow, get out of this fucking town."

"Unless you like this so much that you want to ask Micki if she'd pretty please keep you," I added with a smirk. "Stranger things have happened. Micki has a lot of charisma."

Duct-tape kitty's eyes had narrowed. "Oh, aren't you bisexual? That could change."

Now that Alice knew the parameters of the scene—she'd most likely live, and there were no safewords—Micki got to work. "Go fix yourself a drink," she said to me. "I won't need you for a while." And indeed, when I returned from the bar that stood at the far end of my little rumpus room, Micki had upped the ante on Alice's bondage—everything tighter, elbows jutting up at a painful-looking angle because her wrists were tied more tightly behind her back, and rope in a neat harness fixing her chest securely to the horse. Her ass and cunt completely accessible, spreader bars keeping her high-heeled feet thrust as far apart as they would go—Micki had made a tableau straight out of John Willie. Anybody in the S and M community who said fucking wasn't important had never seen this little setup. This was *all* about fucking.

"You know, we could do a lot of things to you here, Alice," said Micki, "and maybe we will. But it seems to me the most poetic justice would be a nice hard fuck. We'll tape it, of course, and if you ever come up on my radar again, your spread-wide ass is going into the video stores. Don't think I can't get it there. And remember, I know your real name. It'll be on the cover in a real big font." Micki wasn't kidding—Alice was on the horse because my rumpus room digital recorder was pointed right at it. I liked to document my best rumpus experiences, and this was surely going to be right up there with the first time Micki came to visit me here.

I told you I'm a nice guy. I am. But Micki—well, she always had a sort of mesmerizing, awful effect on me. It's why I asked her to do this job. And I would never, ever rape anyone—unless Micki pointed her scarlet nail and said, "That's your end." My cock was suddenly ready to do anything to anyone, and Micki's cock came out of her tote bag at just about the time my pants hit the floor.

Micki assigned me to fuck Alice's face. She took up the rear, and

I noticed the dick she'd strapped on was not one of her smaller ones. Maybe Micki didn't actually have any smaller ones. Whenever she'd lay trussed up under me, spread painfully wide to my own somewhat-better-than-average meat, she would eventually, mewlingly, beg me to get out one of her toys and finish her off. And her toys—well, they gave *me* penis envy. So wherever she was shoving that thing, into Alice's fore or aft, she'd definitely notice. And though more than willing to do Micki's bidding, I let her start first before I slipped Alice's gag—I needed her in a haze before she had a chance to use her perfect white teeth on me.

Micki knew how to put a person in a haze. And though I'm not sure Alice liked what Micki did to her, exactly, she looked to be going under. A cock as big as Micki's will focus a woman's attention, I guess. But as soon as I saw a bubble of drool appear at the edge of the ball gag, I knew it would be safe to take it out and slip myself in. I'd fucked face more than once—sometimes it's just what a tied-up woman wants, and I pride myself on being able to judge the sometimes tiny space between "not quite hard enough" and "just a little too hard." Of course, I gave Alice the latter right away, slipping into her saliva-slick throat and using it almost as savagely as Micki, on the other side of the horse, slammed Alice's ass. I fisted my hands in her hair and thrust so hard the horse rocked a little—or was that Micki's doing? Alice's gulps and sobs around my meat made me so fucking horny, the nice guy I've been protesting I am had taken a complete hike. Her drool slicked me up so that I could have fucked her throat all night. And there was one more thing: Micki and I could look right into each others' eyes while we slammed our bodies at the completely helpless blonde tied between us. We fucked each other, in that crazed-weasel way, right through Alice's immobilized form. It was so hot that every so often I had to close my eyes and scrape my cock over Alice's teeth, just enough reality check and discomfort to keep me going. Because this was better than any fuck Micki had ever thrown me, even at her most cat-in-heat moments tied to my bed. This made me real glad that there was a woman between us who needed and deserved to be punished, because I don't know if I could have taken all that heat directed just at me.

• • •

At length Generalissima Micki called me from my post. She pulled out of Alice's ass with an audible pop—her dicks were usually the big-headed kind, and this battering ram was no exception. She got me to support Alice's weight while she levered the three-quarters fucked-out bondage victim to the floor—still in range of our camera, in fact Alice's cunt pointed right that way—where my job was to hold her down while Micki worked her efficient hand into Alice's cunt while she continued the evening's comportment lesson. This time Micki could look right into Alice's eyes, and from the look in them as Micki slid in past the knuckles, not bothering to do more than spit on the pink cuntflesh first, Alice had never realized anything much bigger than Johnny's dick could fit in there.

"I love surprising sophisticated people," said Micki with real satisfaction, giving her wrist enough of a twist that Alice gasped and yelped. I knelt down firmly on the wrists that had suddenly started to flail.

"Now Alice, here's where I make my point in a way that you just might hear," said Micki, focusing all her feral-beast-in-a-cop-suit presence on Alice. "What we're doing here is sex. It's not especially consensual, which would ordinarily be a problem. In fact, I'm really using sex as a weapon here, which I don't condone, not at all, but sometimes you just have to fight fire with fire. You don't respect sex or desire, Alice, you use it. That's not right. I don't care how you got this way, because you are smart and calculating enough to do anything you want, and you seem to want to do this. And when I get done with you . . ."—and here Micki began to thrust, achieving a surprising amount of movement in and out of Alice's presumably very tight and very full cunt—". . . you'll never again get filled up enough by a rich guy or a skinny big-dicked punk. You're going to need something else. You're going to need to think about what your life is about . . ."

Micki was fucking hard now; her words were coming out in gasps. ". . . and what you're doing with it . . ."

Under my knees, I felt pressure; Alice's body was tightening up like a bowstring bends a bow.

". . . and you're not going to use your cunt to get you furs and caviar anymore, because your *cunt* . . ."

Micki punctuated "cunt" with an especially powerful thrust. I could see her biceps working.

". . . your *cunt* is going to have some needs of its own. From now on, you fucking grifter bitch, your *cunt* is going to talk to you . . ."

Alice came with a howl and I could barely hear Micki's final words: ". . . *twenty-four hours a day!*"

Just like Micki's cunt, I bet, talks to her.

Micki didn't kill Alice, though I can't swear to the behavior of her goons—the same two guys who ushered Johnny off his bar stool gave his erstwhile girlfriend, fucked-out and sloppy and reeking of come, a ride home, or a ride *somewhere*. I spent the rest of the night with Micki, fucking in full-out crazed-weasel mode, which was just as scary without Alice between us as I'd thought it'd be—just not scary enough to stop. When Micki got like this, it was too confusing to figure out who should get tied up, so for once neither of us did.

I don't know what became of Alice. She hasn't shown her face in this town, and every online pervert in the country knows her story, thanks to Micki. That woman loves telling tales out of school, but only when it's appropriate. She has a superego like a fucking steel trap. She also put the word out on the PI wires, so if Alice turns back up in Bangor, Maine, or Tupelo, Mississippi, someone will have a shot at figuring her out before she goes too far with the next rich schmuck.

Micki and I had a good reason for breaking up the first time, and we didn't get back together over Alice—except that one night. I'm a nice guy, but let me tell you—I'm keeping a close eye on Joe's girlfriends now. I'll know if any new grifters try to get their meathooks into him. And if anyone does . . .

I'm sure Micki and I will be able to handle it.

Will You Be My Daddy?
by Brandon Mitchell

In "Will You Be My Daddy?," **Brandon Mitchell** describes one of the most taboo fantasies in BDSM play — that of "Daddy/girl" play. The imagined relationship between a dominant "Daddy" and a submissive "girl" allows these two characters to explore deep realms of her submission, and also lets "Daddy" take on a nurturing and gentle aspect, as well as being sexually dominant.

You could say that Jordana and I have an unusual relationship—but I would prefer the term "rare." You see, I'm her Daddy.

No, I don't mean I'm her father. Her father died when she was twelve. I'm her Daddy.

No, we're not related by blood. As I told you, I'm not her father. But don't even think of suggesting I'm not her "real" Daddy. I'm as real as it gets.

Daddies have even greater responsibility than fathers, and they can be even more important in their little girl's life. You see, Daddies are a very special breed of father figure, and it's not a life I chose, exactly. Rather, it chose me. The first time it happened, it just felt so right. It felt so perfect, so satisfying, that I knew I would never want to be anything else.

The first time Jordana curled up in my lap, she nuzzled her pretty face against my neck with that very special coyness that spells a shy hunger, a need so great and a love so unconditional that nothing can touch it.

And she whispered into my ear in a sexy, coquettish lilt:
"Will you be my Daddy?"

• • •

My little girl is 5'3", with straight, coal-black hair and brown eyes. She's got very pretty, flawless pale skin. She's got adorable little B-cup breasts that, even though she's had them for many years, she still shows to me at least once a week and asks me if I think they're growing. She's got a tongue piercing—I took her to the parlor and watched as she got pierced, though the piercer told me I didn't have to sign the release form.

She's asked me if she can get nipple rings, but I drew the line.

Unlike the real father-daughter relationship, the love between Jordana and me has very clear parameters. In fact, it's the rules that make it so wonderful.

They're not the same rules, by any stretch of the imagination, that a father and daughter can, or should, live by. For all their similarities, Daddies and fathers are very, very different. There are some things Daddies don't have to do.

Daddies don't have to change diapers—at least, not all Daddies. Some of them do, but I don't. Jordana's well out of diapers, you see. In this life we live, she's chosen to be old enough to go to the mall with her friends, but too young to go without a strict curfew. She's also too young to smoke or buy cigarettes. She's too young to be left alone over the weekend. And she's barely—just barely—too young to date boys.

The "too young" part was her choice, based on her needs, her wants, her desires.

The "just barely" part was mine.

Daddies don't have to pay for college—that is, unless they want to. Jordana's already got two PhDs, though, so it's pretty irrelevant for me now. But that last semester of fees for the university . . . I paid for that. I'll admit it was a stretch for me. It was a private school and all—one of the best in the country. But Jordana curled up in my lap and kissed my ear and said "I want to go to a good college, Daddy." How could I say no?

And my pretty daughter thanked me in every way she knew.

.   .   .

You see, Daddies get to do all sorts of things that good fathers would never do. If you've ever had a daughter who's really too young to date boys (but just barely), you know that they're often very, very, very ready to date boys long before you're ready to let them date boys. Jordana's been ready to date boys (but just barely) for about eighteen years.

She's so ready to date boys that she wants it almost all the time.

We have strict rules. She can flirt, she can tease, she can wear sexy clothes. She can even go out in public with no bra on, letting boys look at her small, firm tits when they show through her shirt. She can go without underwear as long as she promises to be good. She can chat with boys on the Internet as long as she doesn't agree to meet them and doesn't call any of them "Daddy." She can even go out with boys, as long as it's in a group. But she's agreed to never, ever let a boy kiss her or touch her down there.

In return, I give her everything she needs.

Daddies get to spank their daughters, too. The one time Jordana let a boy kiss her at a New Year's party, she told me right away. She'd been drinking champagne. I'd said she could, so it wasn't really her fault. I spanked her anyway, and she's never done it since.

I also spank her when she sneaks a cigarette—in fact, she always tells me. She knows she's not supposed to smoke (she quit five years ago after ten years of smoking). Now, when she gets stressed out and just can't say no, she comes to me right afterward so I can smell it on her. And that's when I put her over my lap.

I spank her when she won't do her homework—that is, correcting essay tests for upper-division Psych. When she can't focus, she does things like try to watch TV, play on the Internet (she shows a proclivity for those naughty sites), or read my magazines. She tells me every night when she comes home from school what papers she has to correct. When I see she's not doing it, I give her that look. And she gives me that look right back.

And that's when I spank her.

.   .   .

Spanking your little girl is very different when you're a Daddy. It's not cruel at all, though sometimes Jordana pretends that it is. Sometimes she doesn't want it. If she really, really doesn't want it, she says "You're a bad Daddy!" or "You're so mean, Daddy!" She gets the spanking anyway. Other times, she says "Please don't spank me, Daddy!" or "I'll be good, Daddy!" as I lay her out across my knee, lift her skirt, and pull down her panties. She gets the spanking anyway.

Sometimes, when she really doesn't want to do her homework or she really feels bad about that cigarette, she cries.

To tell you the truth, I like it when she cries. I know she's really getting what she needs.

And whether she cries or not, she gets the spanking. Because she knows it's good for her—she told me.

And it's definitely, definitely good for me.

Sometimes she's really, really bad. Sometimes Daddy comes home from work and I see the stack of papers, untouched, on her desk. I see the TV on. And she's out on the back porch smoking a cigarette and sneaking one of Daddy's beers.

I always come home at the same time, so it's obvious she knew she was going to get caught, but she acts surprised and guilty just the same.

Then, I actually relish the chance to give her what she needs. When she's that naughty, I know she needs a spanking very, very, very bad.

When she's that naughty, she's usually dressed up for the occasion. One of her short plaid skirts. A white crop-top with no bra underneath. Knee-high white socks. Her lustrous black hair is usually in pigtails.

When she realizes she's caught, she turns red in the face and looks down, too ashamed to meet my eye.

I take the cigarette out of her hand and take a puff on it. Then I drop it to the concrete patio and crush it out.

I snap my finger and point toward the house. Jordana follows.

I sit down in the chair we always use—it's heavy enough to hold us both but it has no arms, so she can lay firmly across it and rest in

my lap, bent at the waist. I tell her she's been very, very naughty, so she has to take her panties off.

Red-faced, she lifts her skirt and pulls down her black-lace thong. She knows she shouldn't be wearing underwear that naughty except for a special occasion, and the look I give her spells it out. She hands me her panties and I run my fingers over the crotch. They're soaking.

"You've been thinking about naughty things, haven't you, Jordana?"

She nods, her face reddening still more.

I sit down in the chair and snap my fingers. Jordana obediently lifts her skirt and lays over my lap, her bare ass turned upward, thrust into the air. I know she wants this spanking very, very badly.

I stuff her wet panties in her mouth, just to remind her how turned-on she is.

I run my hand over her pert, firm buttocks, telling her to spread her legs a little. I caress the curve of her ass, and I can tell from the way she squirms that she's wishing I would touch her pussy. I don't. I make her wait.

My first blow on the sweet spot of her ass brings a muffled yelp from her mouth. I spank her again with my cupped hand and she wriggles her butt as if asking for it. I spank her harder. And harder. And harder.

Within a minute her normally pale ass is bright crimson and warm to the touch. I spank her harder. She starts to cry, biting down on her panties and shaking her head violently back and forth. She starts to plead, her words barely discernible through the ball of panties: "No, Daddy, no please don't, please don't spank me, Daddy!"

I tell her to open her legs wider.

I run my fingers up and down in her moist slit, feeling how incredibly turned-on she is. I tease her clit and she whimpers, moaning. I start to finger her and she pushes up onto my hand, wriggling her butt back and forth as she begs for more fingers. I take my fingers out of her and push her down firmly into my lap.

I start to spank her again, this time hitting the sweet spots on both cheeks, my cupped hand rocking from one side of her pussy to the other.

She writhes and squirms in my lap, her nipples hard against the outside of my thigh. I feel her gripping my legs as it gets too much for her to bear. I don't stop, though. I push her right past what she can bear, without slowing or stopping.

She comes, gasping, spitting her panties out halfway across the room. Her soft tears break into overwhelmed sobs as she gives in to the agony, surrendering. Her body shudders as she surrenders it to her orgasm and her sobs.

"Thank you, Daddy," she moans. "Thank you, thank you, thank you, Daddy."

"All right," I say, signaling that she's done.

She can feel my cock hard against her belly. She knows how to thank me for spanking her. How to thank me for being her Daddy.

She gets down off my lap and kneels between my legs. She's done this many times, but she still looks up at me with a tentative, nervous, wide-eyed naivete. I unbuckle my belt, unzip my pants, and take out my hard cock.

When she sees it and smells it, she's overwhelmed with hunger for it—I can see it in her face, in the way her mouth goes open wide and she seems to be fighting the urge to suck my cock. But she still looks up at me, waiting for my signal.

I guide my cock to her lips, sliding it between them.

That's all she needs. Her mouth slides all the way down my shaft as she hungrily gulps my cock into her throat. Her tongue swirls around the head and covers the underside with tender licks as she turns to the side and lavishes affection on the shaft from base to tip. She can't get to my balls because they're still tucked into my pants, but her tongue seeks hungrily around the base of my cock.

When I'm close, she knows. She can taste the increase of precome at the tip. Jordana always wants to swallow.

She covers my cockhead with her mouth, clamping her lips just behind the glans. She wraps her fingers around the shaft and slowly starts to pump my cock up and down, bringing me closer very, very fast.

My ass lifts off the chair and she rides me as my hands rest on her head. She looks up at me with her big, bright eyes and we lock gazes as she takes my stream of come into her mouth. She swallows it all,

pumping my shaft with her hand until she's tasted it all. She keeps sucking me until she feels it start to go soft.

Then she tucks my cock away, crawls up, and sits in my lap.

"Thank you, Daddy," she whispers as she nuzzles her face against my neck. "Thank you for spanking me."

See, my little girl knows exactly what's good for her. And after that, she always finishes her homework.

She finishes it really fast, in fact. Because she wants very badly to get her homework done. She knows when it's all finished she can come to bed. And she wants that very, very much.

Because that's when a little girl gets to do even more wonderful things. Especially when she's done all her homework.

ABOUT THE EDITOR

N. T. Morley is the author of twenty published and forthcoming novels of erotic dominance and submission, including the trilogies *The Library, The Office,* and *The Castle* (all published by Venus Book Club), plus *The Visitor, The Pyramid, The Factory, The Institute, The Nightclub, The Appointment, The Circle, The Limousine,* and *The Parlor.*

Visit Morley's website at www.ntmorley.com to read about upcoming projects and enjoy exclusive excerpts, serialized novels, and short stories unavailable elsewhere.

ABOUT THE EDITOR

N. T. Morley is the author of twenty published and forthcoming novels of erotic dominance and submission, including the trilogies *The Library*, *The Office*, and *The Castle* (all published by Venus Book Club), plus *The Visitor*, *The Pyramid*, *The Factory*, *The Institute*, *The Nightclub*, *The Appointment*, *The Circle*, *The Limousine*, and *The Parlor*.

Visit Morley's website at www.ntmorley.com to read about upcoming projects and enjoy exclusive excerpts, serialized novels, and short stories unavailable elsewhere.